"A wonderful genre-defying adventure, rife with strange heart and weird horror. But most notable is its particular, careful attention to its characters. Premee Mohamed is a bold new voice."

Chuck Wendig

"One of those wonderful books that keeps peeling back layers, not of some cosmic mystery, but of its two main characters. Nicky and Johnny end up being much more complex and ambiguous than they appear at the start of this book, and every reveal is gasp-out-loud astonishing."

Charlie Jane Anders

"A perfect balance of thriller, horror and humour; reminded me of *The Gone-Away World*."

Adrian Tchaikovsky

"A galloping global adventure where privilege and the lies we tell others are as great a villainous force as the budding cthulonic forces the heroes must rush to stop."

Brooke Bolander

"Gripping from the first, arresting sentence to the last, this is unsettling, mind-devouring cosmic horror at its best, wrapped around one of those captivating *noooo-this-is-a-terrible-idea-but-why-what-noooo* relationships."

Jeannette Ng

"The most interesting thing about *Beneath the Rising* is the friendship between Nicky and Johnny. During the course of the novel, Mohamed peels off the layers of this relationship with nuance and depth, and takes it to places where few novels I've read have gone."

Sara Norja

"This book is the offspring of *A Wrinkle in Time* and the Cthulhu mythos, raised on epic poetry, the love songs and rock ballads of the 00s, and the inescapable rhythm of *Gitanjali* if it were a gory tentacle-sprouting punk anthem."

Likhain

"This is a great story! I loved the globe trotting, ancient history and mysteries at every turn."

Stewart Hotston

"Mohamed explores the many layers of Nick and Johnny's relationship with empathy and heartbreaking precision. It will haunt me like no Old God ever could."

Kari the Talewright

"*Beneath the Rising* is a fast-paced adventure story. It's also a story of powerful, complex, often difficult emotions, and the tangle of friendship and devotion and other scary things, and honestly I wasn't prepared to have so many feelings."

Karolina Fedyk

First published 2020 by Solaris
an imprint of Rebellion Publishing Ltd,
Riverside House, Osney Mead,
Oxford, OX2 0ES, UK

www.solarisbooks.com

ISBN: 978 1 78108 786 2

A CIP catalogue record for this book is available
from the British Library.

Designed & typeset by Rebellion Publishing

Printed in Denmark

BENEATH
THE RISING

Premee
Mohamed

SOLARIS

CHAPTER ONE

MY EARLIEST MEMORY of her smells like blood.

I remember just enough.

I woke in twilight, a violet dimness, and looked at the hospital bed next to me: reek of dried blood and disinfectant, the unfamiliar profile of a pale girl visible through a clear mask.

They had loaded me with enough drugs to erase my body. I thought: *I am a head. I am just a head. A head in a bed.*

I suppose they thought it would be monstrous to let a little kid feel that kind of pain.

People used to ask how we met. I would always say, "Our moms are friends. That's how we made friends." Two lies.

* * *

THAT WAS THEN; this was now, leerily waiting for her at International Arrivals. These were unfriendly times to be nervous-looking and brown and alone, after what happened last September—those two planes nearly hitting the World Trade Towers, overshooting, crashing into the river. It didn't matter that the hijackers had failed; what had mattered was that they were Muslims. Kids I had known half my life had hurled slurs at me after school—terms for Muslims that I didn't even know, more generic insults that I did. Kids that *knew* I wasn't Muslim. Who cared, when all you needed to know was that the terrorists had been 'brown'?

And people in uniform had started giving me long, cool looks everywhere I went: mall, airport, walking home from school. News stories about turbaned men beaten at train stations late at night, one kid walking with his hijabi mother shoved into traffic by a jeering group of frat boys at the university while she watched. Someone had spray-painted 'terrorist' on the sides of both a mosque and a synagogue. People were so batshit scared they couldn't even be racist right.

I ignored the stares and tried not to look too anxious as I waited for my best friend to deplane. It wasn't that it was a big deal or anything. Just that she could have gotten a cab or a limo or sent a driver, but instead she had called *me* after we hadn't seen each other for six months—and I wanted that to mean something again. Like the old days, when we silently denied that she was getting more extraordinary and I was getting more ordinary, and one day our friendship would die out in a way that couldn't be rekindled.

There she was at last, caught in the moshpit at the gate as cameras that I hadn't seen in the crowd began to flash. Goddamn digital cameras that people could fit in their pockets, instead of the big black rigs that you could watch out for. I towed her out and propped her next to a vending machine while the tide of people ebbed around us, so that the reporters had to photograph my back instead of her exhausted face.

"Welcome back, Baby Einstein," I said. "Buy you a Coke? I think I've got a toonie. Or straight home?"

"Home? What's a home? Oh my God, Nick, that flight, no words, not in the English language, maybe in Latin... Can we go get a Happy Meal? Or a Starbucks? God, I could really use a coffee. Or maybe not, I dunno, I threw up like three times on the plane and then I ate a pack of Mentos and Mentos aren't really *food* food are they, they're almost sort of a, sort of, you could almost use them like aeronautical epoxy to—"

"Slow down for a second, Johnny."

"I said *IthinkIneedcaffeinemorethanIneedprocessed-poultryproductsbutthejuryisverymuchout.*"

"You sound like you've literally been drinking nothing but coffee for a week."

"Not a *week*. Not *literally*."

"Where's your minder, for Chrissake?" I said. Her assistant Rutger was usually steps behind her. "I thought he was supposed to keep this kind of thing from happening." Being ambushed by paparazzi, I meant. She often managed to sneak in and out, smuggled down airport pedways, through tunnels in strange cities, emerging under her hotel or in university parkades so that people joked about teleportation, when really Ye Shall 'Ru The Day secretly did all that.

"He's coming in tomorrow. We borked up our flights. And don't call him that!"

Back at the car, I cautiously revved the elderly engine and said, "All right, which do you really want, nuggets or coffee? I'm working at noon, I don't have time for both."

Silence. She had passed out, head lolling against the window, her open mouth all pink tongue and razor-sharp teeth, like a cat. Her sleep was so deep that her eyes cracked open, showing a sliver of iris past the lashes. That, too, just like a cat. Not a housecat though. One of the little wild ones.

She roused herself enough to hand me a twenty as we reached the parking kiosks, and then we hit the highway, where the hum of the wheels put her back under. Ever the doting friend, I stuffed a Taco Time napkin under her chin to catch her drool.

HER HOUSE DIDN'T smell as fusty and dead as I would have assumed, but then this wasn't her first rodeo; she'd probably had a service in to housesit. The jungle at the front entrance looked springy and green. Johnny staggered in and started slapping random panels on the wall, opening blinds that let in flecked planks of sunlight.

"Go sleep," I said. "Stop fucking with that stuff. You can turn on all the lights later."

"I had an idea, on the plane. A big one. A *big* one."

Oh no. I knew that tone of voice; insomnia, late-night phone calls, and probably several chemical burns were on the way. "Sleep!"

"I have to get it down first, because there's a—"

"I said *sleep!*"

"You're not the boss of me!"

"Jetlag is the boss of you," I said. "Call me when you're up, if you ever get up."

"Oh my God. If I don't get up, do you still want me to call you?"

"Nope."

"Zombie."

"Correct. Night of the Living Dork."

"Thanks for the ride," she said, already halfway up the stairs, dragging her bag. "There's snacks in the freezer if you want anything. I owe you!"

"*Everybody knows that.*"

Still yelling at each other after all these years. That aura around us both, cursed by our meeting, the smell of blood following us. Or was it? How cursed were we now?

WHEN I GOT home from work, the noisy house stank of burnt toast, so that for just a second I tried to remember if that was caused by having a seizure or a stroke, but maybe one of the kids had set something on fire in the toaster oven again, which happened so often that the glass was smoked black, like a drug dealer's back windshield. Moreover, they weren't supposed to use it without a grownup around, so the system had failed somewhere.

My sister Carla tiptoed into the kitchen, pale, baggy-eyed. Her Mickey Mouse nightgown was faded into transparency; I looked away. Skinny for eleven. You'd expect her to still have some baby fat, but I think she burned it all off worrying. Funny to see that skinniness and know it's nerves, when you consider how fat some of our family is. Me, I'm turning into a perfect copy of Dad: pencil legs under a slowly developing gut, like a ping-pong ball on toothpicks, even though I know—we all know, we're too polite to say it—I'm not eating enough. All my uncles on both sides back in the Caribbean looked like Dad, and so they looked like me too, or I looked like them. Genetics is powerful, Johnny always says. It's powerful. It fights you—whatever you eat, whatever you do, wherever you live, your genes fight you.

Carla stooped to pop the cabinet lock, digging for something under the sink.

"Hey," I said. "You all right?"

She jumped a foot. "Oh my God! Nicky, you scared me. I didn't see you. I can't sleep. My tummy hurts."

"I think there's some Pepto-Bismol above the sink," I said. When it became clear that she was just going to stand there rubbing her eyes, I forced myself out of the kitchen chair.

She headed back to the kids' room still absentmindedly carrying the pink-smeared spoon, the noise clearly identifiable now as music, broken by the gabble of a radio DJ. God knows it can't be easy for the twins to share a room with their sister, but it's not easy on any of us and the rest of us generally manage not to be shits about it. I mean, what's the first commandment of two adults and three kids in an eight-hundred square foot duplex? That's right: Don't Be A Shit. Oughta be our family motto. Matching tattoos.

I shoved at the bedroom door, which moved slowly: Chris and Brent had wedged it with a chair and a couple of phonebooks. They turned drowsy, round, identical faces to mine from the bunkbed, dark hair fluffed straight up.

"Off. Now," I said, pointing to the radio, blasting No Doubt.

"Can we turn it down instead?" said Brent, reaching for the volume knob. Oh, so it was going to be one of *those* nights.

I beat him to it and hit the power button, then yanked the plug out of the wall and picked it up, ignoring their whining.

"Sleep. Now. I don't care if it's the weekend, it's *way* too late for this."

I stowed the radio in Mom's closet, stripped to my undershirt and boxers and climbed onto the couch, so hungry for sleep that I was drooling, like Johnny in the car. Ten hours of stocking groceries is a dog's work—I was exhausted—yet I felt weirdly wired, as if I had just heard a favourite song I hadn't heard for a while.

Was that it? The familiar song of envy and resentment and adoration and excitement of having Johnny back in town? A song I'd heard my whole life in fits and starts, as she flew around for work. She'd missed her birthday (mine too), the anniversary of our meeting, my high school graduation; she'd missed so much.

I'd last seen her at Christmas, and barely at that. I had picked at my plate of caviar and lox while she and Rutger yelled about lecture dates, and all the other party guests, of whom I knew not one well enough to talk to, danced and drank and exchanged presents and air-kissed each other and talked about prions and gravity lensing. At the end of the night Johnny got the caterers to make a package of treats for the kids and that was it. I didn't even get to say goodbye before I left, and she was gone before the new year.

When you miss someone, the best thing is to wait it out till it fades; but the ache had not gone away in half a year, not even lessened. We'd tried to keep in touch—there had been a few phone calls, always her to me. I never knew where she was and could never have afforded to call so far away anyway.

Each time I had imagined her lying on a huge hotel bed, all white sheets and gilt angels, like in a movie, with a decorated porcelain phone, bare feet, unironed dress, her short blonde hair sticking up like feathers, the Coliseum or a medieval castle outside her window. But I never asked if it was true. Too embarrassing.

Nothing new, she always said, yawning down the line. She was tired, the churches were beautiful, Rutger was being ten pounds of crap in a five-pound bag, how do people get married and spend *all their time* together without *murdering* each other? Someone had tried to photograph her in the shower in Berlin, her mother had suggested suing the hotel, she had gone to the Eiffel Tower, she didn't throw up, she threw up *at the bottom*, when she came back she was definitely working on motion sickness drugs, *forget* cancer or malaria, she had bought two geneticists and a geophysicist and would now splash out more cash on English lessons and facilities for her new people, like putting fresh paint and a spoiler on a used car; the purpose of science, after all, was to make more money to buy more science.

"Your nothing new is waaaay different from my nothing new," I told her.

"New is relative," she said. "Like so many other things. You don't know how big a figure is without a scale bar."

"All I can say is, it sure is quiet around here. I can actually hear myself think."

"Ha ha, and then another ha ha," she said. "I was gonna send you a postcard, but now all you get is my unending loathing."

"I had that already."

"Now you get *all* of it. Except what I still need for that piece of shit in Berlin."

"God yes. Fucking pervert. I mean who tries to photograph a seventeen year-old in the shower. Sue his scrotum off."

"*Oh my God you said a bad word.*"

"*Scrotum is not a bad word and I still want a postcard.*"
Shouting down the wires, as if we had been standing right there, laughing at each other the way we always did, like donkeys, all our teeth out. Six months. We had never been apart for so long. And I could never tell her how lonely I'd been, for fear of embarrassing us both. The world wanted so much from her; how could I make any more demands?

CHAPTER TWO

SHE WAS ON the front page of the *Globe and Mail* the next morning. *SHE'S DONE IT AGAIN: Prodigy's New Dementia Drug.*

I skimmed the article in the break room at work. Designed it herself, Alzheimer's and other conditions, five years of testing, Dr. Hans Pfenzc supervising manufacture at official pharmaceutical arm, Ottawa. Worldwide distribution by the end of 2003. In less than a generation kids would be asking their parents "What's Alzheimer's?" if they saw it in a movie or a book.

My sweaty fingers pulled words from the newsprint. *She's done it again.* A tiny photo of Dr. Pfenzc—how would you pronounce that, I wondered?—and a big one of her, the photogenic one, in a white dress with a big red flower at her shoulder. Her hair in the photo was shorter than when she had left, in fact shorter than when

I'd picked her up yesterday. She looked like a nicely-groomed ten year-old boy. I wondered when she had gotten it cut. What city in Europe, what fancy salon, a century-old pair of scissors probably, silver-plated. Must have cost more than our monthly rent.

I scoured the photo for clues. Could be that award banquet she called me from, squiffed on champagne.

("There's no minimum drinking age in Europe!"

"I'm pretty sure there is. Where's Rutger?"

"Beats me.")

She won an award that night—not the big, main one, but a smaller one. Some chemistry award to add to her display case.

The paper didn't go into her background, for once. A tiny relief. No mention of the big white wedding cake of a house, the squash court she only used for experiments, all those secret floors underneath like an iceberg, like a Bond villain's lair; no mention of her labs, her observatories, her factories, her ribbon-cutting ceremonies. Her prizes and magazine articles and thinkpieces and documentaries. She had been *Time*'s Person Of The Year in 1995 for her HIV cure. The laminated cover she'd given me was still around my house somewhere—the golden child perched on a lab stool, posing with a microscope. People keep trying to prove that she's a fraud. They've all been embarrassed, discredited, publicly shamed for it. She's legit. Not like me. If someone tried to prove that I was a fraud, they'd be trying to prove a negative, demonstrate the existence of nothing. A nothing in a nothing life.

What was she doing right now? Hopefully sleeping in her iceberg house—or, more likely, pacing like a zoo tiger, out of her mind on espresso and jetlag, her and her 'big idea.'

It's the way it's always been. State of the union. But like she said: I wouldn't have been so bothered by it if she hadn't come back and held my life directly up next to hers for comparison, like those laundry commercials with the stained shirt and the clean one.

But when I think about not being her friend any more... it wouldn't even be like an amputation, where you lose a visible part of yourself, but some violently invasive surgery, where you are left without organs. I can't imagine that level of pain. And maybe she can't either, because she hasn't abandoned me, either, after all these years, when that would be the easier way. When she has already dismissed so much from her life.

The paper vanished from my hands and smacked onto the floor. "Whatcha got there, Osama?"

I didn't even bother going for it, just sat back on my crate and put on a poker face, the standard when my manager arrived. "Morning, Gino."

He snorted—but that's key with bullies, don't do anything that shows they got a rise out of you—and turned away, heading to the lockup and activating the timeclock so the stockers starting to trickle in could punch our cards. Several people stepped on the paper, right on Johnny's picture. I flinched each time.

* * *

THE PHONE WAS ringing just as I came home; I heard Carla pick up, followed by a delighted squeal. I knew who inspired those kind of noises, and collapsed on the couch to wait.

"It's Auntie Johnny! You never said she was back!" Carla shouted, dancing in several minutes later. "We talked about school! And haircuts!"

"Gross, girl stuff," I said, and took the phone, wet from Carla's eager breath. "J-Dawg."

"N-Diddy," she said, formally. "Or is it N-Puffy?"

"Puff-Nicky."

"My God, we'll never be rappers."

"Well, not with that attitude," I said. "What's up?"

"There's sort of a..." In the pause, I heard a highpitched hum, as if she were standing in front of a running microwave. She finally said, "Something kind of big just happened, I think. If it isn't, then it isn't, but if it is... I want a witness."

"Did you literally just murder someone."

"I'm not answering that question without my attorney present. Can you come over later?"

"Maybe. I'll call first." I hung up and returned the phone to Carla, who was draped, rapt, over the back of the couch.

"Aren't you ever going to ask her to marry you?" she sighed.

"Good Lord, she's not even old enough to vote," I said. "And also, people don't marry their friends."

"Yes they do. I saw it in a movie."

"That's *movies*. Nobody does that in real life."

"Do too."

I tried to get up off the couch, but as often happened after a busy shift, my legs refused to work. I dug my knuckles into my thighs and stared at the TV, showing some weirdo cartoon with extremely muscular mice. "What are we watching?!"

"She's the prettiest girl I've ever seen," Carla said. "Did she really murder someone?"

"I don't think so."

"Maybe don't marry her if she's a murderer."

"Yeah, write that down somewhere," I said. "That's useful advice."

After Mom came home, I reluctantly crawled back into my car. I didn't want to go over to John's; I wanted to take a fifteen-hour nap and not have one single interruption for a missing backpack, broken window, loose tooth, split lip, or stolen diary. And I was keenly aware that I smelled of armpits and rotten apple—like the break room at work, basically, and I had forgotten to put on deodorant this morning. She wouldn't say anything, I knew, but if Rutger was at the house, there would be some dirty looks. It wasn't that he didn't like *me*, exactly, but that it was far too easy to inadvertently do one of the dozens of things he didn't like.

Halfway there I realized I had forgotten to phone her, but there was nothing doing except to cuss at myself. Cell phones were great, but both of you had to have one, and I didn't; Johnny had about six, but I didn't know the numbers for any of them. I was pretty sure she just used them as emergency lines for her various major labs and research centres. I couldn't imagine how much they would cost.

For no reason, achingly, I remembered using walkie-talkies in the ravine when we were kids. We had barely needed them, though: I had always known what she was thinking, she always knew what I was about to say. My other heart, the heart that beat outside of me. Had we grown strange to each other in her absence, grown up, grown away, grown into different people? Flying away from each other like the unknowable planets she had found with her telescopes and calculations?

As I turned into her driveway, I had to pull my visor down to know where to stop. What the shit? Every light was on, every room, every floor, hard blocks of white shining in the yellow late prairie sun. No way had she turned on all those lights. And in fact, hadn't she installed motion sensor lights a couple years ago to make sure only rooms in use were lit? Was she having a party? I glanced around at the mostly-empty street. No, if it were a party, I'd never have been able to park in the driveway. And where was Rutger's Lexus?

Uneasy, I splashed through the lush lawn in what was rapidly turning from sunset to dusk, triggering a set of halogen spots that shone right into my face as I punched in her code, praying she hadn't changed it when she got back. The alarm system was wired to call the police if you fed it the wrong numbers.

But it let me in, and I stepped into a blinding photosphere, forearm over my face. "Johnny?" No reply. I toed my shoes off and tried the intercom. "John? It's me. Where are you?"

"Uh, Hadrian... let me come up and get you, okay?"

"What's going on?" Every single light was on, even some I hadn't known existed, tucked away in recesses in the ceiling, behind floor vents, in sunk tracks on the walls. The heat was intense after the coolness of the evening; sweat prickled on my back. Great. Stupid to believe I couldn't possibly smell any worse. Moisture was condensing under my socks on the cool tiles.

She appeared at the end of the hallway and for a second I thought she'd figured out how to make herself into a hologram—all silver spangles, shimmering and shivering, not really there. I hesitated before following her.

"Sorry," I said, "I thought maybe you were a T-1000?"

"That's the last goal of science, not the first," she said. "But no one will want to be a robot after I show the world what just happened."

I looked at her properly and did a cartoony double-take, making her giggle. She was in a short, white dress covered in silver sequins. On anyone taller, it would have practically been a shirt.

"What the hell is this?" I said. "Like, no offense, but we both know Rutger has to shoot you with tranqs to get you to dress up."

"Yeah, like in *The A-Team*," she said, pausing to do a little pirouette in the steel-toed boots she wore in her lab. "I bought this in Venice; we were coming back from the conference centre and it was just so pretty and there was only one left."

"My God, you're finally becoming a real girl."

"Don't be so gender essentialist, Nicholas," she sniffed. "Anyway, I was trying it on between two mirrors and something just kind of... it was like... you remember that reactor I worked on a while ago?"

"The one you were working on when you were ten? That's more than a while ago."

"You know what I mean," she said, speeding up to a trot. "Listen, I was looking down at the sequins, and I just kind of, I don't know, I had had a lot of coffee, and it seemed like they were sort of moving—"

"Do you mind my asking if you *slept* last night?"

"—no, but listen, listen, moving in a pattern, something I knew, or I knew the start but not the end, I had seen the start on the plane, like when you're at karaoke and you realize halfway through the opening that you don't know the verses but just the chorus, but when the words come up you realize you *do* know the verses after all, so I ran to write it down, and it seemed okay, I mean it seemed like it *should* work if you look at the sequins as electrons? Anyway, I started the same as the old one, but this time I created the graphene substrate by making kind of a carbon snow—"

"Is one of its side effects not needing to breathe?"

"—and it *works*, I switched the house grid off the solar cells and onto the reactor and I'm sorry about the heat, and the smell, I think that's mostly burning dust and bugs on the halogens, I keep meaning to switch them to the LEDs, but there's never time..." She trailed off; her face was slick and hectic, red dots below her eyes, hair not just damp but actually dripping down her neck into her dress, turning the white to gray.

"Okay," I said. "I'll come look. But then we're sticking a cold washcloth on you."

She tapped a long sequence on the keypad, thirty or forty digits, letting us into Hadrian, one of the more familiar of her many inexplicably-named research rooms.

I followed her, barking my shins repeatedly, around a maze of shin-height equipment and reels of cable to an ordinary metal table bolted to the floor, lit with the same blue Ikea desk lamp the kids had in their room. The table was cluttered with tiny bits of metal and plastic and had a shoebox-sized metal case on it sprouting a dozen black cables, one of which snaked into the darkness. It hummed unpleasantly, setting my teeth on edge like biting foil.

Next to it for some reason sat a four-pack of lemon Perrier, one half-empty. I opened a full one and offered it to Johnny, who wasn't paying attention. I drank while she babbled.

"So normally you'd need a Grabovschi Plate to make real carbon snow, but then I thought, what have I got to get it up to the same temperatures but, and this is really crucial, just in the microcavitations rather than on the overall flake surfaces, and I figured if I used the *microwave* instead of the forge in Belisarius—"

I gazed stonily at it. The lab microwave was about as old as she was, smeared yellow and brown, a very ordinary little box dwarfed by the equipment around it. After a minute I said, "I made a Pizza Pop in that yesterday."

"I suggest you not try it today. So, the new graphene torus is a—"

"What?"

"All right, the graphene *doughnut* is—"

"Actually, that's not the word I was—"

"—atomically plated in silver, which I got from melting down my Cartwright medal, but it's okay because if you tell them you lost it or had it stolen or whatever they'll send you a new one, but it's just stainless steel, I already sent them an e-mail, so now we've got this topological graphene matrix, right, and it's creating edge effects because I gave it a fractional angstrom flex and then linked it to the C-398 magnet that I sort of pulled out of the RC-NCI back end over there, it's fine, I'll buy a new one, and in the aqueous matrix, the electrons display independent choice behaviour and they start to generate their *own* topographical material, which isn't real—"

"What?"

"—under the Yerofeyev definition anyway, but it's so close to the border between the definition and the quantum definition that from their desire to return to their original state, because they immediately regret their choice, right, they discharge energy, and bam!"

"Bam?" I said weakly.

"That's the loop. The choice and the second choice. A renewable electron source. *Electricity*. Anyway, I calibrated it to the house draw, but if my calculations are correct there's kind of no upper limit to production," she said, absently tightening the clamps holding the box to the table.

"Wait. Stop. Drink this." I forced the bottle on her, as much to shut her up for a second as to get some water in her. "Are you telling me this shoebox is... powering the house? And could power... anything?"

"Uh, yeah, does that sound okay? Is that too insane?" She choked on the first sip, water trickling down her neck. "Yeah. It's running on a little bit of Perrier because I can't use the sink right now, I sort of welded a—"

"Johnny! You made a powerplant in a shoebox!"

"It's not a shoebox, thank you very much, it's a shielding setup that—"

"Is this going to cook my sperms?"

"I don't think so, but maybe don't hump it all the same, the shielding isn't really necessary, I don't think, but it does seem to dampen down the harmonics, and maybe it'll be quieter when it's not on a metal surface, I don't know."

"Harmonics? Is that what we're calling that incredibly annoying noise? I feel like I'm chewing on tin foil. What's causing that?"

"Beats me. I'm guessing the impurities in the silver."

"Not the artificial lemon flavouring?"

"No, I don't think so. It's just an electron source, after all. Man, Dr. Yerofeyev is going to freak out when he hears about this, you remember him, he was at my Darwin Day party last year dressed as a trilobite—"

"Stop stop stop stop stop. Please stop." I was getting lightheaded, I assumed from the heat, dehydration, exhaustion, and... whatever she was trying to tell me, which seemed to be that she had put a quantum in a box and plugged an extension cord into it.

She's done it again. The headlines lined themselves up. Child prodigy changes world. Child prodigy... makes a million things obsolete.

Coal-fired power plants first to go. Nuclear next. No one liked those anyway. Gas, crude. Except what we needed for the plastic that could not be replaced by her vat-grown spider-silk substitute, which everyone had been using for years. Even her solar panels, her wind turbines unneeded. We could have electric cars, like in sci-fi movies. Electric... planes? Electric submarines. Electric everything, the whole world humming to her tune. No more wars over oil. The entire world looking at each other and thinking: *We could get along now. We might not have to be friends, but we could be neighbours.*

She had changed everything. And I could always make more sperm.

I dimly realized I had sunk to my heels next to the table. Sweat was running down my arms amd dripping from my fingertips.

"Put your head between your knees," she said from far away.

"Hang on," I said, and then everything went black.

I SWAM BACK up an unknown amount of time later, to find Johnny soaking blue shop towels in warm Perrier and dropping them on the back of my neck. "Let's get out of here," she said. "Can you walk?"

"How l-long... was..." My tongue felt thick and dry.

"Fifteen, maybe twenty seconds. Didn't land on your head or anything."

The walk to the main kitchen was a nightmare marathon through shivering black ghosts reaching for me from the edges of my peripheral vision. Johnny, hovering around me, was a silver moth fluttering in and out of my blind spot. The air crackled around me, as if not wind but feathers brushed against my face. I lifted my feet occasionally at dark spots on the tile; the house had a resident population of genetically modified dung beetles that didn't want poop any more but still desperately needed to roll things, so you'd sometimes see them contentedly going along with a stolen satsuma or pingpong ball. They never looked where they were going and I knew that if I didn't do the same there would be a horrible crunch under my sock, and in our condition that was the last thing we needed.

With its theatrical lighting, the kitchen was the hottest room yet, but we got a pitcher of icewater from the fridge dispenser and spent five silent minutes just drinking, leaning on the cool granite counters. My shirt was soaked and stuck unpleasantly to my body, and even the waistband of my boxers was wet through. I put my head under the sink faucet as Johnny got out a laptop and started turning lights off. The sun had gone down, and I watched from under my curtain of dripping hair as all the windows opened, letting in a gorgeous whiff of breeze.

She ran her hands through her wet hair, spiking it up. Sweat collected in the hollows under her eyes, trembling and jiggling like the water glass in *Jurassic Park*. I dug in one of the drawers and found her a kitchen towel.

"Did you eat?"

"Since when?"

"Since you landed, dummy," I said. "Since then."

"Does coffee count?"

"Some genius." I refilled my glass, emptied it again, listened to my stomach grumble in protest. "Even a dog knows to eat when it's hungry."

"I know." She was shaking all over, not just her hands, not just the water under her eyes. "I h-h-have to start the paper to-nuh-n-night, do the writeup... patent... test protocol... if I c-c-call in all my favours, I could maybe get it patented in f-five, six months, published in..."

"Tonight? You are good for nothing tonight except looking cute and drinking water. No offense."

"I'm *offended!*"

"I know you are, but you are also in pieces. A bunch of very small, tiny pieces."

She burst into tears and pressed the wet towel to her face, but that was okay; I'd seen her at various levels of this kind of utter, strung-out collapse before. It wasn't real crying, it was her body trying to get rid of stress hormones or something. Nothing could be done till she was all cried out, so I just moved her water glass away so she wouldn't bump it with her elbow, and politely looked away, down to the backyard, a lake of fragrant grass lit here and there with the starey, luminescent eyes of rabbits.

Look at us, hitting escape velocity away from each other. Look at her, in pieces, letting me watch her be in pieces, as if we were grownups. How old were we when the unspoken agreement came that we couldn't do kid stuff any more? No more Marco Polo in the ravine, no more play wars with imaginary soldiers, memorizing tactics from her old Roman manuals. No more water-balloon fights. No more self-authored plays fighting over who played the boy and who played the girl, ending up with two armadillos of indeterminate gender flying away on their dragon to be emperors of their far-away planet. No more one-legged races or pretending to be dinosaurs or scuffling over colouring books. No more skating on their family pond—although to be fair, that was kind of a mutual decision after she fell through that one time. Maybe that was when we decided it. We hadn't had a referendum or anything.

"Let me make you some supper," I said when she had tailed off to just snuffles and hiccups.

She laughed. "There you go again, trying to take care of everyone."

"Just people who can't take care of themselves," I said.

She put her head on her side, looking at me. I stared back, steadily, waiting for her to smile again. Would I know if I were falling in love with her, I wondered. A different, a grown-up love. Would something tell me, like a bolt from above? Or would it be something as small as that I wanted her so desperately, so uncontrollably, to smile at me and she wouldn't? That I wanted her to look at me the way she looked at that shoebox?

"Yeah, okay," she said, tossing the towel on the counter. "Food. Sleep. Yeah."

"Deal?"

"Yes, deal. What do you get out of it though?"

"Same thing as you."

BACK HOME, I parked and sat on the Geo's warm hood listening to the engine tick down. The streetlights were out on our side—typical—and the night sky was startlingly clear and bright. The stars, that would be the only thing that Johnny's discovery wouldn't change. You'd have to look that far to find something she hadn't touched.

On the horizon, a faint, green shimmer rose over the rooftops. My gut twinged, a memory scratching at my ribs. Dad loved the northern lights, had driven us all out to see them when I was younger. It seemed you didn't get those in the Caribbean, so he and Mom had never seen them till they moved to Canada. Some kind of magic, a small magic, I used to think: how did he know when to go? It turned out he had tracked the solar storm dates using a phone tree round robin with other amateur enthusiasts and the observatory at the University of Alberta. They were good; sometimes the lights would rage for half the night, captivating us on some gravel road an hour from town, no light pollution, just the green and pink ribbons.

Johnny got a much better view from her observatories, but she was always grateful to be invited. In the winter we'd bring hot chocolate, run the car to warm up. The good old days, before everything went to shit. Our parents got divorced less than a year apart when I was in grade eight; we were both shocked, reeling, couldn't even comfort each other. We dove into distraction instead, and spent as little time at home as possible, like it was a prickly sweater we were occasionally forced to wear. Johnny picked up all sorts of weird hobbies: soapmaking, paddleboarding, Japanese flower arranging, three different martial arts (incompetently, as she hated to be touched so much that she never sparred). I learned to cook. Johnny's mom started a chain of private spas.

It was all bullshit, anyway, a Band-Aid over a broken bone. Particularly for us, because Dad's side blamed Mom for the divorce, and Mom's side—fretful, class-paranoid—blamed Dad. At least Johnny had avoided all that. Divorce was so normal with her parents' friends that it was almost a given, like having a live band at the wedding.

Tears rose, looking at those northern lights. Jesus, I hadn't even thought of those trips for a long time. Dad loved the sky just like me, noticed it wherever he went. I wondered if he could see them in Toronto now. Maybe I would ask when he made his monthly call.

Tonight there must have been a really big solar storm; the lights were a silk scarf draped over the black angles of the roofs, gleaming with rich hints of turquoise, even purple—I'd never seen that before. Deep in their wavering centre, something big and fast streaked past. A shooting star? A long, low rumble followed it—I looked up instinctively for a plane, since there weren't any thunderclouds. Then I kept watching for another star. Were we due for the Perseids or the Leonids or whatever else Johnny got so excited about every year? I didn't know what the dates were. But God how beautiful, the silver stripe straight and true across the silky colours like a needle.

And if it really had been a shooting star, I would get a wish. Deserved a wish.

But I stood out there for almost an hour and couldn't think of a single wish that wouldn't be a waste, now that everything had changed.

CHAPTER THREE

THE NEXT MORNING I made pancakes from the big Costco bag of mix and stared out the window as we ate. Another hot one. Get the boys to weed the front lawn. I had to clean the bathrooms. Carla could help with laundry. Grass didn't need cutting just yet. Didn't want the neighbours to call bylaw on us for unkempt property. Who had a year-end book report due? Mom had a late shift at Gold Dust... check the calendar...

The phone rang, interrupting my to-do list. I hoped it was work, but it was Johnny, talking even before I said hello. "Are you busy today?"

"Define 'busy.'"

"A state of occupation, absorption in a task, engaged in an activity which precludes getting everyone dressed and coming out to the Creek for a pre-Canada Day picnic."

"A picnic?" Every set of eyes in the room swivelled to me in the sudden quiet. I laughed, at their double-take, with sheer happiness, maybe even with relief that she had survived the night, hadn't got irradiated or sucked into a black hole or whatever her shoebox did, that she still wanted to be friends, that our family was still her family. "I'm getting some looks here, John."

"Yeah, scrub 'em up, I'll pick you guys up."

"You mean Rutger will. Are you ever going to get your license?"

"How about you shut your piehole and wash your stank ass before I come. You probably smell like the back of the Vengabus. Noon."

She hung up before I could think of a decent comeback, and I turned to the kids and Mom. "Everyone up for a picnic at the Creek?"

I had to cover my ears to drown out the squealing.

THEIR OLDEST FAMILY property, the Creek—which included a creek, a lake, and the pond that had almost killed us—was an hour out of town, but traffic was light for a long weekend and we were out and unpacked before one in the afternoon. Mom had begged off, probably to enjoy a house without us for a while. I couldn't blame her.

Chris and Brent, who should never have been raised in a city, and who had already announced their intention to become scientists like Johnny, vanished into the bush with a "sample jar" and a "net," hastily kludged together before we left. Carla collapsed onto the high-tech picnic blanket, sighing happily in the silence.

"I'm so glad the boys are gone," she said to Johnny.

Johnny chuckled. "They only get louder, don't they, Cookie? I bet you don't remember when you were little, and you asked me to invent something to 'make the babies be quiet.'"

"I would still want it if you made it now," she said under her breath, darting me a sly glance. "I didn't know I was going to end up with all *brothers*."

"Ew."

"Ew."

"I'm gonna sue you both for libel," I said.

"Slander, Nicky."

We got the food out—catered sandwiches, salads, juiceboxes, Nanaimo bars, everything sealed tightly in plastic clamshells.

Rutger stiffly passed me a big thermos of icewater. "Please keep an eye on the children. There are no safety measures at this property."

"Good to see you too," I said, and Johnny laughed. It *was* good to see him, though.

He and Johnny were a package deal, had been ever since she was six and discovered him as a physics student at Heidelberg University. She'd paid for his doctorate, given him his own lab, and asked him to start coming as a technical advisor on her lecture tours—cries of "babysitter" and "pedophile" notwithstanding.

Years later, he had settled into a kind of in-between space between advisor and assistant. He scheduled lectures and flights, proofread papers, filtered her emails, dealt with the 24/7 management of her labs and facilities, booked telescope time, negotiated research contracts, dealt with zoning and environmental permits, and that was just the stuff I knew about. They never struck me as friends or even really friendly, and I knew part of his coolness towards me was simply resenting the time I took away from her science, as if I had bullied my way into her ivory tower—but he was solid, smart, dependable, ever-present. When he was around, you felt like nothing could go wrong. A flat tire, a bee sting, a meteorite strike, all fell within his purview. Anyway, it *was* good to have a qualified adult out here.

He sat on a corner of the blanket, fat and handsome, like a bronze statue in his monotone khakis and polo shirt, and ostentatiously fixed his gaze on the creek downslope from us, watching for kids to fall in. I grinned at him, knowing he wouldn't see it.

Johnny said, "So, big plans for the summer?"

I gave her a look. "Keep the grass cut and the kids from killing each other. You?"

"You know what I meant."

She meant that she wanted me to apply for postsecondary now that I had graduated; we'd had a tense talk about it last year, before she left. It had been so awkward, in fact, that I had wondered whether it had actually ended the friendship. We hadn't talked for a week afterwards. I kept telling myself: *She's busy, she's busy, you're being paranoid, no one's that sensitive, you're both grownups here. You're both* almost *grownups. Act like a damn grownup. No one would stop being friends with someone for that.* And of course at the end of the week she had called and we went to see *The Fast and the Furious*, and everything seemed fine. Was that about to happen again?

"It wouldn't even have to be university," she said, watching my face, where everything I was thinking must have been printed like a tattoo. "Even a two-year diploma at Grant Mac, or NAIT. Your earning potential would—"

"I know that. I'm not stupid."

She ducked her head. "I just meant..."

I sighed. "Listen, don't let's ruin the day by rehashing this, okay? The kids were so freaking excited. See you again, see the Creek. Look, they're not even paying attention to the food. So let's just say: no, I still can't afford four years, or two years, or a year. No, my grades are still not gonna get me any scholarships. No, Dad won't kick in. Still. Nothing's changed except that if I get good shifts and work all summer, maybe, just *maybe*, I can save up enough to not work for a month or two while I look for a better paying job. I can't leave them like this. You know why."

"But if you—"

"You can't just throw people under the bus to run off and do what you want."

"But this isn't something frivolous. It's... it's following a dream."

"If you have to fuck people up to follow a dream, then

it's a bad dream and you shouldn't follow it," I said. "I mean, not that you've ever had to pick."

My ears were ringing, and although I was staring down at the picnic blanket she'd designed—traditional red-and-white check on one side, nanopolymer temperature-and-moisture control foil on the far side, warm under us, cool under the food, emitting repellent pheromones to keep ants and wasps away—I was aware that she was staring at me with her mouth open. Past my shame and the pounding blood in my face, I felt a little thrill of pleasure. She was so hard to shock and I had finally said something she hadn't expected.

Or maybe it was just that it had been said at all, maybe she thought I'd never say it, after a decade of us both realizing that even though she plowed virtually all her profits into new facilities and people, she still had a hundred times more money than we did, and we never talked about it. I had never asked her for money, even five dollars to cover snacks at the movies. I paid my way. My parents, in a thousand ways, had indoctrinated us never to ask for help. No handouts. Ever. Gifts might be tolerated, within reason. So she gave us treats for the kids, took us on trips sometimes, bought clothes or light-up shoes or shrill toys; and not one word was ever spoken.

"I'm sorry," she said. "I'm not trying to be a dick about it."

"No, you're not. You're trying to be a parent. Don't do that either. Come on. We're here to celebrate, right? Celebrate your shoebox. What are you going to call it?"

"Well, the Chambers Chamber, if I can get away with it." She yawned. "I was up all night again writing it up, e-mailing people, translating stuff, doing figures. Getting some weird numbers on each test run, although the wattage stays steady as a rock. And I can't get rid of that noise."

"I guess when you start mass-producing them you can bury them under a mattress or something."

"I was thinking a building. I'll need time to design a basic structure though. Maybe tomorrow."

I laughed. A lot of her peers (you wouldn't necessarily call them *friends*) teased her about how she got her hands dirty all the time. You were supposed to pay people to do that for you, they said. By this stage in the game. Farm it all out and put your name on the final report. But she hated having anything out of her control, and even, I was sure, resented the little that she had farmed out to Rutger.

I cupped my hands around my mouth. "*Hey, gang! Come eat!*"

We fell silent and sat there waiting for Chris or Brent to yell back. It was silent except for the burble of running water; a magpie in the tree next to us opened its beak a crack, then seemed to think better of it. And I felt a sudden, strange, cold wave wash over me, so abrupt I looked down to see if I had broken into sweat, but I hadn't. Johnny surged up from the blanket and planted herself in front of me and Carla, legs spread like a boxer.

"What is it?" I said, scrambling up next to her.

Something dark was moving in the trees across the creek from us—not one of the boys. Something else. Dark and featureless enough that for a second I thought it was a black bear, half-hidden by the thick undergrowth. And no bird sang.

I stared at it—a stranger, had to be, a thin man in a black coat and pants. But it didn't move like a person, and the pale thing atop it wasn't quite a face. Johnny's breath whistled in her throat. I opened my mouth to speak and found, like the magpie, that my voice had been stilled, an invisible hand over my face. My blood became ice, freezing me in place as I tried to turn my head to escape something I couldn't even see.

"Rutger, go start the van," Johnny eventually said. Her face had turned a pearlescent grey. "Nick, get Carla inside. Lock the doors."

I choked on the unseen barrier, straining against it, only a throttled yelp coming from my throat. Her arm snapped out and connected with my chest almost hard enough to stop my heart, knocking me onto the blanket.

"Go! I'll get the boys. Leave the food, go!"

"Are you crazy? If there's something out there, I'm twice your size! I'll get them!"

"*No*, I will. Go, quick, go on. Get inside."

She tore off at a dead run, skidding on the grass. Hazily, I hoped the boys hadn't crossed the water towards the thing in the trees. It skulked there still, drawing the eye and yet impossible to look at, not even following Johnny as she splashed into the shallow water, simply turning to watch her.

But the fall had released me, and I rose to find Rutger already rushing Carla back to the gravel road. I glanced back to see that the dark thing was gone—oh Jesus, where did it go? Was it going for the van?

I ran, half expecting the thing in the trees to flutter up behind me and smother me, all of me, not just my voice, bury me in its light-absorbing blackness, crunch into me with the razor teeth of its skull, *yes, that's what it was that's why it didn't look like a face it had no features because it was just a skull—*

I fell into the gravel and screamed when something grabbed me by the belt and pulled me up, turned flailing and kicking to see it was just Johnny, easily dodging my panicked blows, the boys behind her. The dark thing was nowhere to be seen.

We packed into the van and Rutger peeled away, throwing me around the back, spattering blood from my skinned palms onto the leather seats.

Everyone was yelling—"What's wrong? What happened? Nicky? Nick? Johnny?"—and as I scrambled up from the floor, I caught a glimpse of Johnny's face, which scared me almost as much as seeing that thin black thing. My heart was hammering so hard I wondered whether it was just going to stop, whether Johnny's push had fucked it up somehow.

"Rutger," I finally called up front. "Ru! Can we put on a movie?" It was the only thing I could think of, and for a minute, while the screens slid out of their recesses in the ceiling and the opening strains of *The Lion King* filtered through the van, it seemed like everything was okay. I was panting, drily wheezing as if my throat had been lined with dryer fluff.

"Johnny, what happened?" Carla said. The boys looked up.

"Yellowjacket nest," Johnny said. "A big one, and they were so mad I couldn't yell to warn you about it. I'm so sorry about the picnic, guys! Tell you what, let's go into town and get burgers and shakes, okay?"

She was shaking, despite the cheerful, Mary-Poppins voice that lulled the kids almost visibly as they settled in to watch the movie. I caught her eye in the rear-view mirror, her green irises dull, almost the colour of the sockets around them. *We are going to talk about this later*, I told the eyes with my eyes.

She nodded.

"WELL, TODAY WAS a goddamn disaster," I said. "Also. Why are we meeting here?"

"No connection to either of us," she said. "Harder to find."

I had to run that through my head a couple of times, rubbing my chest, where the heel of her hand had left a bean-shaped bruise. Wouldn't have thought she had it in her. *Were* we harder to find now? By whom?

Rutger had dropped me off at home, but I'd barely managed to get the kids in bed before Johnny had called me demanding, in whispers, that we meet again. And at her insistence we had walked to this park instead of driving, a long way from both our houses. It was almost midnight, no traffic, nothing open, far from cameras and sirens. I hadn't left a note for Mom, and hoped she wouldn't freak out at me being out so late. She worried so much now.

I had arrived to find a swing moving apparently on its own, a black smear in the darkness, for a moment something unknown—a form without identity, without shape, black hackles and claws like a cat. But the flash of her pale palm had been enough to reassure me. It was cool and still, just starlight and the reflections of the streetlights, and the familiar, beloved glow in the horizon.

"Hey. Look—northern lights."

She glanced up, in the wrong direction, then kicked her feet in the sand, setting her swing going. I clenched my fists.

"Joanna Meredith Chambers, you better tell me what the fuck happened today, and don't tell me yellowjackets," I said. "What *was* that in the trees? I thought it was a bear for a second."

"No."

"Well no, I figured that out, because we wouldn't have run like that if it was," I said. It still felt like there was something in my throat, not a hand now but a lump, a blood clot, through which voice and breath could barely emerge. "Do you know what it was?"

"Not for sure. But it wasn't human."

"All right. Not a person. Not a bear. But dangerous. Now we're getting somewhere." I didn't dare sit in the swing next to her; it was made for kids and the chains might snap under my weight. I leaned my forehead on the support pole, cold metal thrumming with all the earth's invisible vibrations, a train ten kilometers away, electricity in the streetlights, footsteps of people in their houses, distant traffic. I wanted to tell her about the shooting star I'd seen yesterday and the wish I hadn't made.

After a moment, she said, "I think we dodged a bullet. Maybe we didn't. It might be a while before I know."

"*You* wanted me to come out here to talk about it. So I came. Are you just yanking my chain or what?"

She sighed hugely. From anyone else it would have sounded melodramatic. Or maybe on any other day. "I thought I could, but now I'm just worried you'll think I'm nuts. Or sleep-deprived. Or have caffeine poisoning."

"I think all of those things *all the time*."

That squeezed a real laugh out of her, if flimsy. Her eyesockets were dark pools on her face, like a skull, untouched by the scanty light. I shuddered, hoping she didn't see. Then she swung forward into the streetlight and was just Johnny again, the small, fey, familiar face, ninety pounds of blonde bullshit in a raccoon-print t-shirt. "Well, only two of them are usually true."

"Which ones?"

"Listen..." she said, the chains squeaking minutely as she swung. "Listen, did we both pass out yesterday because I had changed the world? Because the whole world changed and no one else knew?"

I looked at her for a moment, trying to tell whether she was joking or whether she'd just unintentionally put her ego on display again. The way her mind works, I have always understood that it is very different from mine, and we had to overcome that to be friends; but sometimes I needed to remind myself that it works differently from everybody else's too. The things that interest her are not above but aside from the things other scientists are interested in, behind and underneath, so that she didn't progress linearly on her preferred problems but zigzagged around, failing quickly and discarding things at lightning speed. That's the way she wants it, as many problems as possible, as if she were the only one put in charge of the world's collective future. There's always been an added layer to the world she inhabits, one I can't live in, one in which she asks questions meant only for herself. I couldn't tell where she was going with this, but she really did seem to be waiting for my answer. I said, "Maybe. I thought it was the heat, though."

"Well, what we saw at the Creek is, I think... a thing that... is called when that happens. That has been set in place to watch for it, its face... pressed to the membrane separating the places where things like that never happen and where they can and do. Which, I will now admit, sounds stupid."

I stared at her for a moment, trying to figure out a polite way to agree. "It doesn't sound stupid, it just doesn't sound..." I groped for a word. "Real."

"Well. What's real, anyway." She laughed. "How do we know what's real?"

"I don't know, but that thing was real enough to see, I guess, since we both saw it."

"What did *you* see?"

"A thing, a black... tall... thing..." I hesitated. Now I knew what she meant about it sounding stupid. Anything sounds reasonable until you have to explain it to someone. I wondered if this was why she got so famously short-tempered on her lecture tours. "With something white or yellow on top, but not a face or a hat. I thought maybe it was a skull, later. Why? What did you see?"

"'Bout the same."

I sat on the ground, looking at her feet instead of her face to spare my neck. Her scuffed black-and-white off-brand Nikes half-full of playground sand next to my equally scuffed off-brand Converse.

She kicked ferociously at the sand. "I'm an idiot. Should have stayed in the house. Wasn't thinking at all."

"Good one," I said. "Some prodigy."

"If I had a nickel for every time you've said 'some prodigy,' I could literally afford to send another spaceship to Mars."

"Yes, but I'm always justified. You sound scared," I said.

"You too."

"I don't know what we're dealing with," I said, more sharply than I meant. "And I don't think you really do either. That's what scares me. You being scared."

She fell silent, swinging, not looking at me. I thought again, unable to help it, about the day we'd met. Which I couldn't even remember.

We were eight and nine when I learned the whole story. We had been dancing to Thriller, hopping and twisting through the sprinkler in her parents' backyard, trying to moonwalk on the wet grass. The hose we had unwisely left exposed on the dark patio stones produced a blood-heat shower stinking of metal, evaporating in seconds off our sunburned skin.

"Joanna!" her mother called from the house, or maybe it was the au pair. "Snack!"

"Coming!" Johnny yelled. We turned off the record player—a beautiful, vintage machine in a real wood cabinet—and were stopped at the glass doors by another shout, this one actively hostile. Johnny rattled the handle.

"Change before you come in! And don't track in any dirt!"

"But we're clean! We were in the sprinkler!"

No one came to unlock the door. Johnny sighed.

I stripped like a snake behind a topiary and whipped into my dry clothes, then trotted across the hissing flagstones to see Johnny wrestling with her wet t-shirt; for the first time I saw the scar on her back, a shining coin stuck to her golden skin. Then it was gone, covered with the silkscreened face of Optimus Prime.

Inside, we speared grapes and cheese with toothpicks, like grownups.

"What's this?" I said.

"Feta."

"And what's this?"

"Smoked gouda, I think."

I gulped my strawberry milk and said, "And what's that thing on your back?"

Said like that, I expected her to get mad, or go quiet, or just cry. Instead, to my surprise, she answered me.

"It's from the same thing as the scar on your shoulder," she said.

I blushed. I always had a shirt on when we played, even when we were swimming. I thought no one outside my family knew of it. "Mom said I was born with that."

"You weren't," she said. "I wasn't born with mine either. We were shot."

"We were *what?*"

She finished her Snapple in lingering sips as she looked out the window, telling the story to the backyard instead of me, exhaling fake peach as she spoke.

ONCE UPON A time, she said, spinning the Snapple lid like a top, there was a charity choir performance at City Hall, and lots of inner city kids—such as myself—had attended because it was free, and a few kids whose parents had donated lavishly to the charity—such as herself—had also attended, and it so happened that a group of domestic terrorists selected the event for participation in negotiations with the federal government. They segregated the children into a store closet as hostages, ejected the adults, and installed men at exits and entrances, which they welded shut.

Their wish, they said, was no loss of life.

News helicopters hovered, sparring with the police 'copter till threatened with obstruction of justice; for days the government negotiators asked our captors to let us go, then begged, cajoled, threatened. One child from the choir died early on—diabetic, they said. Then another: unknown causes. Then another and another: dehydration. And when eight of us had died the Army sent in men with guns and it all went wrong.

We were the only survivors.

And even so, it was a very near thing: a round went through the door, then through Johnny, then attempted to go through me, where it stuck against my shoulderblade. They operated on her first because she had lost so much blood; me next, because they had to phone some people, as no one knew who had fired it, and whether what had lodged inside me was explosive and might have maimed the surgeon.

Recovery was in the same hospital room, infrequently separated by the blood-smelling curtain. We shared our nightmares for weeks, staring in mute pain at each other when we woke, brown eyes meeting green. Our mothers bonded, superficially but tightly. The round, as it turned out, had not been explosive.

"The end," she said.

I stared at her. She told good stories, and I was old enough to know that that sometimes meant she could recap a movie she'd seen or a book she'd read, and sometimes it was an original work for our month-long games of pretend in Braeside Ravine. But which was it this time?

I thought as hard as I could about that dim, violet scene. Had that really been her, that glimpse of blonde hair, clear mask? Or had it been a dream? "That didn't really happen," I said.

"It did," she said.

I hesitated. There *was* something... the sickly, lemony smell of the hospital, the rusty smell of soaked bandages. My kindergarten teacher sending a card with an animal on the front... a hedgehog or porcupine, its leg in a cast. And there *had* been a little girl who talked like a grownup. Hadn't there? "Mom said I had to have surgery..."

"That's true."

"You were there," I said. "I mean, *were* you there? Are you sure? How come I don't remember that?"

"Because many anaesthetic drugs cause retrograde amnesia, so you might not remember the period in City Hall at all, and because most people have incomplete memories before the age of approximately seven," she said. "I'm mostly eidetic, which means I don't have that problem. I remember everything. You're not just dumb."

"I already knew *that*."

But of course, when your best friend was the world's most famous child prodigy, it bore repeating. I felt dumb for even needing her to explain it. "It just means *early*," she insisted. "Not *better*." I knew she was lying, though. She hadn't even spoken till she was three years old— that wasn't early. Her parents hadn't taken her to the specialists to see if she was gifted; they were worried she was the opposite.

But when she decided—and not before—there came the torrent of words, the books, the tours, the newscasts, the patents. All her parents could do was get out of the way, shading their eyes against her light, as the labs and observatories began to go up, till her very name became shorthand for young genius—a piano Chambers, a math Chambers. Nothing that applied to me, to the ordinaries, the anti-Chamberses.

Now, sitting on the swing and still avoiding my gaze, she said, "I don't even know if I would tell you if I did know. It might be dangerous for you to know."

"Dangerous how? Should you be out here without security? Do you even *have* security right now?"

"I hate security."

"Well I don't care what you hate, if we're in danger." She fell silent.

I stood up, dusted myself off. "Is that what you wanted me to come here for?"

"I'm sorry." She looked up at me; her lips were chewed red and raw and I felt my anger waver for a second, replaced with the old love, or maybe just pity. I thought about that dark time at City Hall, and the dark times afterwards, unable to help it. For a long time I'd thought it was a darkness that we carried inside us, whole and complete, like a stone; but it was more like a coat, something we wore and couldn't take off, always visible in how we moved through the world. Our fear of small things, large things, made-up things. The way it took forever to trust someone. The way we clocked exits now when we went to an unfamiliar place, glancing at each other, knowing we were doing it. We'd never be able to train ourselves out of any of it.

I pointed again, and she finally looked up at the right place on the horizon, then started back, nearly toppling out of her swing. The northern lights danced, surging like waves, punctured by stars so bright and hot they barely twinkled. There was another faraway roar, the scream of a big plane passing.

"See? Told you they were out tonight," I said, pleased by her surprise. "They were out yesterday, too. Nice: more blue and purple than usual. I even saw a shooting star."

"Did you," she said softly.

CHAPTER FOUR

I INSISTED ON walking her home, despite her protests that it was safer if we were separated; I couldn't quite get over how she had dismissed me at the picnic, and gone after the boys herself. She wouldn't tell me safer from what, either, and so we walked down the silent streets, dodging between pools of streetlight, with the obvious question hanging over our heads like a cloud. I was not quite at 'How did you know what that thing is?' but I could consider 'Where did you get the idea that it could be a real thing?'

I couldn't think of a single answer on my own. It was one thing for her to be intelligent, which no one doubted; it was another thing to be the holder of knowledge that *no-one else had*. Was it an alien? Some kind of secret government project? A genetically modified animal? Who would make such a thing, and from what? A... a black bear, and a vulture, and a snake, and a bat?

But there was something about her caginess, her disavowal of all certainty. Her refusal to speak now, as if it would appear again upon hearing her voice. I shivered, thinking about it, looking behind me.

Johnny lived in a quiet neighbourhood—rich folks don't like traffic noise or screaming kids—but it was absolutely without sound tonight, only the wind, so quiet I could hear my heart beat. I kept glancing into the black, shivering trees between the houses, wondering if something hid behind the slender trunks. Watching us, as it had watched earlier.

Things seemed to move in the corner of my eye as Johnny unlocked the door. And she could see them too—she kept jumping, fumbling the numbers, peering nervously around us. Well, at least one of us got home safe. "Goodnight," I said. "Listen, if you see that thing again, call me and I'll—"

She jerked away from me, hitting her back against the door; I instinctively looked behind me. Nothing. Darkness. All the shades of darkness, and streetlight soft and orange on the shadowed lawn, patchy beneath swaying leaves. What had she seen?

Before I could ask, she beckoned me inside, and slammed the door. We stood panting for a moment in the oval of light from outside, as if we had been running.

Probably a squirrel or a rabbit or somebody's outdoor cat, for Christ's sake, not the... thing. Alien-thing. Probably *shrubbery*.

I slumped against the wall and laughed. How obvious

was it that it was a stalker, someone in a cheap black Grim Reaper costume left over from Halloween, with a skull mask on top? It was probably glow-in-the-dark, too. For fuck's sake, me thinking it was an alien or a yeti or some weirdo genetic splice. Our government couldn't even get running water on reservations, there was no way it could clone a bear with a snake. If anything, aliens were *more* likely than some garbage animal cooked up in a *government* lab. And less likely than another pedophile stalker, like the ones that came creeping out from under their rocks after that *Time* cover.

She'd gotten a lot of zoning concessions to build this house so that it looked like its neighbours outside; it wasn't till you got deep that you'd know it was hers. Or a supervillain's, maybe. But a stalker would know. Might be out there now, dressed in black. Wouldn't even need to have followed us, if he'd done his homework and figured out her address.

"What's going on?" I whispered.

"I saw... I mean, I thought I saw..." She shook her head, and moved away from the decorative glass pane of the door, as if someone were peering through it right now, inches away. "Don't leave. I need to go make some phone calls."

"What? It's the middle of the night! I have to get home, I have work tomorrow!"

She disappeared into the darkness, and I took a single step to follow, then stopped. You can't just boss me around! I wanted to yell, but frankly, there would have been no point.

Something dark fluttered again on the lawn, the cat or leaf or shadow, the *perfectly ordinary thing*, I told myself as I fled from the door, no longer laughing. There was something out there. Something that had frightened her. How safe were we in the house?

I took a deep breath and headed to the stair tree. The Red Line would lead down to some places I knew—theatre, games room, a couple of small chemistry and biology labs, a tissue culture room, and Ben's tank. It was Ben I wanted to hang out with now, and I don't know what kind of world it is where a Pacific giant octopus becomes a symbol of safety, but there you are.

He had been an accident—a test survivor of a batch of drugs meant not to slow aging but to improve heart function, back in the day. Johnny had patented the heart drug just a couple of years ago, and kept Benjamin Franklin, Science Octopus (his full name) a secret. Even the contractors who had knocked out walls and built the reinforced tank hadn't known what was going in it, I recalled. She'd told them the triple-thick plexiglass and airtight seams were for physics experiments with dark matter. Conniving little weirdo.

"Where smarts won't do, cunning often will," she'd say. "People think I'm an owl. I'm a fox."

"You're a mutant," I'd tell her. "Like the X-Men."

"Clearly you have no idea how hard it is to be a girl, and my age, and a scientist, in a world where the old boys' club still holds sway," she'd said. We had been hanging out in her room, the usual mess, floor crunchy with pieces of molecular models. "Everything *I* do has to be checked a hundred times; Doctor Joe in Kokomo gets published after one half-assed attempt. They can call in favours I have no access to. And they call me a freak so often I keep thinking I need to get it printed on my lab coats. They have peers. I have *fans*. One sent me this huge scrapbook he'd made of all my tabloid appearances. It was as big as a phonebook. *Genius child really a thousand year-old alien. Johnny Chambers: nanotech monster! Prodigy says 'I'm taking over the world!'"*

"Aren't you?"

"Maybe later."

"Well I don't feel sorry for you," I said. "You don't know how hard it is to be brown. Like, you can't know that, no matter what else you do. I'd take being white and rich and pretty and people thinking I'm an idiot any day."

"*And* a fake," she'd said, turning it back to herself again, as she always did. Insulting even though I hadn't wanted her pity. But that was how she thought about everyone in her life: whether they met her standards, not whether their standards might be different from hers. You got used to it after a while.

Ben's room brimmed with warm green light, the tank bulbs shining through the giant kelp. Her dad's hand-me-down reading chair leaned against it, overstuffed blue leather bulging at all the seams, brass nailhead trim hanging on for dear life. I stepped over the piles of books on the floor and curled up in the cool leather, pressing my palm to the wall of the tank. Ben floated out of his castle carrying three toys, a tangled mass of red-brown muscle topped with golden eyes the size of grapefruits.

"What is up, Science Octopus," I said, holding my hand there until he touched the glass on his side with one tentacle and then backflipped off to another part of the tank. You couldn't quite meet his gaze; it wasn't set up that way, not to be eye-to-eye with the human eye. You felt like you were looking at a toy or a robot instead of an animal. Something about their shape. Even the kids' stuffed animals were easier to make eye contact with.

And yet, simply having another living thing here made me feel better. Less scared. In my house you never knew how used you got to other people being within three feet of you at all times till they suddenly weren't. Johnny swung the other way—she could barely stand a crowd for more than a couple of hours before getting snappy and twitchy, and she hated to be touched. I remembered the summer she'd picked up krav maga, some old guy—a professor, I think—put his hand on her bare shoulder at an awards banquet and got thrown across the room before either of them realized what was happening. After that she wore a sweater over all her evening gowns.

I asked her once about why she flies commercial, since she could obviously afford her own planes and pilots, but there she is, right there in that shared metal tube with the common man. "I gotta keep exposing myself to people," she said apologetically. "Otherwise I forget what they're like. You spend too long in the lab, or in the numbers, or at the observatory, or in the field, and then you look up and it's like—oh no! Look at all these *people*. Brrrr! Like a shock to the system. I gotta keep my immunity up."

"Is that why you keep me? So you can keep your immunity up to normal people instead of scientists?"

"I keep you," she had said, "because you are *mine*."

"And you don't like people touching your stuff."

"No I do not."

Couldn't deny it. She'd moved out of her mom's house at eight, with her blessing, when the publicity was at its height.

("Oh, so what. Eve Plumb bought a house when she was eleven!"

"Who's that?")

Somewhere that no one might touch her stuff except her. The pique of a child, you'd think, but she's never really been a child with anyone except me. And it hadn't been a snit. It had been as calculated and rational as anything else she'd built—the telescopes, the dark matter labs, the experimental greenhouses with their frankencanola and monstertatoes and byzantine ventilation systems to prevent a molecule of pollen from going the wrong way, her institutions and plants and warehouses and farms and factories. Like the tank for this strange squishy thing, floating past me occasionally and showing off his toys.

"That's real nice, Ben," I said.

The other thing in the room whose gaze I couldn't meet seemed to be watching me anyway: her chemistry robot, which I'd always been leery of. I hated its two huge depthless lenses, like the eyes of a shark. ("It's not looking *at you*," she had said again and again, "it's just that it needs two lenses for depth perception, and you've got pareidolia."

"I think there's a cream for that now.")

But I knew it wanted to do science on me. It had once, for example, electroplated a dung beetle that had wandered in there by accident (admittedly, it had survived; you saw it walking around the house every now and then, although in a very shaky gait). The solid tapestry of puffy and scented rainbow, unicorn, and cloud stickers all over it made absolutely no difference to my feelings towards it, nor did the fact that it was one of her prized possessions—she had created a huge database of potential drugs, and used the robot to synthesize them automatically before doing some kind of ultrafast modelling on another computer, then cells on a chip, then something called 'organoids.' It cut years off her drug development process and had probably saved a lot of lives, but it also looked a lot like a praying mantis with several stabbing limbs, and I had seen enough movies to know how it would move when it finally attacked me.

I realized I was falling asleep, or my body was simply taking matters into its own hands, as the chair warmed under my body. No big deal if I spent the night, I supposed, providing I called home in the morning, but how would I ever wake up in time for work? Might have to risk it. Tired. Johnny would wake me up, when she came back. Whenever that happened. Should be soon...

I floated down into black and green light.

a dream of darkness, a dream of light that was not light, streaming past me
a stench, rotted meat and ashes, a stink of solvent, swamp gas, a bloated deer at the side of the road, old blood, cancerous chemicals
a dream of stones
a dream of stones over me, blue and white, thrumming to shake me apart
to cry out and cover the ears only, to pretend courage
to scream, to go unheard
light not meant for real eyes
a warm pressure, a multitude, a moist stink of licking shadow

the stones!

the watchers!

I woke up screaming, woke myself up, not a real scream but a hypersonic bat-high whine like an infant at the edge of its pain threshold, hands over my ears to block even that out.

The world had ended, there was nothing we could do, not even witness it, the noise and the shaking drove us down like animals to cower, eyes shut and ears hidden to block it out, unable to, the entire body ending like the world ending, tearing apart in precisely the same way. A dream of blackness in which everything was both visible and wrong.

My throat hurt; I tasted blood. Ben floated over, tentacle-tipping the glass tentatively near the chair, like he wanted to pat me on the shoulder. I put a hand to the tank and waited while he touched it on his side. I trained him to do that. Like a dog waiting for "all right" before it could eat. She wanted to see if he would remember.

She. She who? I felt fuzzy, as if I'd hit my head. My watch said I'd been asleep for two hours. She should have come back. Had something happened? No, ridiculous. We were safe. House a fortress.

All the same, I felt intensely as if I were being watched. Not by the robot or the octopus, who had both looked away. But something else, in the empty room.

I crawled out of the chair, wincing as my gravel-scraped palms stuck to the leather. It felt like leaving sanctuary. Like in movies where the hero steps off the churchyard dirt, hallowed ground, and the vampire or werewolf gets him. I swallowed hard—more blood, Christ—and forced myself onwards. At the staircase, a faint glow from above reflected down the handrail, promising safety, or at least company.

It was coming from the main kitchen. All the blinds were down, barriers of tasteful dove-grey that matched the walls, reflecting back the silvery light of the halogens.

(not like the light at the end of the)

(be quiet)

(it was a dream)

Johnny was at the island, staring at the coffeemaker, a big Italian thing enameled in cherry-red like a Ferrari. It looked like a transforming robot from one of those

Japanese shows the kids watched. Johnny never did things in half-measures. It was just starting to hiss, but she heard the sound of my socked feet on the floor anyway.

"Hi," she said without turning. "You okay?"

"Glk," I said. The pain in my throat prevented anything else. I got a glass of water from the fridge and stood beside her. She smelled of raw coffee and her mom's line of expensive soaps, herbal and sweet, the smell of money; but her Spongebob Squarepants pajamas smelled of the same fabric softener we used.

"Fell asleep in Ben's room," I said. "What's going on?"

"Don't leave tonight," she said, voice so low I could barely hear her.

"...Uh..." My brain gummed up, stalled out. That's the problem with naps really, you never feel a hundred percent afterwards, even if you really needed it. She wanted me to stay? No. She just didn't want me to leave. She didn't particularly want us to be together, she just didn't want me outside.

Sweat broke out on my neck, and something else, a buzz, as if it had been asleep and was just coming awake. I rubbed at my nape, fingers tangling in sweaty hair.

"That's why," she said, as if I had finished my thought. "Feel that?"

"What?"

"Yeah. It's watching the house."

"Who is? 'It' *who?* That *thing?*"

"You shouldn't have walked me home," she said. The coffee machine finished and left a gaping silence punctuated with little clicks and beeps as it wound down. The glass cup of espresso was small enough to look proportional in her shaking hand.

"Hooooly shit, that is not an answer," I said, feeling hysteria rising, trying to push it back down. I'd never heard her talk like this before. "You let me, anyway. You should have stopped me if...Is it *the thing*? And how do you know all this? And what were you *doing*? Jesus, I woke up freaking out, I had the worst fucking dreams—"

"What?"

"I *said* how do you know this and who's watching the house. You can answer in either ord—"

"You fell asleep," she said. "And you had... you had a nightmare?"

"Answer the *question!* Jesus Christ!"

She turned at last, fixing me with the full wattage of her green stare. I tolerated it for as long as I could, then winced and turned away. "Well, I guess you're involved whether I like it or not."

"Involved in what?"

"There's a long answer and a short answer," she said flatly, "and both of them are going to require the willing suspension of disbelief."

"I watch a lot of kids' movies. Do your worst."

"The short answer is the *thing* is yes, currently, probably, watching the house and deciding what to do next; and I know about it because I've always known it knew about *me*."

"That's the *short* answer?"

She shrugged, and sipped her espresso.

I felt as if the room was revolving slowly around me, and eased myself onto a stool, hanging onto the island. Fainting twice in two days couldn't be good for you; and here, I'd hit a slate floor instead of vinyl tiles.

"If I go," I said, "it would follow me... back to my house."

"I think so."

"And that would be bad."

"Definitely."

"But it hasn't... it hasn't *done* anything."

"Not yet."

"The dream I had...was just a dream. Right? It doesn't mean anything. It just..."

"It might mean nothing. Proximity effects. It might mean that it... it's watching you, too, and not just me. I just don't understand how..." She trailed off.

I drank more water, diluting the blood still in my throat. I could barely remember the dream now—something about colours—but the screaming had been real enough. The kids. Mom. If just watching me had led to that, I couldn't let it get anywhere near them.

"Don't you have another way out of this place? It's practically a fortress. And fortresses have secret exits for when things go sideways. Like castles do, like medieval castles. Tunnels. Buried lakes with ferries. Secret monorails. Panic rooms..."

"I *do* have a panic room."

"What about the secret monorail?"

"Never thought I'd need one. And didn't we have

the conversation about being a supergenius versus a supervillain years ago?"

"I think we need to have it again. What about a secret getaway zeppelin hidden in the roof?"

"Blimp, Nicky. A zeppelin has rigid sides, I'd never fit one up there. Anyway, no."

"I cannot believe that you have all this money and you don't have a secret getaway blimp for when monsters are watching the house," I said. "What's the point?"

"I know, I know. But even if we got out, there might be nowhere we can go now." She put her empty cup down and pressed the button on the machine again. "You don't believe me, do you."

"I..."

"But do you believe that *I* believe it?"

"Yes," I said. "Absolutely I do. Because I saw your face at the Creek today, if no other reason. You're the thing I believe."

She dropped her head into her hands for a second. "Listen," she said, breathing fast through her mouth as if she'd been running. "I think... I'm gonna have to get you up to speed on this before things start to happen."

"Things? What things? Things like *what?*"

"Think of a house, right? A house is a house. But also, our world is a house."

"All ri—"

"Lots of doors. Any locked door, if you've got a key you can get in, or if it's a keypad, you have to know the code, or ask somebody for the code."

"Got it."

"Then once you're inside, what have you got? More doors. Doors to bathrooms, closets, bedrooms. You can move easily between them too."

"John, why are you panting like that?"

"Listen, this thing, this watcher? Part of a cabal of things that have been invading Earth and other places for a long time. The first one was about seventy million years ago. Nothing had evolved that had keys or codes to keep invaders out. Whatever you want to call Them—I guess 'the Ancient Ones' is as good a shorthand as any, or the Watchful Ones, Those Who Live Outside—They've been locked out from Earth before, but They're used to being able to leave and come back whenever They want. They open the doors and come in, and only evil follows, because They are nothing but evil. Only evil. All of Them. They don't just want to occupy, They never have. That's not enough. They want to conquer."

"Johnny, you're freaking out. Put down the coffee and—"

"No, sit down, listen to me. Shut the fridge. *Listen.* The first written records of Them are from Sumeria—the destruction of Ur, the flood in Shuruppak, Khorsabad, what happened in Nineveh, and not just there, *hundreds of places* where the records were murals or paintings, pre-literate, or no survivors to leave an account at all, do you understand me? Not one survivor. The fall of Carthage. What They did to Kahuachi, in Peru. What They did in Vilcabamba, the Harappas people exterminated in India, ancient Jericho, Çatal Hüyük in Turkey, Newgrange in Ireland, the Minoans, the Mycenaens."

She was trembling so hard she was almost flickering, like a poorly-tracked VHS tape. But fear alone wasn't proof. "All right," I said dubiously. "If They're so powerful, why aren't we one of Their colonies right now?"

"No one's really sure. But sometime in the past, we did figure out a few things when They appeared. How They travel, where They can come in. The thin places, gates and veils, were mapped. Someone learned how to use Their magic to fight Them, push Them out, even knock Them out. It's not sleep. It's something else; it takes work. Almost like anaesthesia. But it's so light, anything can wake Them. They are *infuriated* by having Their paths barred, especially by things that, to Them, are barely better than, or different from, insects."

"Us."

"Us. It's not just entitlement, it's revenge. There's so much more I could tell you, but just take away that They are gods, but not like the gods we write about with love in the Bible and the Bhagavad Gītā and the *Silmarillion*. I only say 'god' because I don't know another word for that much power."

"And these gods, They're... here now? Awake, back? Or just *one* of Them is back?"

"No. They still can't come here; the doors are still locked to them. But magic always seeps through, and lesser things, like... like flies coming through a window screen. This thing, it's a servant, an ambassador. A former apprentice. But now that it's come, evil things will happen. They generate magic like poison, powdered cyanide, like a fungus shedding its spores, invisible, everywhere, a crawling ugliness and wrongness that... that... that dusts down and catches and grows and creeps. Anything that is Theirs can scoop it up, use it. And now that it's here, more may be able to come."

"You don't know."

"No."

We stared at each other for a minute, tense. Eventually her breath slowed, and she reached for her coffee with steady hands.

"Jesus Christ," I said, "I have work tomorrow, I can't stay. What are we gonna do?"

"Stay over. Don't take the bus in the morning. I'll get Rutger to give you a ride."

"What if it follows me to work when we leave?"

"I'm hoping it'll stay here and watch me instead. Maybe I can... I don't know. Distract it by running the reactor. I think that's what it's interested in. What drew it here."

"You're *hoping* that... oh God. Is Thou Shalt Greatly Ru This Day in on this? Does he know about the... Ancient Ones?"

"No, and stop making fun of his name."

"Does anyone else know?"

"Yeah. That's who I was calling."

"Can they help? Can they... can they do... God, it sounds stupid to even say it. I'm sorry, I'm freaking out but I'm working on it. I need a minute. This isn't *The X-Files*, you know."

"I think I'd look cute with red hair."

"Who says you're the scientist in this scenario? You're clearly Mulder. Look what you're asking me to believe."

"Don't, then," she said, draining her cup; her face was gray and glistening, all the blood hiding. "If it makes you feel better about all this."

"It does not. Can They get in the house?"

"I don't know. I mean, it's set up to be hard for humans to get into, not... other things."

"Great news. *Not*."

We dug up an oversized t-shirt for me to sleep in, and I made Johnny promise to stay in the hallway while I showered, repeatedly dropping and chasing one of her mother's spa soaps around the huge glass box. My hands were shaking so badly I cut my thumb opening the toothbrush package, a bloodless gash on the sharp plastic edge.

I kept telling myself it wasn't fear, not really, it was something else—exhaustion, dehydration, like yesterday. And that was easy enough, because what had I had to fear so far? In my whole life? Just the little things that were scary but survivable: getting grounded, being bullied at school, one of the kids going missing in the mall. This felt more like something from *outside* of me, like secondhand smoke, greasily invisible, sinking into my pores, blown from someone unseen. Not something I could scope out and assess, feel the shape and edges of, decide for myself whether I should be scared of it. The dark thing. Harbinger of the Them. Only her word for it, and this placeless, nameless adrenaline.

We took the Indigo Line, a seldom-used route that never meets the main staircase, descending until I convinced myself that the air was growing warmer from the earth's core, and our thighs were stinging and trembling. Finally we reached a long hallway with a couple of doors on each side, and Johnny let us into one with a thumbprint scanner. It was much cooler than the hallway—and, of course, down here, windowless.

"What is this place?" I said, looking at the two couches kitty-corner to each other, the piles of magazines and blankets, the single phone and lamp.

"Reading room," she said. I lay on one couch and looked at the ceiling—matte metal, dark gray, studded regularly with screws or rivets, trying to figure out if it spelled anything. A beetle bumbled past on the ceiling, iridescent green and blue.

She said, "I don't even know if we're safer down here, but if we're being watched, maybe we're harder to see now."

"Thanks. I'm gonna sleep great now. Wait, *we*? Are you staying—?"

"Yeah."

"After all that coffee?"

"Honestly, it just goes through my system like lemonade now. I'll get you up at six," she said, snapping the light off without ceremony.

I wrapped myself in the blanket and closed my eyes, unnecessarily; it was pitch black either way. Jesus. A reading room buried in the dead centre of her fortress, protected from anything and everything we might have worried about as children. Nuclear blasts, anthrax-hurling madmen, civil war, serial killers. Bullies. Mean girls. The fashion police. It wasn't the billions of people she'd helped who hated her; it was the ones whose lives had been essentially unaffected, and who lived in jealousy and suspicion of what she was. She'd almost burned herself out when she was ten or eleven, working hundred-hour weeks, never sleeping, publishing paper after paper and combining them with press conferences and lecture tours, till Rutger and her parents had put their collective foot down. Don't, they'd said. You'll die.

I don't care, she'd told them—I remembered that, how I'd jumped when she said it—I need to get as much done as I can. How had we convinced a ten year-old kid that she had lots of time left and didn't need to die trying? I couldn't remember. Maybe we hadn't. And then at the Muttart Conservatory a few months later for their holiday concert, her white arm emerging from a puff of burgundy velvet, pointing at the skinny stalk similarly poking from an unremarkable pile of grey spikes. "That's a century plant," she'd whispered as the orchestra set up. "They save up and save up and save up for years, decades, and then they suddenly send up one flower shoot and then they die."

"That's stupid," I said. "Most plants do it every year. We talked about it in school."

"Yeah, but they don't make anything like that," she said. It was true; the spike had grown so tall and so fast that they'd had to clip it at the top, lest it try to break the glass of the pyramid and shoot out into the icy prairie air. "Look at that. How nothing could miss that it's flowering; that that's the biggest and best thing it'll do in its whole life."

"And the last thing."

"Sure. But look."

"I *am* looking." Looking but not seeing. It was years before I knew what she'd been trying to tell me about herself—not a confession but a warning.

Before she'd left, this would have been my dream night—there would have been hope, excitement, anticipation. Maybe this night, this one sleepover, would be the night I'd admit that I was in love with her, and she'd say it back, and we'd agree that we'd grown up, that we were ready for grown-up love very different from the fierce, childhood devotion we'd always had, and then we'd kiss, and then...

In the silence, I heard my stomach gurgle, Johnny's soft breathing, the scrape as she turned over on her couch. Far from becoming accustomed to each other's noises, I thought, in a few moments our ears would sprout new hairs, new bones; we would be able to hear each other's heartbeat against the blankets, thrown out and resonating like a drum, we would be able to hear the scrape of eyelid against eyeball. I swallowed nervous spit, sounding like a firehose.

As many times as we'd played together, stayed up late talking, driven around, eaten side by side, boosted each other over fences, removed splinters, tried to hypnotize each other, this was by far—I thought—the most intimate we'd ever been. It was as if we were trying to fall asleep inside one another's mouths. It was far from romantic; it was disgusting. But we'd always been like this, hadn't we? That unhealthy, stifling closeness, just like this, like conjoined twins who could have been separated and always refused the operation, face to face breathing each other's breath, too close to be normal friends. Too close to love. That was it, wasn't it? We'd never say it. It couldn't be said—that we were not *ageing*, precisely, but *maturing* at two completely different rates, that both were outpacing the friendship, which was a third rate, a third line on a graph we never thought about. Independent of her, independent of me. And yet we couldn't leave each other.

I lay awake while Johnny's breathing grew long and slow—asleep, or faking sleep. Not kidding about the coffee, apparently. I was thirsty and also had to piss, but there was no way I was getting up to fumble around till I found the door and let myself out into the dark hallway to grope along till I found a bathroom (not likely) or the stairs (definitely not).

In the morning, I thought, in the morning I'll ask her questions and she'll answer them, she'll stop talking about things that happened thousands of years ago and just tell me what we can do right now. No. Not what we can do. What *she* can do. She's the one They're watching. She said so. I'm just in the wrong place at the wrong time.

I finally began to doze off, my heartbeat growing muffled, a faint impression of Johnny whimpering and even speaking a few feet away, the sound of her voice no less familiar than that of my fading heart, though in a language I didn't know.

Wait. Don't fall asleep yet. How does she know any of th—

> *the sky is*
> *not a sky*
> *the sky is torn, ragged at the edges*
> *a spill of struggling bodies*
> *light by which one cannot see*
> *a march in the dimness*
> *cover eyes and ears against the*
> *against*
> *the light which can be heard*

I woke up on the floor, grit in my mouth, spitting and gagging even before I had come fully awake, and I couldn't take it any more, I banged around till my hand hit the slim metal pole of the lamp and I switched it on, already apologizing to Johnny— who, I saw with a shock as my eyes adjusted, had slept through the commotion.

But it didn't look like real sleep—in fact, I realized with a jolt, it reminded me of the twins and their night terrors. The first time it happened I thought they were having a seizure, they were so stiff, trembling, unwakeable. Just as I had run for the phone to call 911, they had woken simultaneously and burst into tears, and the rest of the night was spent comforting them. They either didn't remember what they had dreamt, or couldn't express it in their childish language. Just like me, a few minutes ago. Except that I had woken myself up and she hadn't.

In the clear light her skin was green-grey, beaded with sweat that shook down her face with the trembling, her hair glassy, bleached of colour, hands fists. I reached for her instinctively, then forced my hand back. No. She'd hurt me if she woke up—not on purpose, but that wouldn't make any difference. As I looked up, a corner of the room seemed to recede, sprinting as if down a long corridor—and then it was perfectly normal, just like the other one, a mirror image. The lamp creaked under my grip. All the shadows looked too black, not sharp enough. There had been *depth* in that corner. Hadn't there? Just for a second?

"Johnny, wake up. Wake up!"

Her eyes flickered open, gazing straight past me to the ceiling. She screamed.

I backed away, hitting my thighs on the couch and toppling over it, and struggled up. "John! Snap out of it!"

"Nicky?"

"It's me, it's—Jesus. Are you okay?"

I finally flipped myself off the couch's sucking grip and crawled over to her, stopping at a prudent distance. "You're, uh, bleeding a little bit."

"Bit my tongue." She ran her forearm over her lips, producing a long streak of pink-tinted saliva, like lipgloss. I looked away. "What... happened?"

"You were having a bad dream."

"Was I? How do you know?"

"You just looked like you were." I sagged onto the floor, rested my wrists on my knees. I wanted to sleep for another eight hours. Real sleep, not this nightmare garbage that left me even more tired. "You looked like the boys did when they were having night terrors. Don't you remember what you were dreaming about?"

She shook her head, wiped her mouth again. "I dreamt I was... somewhere else... and I couldn't see. I mean, I could *see*, but not..."

"The light was wrong," I murmured. "You could hear the light but you couldn't see in it."

She stared at me.

"John," I said. "Did They get into the house?"

Silence. After what felt like a punishing length of time, she lifted her wrist and said "Well, it's 5:45. We'd better get you to work."

She threw off the blanket and stepped past me. The hallway was as dark as our room had been, lit by the lonely triangle of white light interrupted by our silhouettes. Shadows seemed to squirm at either end. I watched them till I was sure they weren't moving.

CHAPTER FIVE

I TURNED AROUND so many times as Rutger drove me to work that I wricked my neck, but no shadow followed us, no black streak floated or loped behind the car.

"Joanna seemed upset this morning," he said abruptly when we stopped at the lights on Hebert; I nearly jumped out of my skin. I hadn't expected him to say anything to me, let alone something I couldn't really reply to.

Well, I'm not fucking surprised, I almost said. Instead I shrugged. If he didn't know about this... this new stalker, this new situation, then it wasn't up to me to tell him. I stared at his profile, hoping to get some clues from it, but his expression was fixed.

"She's tired," I said carefully, unable to bear the silence much longer. "She's working on something big."

"Renewable energy, yes. She described to me the design of the reactor."

"...Oh. Good. That's good."

"It does not seem to me," he said quietly, the end of his words a little clipped, as we turned into the parking lot, "that it *should* work, however."

I glanced at him. That was the closest to real anxiety I'd ever seen him express. For a moment I debated spilling everything, telling him what she'd told me, begging for help; she couldn't deal with this alone, not if They were everything she said They were, and who knew how she'd come to that conclusion anyway. I mean she was smart, yes, absolutely, but she was still just a kid, we were just kids, I couldn't help her, we needed... but I knew I couldn't. "I guess that's why she's tired. You know. Testing it or whatever."

"Perhaps."

We had taken, at her request, a twisty route; I ran from the Lexus and managed to clock in just in a minute before my shift started.

"You all right, Nicky?" asked the bakery manager, Barb. "You sound stuffy. Coming down with something?"

"Hm? No, I don't think so. Allergies," I said.

"You look sketchy, baby. I got some Benadryl in my purse, come see me after you check the bread numbers, okay?"

Everybody wanted to be my mom. I sighed and headed into the bakery storeroom, then stopped, confused. Something stank, something that would have been just as out of place but more comprehensible coming from the meat locker: a rotten stench, green-black in colour, not the fuzzy apologetic blue of bread mould. I hesitated near the tall shelves, sniffing—and then the door swung shut behind me and the lights went out.

For a second I stood in complete darkness, and then I spun and scrabbled at the wall for the switches, feeling them under my fingertips as up, thumbs-up, yes sir, we're still on. I flicked them anyway, up and down a dozen times. Nothing. *A darkness, strangers, the sound of gunfire.* I reached for the handle, and cried out as a hand closed around my wrist.

"Uhh!" I yanked back, but the grip was like a handcuff—scaly, hot, carrying a wave of stomach-churning smell so that I had to spit quickly onto the floor to empty my mouth. The hand didn't budge. I wrenched at it, this can't be happening, I was just too tired, that was all, hallucinating, or some fucking prank you guys, some fucking *prank*, but the hand wasn't human, and I was only, I knew, using the word 'hand' because 'appendage' would have made me scream. Even now I wondered if I should be screaming; my affronted grunt wouldn't have attracted any help.

It wasn't completely dark; there was a little light, ordinary fluorescent light filtering under the half-inch gap under the door. As my eyes adjusted, the thing holding me came into focus—yes, of course it was the thing from the creek, a limb extending from the raggedy blackness and clamped tight around my wrist.

I was sure that if I kept squirming it would simply take the skin off, and a dim embarrassment soaked through the terror: that it was not the pain I feared exactly or the injury itself, but how I would explain it when I got out of the storeroom, if I ever got out. Because everyone would ask how it happened and if I couldn't explain I would be in trouble. I became aware of my panting breath and willed it to slow. Okay. All right. Found me. I believe.

I believe. *I believe.*

"Let me go," I said.

A long hiss, almost laughter. I turned my head away from the fresh torrent of stench, the tangled mass of ugliness inside the hood. And the white, straight, shining teeth—I had seen them for a fraction of a second, and that was long enough. My skin kept trying to crawl away from the sticky, rasping grip, the way the claws of the velociraptors in Jurassic Park might have felt.

"What has the child told you?" it whispered.

"What child?"

"You know of whom we speak."

Nothing you don't already know, I thought. Nothing new. Nothing you haven't known for, what, millions of years? And why would I tell you anyway? "No, she hasn't told me anything," I said after a second.

"As I thought." Another crackling hiss, like the cockroaches in the museum. The hand fell away and I stumbled back towards the doorway, rubbing my arm on my apron and yanking on the handle, which creaked and failed to open even under my full weight. It emitted a faint purple glow, sickeningly wrong and yet familiar, the light I knew from a dream, growing brighter the harder I tugged. Finally I turned again.

"The child called us," it said, drifting closer; I stared

at the floor, where the ragged ends of the robe, outlined in silver light, hovered above the tiles. "We heard it in our slumber. A new thing has come into the world. No human should possess such a thing. Even her. She does not know its true power. And still she called."

A sickly mist fell from the thing, just visible in the thin band of light. What had she said? A contagion, spreading, like the spores of a fungus... I thought about it settling on the plastic bags of bread and buns and tortillas and croissants, sinking through the wrappers, sending black threads into the soft white contents, filling each pore with a little droplet of black, the light all wrong, the sky that was not the sky.

"I don't know what you're talking about."

"She will not give it to us willingly. But it is the way of the world for power to go to the powerful. Not to the weak. It is... inevitable."

It was still coming; my back hit the door. But there was nowhere else to go. I didn't dare close my eyes and lose the tiny bit of light; to be in complete darkness with this thing—never, I would go insane. Maybe that was what it wanted.

"Take it from her," it whispered.

"No."

"You have seen it. You know it. Bring it to Us. Speak to her, ask her to see... reason..."

"Reason? What reason? She's got no reason to turn that thing over to you."

A long silence. But if it were going to kill me, it would have by now. Right here, right now, in the darkness. All it would take was that scaly, stinking hand at my throat.

"We will reward you greatly," it whispered. "To bring it. Or to destroy her."

"*Destroy* her? You're asking me to *kill* her? What the fuck, if *you* can't have it, no one can have it? No. I won't. I can't and I won't. Fuck off. Let me out."

"There would be... rewards... we have... great rewards..."

"You've got nothing for me. She didn't have to tell me shit about you for me to know that."

Darkness, the icy edge of a limb extending. I shuffled sideways along the door, headbutted a metal shelf hard enough that red stars exploded behind my eyes, and then the hand was scraping along my face, hard, sticky, moving from jaw to forehead. I froze, lids now clenched shut, picturing the appendage popping the unprotected jelly of my eye like a paintball.

"*Have* we nothing?" it hissed. "Nothing to offer? Everything will be taken from you, human. Understand us. Remember. Everything will be taken from you."

And then it was gone—my face set free, the lights shamefacedly creeping back into life. I stared wildly around at the untouched bread, at the clean floor. Nothing. No dust, no footprints. The handle behind me gave so suddenly I fell out of the room, catching myself at the last moment. Riva from the bakery stood there with one of the other stockboys, a kid I didn't know. They were staring at me.

"Are you all right?" Riva said, confused. "Nicky? What happened to your face?"

"Nothing, I... the lights went out and I fell..."

"The lights went out?"

I shook my head, rubbing my cheek. The skin hadn't been broken, but I could feel welts, hot, rising as thick as licorice ropes. "They're fine now, Riva. It's okay. Maybe we could, uh, get Mike to put them on the maintenance schedule for next month or something."

I nudged past her, grabbed my clipboard from its slot, and filled in lines and lines of bullshit numbers. It was as if fear had emptied everything else out; I was an animal, running scared. But the bills still had to get paid. I clicked myself into robot mode and forced myself to get back to work.

The horror faded after a few hours, the mundane duties that had become second nature by my third year in this job: checkmarks and clipboards, lifting boxes, stacking produce. There was a litany running through my mind in the voice of reason, the voice of Peter Mansbridge, a gentle, rational voice. If the thing wanted to kill you, the voice said, it would have. It would have killed you. It therefore didn't *want* to. And it could have, easily. You felt that strength. Look at our fragile bodies, with our squishy tubes and internal skeletons, no claws, no fangs. It kept you alive. Because it *needs* you. It wanted you to do something and you refused, but it didn't kill you when you refused. And so. There must be something else it wants. It offered a reward before it offered a threat. Remember that. Tell Johnny that. Don't forget.

As if I could forget. Its words had seared into my memory—if someone X-rayed my skull they would see everything written on there, like a branded steak in a commercial. And the words would not be in English but the dark language that was its first tongue. English was probably not even the thousandth language it knew.

AT THE END of my shift, I took the bus home, got the car, and let myself into Johnny's house, both hoping and not hoping that she'd be home. I hadn't really wanted to come; I had wanted to go home and be with Mom and the kids. Someplace safe and normal, free from magic and monsters, someplace I wouldn't be watched. But it seemed more and more now that what I wanted didn't matter. I had to tell her what had happened first. Tell her about the deal I had been offered.

Inside, I felt woozy, dizzy, reaching to steady myself on the walls as I wandered to the main kitchen, tracking the sound of the red coffee machine. The pleasant smells of melting cheese and fresh coffee wafted down the hall.

She looked up, apparently unsurprised, juggling something from a plate to a pan. "Grilled cheese," she said, waving the spatula at me. "Want one?"

"Maybe in a minute," I said. Four pieces of bread. She knew I would come here. "Stomach doesn't feel too good."

"Go get a yogurt from the fridge. That'll settle it."

I did, then perched at the counter to watch her flip her sandwich. It smelled like kimchi—she liked all sorts of things in her grilled cheese, olives or apples or tomato or Cool Ranch Doritos, with kimchi and fries being particular favourites. I cracked open my yogurt—one of her weird flavours, passionfruit and lemon. It occurred to me that I didn't even know what a passionfruit looked like. I ate it anyway.

"John," I said. "Listen, I just came to tell you about that... thing... it cornered me at work today."

She went very still, hand halfway to her sandwich. "Let me clarify that in a way that gives me useful data," she said. "It found you at a place that you have not seen it before, a place with other people nearby, and confronted you directly, though not—I assume—in view of witnesses?"

"Yeah. All of that. It must have been waiting in the storeroom. I didn't ask, but I assumed no one else saw it. I didn't hear any screaming." I scraped my spoon in my empty cup and looked at her, a hectic red glare under her eyes that I was starting to recognize as absolute bolting panic, just barely hidden by her iron will. It was as if her fear was the ocean and her rationality a tiny submersible, one of those round ones with a two-foot-thick viewport just an inch or two across, only looking at the world through that lest it be crushed, able to resist the pressure specifically because of it.

I began, weakly in the face of that panic: "It... it wanted..."

"Did it offer you a covenant?"

"What?"

"Try to make a deal?" she said sharply.

"Yeah. Tried. It asked me to get them the reactor."

"In exchange for?"

"It just said 'reward.'"

"And that was it? That was all it said? Nothing else?"

"Yeah. Well, I mean, after it said it would reward me and I still said no, it sort of threatened me instead." I closed my eyes, remembering—oh Jesus, the stink, the darkness, the line of blue light on the floor, the pressure of the air as its limb approached me, that I should never have been able to sense. "It said everything would be taken from me."

Her shoulders slumped as she stared down at the counter, like her reply might be coded in the millions of tiny dots in the granite, a secret language just like Theirs. I knew what it would say, I had read the same thing in the ragged edge of the thing's garment: unhappiness, everything good in me emptying out like a lake over the edge of a cliff, vanishing into the dark and the cold for years, nothing ever returning to me. To conquer, she said. Not occupy. Of course They would not want to live here as equals. It was not in Them; I knew that now.

I took in the softness of the blonde at her temples, how thin the veins were there; the curve of her lips, the angles of her hands, the sleek sweep of her back under the cheap cotton polo shirt, the gloss and curl of the lashes. My nose knew every molecule she gave off, because that is what love does, turns you inside out until you are nothing but a pile of nerves and senses—the sweet, hay-like smell of her hair, the cherry of her cheap lipgloss. Makes a million dollars in a month and spends precisely one dollar and nine cents on her cosmetics in about the same time.

Could I possibly tell her that I had been asked to kill her rather than let the reactor be used? No. No words for it. And, I thought, she had probably figured that out already.

"Everything will be," she finally said. "And everything will be taken from me, too. All of us. All of the world. That's what it meant."

"How do you know?"

"Because that's what They do," she said, slowly. "Because Their evil takes that form: taking, destroying. Because that's all They want. They know we want this. That's why They want it. Because anything we love is something They want to take away."

"But—"

"It's got to be that the doorways are thinning. Maybe not opening, not yet. Conditions must be lining up for them to be able to open, though. There *has* to be something. Historically, there's always been something. A... volcanic eruption maybe, an earthquake. Something big. Something soon."

"And what happens then?"

She shook her head, a sharp snap like she was dislodging a fly, and reached for her cooling sandwich. "I told you. You read the mythologies, a pattern starts to emerge. You have to remember that history, which they say is written by the winners, is in fact written by the survivors; you can't write shit if there's nothing left after you win. Look at Sumeria, look at the whole Middle East, look at half of South America."

"What... am I looking at?"

"Patterns. Repeated, like wallpaper. The big man rises, boosted by the gods, till something goes wrong. And something always goes wrong, because the gods are finicky fuckers, they're like my Aunt Edna on meth, they scream when you move the doily on the coffee table. A renovated shrine, a skipped sacrifice, a missed syllable in a hymn—everything suddenly becomes a blasphemy. The city is destroyed, or the country is destroyed, in moments, but so violently and visibly that horrified witnesses can describe it from miles away. Every last man, woman, and child killed, all the animals burned, the rivers erupt and boil, the buildings toppled, the sky torn apart. Sometimes there's a crater, sometimes there isn't. What happens when the gods are no longer on your side? You're not the big man any more. You're nothing. And everything is taken from you."

"*That* isn't happening here," I said firmly. "It could have killed me. It shut the door and turned off the lights and grabbed me, and that was all it did. That must be all it *can* do right now. Nothing was stopping it."

She looked away, and a silence drew out. "Making the reactor woke Them up, I think. But now They're getting ready for bigger things. Their powers are... we don't have good words for it. Not in any language. And that thing is more of a scout than an ambassador, if it's who I think it is. It likes to make deals, they say."

"You... know it?"

"I think it must be Drozanoth. No one else watches Earth enough to know what to watch for."

"It just watches?"

"It's a powerful *igigi*, one of those who wander under the waste, created in Dzannin, Apprentice to Azag-Thoth," she said quietly. "So its teacher is the worst and strongest of Them, and one of the oldest. It's had many apprentices in its time, but Drozanoth is the one that watches and waits for a chance to let its masters back in."

"Like... those fuckin' houseflies that wait right outside the door."

"Just like that. It knows humans, humanity, it's seen enough to derive the patterns we make. The way things change just before the world surges toward something new. If everything is thinning out, then simply thinking about the reactor might have shocked it into action—like a goddamn airhorn."

"Science as an airhorn. Great."

"Not science. More like... possibilities. And this is just from the old readings, you know." She groped for words, chewing, waving her hand in the air as if writing on a whiteboard. "Some things are like a light in the darkness to Them, tiny but real, because it's so dark where They are that any light seems incredibly bright. And the more ways it could change things, the brighter it seems. It was like that for writing, and the wheel. And the atom bomb. It can see a little ways into the future, not far and not well, but it sees possibilities the most clearly. Goddammit. *Goddammit*."

"The... bomb?"

"Yeah, it, I... I just, is there a way to keep talking without sounding totally insane? I don't know. Who's the best judge of that? Not Them. Not me. Maybe you? I don't know."

"Not me."

I wondered if the thing was running some scheme it'd run before, like some kind of... little-known magic Mafia. I knew the story from Hollywood. The mobsters don't go to the poorest neighbourhoods, because what can they steal, who can they get protection money from? You bust up a pawn shop, the owner simply vanishes overnight. No, you wait until a bigshot comes into your neighbourhood, or you cruise the ones where the bigshots live, and you pick the biggest white-painted wedding cake of a house, and you roll up with your Tommy guns and your goons, and you say: *That. I want that. I have found something that is worth taking; and that is what I will take.*

Limitless, clean power. That was what they wanted to take from us. All the same, the human race would be fine without it, wouldn't we? I mean, eventually we'd poison the air and kill the oceans, run out of oil and coal, but there was always nuclear and solar and wind and hydro, and they hadn't tried to destroy those. The entire world already used Johnny's solar panels for power, mounted on the flexible nanoceramic she'd invented when she was five, which was also everywhere and in everything. Most of the plastic out there was one of her bioplastics, or that bamboo polymer stuff, and she had built recycling plants to break existing plastic down not just to bits but molecules, ready for re-use. Already it was clear we'd never be knocked back to the Stone Age. And as for nuclear—Johnny declined to even re-engineer the CANDU power plant when they asked her, saying that the power output for the amount of waste they got—she demonstrated by crawling under her lectern—was perfectly fine without any sort of quantum shift in efficiency. I'd written an essay about those reactors for school. Hell, I'd cited her. We'd be fine. If the mobster had wanted the reactor with the intent of ransoming it back to us, I couldn't see who'd pay. No one in the whole world.

"It's bluffing," I said. "It's got no hand to play. It's just trying to scare us."

"We'll see." She crammed another bite of grilled cheese into her mouth, pieces of spicy cabbage plunking back into her plate and leaving blindingly red splotches. "Want the other half?"

"No thanks."

"Are you sure? It's good. And the kimchi's not that hot. I get it from one of my grad students, her mom makes fifteen or twenty jars at a time and sells it to all her friends."

"Nah, I'm good. Asian hot—you know, Thai and Korean and stuff—that's a much different hot than Caribbean hot."

"Yeah?"

She looked relieved to have a break from the subject of Them, so I gamely kept going. "Yeah, we're all habaneros and weri-weris, those little ones in the fridge that you thought were cherries the one time?"

"I would have *died*."

"Probably. I used to be able to eat a lot of that kinda hot before Dad left. He did most of the cooking. The twins used to eat scrambled eggs for breakfast that were orange from hot sauce, hotter than I could eat. Grace brand. Tiny little hole in the bottle, much smaller than a Tabasco hole, because you sure as hell did not want more than a couple drops in your food. Dad, he'd mash whole peppers into his curry and we all had to eat it or go hungry. And then when Mom started doing most of the cooking, it was all salt, no pepper. She never liked things as hot as he did."

"So your capsaicin tolerance went way down; interesting. The kids too, I bet."

"Yeah. They can't even eat the red sauce that comes with Mexi-Fries at Taco Time now."

She laughed out loud, the colour returning to her face. "I love that sauce. I wish they sold that sauce in bottles."

"You'd do shots of that sauce."

"I'd drink that sauce over ice like a highball."

"You're the grossest thing in the world."

It was good to see her smile again. Might be the last one I'd see for a while. She finished her sandwich and wiped her fingers slowly, one by one, with a napkin, not looking at me. Then she said, "You guys should leave town."

"That came out of left field."

"Only if you weren't paying attention. Drozanoth knows where you work now; why wouldn't it know where you live? It might escalate, since you claim you refused its offer. They don't like to be refused."

"I *did* refuse it!" I said, startled. I felt as if she'd slapped me. "What, did you think I'd lie about that? To... come over here, grab the reactor, and run? Jesus Christ, Johnny. What do you think of me?"

"I think you're in danger," she said, as if I'd said nothing at all. "Think about it for a second, Nicky. You're alive. Why? Because if it can't fuck *me* up, because I'm the only one who knows how to make the reactor, then maybe it can apply strategic pressure to someone else. Someone close to me."

I stared at her. Strategic pressure? Did that mean what it sounded like?

"It'll get stronger, it'll summon more magic to use," she said. "And your chance to get away will get slimmer and slimmer. Imagine being in an empty room and being asked to write a novel. You can't, of course. But supposing paper starts to blow in under the door, suppose it starts building up, supposing one day you get a pen..."

"So right now, it's in the room, it's... getting enough paper to... do that?"

"Yes. There's still a chance, there *might* be a chance, to get away—and if you're far enough away, it might not be able to find all of you right away. It might decide to save its energy and turn its attention entirely back to me. You'd be safe."

"Strategic pressure," I said, through a slowly closing throat. I couldn't believe I had just dismissed Them as incompetent mobsters. "Using me as leverage against you, because it knows we're friends. And since I said no, then..."

"Using your family as leverage against *you*. They're not rocket scientists, Nicky—they're brutal and crude and not very bright—but they understand pain. They know it well, after all this time."

They understand pain. I'd known that from the start. How? *Everything will be taken from you* was a promise, not a prophecy. "All right," I said. "I'll... I'll go talk to Mom about it."

"I can help. I can get Rutger to help. We can find somewhere to hide all of you."

I nodded, not really paying attention. Things were moving too quickly for me to keep up with. The kids were still in school, could we pull them out with a week left? Mom's job, who would cover her shifts? If I missed work, Gino would be as much of a dick about it as possible, and I would lose *my* job. How long would we need to hide? Who would check the mail, who would look after the lawn? The city would cite us for weeds. They'd done that before. The neighbours would call bylaw on you. Maybe Mrs. Li could watch the place... unless that put her at risk too...

"If we called the police," I said slowly, "and said that... you had a stalker, and left all the magic and gods out of it..."

"They can't do anything."

"How do you know?"

"What do you think they would do?"

"Well, they... I..." I stuttered into silence, feeling like an idiot. Of course they wouldn't. What *could* they do, against something like this? Assign her bodyguards?

Trail her around? "But there's other help out there, right? You said you called them."

"I called for information. They're not qualified to deal with something like this."

"*They're* not qualified? How the hell are *you* qualified? You've never dealt with anything like this before, you said you read everything in books. Maybe there are people out there who... like you said. Like back in the day. Who could shut the doors again when they're being forced open. We should let them deal with it, we should—"

"I meant it," she snapped. "They can't. They're more like librarians, they gather information about Them, that's all. I don't need librarians."

"Hell no. You're in way over your head if even half of this shit is true. You need an army, you need—"

"Listen," she said, sounding strained. "I know you want *grownups* to rush in and deal with this. But they'll only make things worse. Trust me. They won't know what to do, they won't even know where to start. No one does except me. And if they get involved and throw barriers in my way, I don't even know what'll happen next, and I'm the only one who can figure it out."

I fell silent, stunned not only by the assertion but by her arrogance, even though I knew I should have been used to it by now. She sounded convinced, convincing. As if I had needed any more evidence after what had happened in the storeroom.

"All right. I'll talk Mom into it somehow. But don't call Rutger in just yet. I need to think," I said.

"He's not here. I asked him to run some errands."

"What? I just heard him in the hallway."

She looked up, rabbit-alert. In the silence, as you'd expect, as if in a movie, we both heard the long creak of a door opening. Which shouldn't have been possible; no door in her house ever creaked. She was too sensitive to that kind of noise.

"Stay here," she said, sliding off her stool.

"Like *balls* I'm staying here."

CHAPTER SIX

WE MOVED INTO the empty hallway. Nothing. Just a hard, cold breeze where there should not have been, and a faint whiff of something both disgusting and familiar. "Oh, holy shit," I blurted before I could stop myself. "If They get in here..."

"Yeah." She put her hand flat on the wall, as if checking for a pulse. I shook my head, wondering why that should be the image I thought of.

I followed her at a fast dogtrot to first her workshop, where she unhooked the shoebox and tucked it under her arm, and I admitted that I was shocked to find it still there, then to Ben's room. I felt safer as soon as we were bathed in the cool, green light, unsure why. I went to the tank and put my palms on the glass. Behind us, she dragged a gigantic toolkit up to a table, the box painted in battered black enamel just visible beneath dozens of old scratch and sniff stickers.

"They've been sleeping for a long time," she said. "Waiting, even the ones who don't know it, for the signal to come through. Drozanoth set off an alarm in 1945, when the Americans used the A-bomb on Hiroshima and Nagasaki, because it thought They should come back before we destroyed each other and They had no one to rule. But They couldn't enter then, and it made Them angry, growing more restless by the day, swimming up through sleep. Or over. Or... They don't really live *beneath* anything, *above* anything, physically. They live... over *there*. Sleep over there."

"So we must have changed the code on the door," I said. "The last time They came. To keep Them out."

She shook her head, cracked open the toolbox, and got out a set of screwdrivers with heads more complicated than anything I'd ever seen. "They'll figure something out, I know They will. New, fresh magic is coming in from somewhere and Drozanoth wants nothing more than to turn the key when the time comes. And the time is coming. It might have the means to do what it wants soon. And it wants Them back. Wouldn't you?"

"I find it extremely scary that I can hear you capitalize Their name," I said. "What are you doing?"

"Fucking this up," she said. "But I was working on the surface calculations last night and...I don't know if I'll ever be able to make it again."

"*What?*"

"They can't have it. They can't take it from us. They *cannot*."

"John, wait. Don't. If that's the only—"

"Here, toss this into the sonicator and press the red button." She was disassembling the reactor with startling speed, her hands a pale blur, pausing only to hand me a tangle of wires with a thumbnail-sized computer chip embedded in the middle. I glanced down as I took it; the inside didn't even look that complicated. I realized I had been expecting a mystical glow, like the Ark of the Covenant, or the briefcase in *Pulp Fiction*. She smoothly stripped the wires and tied them into knots, took out a gleaming circle from the center and set it on the table.

When I came back from the sonicator, she was almost done, the reactor just a metal shoebox again. Several components seemed to have disappeared entirely; I wondered where she had put them.

"Even if it could be recreated I don't want Them to try," she said, hefting the circle in her hand, a dense brick of circuitry with gobs of clear epoxy on the edges and a spherical cavity in the other. "They'll have to settle for having me, if they can't have the reactor. And They can't have me either."

"Says you."

"I know. But it might give you time to run." She took the brick to a fume hood in the corner and pressed buttons till the plastic cover came down and an open flame erupted from a spigot in the middle of the cabinet. The brick sputtered and caught, a greasy, tall fire drawn into a long streak from the fan. Her breath slowed while we watched it burn. Not just shattered to bits, but eliminated from the world entirely; not even the memory of its pattern remained now.

I thought: Why even tell me these things, why draw me deeper? A child's bedtime story for a child you wanted to scare into insomnia, the story dug up from some unholy library book. I know those gods, now that you have named Them. You are not the only one They know. Tentacles, in board games. Books bound in human skin in jokey horror movies. Statues and a buzzing chant at the start of *The Exorcist*. But now you're telling me all that is based on something. As if the truth of Their existence were the piece of grit inside a pearl, coated with years and years of denial and the deaths of witnesses, until finally all that was left was a palatable white surface that we could make movies and games about, write short stories about, without fear of repercussions from anything trapped so far down in the gem. So you say, knowing I have no way of contradicting your story, that I never have.

"And you think no one else in the whole world, ever, could re-invent that thing," I said.

"No one else could ever come up with it, no."

"You know what you've got?" I said. "A really healthy sense of self-esteem. Like we talked about in school. Like, a *battleship*-class ego."

"Thank you." She shut off the flame and we watched the clouds of black smoke spiral up into the hood. Her face was still, calculating. "The..."

Her voice trailed off. I turned, knowing what was in the room just as before: there was no way you wouldn't know. Neurotransmitters millions of years old cried out in fear as it drifted into the room, leaving a black smear on the door. We had destroyed the reactor just in time, I realized. My God, in five minutes it could have laid its actual hands on it. As if Johnny had known this would happen. As if she knew just when...

She whispered, "Too late. You could have taken it while we slept, Drozanoth."

It hovered feet away, dripping and hissing as before, a dirty black sheet of translucence and impossible darkness in the center of the room, teeth gleaming in the featureless face. "Too late? We have held counsel, much has been made clear." Its voice was a stream of clicks, like in the store room, like the collected speech of a thousand random noises. The stench was unbelievable. I put my wrist over my nose. "And greetings to *you*," it added, making me flinch. "I see you are together again. Very wise."

"Don't talk to him. You can't be here," Johnny said sharply, voice hoarse, as if she had been yelling instead of whispering. "Even if you survived the crossing. There isn't enough..."

"There is. And ever more. With every passing moment. Cannot you feel it all around you? Time!" it gasped, and made a creaking noise I took to be laughter. "I had forgotten the thrall of it. To be subject to time again. It is no wonder your puny minds fly into dark places. You will never evolve past that."

"It's gone, the reactor is gone. It'll never be remade." She backed up, gesturing me to follow, getting the table between us and the thing. I moved as if on stilts, unable to feel my legs. "You have no reason to stay. Get out of my house."

"Hear me out, child," Drozanoth hissed. "You do not know what it did. What it can do. If you give it to Us—"

"No!"

"You think you cannot be persuaded this time," it said, still floating closer. Below the ragged edge of its skin, bilious mist dripped onto the table, melting the metal, fouling the air.

Was that a threat? Was it threatening her? Us? *This time?* I whipped my head around, but Ben's was one of the few rooms of her labyrinth that only had one door. Behind me, Ben faintly pounded on the glass—how could that even be heard through such thick material?—making a rhythmic squeal and bump as his arms reached out for Johnny and failed to shield her. I knew how he felt.

"No, I can't," Johnny said. Her voice sounded very far away. I looked at her in alarm and saw that she was clinging to the table with one hand, keeping herself upright. "The laws of physics won't alter at your whim, monster."

"*Monster*. You don't know the meaning of the word. That will change."

"Not if I can help it. So get out of my house. *Get out of my fucking house!*"

"Of all sentient creatures in the *universe*, you, child, have least claim to give me orders," the thing said, and laughed—a screech that made my skin ripple, like the scream of a wounded animal. "Do you not? Deny it. Deny it."

It had nearly drifted, burning, through the center of the table, and I recoiled. I hadn't realized how close it had gotten; we were backed all the way to the bookshelves, nowhere to run. The remaining junk on the table jumped and glittered as it approached, the metal surface blurring at its passing, as if the monster were immensely hot, immensely heavy, a different class of being than anything on Earth that could float. This was no innocent jellyfish or butterfly but a hovering mass of poison as hot and dense and dangerous as depleted uranium. Or not even comparable to something as banal as that. Nothing we knew. No element. No phase of matter.

"We suggest you work on it," Drozanoth went on, an antenna or feeler extending from a wet slit in its front, reaching for her with trembling tendrils, glowing at the tips like an angler fish's lure. "With haste, not with leisure. It is for Us. Not for you. Not for your kind. You have made it for us, and you did not even know it. Till now. Till I have come, bearing this gift."

She froze, the feeler nearly to her face. I snatched at the back of her t-shirt and yanked her away from the thing, stumbling heavily into the bookshelf, which teetered but, weighed down by cinderblocks of math and biochemistry texts, did not fall.

"Because I will return," it continued. "You must finish before then."

"I'm telling you, I can't."

"Won't," it clicked, the feeler still groping in the air.

Its pale yellow light looked sickly and wrong in the rich glow coming from the tank. "Can't, or won't, child?"

"Both!"

It paused, bobbing lightly, and then howled something at her in a different language, slimy and hissing. But Johnny understood, because she rose screaming from the floor like an arrow, hands claws. Drozanoth dodged easily, sending her crashing into the side of the table; tiny wires and pieces of shattered plastic rained to the floor. And then it was floating towards the tank. Towards Ben.

It happened before I even drew breath to scream—the crack of dark light that smashed open the glass, the tidal wave of its contents crashing over us, my arms crossed in front of my face, books raining onto me, their impact softened by the foot of stinking saltwater over my head, gone in a heartbeat, and then Ben—his huge, golden eyes meeting ours—grappling for a pitiful moment with Drozanoth before being ripped to shreds almost at Johnny's feet, splattering us with blood, ink, and water.

"Can't, or won't?" I heard through ringing ears as Drozanoth vanished.

CHAPTER SEVEN

I GOT UP painfully; I was soaked through to my briefs, and my body refused to cooperate. Had we been *submerged* for a second? Sheer luck that we hadn't inhaled. Shaking, I crossed the room to Johnny, nudging aside huge shards of broken plexiglass, stunned and dying fish, crushed coral. The sand that had flooded from the aquarium formed a beach, once white, now black and blue with the pulped remains of Benjamin Franklin, Science Octopus. Johnny was folded over in a pool of ink, not weeping, just gasping for air. I squatted next to her, bracing a hand in the cold, wet sand for balance. The only sound was the roar of water escaping down the floor drain, bubbling as things got wedged in the grate.

The room was destroyed. Even the ceiling had not been spared, cratered as if hit with gunfire. A thick hardcovered textbook had been driven into the wall—two feet of reinforced concrete and nanoceramic. Drozanoth showing off its power. The lights flickered uncertainly; I wanted nothing more than to run before they died and we were left in the dark. But I couldn't leave Johnny, and there was no way she was moving.

I looked down to see that she had filled her hands not with Ben's poor flesh, but a dead mantis shrimp, its riotous colours barely faded. Her face was a mask under the short, wet shards of her hair. Under her soaked t-shirt—though I told myself not to look—I could already see bruises angrily forming, black as tattoos. She had a bad, raggedy divot on her upper arm, maybe from a book, maybe from a piece of the glass. It wept fat drops of blood down to her elbow, soaking into her shorts and mixing with the ink.

Drozanoth didn't want to hurt her. It could have hurt *me*, but instead it went for Ben, who could not even defend himself, who never even saw it coming, who had not understood what we were doing. It wanted to make a goddamn point.

My throat closed off with grief and rage. Fucking unfair. How fucking *dare* that monster. Ben had done nothing except be loved by Johnny, and for that he died. What had we gotten ourselves into, where something like this could happen in a matter of seconds? Without a moment of hesitation, without even so much as a warning. Or maybe—thinking of Johnny launching herself at Drozanoth over the table—there had indeed been a warning. Just not one I could understand. We were in so far over our heads that for a moment I could not even breathe.

I wanted to ask what the monster had meant by *this time*, but realized I was terrified that she would tell me. Instead I got up, and began to pick up the books that had fallen into the water, stacking them in the driest corner near the wall, carefully aligning their corners with the concrete. I couldn't think of what else to do, just picking up and carrying cold, wet bricks of paper, cradling four or five in my arms at a time and building them into neat stacks.

After I had done three hip-height towers, Johnny got up and did the same, weaving around me to get books I had missed. Water oozed from the bottom books, compressed by the weight on top of them. Maybe the ones at the bottom would be okay in a few days, pressed flat like that, provided they didn't go mouldy. The top ones would inevitably fluff and curl, blooming into illegibility. I wondered if Johnny knew how to fix them. Or knew someone who knew how. Or maybe she would just re-buy them. Morbidly, as I walked and stacked, I watched for one with a rusty smear on the cover, showing where it had cut her as it fell.

After we finished the books, still not talking—a painful, stretched-out silence, with me hovering just on the cusp of trying to say something comforting, and her simply locked into some wordless prison of grief and shock—she opened a closet filled with cleaning and aquarium supplies and began to carefully sweep the floor, piling everything into a jumbled heap of colourful fish and clear glass and dirt and torn seaweed and pieces of the ceiling and walls. I got another broom and started from the other side.

The artificial rock that had served as the castle in Ben's kingdom rose nakedly into the gloom, illuminated by the few unbroken bulbs, like an ancient ruin lit up for tourists at night. I wondered if anything had survived in some tiny pocket of water caught in the craggy faux-stone. It didn't seem impossible.

What did seem impossible was getting this debris, which I belatedly realized we had piled right over top of Ben, out of the room. We both leaned on our brooms and looked at it. Some of the pieces of plexiglass had been too big and thick to shift, but the rest looked like a sinister iceberg, where tropical fish sent their elderly to die. Water dripped ceaselessly from it. It would be a long, long time before this room was completely dry.

"How are we going to get all this out of here?" I finally said, my voice broken and too loud in the quiet.

"Rutger and I can do it with one of the mini-lifts," she said. In contrast, her voice sounded startlingly level. I wondered if she was in shock.

"Johnny. I... I'm sorry about Ben."

"Me too. He was a good octopus." Tears started down her face now, slow and undramatic. Her shins were dyed black from his ink. "This is all my fault."

"Don't say that. You couldn't have said yes." I swallowed, reached out, pulled my hand back. She tugged her shirt up and dried her face with the hem. "You couldn't have. It said..."

"It said They want it, not that They don't want us to have it," she said, and laughed, a slightly hysterical caw. "I think I know what They want it for. They think they can weaponize it. I bet that's what they think. All that power... like the old *Y'g D'bzan'ithot Ul-Nbdar*. The strangest weapon that's ever existed. A doomsday device. Like the one that destroyed Ur."

"*What?*"

"It's in some of the carvings in the cities the survivors fled to," she said. "And it's the same one pictured in Macchu Pichu, and Mohenjo Daro."

"But the—"

"You should go home."

I stared at her, mouth hanging open as all my gears clashed. "Go... *home?* Are you fucking kidding me?"

"Why would I be kidding? You want to stay and deal with, with...?" She waved her arm around the room, then flinched as if she'd just noticed she was hurt, without looking down.

"Yeah," I said. "I do. And I don't want to leave you. Not like this. Jesus, Johnny, it... it just... it..."

"I know."

"Do you know that that's the thing you say *the most goddamn often out of anything* and it is driving me *insane?*"

"Well I can't help it if I know things!"

"You think what you know is always right! Except now! Now you just *think* you're right! But you're wrong!"

"How do *you* know I'm wrong? Are you going to take that thing's word over mine?"

"It's not a matter of words! It's that it killed Ben! Right in front of us! *Right in front of us!* And now you're telling me to just leave, like you can handle this alone, because you want to handle everything alone! Well look what's happened now that you're trying to do it alone this time!"

"I *told* you, I can get this under control! You don't know the entire story!"

"I would if you would just fucking tell me! We used to tell each other everything!"

She caught her breath, and leaned her broom against the waterlogged armchair that had borne the brunt of the water, now pushed almost to the opposite wall. Her face looked slack somehow, dark, all the light gone from it. Hours seemed to pass before she looked up and spoke, just when I was about to apologize for yelling at her.

"All right. I'll tell you. I should have told you years ago," she said quietly.

It felt as if a wave of hot air washed over me, head to toe, physically staggering me. Nothing good had ever come from someone saying that, I thought. In the history of mankind, there was no more ominous sentence. I braced in the silence, listening to water drip from a broken pipe in the ceiling.

"It was better for us both if you didn't know," she said. "But I can't protect you any more. Or so it seems."

I felt myself bracing for impact, as if she might slap me. My stomach churned and gurgled, always my first and most reliable barometer of something going wrong.

"Drozanoth knows me because it was the one who... made me what I am."

"Made you... what... what? *What* did it make you?"

"A prodigy. A genius. Smarter than the average bear. Whatever you want to call it." She laughed, a dull noise, still staring at the floor.

I stared at her. All I could see for a second was that *Time* magazine cover, her beloved face under the crisp, familiar typeface. Person of the Year. When she was *nine*. And now she was saying that that thing, that groping tentacle-tip of a clamouring pack of monsters, had... had caused that to happen? "I... how?"

"It came to me when I was very young. Before you and I met."

"But—"

"I was about three. It made the offer, I accepted; it gave me what it wanted to give: the memory, the processing ability, the speed, a few other things. Then it came back a few months later, when I was working on my wormhole book proposal, and said: Do you want to *keep* it?"

"So you..."

She nodded, the barest movement of her chin. "I asked it what it wanted in exchange, and it said time. We hammered out the details of the covenant. It took days."

"...Time."

"Can't get something for nothing. But I didn't have anything to pay with. So I buy my empire in time. One to one exchange rate. Every minute I allow myself in prodigy mode, in the grip of Their gift, is a minute off the end of my life."

"Holy shit," I breathed. I thought I might faint. "Jesus Christ."

There it was.

More even than the covenant, that was the secret: her payments. She could have told me the first part and left out the second, I thought. Could have spared me that. We had known each other long enough. And hearing that it was magic would have been no barrier, after today. I wondered if she knew exactly how long she would have had, and could pace herself accordingly. Or if they had just... just made the agreement, left it at that. Not saying that she would be killed by a bus at thirty. Die of cancer at sixty. Something like that. Something you'd never know, and one day she'd simply run out of time. What then? Vanish, on live TV? Collapse to the ground and die like anyone else?

I realized I was shaking. "Can... you go back on it? Be normal now? Would that get rid of—"

"A covenant is unbreakable. Just hope you never get offered one."

"I..."

"You think you can say no. And then it comes and you... can't."

I nodded, head moving as if on autopilot. I just couldn't stop picturing it, how horrible it would have been. All those years. Clicking it on and off like a light, trying to do as much as she could on her own, surely, to save that time, but as a child, with the mind and stamina of a child. Exhaustively researching articles and books and then going into prodigy mode for an hour or two, eyeing the clock obsessively, worrying. All those years not knowing which would be her last.

"John..."

"I'm sorry. It changes everything."

Of course it did. I held down a wave of revulsion and said, "It doesn't change anything."

She looked up at me uncertainly, tears bright in her green eyes, more blue than green down here, in the flickering lights.

I thought: I was wrong. If anything has formed between us, it isn't love. And it isn't that... vast, empty chasm I thought it was, with no bottom, and us looking at each other across cliffs of impossible heights. It's an ocean, huge and deep and polluted with monsters. Yet it could be crossed. Either of us could build a boat and cross it. Neither of us will, since it's easier not to cross than to cross, and what do we have to spare, in terms of time, wood, canvas? We have nothing, not one thing. We will never sail to meet each other.

But both of us wept into this ocean. That's our salt in there. There is a duty that remains, if not love.

"You didn't know what you were doing," I said.

"Please, no platitudes," she said. "I knew precisely what I was doing. That was what the deal meant: that I had full knowledge of what saying yes would mean. Of what saying no would mean. I accepted knowing that the lives I would save outweighed mine... qualitatively, quantitatively. That more people would live better. That even if I said no, I would still be... still have a good life... like..."

"A little blonde princess," I said. "A Disney princess, with everything you ever wanted, and no one ever saying no to you. The money, the jewelry, the dresses. Maybe even the castle. I mean, look at what your mom lives in. And she's got her MBA; your dad's a professor. You'd still be brilliant. You'd still be special. You'd still be beautiful. You'd still be famous, even. You would still have changed the world."

"Yes."

"But you wanted to *save* it."

"They gave me the chance," she said. "You'd have said yes."

I was still shaking; I wondered when it would stop. Out of the corner of my eye I still seemed to see Drozanoth raising its feeler, moving it towards her face. All I wanted to do was turn and run. It didn't matter where. Just out of the stupid white house, away from the smashed glass and water, out into the street. Helter-skelter down the middle of the road.

I restrained the impulse and said, "You could weaponize a nuclear power plant too. And there are lots of those."

"This weapon is not like that. Trust me."

"So it... *could* be made into that? You were lying?" I swayed, and sat down with a squelch on the soaked armchair, re-soaking my pants, which had just begun to dry. "Jesus Christ! Johnny, how...?"

"With the amount of *potential* destruction available to it because of the amount of power it could generate, yeah. They could hang that over our heads and ask for anything They wanted. The main thing that humanity has learned from thousands of years of dealing with Them," she added, "is that only evil comes from evil. That They only give with the expectation—not the hope, the *expectation*—that Their gift will always go wrong. I knew that, and I knew this day might come. I still said yes."

"What are we going to do now?" I said, after several minutes of trying to work through that and failing.

"What's this 'we' business?"

"I already said I can't let you deal with this alone."

"And I already said that you have to."

"Sucks to be you then."

She sighed, running her fingers through her wet hair. "They know how to find both of us. And They will, if that's what They want. So I'm gonna sleep here. Go home and see if you can get some sleep. No, don't look at me like that. I'm not sending you away so I can sneak off and do something stupid. I'll have a plan in the morning."

I waited for her to say something else, then gave up and left, just walked back to the car, my shoes squelching, smelling of fish and death.

I should have guessed. I should have known. How else could she have known so much about Them if she hadn't been dealing with Them her whole life? Thinking about her watching me watching her all those years, knowing I could never be told, was too dumb and ordinary to be told. Once, just last year, I had watched her walk away from me at midnight and had paused teetering on the corner, on the verge of sprinting after her and begging forgiveness, when a police cruiser had come by; and all I could think about was the light, watching the light. I thought I had changed but I have never changed enough, and all I will ever be is the boy on the corner waiting for the light to change. And I thought she was a hero. But could you be a hero under those terms?

This wasn't like Clark Kent getting his powers from a yellow sun. This was bargaining with the Devil, like in that play we'd gone to, *The Black Rider*. How she must have been laughing at me inside, knowing what she knew. That she was a made thing, no different from that young clerk with his handful of magic bullets. Except he'd done it for love, and she'd done it for... what? Power. Dealing with the Devil deliberately, consistently, willfully, for years and years and years. More power than anyone on Earth had. Maybe more than anyone should have.

Remember. Don't forget. Remember the day Johnny told me the story, remember that I didn't doubt her credibility, too young to know the word, only the word 'prodigy,' know that it meant she was better than me, had been born better than me, that the only thing joining us at first had been that bullet, and that nothing should have joined us when we got out.

Coming home that night, I scrubbed at grass stains in the shower and ran my fingers around the puckered edges of the scar. The way the surgeons had fixed mine, it looked like a frowning mouth, not like Johnny's. A crescent rather than a disc. Like two phases of the same moon. Maybe because it had hit her first and hardest, as nothing else would ever do again.

Shivering in the warm water: not remembering but imagining the bullet spearing through the door, then through her, and then barely slowed, lubricated with blood, into me, like a wild animal darting into a dark place to hide.

CHAPTER EIGHT

WHEN I PARKED at home I had taken so many twists and turns on the back roads and gravel highways past the grain elevators, trying to make sure nothing was following me, that it was past dinnertime. I knew even before I walked up the steps that I was in trouble; a shadow loomed behind the screen door.

I opened it partway and waited for Mom to get out of the way. Her face was pinky-red, gleaming with angry sweat. I opened my mouth; she cut me off.

"Where have *you* been?"

Shit. Forgot to call. "I took an extra shift," I lied. "In Seafood. I was so busy I didn't have time to call and say. Sorry."

The deep rut between her eyebrows got even deeper. "You were supposed to be home at noon. What the hell did you think I was going to do with the kids?

On goddamn Canada Day, when everything's closed? Huh?"

My stomach sank. "Sorry, I—"

"—You didn't think? You weren't thinking! That's what it is. What did you think we were gonna do? You didn't! I had to leave them alone while I went to Gold Rush! They thought they were gonna go downtown with you and do Canada Day shit at City Hall!"

Oh, shit. Shit. I felt actually sick now, my guts making alarm noises that I tried to ignore, like the stench of the fishy water still drying from my clothes, heat rippling up and down my face. Canada Day was our big day, had always been our big day after Dad left; we'd take the bus down to City Hall in St. Albert and get flags and temporary tattoos, make the masks or crafts they laid out, eat hotdogs and ice cream in the sun—every year, year after year, all of us, often Johnny too—and then home for even more junk food before heading back out for the early fireworks at ten. Just us, a little brown blob amongst all the white families, waving the same flag as everyone else. This year our very presence would have been half a protest.

And I had missed it. And I couldn't tell her why.

"Look, I couldn't turn down the shift," I said weakly. "They didn't have anyone to cover for—"

"Neither did we! That was just selfish of you, it was just selfish. And thoughtless. Like you never think at all. Just a complete lack of consideration for other people."

Each word was delivered flat and hard, like a slap; I couldn't meet her gaze, was staring around the living room at the scattered toys and books, drawing paper, candy wrappers, dirty plates. What the hell had those three been doing? Mom would have gotten in less than half an hour ago and banished them to their rooms, whatever it was. Moping, probably mad at me. For a moment I wondered if they were listening to this, believed her because they'd heard it so often: *Dumb Nicky. Never thinks.*

No reply ever ended these arguments. Silence meant you were giving her 'the treatment.' Talking back was 'giving her lip.' Trying to reason with her was 'disrespect.' I knew what came next: who was the parent and who was the kid, who did all the work in this house, and so on, the same script we'd heard even before Dad left. That me thinking my paycheque made me a provider in the house, a big man, when I was just off with that goddamn girl all the time instead of being a *real* provider...

In the long silence I realized with a start that she was going grey, brightly silver-blonde in the black; I wondered why I had never noticed it before. But I had never been so tall before, so old before, overtopped her by so much. My stomach was somersaulting. I had to get to the bathroom.

"I said I was sorry," I said again. "I'm gonna go say sorry to the kids, and then I gotta shower, and then we've gotta talk about—"

"Well, why don't you just talk down to me some more? Huh? Just ignore what I'm saying?"

"I'm not igno—"

"And you're interrupting me! Did you think I was done?"

Only now was her voice starting to rise; sweat broke out on my forehead. It was like being a kid again. You're not, I tried to remind myself. And don't forget you have to be taken seriously about getting away. A little while. Don't say why. Just come up with something. Just lie. Christ, she won't listen to me at all, will she?

A shadow flickered across the hall behind her so fast I wondered if I'd really seen it. And then her face was shifting, slackening with shock, finally falling open in a scream. The shadow was there and true, black and sharp-edged across the floor. I turned at last and saw what was flying towards the window, and immediately wished I hadn't—a shivering tangle of wrong angles and tentacles, as if everything had bones that had been broken and were about to jut from the skin, covered in dark, slimy skin, studded with glowing red eyes. It hit the window with a thud; the glass shivered visibly but held, streaked with cloudy slime and hairs.

I couldn't even tell Mom to run, I just spun her by her shoulders, shoving her out of the living room towards the hallway, trying to get something solid between us and the thing, some doors, some walls, less glass. I got her into her bedroom and pushed her into the closet, like shoving a pile of warm dough. It was after me, had to be. Knew me. Didn't know them. Had to stop it.

It was only then that her screaming formed words. "What was that? What was that? *What was that thing?*"

"Stay here where it can't see you! Where are the kids?"

"What was that *thing?* Don't let it get in the house!"

I shut the closet door, hearing first a bang, and then—oh, shit—the musical tinkle of falling glass from the living room. A multilegged shadow, all spikes and floppy appendages and translucent nodules, firmly struck the hallway wall, like an ink stamp. I cast about, left, right, left, right. Kids. Bedroom. Two quick steps: empty.

Check the backyard, last place left to look. But the door to the backyard was in the kitchen, and that meant going back into the hallway. The hallway where something was bumping and slithering along the shag carpet, hissing like a snake, a shrieky tortured breathing that made it sound like more than one thing. Maybe it was. Jesus, maybe the whole house was filled with them.

I slammed the kids' door shut and looked for something I could tip in front of it, but the desk would take too long to drag and the bookshelves were too far away. Forget it. I yanked the window up and used a pen to rip a long diagonal slash in the screen, then clambered through it at speed, not glancing back. I skidded on the grass as I ran, hearing screams from the backyard.

Mother*fucker*.

The kids were pelting towards me, heading—thank God—for the street rather than the house, pursued by two low, bulbous pink things like scorpions that were pulsating patterns like TV static, almost but not quite distracting from the shining black claws. Carla grabbed me around the waist, sobbing and shrieking, as one of them leapt for her, missed, and clawed a chunk out of the tree up front.

I peeled her off and pushed her towards the twins. "Run! Don't go back to the house. Run, get down the street!"

I couldn't check to see if they were doing what I said, because the things were on me. I pivoted and ran back towards the front door. Shit. Nothing out here. Any weapons would be in the garage—a shovel, a crowbar, something. Would they even damage these things? Better than doing nothing.

I pounded back up the steps and flew through the open front door, where two of the black things with red eyes were systematically tearing the kitchen apart, which stopped me in my tracks—the noise, the screeching, the crashing and thumps as the cabinet doors fell off and the drywall was shredded. Behind me, the two pink things hit the closed door hard enough to make it judder in its hinges. Dumb things. Weak and dumb, Johnny had said, until the gods Themselves came back. But not *so* weak. Not so dumb.

I ran for the garage, already hearing something coming after me, and wrenched the door open, sliding across the hood of Mom's Sunfire. No shovel, no crowbar; where were they? Buried somewhere in the junk? I snatched a rake from the corner, turned it handle out, and came back to the house swinging and yelling hoarsely, hoping they'd be drawn to me.

One of the pink things reared up like a cobra, its claws shining and flashing so that I could barely see for a second, and then fell onto the other one as I thrust at it with the rake. There was a sickening pop as some plate or scale gave way, a torrent of viscous slime cascading onto the kitchen floor. I retreated as they all turned, a thousand eyes focusing in multicoloured hatred, and pursued me across the shattered remains of chairs and table, couch and TV. That bought me a few seconds as they clambered frantically over the junk; I swung the rake again, caught one of the black creatures in the eye region, sending it reeling.

Something swished past my face, a projectile blob of hairs and venom that scorched the wall at once, sending up blue smoke. My chest seemed to catch on fire too—I started coughing so hard that I began to gag, and watched through tear-filled eyes as they approached, knocking debris out of the way.

"Get down!" someone yelled over the screeching; I dropped flat, and something whizzed above my head, exploding in a deafening cascade of white sparks. For a second I could barely see or hear, then realized something was heading for me, end over end—the couch frame, oh no—and I just managed to cover my face before it landed on me.

BY THE TIME I dug my way out it was all over. I felt as if my head had been wrapped in cotton wool. Through pink-smeared vision, Mom approached from the hallway, and finally the kids from the front door—thank Christ—all three unhurt, it seemed, though sobbing and shaking. I reached automatically for them.

"No, uh-uh," I dimly heard Johnny say. "There might

be things left in the house, hiding. Get out into the street, go find Rutger. Get ready to run."

"Listen to Johnny, guys," I heard myself say, through a wrench of loathing. Her fault. Her fault this had happened. Her fault I got dragged in, then my fault they did. But hers to begin with. Like we were all strapped to the mast of a sinking ship, the innocent and the guilty drowning together. "I'll be out in a minute, after we check the house. It'll be okay. I promise."

They stared at her. At me. Their eyes were so full of betrayal and confusion that I wondered how I would be able to even speak to them when I could again, what words I could find except a senseless stream of apology. Or lies. But they filed out, and from the corner of my eye I saw Rutger, disheveled and harried-looking, in a dark suit, beckoning them.

"Up you get," Johnny said, and I squinted at her lips as if it would help. We quartered the place for more monsters, finding nothing except their remnants—slime and chemical burns, stray hairs and broken claws, and the smashed remains of half the house. They had gotten down to the studs in places, the drywall peeled away like flesh from bone. Holes gaped in the ceiling, leaking ropes of torn pink insulation. I looked down and realized that one of my shoes was gone. How had that happened?

Back in the kitchen, I said, "What did you do? Was that magic?"

"Experimental weapon. Definitely not magic."

"But you *can* do magic?"

"Listen, we'd better talk about what to do next, and quick."

I swallowed, hard. She hadn't answered the question, and she knew I knew. "There's a next? What's next? Look at the house, I... we..."

"I think I have a chance to fix this," she said. "A slim one, razor-slim, but the best one for a while. I kept thinking: something's coming. But where's all the magic coming from? Are things thinning out? So I did some research and... signs are pointing to a window soon, a window in time, an alignment. Like all the doorways in a house moving till they line up in a row. It might be a short one compared to historical windows—maybe just a couple of minutes—but while it's happening, the biggest and oldest gate in the world could open, and who knows what could get through. It could be everything. All of Them."

"Not just the ones small enough to fit through the screen door, like now."

"Yes. The big ones. The real gods. And other things. Other... but there's a chance that I could, I mean, it's not definitive..."

"A *chance*."

"A chance that I could prevent the door from opening. In those few minutes. Slam it shut, lock it, and maybe keep it locked for a long, long time. I could beat Them there if They don't know I'm coming. If they think I won't go on the offensive."

"That sounds pretty good," I said. My voice felt as if it were coming from a long way away. I wondered if the attack, or her experimental weapon, had damaged my eardrums. "For the planet, I mean. That's cool."

"Nick."

"Did you see where my shoe went? I'm not really... like, *swimming* in shoes. I have three pairs of shoes. So that's like a... seventeen percent reduction right there."

"Nick, you're in shock. Sit down."

"Is my math right? Did one of the things eat my shoe? Where did Rutger go? Where are the kids?"

"Sit. Down."

I sat, heavily, on the lone unbroken kitchen chair. Those sonsabitches destroyed *one* room in *her* house. Unfair. What the hell kind of weapon had she used? I searched my memory and found a hole in it, a missing minute or two, funnily angled at the sides. I stuck a finger in my ear and twirled, looked down at my socked foot. A sparkling shard of glass had lodged in the dingy fabric, but I didn't see any blood. Lucky. I carefully pulled it out, half-listening to Johnny.

"You said you wanted to help," she said. "Come with me to the gate. I can't do this alone."

I laughed. "You do everything alone. What do you need me for? Or what do I need you for? To protect me?" Something popped in my ear, and everything sounded much clearer on that side.

She watched me for a moment, her face calculating, serious. Waiting for me to figure it out.

Leverage, I thought. Me as leverage against her, my family as leverage against me. And if They couldn't get ahold of Mom and the kids to use, then they were safer away from us. But not me. I was still fair game no matter where I went. "Shit."

Softly, she said, "I need your help. Isn't that what friends do?"

"Of course it is," I said automatically. But even as I said it I wasn't sure if I was lying. We were friends because we had always been friends, but... why? What did she ever see in me, and what did she see now? We had fought about it, as kids; I had accused her of being a grownup in a child's body, humouring me out of pity and habit, secretly preferring time with her grownup friends. And she had raged at me, cried. I had been shocked at my ability to hurt her, taking that—rightly or wrongly— as proof of her love. After all, I thought, no stranger had ever brought her to tears. But now I wondered if she had cried because she didn't *have* any grownup friends. Because she had no one but me. Never had. When we were little she'd confided that she felt she had no one to communicate with, no community. Then, after meeting me, she had a community of two. Always us against the world. The world that demanded different things of us, but which we had always faced together.

I took a deep breath, attempting to pull myself together, and said, "When's the thing? The alignment? Are those things going to come back? I have to talk to Mom, the kids, call the—"

"I put Rutger in charge of all that."

"What? In charge of what? All what?"

"Don't worry about that. Do you trust me?"

"Yes. You know that. But..." I waved a hand helplessly

at the house. "What are we going to do about all... this? This isn't livable. The management company is going to freak out. We—"

"I'll deal with it," she said firmly. "Here." She turned and dug in her bag, coming out with her chequebook and a fountain pen. I watched numbly as she tore off a cheque and put it on the table next to me to scrawl a number—the zeroes tumbling, never seeming to stop—signed it, and handed it to me. It was made out to Mom. "To fix the house, for your rent, and for the work you'll miss."

I stared at it. She always got novelty cheques and this one was particularly bad, some old-styley dinosaur painting with a tiny-headed, big-mouthed T-rex attempting to maul a triceratops that looked like a rabid dog. Their pastel colours were insubstantial behind the bold, black strokes of Johnny's writing. "So you're... renting me," I said.

"Oh, for God's sake. As if you're worth the late fees. You said you were coming anyway. It's *compensation*."

"Buying me, then."

"Do you even know what that word means?"

"You picked a really excellent fucking time to talk down to me," I said, feeling anger tower like a thunderhead, fed by the look of nonplussed defiance on her face, so sure she was in the right. I shoved the cheque back at her.

"N—"

"Look at this house! Look what They did to it! Or what *you* did to it! You know, you can write a cheque as big as the moon, it'll never make up for this, for having this taken from us when we finally had something to take. And now you think *money* will fix it? Just like money fixes everything else? You want to deal with me the same way They dealt with you? Yeah, I can see who you've been taking lessons from. The truth is, you've finally found something you can't buy your way out of! Something your goddamn money can't fix for once!

"This is a *life* you're trying to buy, Johnny, and a life isn't *stuff*, the way you—you *joke* about buying researchers, the way you laughed about buying Rutger when you paid for his replacement. Maybe because *you* got bought, you think of us that way, I don't know. I don't care. And you know what? The bank won't let Mom cash this fucking cheque anyway. It's too big."

Her eyes went wide. Very clearly I thought: I used to think I was in love with you. You, of all people.

I also thought: I wonder how long I had that speech building up. Most of it, anyway.

Influence clusters, contaminates, then maims; and it is made out of money. When you have money you think the way people with money think, because that's the influence. Ordinary rich people buy homes, plural. The super-rich make homes everywhere. People like her, though, don't need a home; they have nothing that they are worried about keeping, they know they can replace anything, literally anything, even if it is supposed to be one of a kind. She doesn't have those voids that other rich people have, the ones they try to fill with paintings and cars. She doesn't even try. She just lets the voids sit, and races past them trying to save the world. Even her house is a decoy, almost, isn't it? Not like ours, a knowable thing. Inside her castle you never know where she is. You go looking for her, you can't find her. I never knew why that was, only that she made it that way, and everything she wants made a certain way is made a certain way.

"What about cash?" she said, quietly.

"Did you hear *one* thing that I just said? It's not about the money!"

"I'm trying to help!" she cried. "What, you think it's better to walk away, leave them with nothing?"

"I'm saying the *leaving* is the problem! Why can't we—"

"I'm thinking, Nicky, and all *you're* doing is—is— is reacting! Like an animal! You think insurance is going to pay for this? I've talked to enough insurance companies to know they won't. You want the kids out on the street? Hunted down by monsters? I'm trying— to—help—you!"

"Fine!"

We both ran out of steam, and she slumped, still braced on the table. I wondered why it looked so familiar, then remembered: Ben. The smashed aquarium. The delta of artificial sand, her curved back. I am not the only one who grieves here. No, we all grieve.

"I'll get Rutger to do it in cash," she said after a few minutes. "Go pack a bag."

"Where are we going?"

"I don't know yet."

The monsters hadn't gotten to Mom's room, where I kept my clothes, so I was able to shower and change, even shave—quickly and badly, without letting the shaving cream soak in enough. I still hadn't found my other shoe, but my older blue-and-yellow Nikes were intact in the kids' closet; I put them on, then headed for the front door just as Johnny came through it, almost bumping into her.

"What are you doing?"

"Uh," I said. "I need to talk to Mom and—"

"I told you. Rutger took care of all that."

"Say again? All what?"

"They're still in danger," she said. "I asked him to hide them till we get back."

"*What?*"

She held up a hand, tiredly. "Please don't start," she said. "They're not safe here. You know it, I know it, Rutger knows it, they know it. Do I need to go on?"

"No, but sometimes I'd really like to punch you in the face," I said, through gritted teeth. "You didn't let me say goodbye, you didn't...all right. Where did he take them?"

"It's better if you don't know. In case."

"In case of... oh, Christ."

"Nick. I'm sorry. I'm sorry that my help looks like this. I would do anything for it not to. I'm sorry you didn't get to say goodbye. I wasn't thinking. I just wanted them to be safe."

You don't love anything, I thought, clearly, as if the

words had been spoken to me by someone else. *You don't know what love is. You didn't think I needed to say goodbye because you don't care enough to say it. What am I doing. What am I doing.*

"Okay." I wondered if I were still in shock. "I don't have a passport," I said. "If we're going anywhere that needs one, I mean."

"I know."

She dug in her bag and handed me a brown envelope, smelling powerfully of fresh ink. The passport inside looked real and official, with a textured blue cover stamped with gold and pages that, tilted, showed security holograms of maple leaves and the Parliament Buildings. My picture looked like what you'd think a passport photo would look like—wan, resentful. *Nicholas Prasad, Noted Grump.* Where had she gotten that picture?

"Digital mockup," she said. "I had Rutger do it. He's very good."

"At faking official documents," I said. "Does he do this a lot?"

She shrugged.

"If he gets caught..."

"It's not him that has to worry. It'll be me." She thought for a moment. "They'll probably prosecute me as a juvenile, though."

"Hope so." I weighed it in my hand, then put it my back pocket. "You brought this with you. You knew I didn't have a passport."

"Lots of people don't have passports. You still don't

need them for domestic flights if you have other photo ID." But in the tactful silence she left I thought: Yeah, but you also knew that there are types of people who just don't have passports. People who don't expect to fly out of the country. People who, not to put too fine a point on it, can't afford to fly out of the country.

"Can I call Rutger, talk to Mom and the kids?"

"No. It's better this way."

I closed my eyes. Did she know how close I was to the end of my rope, or could she, as an intelligent creature, guess?

Count to ten. Count to ten before you slam her into the wall. Or burst into tears. Or both.

The way she wasn't able to distinguish between her decisions for her work, her research, her science, and her decisions for people. The way she saw it all as the same thing. An equation where the variables were unspeaking and fixed, rather than living, breathing humans making choices out of fear, love, courage. The way she saw no ties between people—no, between anyone other than her. The way everyone ranked below her, in some great misshapen pyramid of humanity where she was the tiny point at the top and everyone was simply spread out below her. The way she saw our ties as trivial, easily broken for the sake of logic, or convenience, or boredom. As if... as if her inability to love her family meant I didn't love mine. As if "I'll be back in a minute" were acceptable last words.

"There are rules," she said softly. "They have rules. For me."

Count to ten. Count to ten. Rules for the rich. Rules for fucking *money*. Rules for pretty people. Rules for scientists, the elite. Rules for the famous. Rules for people who said 'Talk to my people.'

She said, "There are no rules for you."

She had done the math, as always. Because math is pure. The rules of math are pure. And the rules of love are dirty and messy and bend and flex and break constantly. Count to ten. Don't lose it.

"Do you need me to pack for you?" she said tentatively.

"I'll do it."

My schoolbag was wearing away at the bottom; I took my old messenger bag, packed a handful of clothing in a daze. "I'll be back soon," I said to the empty closet. Maybe it would hold the vibrations of my voice, bouncing between the soft fabrics, maybe it would hold a few molecules of my breath till I returned, maybe it would just hold the idea, not even the words, just the intent, just that I said it.

Back outside as we walked to the car, my neighbour came out of her house, quivering, phone in hand. I nearly ran over to steady her. "Mrs. Li," I said. "It's all right, it's all over."

"Nick! What happened?" she gasped. "The *noise*..."

"Um," I said. "Break-in. We... already called the cops." She was pretty old, there was no way the word 'monster' would be uttered anywhere near her. Second death of the day, two too many. She clung to her doorjamb, staring at the smashed window, the scratches on the tree, the siding, the doors...

"Who broke in? They could break in *here!*" she said. "Where are the babies? Nick! Come back here!"

I slung my bag into the car. Johnny got in next to me, the bag between us like a chaperone. I glanced up front to the driver: not someone I knew, a heavy, silver-haired older guy, the back of his neck crisscrossed with wrinkles, smelling powerfully of cologne. A bodyguard? No, not after all this time; she hated bodyguards. Rutger was enough, she always told me. Even just the sight of his big body, the shoulders that seemed like they couldn't fit through a doorway.

Where had the bastard gone? He had vanished like a ghost, taking the people I loved with him. Vanished all. Like ghosts.

"Do you think I'm gonna need this extremely illegal passport?"

"Mm. Not sure."

She wasn't even listening. She was looking out the window at the long sunset, grey and pink, sparks of gold. You could barely tell the sun was going down except for the slow diminishing of the light. Where it would normally sit on the horizon was merely a brighter westerly glow than the rest of the sky. Her familiar profile was outlined in the last of it, amber and violet, like a salute to her beauty, a hat tipped to it. But if we failed, everything beautiful in the world would die, not just her.

"Look," she said softly. "Whatever's happening, it's already affecting the light. See that? The books say it starts at the shoulders of the day. Dusk and dawn. And They're gathering around us too. Getting ready."

"Where—"

"I mean, gathering around the world. The planet. Those northern lights we saw the other day, we shouldn't have seen those. I knew right away something was wrong. There hasn't been enough solar wind activity to cause that. But magic in transition seems to cause a kind of similar ionizing effect."

She slumped, forehead against the glass. "They know. They know something's coming."

"Well, we know too."

"Knowing isn't enough. We'll never know as much as They do."

I thought: but someone has to fight Them, all the same, even if no one knows how. In the books, in the movies, someone always has to fight back. Not to end up in the stories later, not to be rewarded with fame and praise and book deals. They just knew someone had to fight.

Had to.

CHAPTER NINE

BACK AT HER house, it was clear that she'd already begun to pull out the big guns, cranked Prodigy Mode to 11. Burning time, I thought. Every flat surface in the Baskerville room, her biggest library, was covered in printouts and photocopies, maps taped to the walls where she'd run out of space at the plastic tables. All five computers and both fax machines were on, singing a quiet chorale of uninterrupted chiming beeps. The heat from their monitors and processors turned it into a dry sauna.

I put my bag on the couch and slumped down, sinking into the dark leather till I was almost folded in half, hearing springs crunch.

"Holy shit," I said. "Buy a new couch."

"If we survive, I'll take you couch shopping."

"Are They gonna get in here, too?" I said. "Mostly,

I'm too tired to care right now, but I just need a yes or a no."

"They will if they want. But I hope we won't be here much longer. I'm close to figuring out what we've got to do. Here, I got you a cell phone. I already put my number in it."

I accepted the silver scarab reverently, flipping it open—a huge full colour screen, almost two inches across. No signal down here though, under the concrete and the metal and the earth. In my pocket it felt heavy, reassuring. It was obviously one of her cast-offs, but I felt better having it.

"What are you doing there?" I said, pointing at the humming monitors and piles of papers.

"Half of it is a half-assed research plan," she said, handing me a stapled handful of papers covered in her dense, small writing. I flipped through it, understanding maybe one word in three. "Working backwards. To shut any gate during an alignment, you have to find it. I don't know exactly where this one is—I only know it's not the Gate of Ganzir, of course, because that got destroyed in Ur."

"Oh, yes, of *course* not that one."

"*Then* you have to fulfil the conditions that were put on it. I don't know what those are either. I'll have to access some source material and there isn't much that can be relied on, *and* the good stuff is mostly in languages I don't know."

"So first step is..." I said, lost.

She counted on her fingers. "Teach myself ancient

Akkadian, Sumerian, and Babylonian. Start hitting up museums, archives, libraries, universities, and collectors to see who's got things I might need. Contact some people who might be able to provide information on short notice."

"Just information?"

"Mostly people in the Ssarati Society. They used to worship the Ancient Ones. They've had a hundred different names over the years."

"What can they do? Magic?"

"If there's enough magic in our world, yeah, but the ones who know that They're real, who aren't playing, won't. Because they truly understand what the threat is. The harder you fight, the worse your punishment is when They come through. You're disincentivized to do anything but lie flat and hope for the best. Ironic, huh?"

"Son of a bitch," I said, and meant it. A gold-and-blue dung beetle wobbled hopefully towards me on the back of the couch; I found a receipt in my jeans, wadded it into a roundish ball, and handed it over. "They take all this seriously. Will they take *us* seriously?"

"Yeah."

"...They know you too. Or you know them."

"It's a long story. The great weakness of humanity is the one everybody knows," she said. "It's that we've always hungered for the fruit of the Tree of the Knowledge of Good and Evil. But the reason we hunger is that knowledge is our only power; it's the only thing we've got to fight Them. It always has been, and it always will be."

"Is there anything I can do?"

"Keep the printer refilled with paper and do coffee runs?"

"Oh my God."

"For real, though," she said. "You know how to work the Gaggia in the main kitchen, right?"

"No, I meant... well, first of all, up yours, and secondly, I thought you were further along than this. I thought maybe..."

"That I had everything worked out? No. I'm working on the ghost of a hope here, and whatever records survived through the years. That's a ghost too." She waved a hand above her head, a few staticy hairs rising to her fingertips like obedient soldiers. "This, what they gave me..."

"Your... covenant."

"It doesn't make me *magic*. It doesn't make me smarter than your average smart bastard. Just faster. It's as if... I can just put together the same puzzle a hundred times quicker than the smart bastard."

"Wish someone had told my parents that," I said.

"What do you mean?"

"Well," I said, "remember that time I, a ten year old, and you, a genius, decided to wash my dad's car, and it was parked in the sun, and you threw a bucket of cold water on the windshield and it exploded?"

"Shut up."

"Man, and they used to think you were a good influence on me," I said, shaking my head.

"Really? They never wanted us to hang out."

"It wasn't you they didn't like," I said. "They didn't want me to be *distracted*. They wanted me to study. I mean, Dad, mostly. Mom was much less of a hardass. He thought girls would keep me from getting good marks."

"Joke's on him," Johnny said. "I'm not even into that kind of thing."

"What...kind of thing?" I said nervously.

"Oh, you know. Dating or whatever. 'Romance.' Boys."

"Excuse me."

"I mean, have you *met* boys?"

"*Excuuuuse me.*"

"I dunno," she said vaguely, shuffling a thick deck of printout. "Just not interested in the whole idea."

"Well, maybe you'll find it interesting later."

"Could be. Don't really care either way."

That kind of thing, I thought; was she trying to tell me flat-out that she'd never feel about me the way I felt about her? Or wasn't sure I felt about her? Or had, at some point, recently felt about her? Maybe it would be another fourteen years till she told me that. I said, "I got good marks anyway. Well, good by my standards."

"Look, maybe he didn't get a genius in the family, but neither did the Chambers. Technically."

"Technically. But you were talking about... about puzzles?"

"Yeah. I'm still gathering pieces. I'm going as fast as I can. But I can't do anything until I have enough to at least start the frame."

"And when you do?"

"Then we go wherever we have to go."

"This is going to be like *The Road to El Dorado*, isn't it?" I said. "We let you watch that movie too many times."

"It is not!" she said. "The *only* similarity is our hair. And I've only seen it six times. Besides, we're trying to save the world, not get a million tons of gold."

"Man, are *we* on the wrong mission."

I looked at her for as long as I could stand, like staring at the sun, trying to take it all in—her eager, frightened, golden face under the ruff of feathery hair, the piles of paper and books, the monitors all showing photos of pottery with stick writing on it. The great hope for everything. I wondered if the slow, rolling boil in my gut was anticipation or hatred. For this, I had been torn from the people I loved. She had promised they would be safe. I clung to that, wished I could write it on the wall. For both of us to remember. "I'll go get you some coffee," I said.

AS SHE WORKED, I ended up not being useful for much more than to lie on the couch and, just as she'd said, fill her with espresso and the printer with paper, occasionally unjamming both. She was so focused on what she called the 'wet problems' of the world that her particular genius had never really turned to mere gadgets, so she used the same office stuff as anyone else—high-end, of course, but nothing special. "That's not what needs fixing," she'd say, when I complained about the limitations of cars or TVs. "People. People need fixing." All our lives I'd never argued the point. After all, who was better qualified to fix people than her, the—inarguably, publicly, photogenically, financially—best person there was?

Her voice was a soft drone in the background in a dozen languages, phone cradled on her shoulder as she typed on one of the computers. I watched pottery shards flick past almost too fast to see, photographed on white backgrounds, maybe from museum catalogues. Bricks of clay, then bricks of text, black on grey or black on purple, old mimeographs. Colourful vases of glass or pottery, swirled with drawings and words, then tablets like the ones in *The Ten Commandments*, things chipped or stamped into them. It was dizzying to watch.

With a little start I realized I could see something rising off her like pollen, exactly like pollen, a thin, golden mist blowing from her hair, just visible in the lights of her desk.

"John? You look like you're... like..." I cast around for a word. "Steaming."

"Mm." She laughed, a tired wheeze. "Prodigy mode. That's time coming off."

"I've never seen that before."

"You'd never have been able to. Magic is coming through from somewhere, like I said. Whenever it does that, anything of Theirs becomes more powerful. You've been... exposed at close range for a couple of days, so

I'm not surprised you can see it now. More proximity effects."

"Jesus."

"What does it look like?"

"Like pollen. Spruce pollen. Like, blowing off the tree and sticking to my car."

"Gross. Tree sperm."

"Super gross. Ent jizz."

"Oh no, ew," she said, turning away from the keyboard, "I just realized there are going to be *so* many ents in the second *Rings* movie and now that's all I'll be able to think about."

"Ew." I dug my way out of the couch and walked to her desk. "How close are we to everything being fixed?"

She rocked her hand in the air. "I thought Germany might be the next step, because they might have some documentation about what happened in the war. But I don't know if I'd trust it, and I don't think I'll be able to get access to it."

"...What... happened in the... war?"

"Same thing that always happens with Them," she said. She picked a printout from a pile—a mosaic, black and white, showing a seething mass rising over a small town on a hill. The houses looked so defenseless under the shadow of the monster that I shivered for a second, thinking of my own house, the exposed bones of the frame.

She said, "Like I said. The big man says he'll pay Them back. Time, human sacrifices, animals burned on the altars. The Ancient Ones love life force, the way it feels in Their teeth. For years, the cults feed Them, the big man thrives. But it falls through, or he cheats, or there's a terrible insult, or maybe the big man in the next valley simply makes a better deal. They come up, and destroy everything. Many, many times. Noah's flood. Atlantis. Heraclaeion. Mu. Tunguska. Uruk."

"You're just saying random syllables now." I stared at the picture, then her, then the picture again. Someone had depicted this disaster in tiny rocks, long after it happened. Maybe just from stories. Second-hand, third-hand, a hundred years later. But in *Germany*, just sixty years ago, almost close enough to touch... "Are you saying that Hitler...?"

"Yeah. The thing is, his magic didn't work and he never did open the gate underneath Berchtesgaden. He screwed up, the Nazi researchers screwed up. So do I want to get into the Nazi archives? Even if I could, I don't think so."

"Jesus. Not if they did it wrong. But where else can you look?"

"Do you know where the oldest library in the world is?" she said.

CHAPTER TEN

RUTGER WAS WAITING at the airport for us, standing awkwardly between the rows of empty seats in Departures, clutching Johnny's brown waxed canvas bag. It was bulging, like he'd stuffed a watermelon in there. I knew it well—she took it everywhere, lecture tours, trips to the mall, whatever. She used them till they fell apart, which took a long time, but she loved things like that, very expensive things that looked cheap, except that a cheap imitation would never survive so many years of her abuse, soaking it in the rain and throwing it off luggage carts and dropping it off train platforms, dragging it along conveyor belts and the sharp teeth of escalators, cramming it with razor-edged textbooks and unsheathed soil knives, having lipglosses and yogurts and bacterial samples explode inside it.

The company had offered her free ones because of all

the free publicity, but she always turned them down. Turned everybody down. I would have taken one of those bags no problem, but she never offered to buy me one and I'd never asked. Part of our unspoken nod to basic economic facts: I gave gifts that I could afford, and she gave at the same level, so that we wouldn't embarrass each other.

It occurred to me, with a pang that felt like someone had poked me sharply in the neck, that Rutger was at the airport not only because he had packed for his employer, but because my family had been put on a plane, no doubt kicking and screaming, and sent far away. I opened my mouth to ask him about it, then thought better of it, seeing his face. He wasn't even looking at me.

"Thanks," she said, slinging the bag on her shoulder. "Um, this is a bit much. Hang on." She fished out handsful of clothing; I turned my head as she got to a layer that seemed inappropriately silky and patterned for me to look at. Now was not a good time for an unexpected hard-on, not that there ever was. "We won't be gone for long."

"I am against this," he said, holding the discarded garments in both hands, nearly but not quite hiding how his knuckles stood out white against his tan. His face, usually so impassive and consistent, with its painted-on expression of polite curiosity, was trembling, wavering as if seen through water. I wondered how much he had seen at the house. How much he believed; how much she had told him. Whether I should pity him. "I am going to ask you again. Don't go."

"That wasn't a question," she pointed out, repacking the bag and hefting it experimentally.

"Will you stay?"

"No." She looked up at him. "I know you're trying to find some loophole that will result in me agreeing to stay put. And I know you don't like this. But we have to go."

"I will go with you," he said, all in a rush, as if it had just occurred to him. "Don't take... this one. Take me, instead. Whatever is happening, I will be of more help."

"No."

"But—he isn't—I would—"

"Usually, I'd tell you that was true," she said, trying to find gentleness in her voice, to remove the unintended insult he felt he'd received. I wished I could tell him that my going wasn't a slap in *his* face, that it wasn't that I was being preferred over him because of some talent I had or skill she wanted me to exhibit. That we might be flying to disaster and death.

She said, "We'll be back by the sixth. At the latest. Maybe the seventh, if I have any trouble booking our flight back."

"If you have trouble, call me and I will book it," he said at once, then checked himself, like yanking a puppy back on a leash. "But I am telling you again, I don't see why you are doing this. Why you are going there. Why you won't tell me."

"Just promise me you won't tell anyone where I'm going or who I'm with," she said. "Promise me. Tell people I'm just going on a business trip like usual, if anyone asks. Anyone. Police, mom and dad, anyone. Promise."

"For years I have closed my eyes to many, many things that you have done," he said, after a long, stunned silence; he wasn't looking at her any more, just me, his bronze-coloured eyes sparking and seething. "Where I could not close my eyes, I closed my mouth. Sometimes, as you asked. Sometimes, when you did not ask. But I cannot promise this time. Especially because you are going with *him*. If your mother—"

"Her especially. Tell her I'm going to... check up on the university endowments from last year."

"If. She. Asks."

"Just tell her that!" she finally snapped, taking a step towards him; both he and I backed off in actual fear. "And I want to hear you promise it!"

"Joanna, the house, these things that have happened, I cannot lie about everything to everyone. You don't know what you're getting into. Whatever this is, whatever you are doing, you can tell me, and I will help take care of it. I know you are... I know you are..." He cast around for a word, his face writhing. "*Special*. That you have done much more than a girl your age would normally do. But sometimes, adults have to—"

"We have to go," she said, cutting him off. Reminding him of his place, I thought, wincing. Not a friend. Not a parent. Just an assistant. "I said, promise."

"Yes," he muttered, fists shaking at his sides. "I promise."

"Thank you." Something deep in her chest wheezed

like an accordion; stress bringing back a whisper of her childhood asthma, long outgrown. I wondered if it would resurface on such a long-haul flight, in that dry air. Shit.

"We'll be *back*. Wait for my call. And water the plants," she added as she walked away. I scuttled after her, giving him a half-hearted wave. I didn't like the guy, but I hated for that to be our final goodbye. He lived for her in a way that I didn't; the ways we loved her and worried about her were so different.

I wondered what he would be doing if she hadn't found him. The way she talked about him in interviews, two prodigies finding each other, as if it was meant to be. No mention of his parents having kicked him out of their house, how he'd been homeless for part of his degree, his tuition paid for but nothing else. I didn't know the rest of the back story, and he didn't like that narrative anyway. In interviews, he'd simply say that he decided to work for Johnny because he believed she was doing good work, work that would make a real difference in people's lives. "She made me a generous offer and I saw that we could be of assistance in each other's research." His face in those TV spots like I'd always seen it—sharp, bright, focused, just like hers. Maybe that was what she had seen in him. A mirror face, a brightness.

What had she seen in me? Not that, obviously. Maybe opposites attracting. I wasn't her other half the way Rutger was, and that had been his goodbye. I wondered what mine would look like.

In gloomy silence we got dinner at one of the few

restaurants still open, apathetically shoveling noodles and rubbery shrimp into our mouths, not really tasting it, fueling our engines.

"You'd think we'd be having filet mignon and fancy champagne for our last meal," I said.

She choked on a laugh, the first real one I'd heard in what felt like forever. "You'd think so, eh? Like, um, garnished with a whole lobster."

"And a big fuckin' truffle."

"Yes! A truffle as big as a volleyball. And some gold leaf."

"And... what else is really fancy? You'd know, *Richie Rich* fancy. Some rare cheese? Made with like, whale milk or something?"

"Ew!" She thought, looked at the ceiling. "But there's somewhere in Sweden that makes a cheese with moose milk and that's a couple of hundred dollars a pound."

"Yeah. A grilled cheese sandwich with moose cheese and truffles and gold," I said, pushing the remnants of my meal around on the bamfoam plate. "*That's* what we should be eating."

"I would destroy a civilization for a grilled cheese sandwich right now. I'd go full fucking monster."

"Me too." I smiled at her, dragging it up from the depths with muscle-tearing effort. "But actually, let's not call this our last supper."

"Of course it isn't. We're not gonna starve over there. All the stereotypes about the Middle East are wrong except one: they want to feed you. All the time."

"Have you been where... where we're going?"

"Sort of." She jerked a thumb at my bag, where she'd stashed a double-sided wad of her printouts, drawings, and notes, as thick as my forearm, like a book manuscript. "I've been to Morocco twice, but not Fes, which is where we're going."

"*Morocco*. That's amazing. Jesus. I've never been to..." I trailed off. I'd never been anywhere, really. Incredible to think this would be my first real trip.

She said, "A library there might have documents about the alignment. Right now all I know is it's close, it's breathing down our necks. There's so much magic in the world I can almost taste it." She lowered her voice. "So much that Drozanoth might be able to start using human agents to do its dirty work. And then the rules go haywire and we are in the shit."

"We are already in the shit."

"We are currently shin-deep in the shit. If that thing starts conscripting people, we will be chin-deep and treading." She took a pen from her bag and scribbled briefly on a napkin, then turned it to me: *Man in blue coat behind me.*

I jerked my head up, then immediately pulled it back down, pretending to scrape the last noodles off my plate. A nondescript white man in a blue and white Adidas jacket, head down, dark hair, a fragmentary memory of a pair of intensely blue eyes staring at us in the millisecond before we had both looked away. "Well," I said, pitching my voice as low as I could while I tore up the napkin, "people stare, you know? I mean you were just in the paper two days ago and you got moshed by photographers right in this airport. Or did you forget that you were famous?"

"Look at his face, his skin," she said, so softly I could barely hear her. "Like something's being taken out of him, moment by moment. Look how pale he is."

"There's a lotta pale people in the world."

"Yeah, there are. But remember his face. Don't forget it. Watch for it, later."

"All right."

"If there's one, there could be others."

"All right, all right."

"Hey. This isn't paranoia," she said.

"After what I've seen today, nothing is paranoia," I said.

"Write that down somewhere," she said. "Nothing is paranoia."

I WAS WORRIED about the passport setting off some kind of alarm when it was scanned, but it didn't—Rutger did good work. My God, these days I couldn't imagine what would happen if I had tried to get on a plane with a fake passport and got *caught*. The private room, the rubber glove, a million years in jail. It was traveling with Johnny that got us through, I realized, even though they had given her some flak for the ticket purchase because she was under eighteen. It was traveling with a white girl, traveling with money. I would take it.

It wasn't till we were on the plane, buckled into our first-class seats, that I let myself relax. Nothing could get us up here. The man in the blue jacket hadn't been in the line to board. And he sure wasn't in first class— we were separated from economy not by a curtain but a sturdy door, and there were only six passengers for twenty seats, none of whom seemed to alarm Johnny the way he had. First class even had its own bathroom, which I proceeded to destroy ten minutes after takeoff. I half expected the flight attendants to wear hazmat suits as I sheepishly crawled back to my seat.

"Are you okay?" Johnny whispered. "Do you have the anxiety poops?"

"I have *not* got anxiety. I've just got the poops."

"Uh huh. Drink some water."

My stomach is too damn sensitive; it's like a burglar alarm that goes off when a bird lands on the house. I wondered how it would react to being in a new country, all that strange food and foreign water, unless Johnny had something for it. I hadn't even had time to get all my shots before we left; Johnny hadn't even brought it up. Probably because she had had all of hers for years, and I'd never even left Canada before. If I shit myself to death, would she pause to memorialize me before racing ahead to solve the mystery and close the gate? The greater good, you know.

She had this mantra. Or manifesto. Anyway, this immovable hierarchy in her head, that she'd tell reporters, students, anyone who asked. About how you had to get people food and clean water and a roof over their head before you got to anything else. How you had to vaccinate their babies, prevent the early childhood diseases, quickly and completely treat whatever you had failed to prevent, and then leave people to it. At once. And in totality.

She had invented these... I can't remember what she called them. Something Pods, missing out on the chance to call them Chambers Chambers before the reactor ever came along. A self-contained flat-topped cone, for refugees and natural disaster victims and so on. You'd do your stuff on the main level and then there were a couple of steps up into a loft area, for sleeping and food storage, a fold-out solar array for powering flashlights and phones, a little water capture device that could get a certain amount of moisture out of the air. And depending on how you shut the portholes and flaps, your cone could withstand being hit by a hippopotamus or washed away in a flash flood. And you'd be fine. Safe, fed, dry. I think there were something like a half a billion of them out there now. Stocked with her vacuum-packed protein pastes and cubes, and the chemical toilet, and the compact fuel packs that burned for days.

And people would say "So now you're going to stop the local warlord? Arrange a treaty with the neighbouring assholes? Take away their nukes?"

But every time, she'd say, "No. I'm providing necessities. Anything else is up to them." Adamant, unbending. You don't treat the symptoms, she always said. You treat the illness. If there is lingering fever or coughing, the patient can deal with it themselves.

I remembered the summer she'd developed that ration paste, looking for something heavy in fats and proteins, savory and sweet, shelf-stable. She processed nuts, seeds, protein gunge cooked up by bacteria in the labs, whatever she could think of—obscure beans, bark, seedpods, the coverings of strange fruits, stopping just short of mealworms. I ate sample after sample and kept getting sick. She'd yell at me, seeing the empty spot in the fridge, one grid missing out of nine or twelve or fifteen, fucking up the whole experiment, and I was always unable to explain why I simply picked food up and ate it when I saw it. I was ten or eleven and I simply could not explain myself.

I looked across the aisle; she was blackout asleep, curled around her music player, all cried out. "CDs will be dead soon, Nicky," she'd told me when she released the players, one of her few forays into gadgetry. "This is what people will want, and Apple will make millions of them. Digital music will take over. Better than what you can get on Napster." She had been right, of course, at least about the players. The first batch had sold out in a month, the factories scrambling to keep up. The glass ones, that looked like a bottle of perfume; the metal ones, like a flask, satisfyingly heavy; the plastic and rubber sport ones in black and blue and red and white that everyone ended up buying that showed fingerprints instantly. And hers, the only one of its kind, made of wood that only grew softer and smoother over the years, her thumb slowly rubbing away the design of leaves and vines on it, pale gold against the sepia of the wooden casing. If you didn't know better, you'd think she'd fallen asleep cuddling a yoyo. Always wanted to be special.

Always *had* been special. Even before I knew. I thought about City Hall again, the shooting. The first day I ever saw her face.

What else did those old memories hold? A perpetual darkness, smell of urine, someone big who smelled of cigarette smoke, pushing me... faint sunrises and sunsets, broken by flashlights and headlamps...

Years later, when I was in junior high and Johnny was arguably more famous than Vanilla Ice, Lifetime made a straight-to-TV movie about it, based on a novelization we hadn't known about called 'As Angels Sing.' Looking back, the title was the only thing that didn't make me physically cringe to think about. John's parents sued—unsuccessfully, I think. Mine didn't care; my character in the movie was only onscreen for a minute, and he was played by a black kid instead of brown, as if any colour would do.

When I found out about the movie, Johnny was away as usual, working at her maize lab in Georgia. I called main reception and patiently waited out five or six transfers till someone found her and I broke the news.

"Oh my God," she wailed. "A Lifetime movie; please, God, no. I can't come home now."

"You have to," I said sadly, "we have to watch the Canada Day fireworks with the kids."

"I'm flying back out on the weekend. Do *not* bring up that movie."

Even now there's no indication that it happened, not even a plaque commemorating the deaths, because City Hall was renovated around the time the movie came out, swapping the bullet-pocked brick for tile and adding a glass pyramid. I was pleased—I wanted it changed, unrecognizable, something entirely new, something where no darkness could live. Johnny was upset. She wanted the city to knock it down and make a park.

At the opening ceremony, we sat between our moms so we could talk. "Treehugger," I whispered, looking straight ahead.

"I'm an aesthete, not a treehugger," she said. "Look it up."

"I like how you think I wouldn't know what it means."

"I like how you're pretending you're not going to go home and look it up."

"I'm *not*."

Now, salt was crusted solid across the bridge of her nose, a wet channel running through the middle of the crystals, her upsprung hair shorter than mine. It had been years since she'd had long hair; I remembered it blowing in the wind once as we said goodbye on a summer evening, the silkiness and loft of it with the sun coming through, seeming blonder in its length, a shining scarf afloat on her shoulders, weightless.

A younger her, a younger me. We could never go back. And I was the only one who wanted to, anyway. Because I was the only one who loved or even knew how.

the teeth in the night, approaching
red the sky
stars turn and dance

the cathedral of black stone has shattered
the cathedral has been buried
water seethes at the foot of the cliff

in the snow we come, in the sand we come, from
the waves we come
a curl
a curling plume of burning flesh
dance to the

stars

I woke up slowly, not the way she always did, snapping awake, and became aware of the airplane's hum, my dry, sticky mouth, the blanket sliding off my shoulders, looking automatically for Johnny. Bad dreams, I thought. Proximity effects. I thought about telling her I'd had another one, letting her do some dream interpretation or whatever, but there was something strange about her. She was awake, alert, hilariously so, like a cartoon of herself—still wrapped in the blanket, only her nose and her wide, alarmed eyes showing. I followed her gaze to two pretty flight attendants chatting near the cockpit door, not in English.

"What is it?" I whispered.

She glanced quickly at me, then back to them. But it wasn't till they eventually wandered off that she turned and whispered "Go get your bag out of the overhead storage bin. When we land, put the strap across your body."

"...Why?"

"Because we're going to be held in custody at the airport and I want you to have it on you in a way that they can't easily grab it off."

"What? We're going to be *arrested*? For *what*?"

"Not arrested. Held in custody. For our own safety."

And I looked at her grey face over the blanket, stony with not just anticipation but rage, and thought: Oh shit. Rutger. We asked him not to tell, she made him promise not to tell, but we both saw his face as we left, and he told. She was gone all the time without comment, but now we had been reported as missing.

I thought: We're going to be put right on a plane back home as soon as we land. If we're lucky. If we're not...

I pictured a tiny room crawling with earwigs and cockroaches and scorpions. Dusty, terracotta light, unchanged for hundreds of years. Like the scenes in *Robin Hood* or *The Mummy*. Screams from down the hall, the sound of a metal rod scraping on the bars of our cells... no phone calls allowed and the only person I could think to call buckled over the stinking pail in her cell a few feet away, or with a guard pinning her to the wall with his crotch... oh man, why hadn't they just put me in jail on *our* end of this fucking trip?

"Look, stay calm," she said. "Remember your bag. We need those papers. The language keys are in there and I can't work without those."

"Stay calm, she says. You got a plan for this, Li'l Miss I Have a Plan for Everything?"

"Gather relevant data, formulate next steps,

implement, return to original parameters," she said, blinking innocently at me. "The usual."

"Isn't that what you said right before we tried to eat ten pounds of marshmallow bananas at your grandma's house?"

"Shut up."

How would it go down, I wondered. Did they have guns, or Tasers, or those tranquilizer things that, ironically, Johnny herself had invented? Nowhere you looked was free from her touch. Nowhere good. Nowhere bad. Eventually it would get all garbled and the history books would say she had invented electricity and screws and the horseless carriage and the letter E. Before dying at the tragic age of seventeen, I added. Good thing she'd started early.

Sweat kept breaking out on my skin in visible, tiny droplets, then evaporating, leaving me chilled. I wrapped up in my blanket and sweated and worried, teeth chattering. Would they tackle us? Shoot us? Quietly pull us aside? I doubted it, knowing what I knew about the Middle East, which wasn't much, just a few dozen viewings of *Aladdin* with the kids; and the news now, shouting about Saddam, oil prices, embargoes, terrorist groups in the desert, the smashed Bamiyan Buddhas that Johnny had sobbed over. I barely knew what people looked like where we were going, even, except angry brown men with moustaches, and women in masks or veils. Just the stuff they showed on CNN. Jesus. Custody, I thought. We hadn't done anything illegal except the faked passport. They weren't going after real criminals, right? Just runaways. They had been told that.

Right?

It's so tough to be young; it's so tough that the only way I assume adults are able to function is that they have forgotten this, that they don't remember a time when they didn't know anything and knowledge was kept from them, and they railed at the gatekeepers. And whatever the gatekeepers were—time, bosses, parents, teachers, luck—they would not have remembered being young either. School was a fucking waste if all it did was let you graduate with a head full of questions and no way to get them answered. And always, always knowing less than Johnny.

And even so, she'd never be able to talk our way out of this. I looked down at my hands: a shine, then dull again. As if waves were crashing over me, cold, heavy. What if Rutger had let something slip to the news, what if wherever Mom was, she was watching CNN and wondering what the hell was going on, and why we were going to Morocco, of all places? She'd be trying to explain it to the kids—and the boys wouldn't even be worried, they'd think it was an adventure, that I'd gone on vacation with Auntie Johnny. It would be Carla who would see through it, who would worry and cry and fret till her stomach hurt.

"How long till we land?" I asked Johnny, who was nipping at her water bottle and swirling it around her mouth, a nervous tic that had earned her an unfair reputation in the press as a wine snob.

"Three hours."

Three hours and then the great unknown. Jail, a fifteen-hour flight back. The end of her plan and the end of the world. Or no. The end of... how did she say it? Not the world itself, but the world that didn't have Them in it. The sky is not the sky; the light is not light.

CHAPTER ELEVEN

THEY DID IT when we landed, wordless, simply pulling us aside as we deplaned into an unbelievable blast of heat mixed with icy currents of air conditioning, swirling a weird cyclone of odours into the high ceiling—spices, sweat, lemon floor polish, cigarette smoke, coffee, trash. I got one glance at the sign that said *Customs*, in English and a dozen other languages, before we were herded away from it, separated from the rest of the passengers.

A hand clamped hard on my forearm, fingers digging in, and before I could tell them not to touch Johnny—I don't know why I thought she couldn't do it herself—the words were whipping out of her, sensuous soft-edged things delivered like the edge of a straight razor. I looked up into scratched aviators over a heavily moustached face, a tan uniform, red-brown face. His expression wasn't angry, despite the power of his grip.

Just... immovable. Like hers. Could not be swayed.

My head began a slow spin, and I looked over at Johnny just as they put the cuffs on her.

"Wait," I finally said, "don't, don't do that—"

My arms were wrenched behind me and something hard and hot went around my wrists—the cuffs must have been in the cop's pocket, I thought feverishly, to be so hot. They were ready for us. Ready for us to not go quietly.

Still no one had said a word except for us. Johnny was talking more calmly now, cuffed like me, hands behind her, looking up at the grey-haired cop who had his hand around her upper arm, fully encircling it. They didn't like girls to have bare arms here, did they? Not like her to forget that. Had she left her jacket on the plane? She was completely white except for two red dots, like stickers, above her eyebrows. I felt boneless with fear, watching her mouth move.

And suddenly I couldn't hear what she was saying, because my ears started to ring, a piercing whine.

"I'm gonna be sick," I said to the cop, voice already thick with it. "I'm—"

"What?" he said.

It all came up, everything I'd eaten on the plane, plus the noodle salad I'd had in Edmonton International, but I'd been drinking so much water that it was a clear jet studded with orange chunks—and why was it always orange, I wondered dimly, coughing and spitting to clear my nose just as another jet burst out. Both cops yowled and stepped back.

And in that split second, Johnny flattened them both—elbow to the throat, kick to the balls—and grabbed the front of my t-shirt, and we took off.

I stumbled on my wet shoes, actually falling to my knees at one point with a sickening *crack*. She hauled me up and hissed "Come on!" but I couldn't pump my arms, I kept trying to even though I kept also reminding myself that I couldn't, just wiggling my shoulders like a pigeon. I saw Johnny checking her speed for me, as if shifting down to a lower gear, and felt a brief stab of gratitude and annoyance, cutting through the green haze of the nausea. Someone screamed behind us, loud over the patter of footsteps. I didn't dare look back. We weren't even the only ones running in the airport, though most of the others were headed in the opposite direction, towards flights they were about to miss. They made good camouflage, though, as we raced towards the sunlight they were leaving behind.

Where were we even going? The baggage check carousels were in the way—easily leaped—and then through another, unmanned security gate, and bodies congregating at the door.

"Quick!" Johnny gasped, and we darted left, my shoes still skidding horrifyingly, into a door marked *EMERGENCY EXIT* in several languages. It was one of those ones you had to push for thirty seconds before the door opened, but Johnny did something to the wiring under the handle, spun back around, and we were through.

We banged down a hallway and finally through a set

of revolving doors, my bag—my God, how had they let me keep my bag? They must have wanted to search it— briefly getting caught. Then we were free and running into the street, dodging cars and donkeys and horses, miraculously it seemed, before I realized that they were all at a standstill in a miles-long traffic jam surrounding the airport. The air, a damp slap, smelled intensely of unfamiliar things—exhaust, salt, ammonia. The ocean? Where *were* we?

It was so hot and bright that my pupils screamed and I felt my stomach heave again, as if it weren't completely empty, and we pounded through the crowd, deking between dusty bumpers, and out the other side. Huge hotels flashed by, marked with names even I could read: *Hilton*, *Sheraton*. What? Not safe yet, I knew; she didn't have to tell me. Never been so far from home, never been so far.

We ran and ran, sliding around cars and hopping barriers, past houses and trees and yards, people staring at us in a blur, until I got a stitch and we stumbled to a stop in an alleyway, pressed to a rickety iron gate that flaked rust into my hair as I leaned against it and heaved.

"We can't stay here," Johnny gasped. "We're still too close to the airport."

"I'm good," I said, but it came out as a croak and I immediately retched again. "Holy shit. What just happened? Where are we?"

"Casablanca is the best I can do. Otherwise, no idea. I'll check my map when we stop for real." She took a breath that wheezed in her lungs like a toy whistle, and pushed something warm into my fingers. "Hold this still."

"What am I—"

"Sunglasses. Grabbed 'em from one of the cops while we were heading out. We can't keep running with cuffs on. Hold 'em real tight, just like that."

She reversed, like backing up to a trailer hitch; I felt her break the arms off, then pop the lenses out of the frames and use my grip to bend and eventually break the cheap rims. My stomach twisted and gurgled, and for a moment I wondered whether it was going to be projectile puking or just a bout of explosive diarrhea right there in the neat, blue-painted alleyway. I pressed my face to the iron gate, a tiny bit cooler than the blast furnace of the day, and willed my insides to shut up.

"Where did you learn how to pick a handcuff lock?" I said.

"It's not that hard. Most of them are just a single tab, and if you push on it hard enough, it... ah."

I felt mine go free, and as I turned to thank her I leaned over and puked into the corner again. Nothing came up but a few mouthfuls of water; I guessed it was in reverse order of the things I'd eaten. My nose burned and stung. But I'd put water in both our bags on the plane, and I fumbled at my bag zips while she cursed, muttered, and eventually got her own cuffs off.

"There. Always easier on someone else's. Finish that and let's go."

I put the empty bottle back in my bag, and though I didn't feel any less pukey or lightheaded, I did feel as if

I could move now. I followed her out of the alleyway at a fast walk.

Outside the alley, it was chaos and sun and dust—cars honking, bike couriers zipping past, people with actual donkeys or mules screaming "Balak! Balak!" everyone on the narrow sidewalk shoving and pushing between us. I reached automatically for Johnny's hand, as if she were one of the kids, but checked myself and instead followed her as close as I could. Sweat sprang out all over my face, trickling down my neck and soaking my hair.

In the moment of relative safety I craned my head to try to take it all in, wishing I had sunglasses or a hat—it was so bright it just seemed like a spangled kaleidoscope of car windows, men in suits, tiny booths hawking electronics, sunglasses, clothing, CDs, food, tiles, everyone gabbling around me in languages I didn't know, plus blessedly recognizable if not actually comprehensible French and English. People bumped and buffeted me apparently without even noticing. I had been picturing... I don't even know what. Some mud-brick city from *Raiders of the Lost Ark*? Flowing white robes? Tintin books, for absolute sure.

Not so many trees or plants everywhere, or of so many kinds. Not so many fountains, covered in glossy tile. Lots of men with their cheeks ridged with scars, parallel lines high and fierce on their dark skin, mainly older men. A lot of Western clothes, more than I had pictured, interspersed with the loose robes: university t-shirts, Disney, Looney Tunes, over blue jeans or Gap khakis like Johnny's. Older cars, newer cars, hundreds or thousands of little motorbikes, barely dirtbikes. Tons of sidewalk cafes with no regard for the rest of the sidewalk, forcing us to step into the street, widely umbrellaed in blue or black. Silver daggers gleamed on the occasional hip. Everything smelled of sweat, onions, herbs. Bicycles everywhere. Most of their solar panels were the old kind Johnny had first invented, black and iridescent, like the feathers of a starling. Everywhere the roofs of buildings looked like dark wings.

Johnny paused at a stall, negotiated briefly with the bearded man there in French, who kept staring suspiciously at me, and came away with two black-and-white checkered scarves with fringe around them. We ducked into another alleyway, something there was no shortage of in Casablanca apparently, and she showed me how to tie mine around my head before tying hers in a completely different way. After she hit up an ATM in a convenience store—"A haroun," she explained, "they're kinda everywhere"—to get a wad of cash, we kept walking, past mud-brick buildings painted in white in an effort to bounce back some of the dry, burning sun. My head felt much cooler in its own coat of white.

"Sort of a disguise," she said. "Obviously not great. But it helps us blend."

"Yeah. You look much better. Lots of people here have green eyes and you're almost tan enough to get away with it."

"I think that's my dad's side," she said, holding out her bare arms and admiring them next to mine, ringed with red from the cuffs. "I'm almost as dark as you!"

"You wish." I looked around, seeing nothing I recognized as a street sign. "Holy shit. We're in *Morocco*. Man! Can we check your map here?"

We pulled into another alley and she got out the tiny laptop she'd built last year, its solar panel flashing onto my face. The screen was hard to see in the sunlight. "Turn. I need some shade. Thanks. Uhh, shit. Jesus. *Shit*."

"Oh, that sounds so hopeful. So encouraging."

"I didn't take into account that we might not be able to use the airport," she said, pointing at the screen; I didn't understand what I was looking at, but nodded. Two large round black dots were connected by a long wavery line on the green background, surrounded by smaller dots, none of them labelled. "Because it's not a long flight to Fes—it's about an hour—but it's almost a four-hour drive."

"Oh, shit."

"Come on," she said, starting to walk again, briskly. "I'll figure something out."

WE ENDED UP circling back to the airport like movie spies trying to lose a tail, walking then taking a bus from a random stop, Johnny pushing bills carelessly into the farebox. Even from a distance I could see dozens more uniforms at the airport's doors than I would have guessed. Not all for us, surely. Or maybe they were for us, because we'd gotten into a fight?

But the nearby bus depot was so crowded that I doubted anyone would be able to spot us, and half the crowd was wearing scarves like ours. My height was the main conspicuous thing about us—at six feet, barely remarkable back home, I towered over this crowd. I slouched as I followed Johnny.

The heat was like nothing I'd ever experienced, like being trapped in an oven. Waves of it coming off the white sidewalks, practically a physical force, pushing me around with every step. The occasional humid ocean breeze barely cut through it. She walked purposefully towards the ticket office, elbows out to nudge people aside.

"Keep a hand and an eye on your bag," she said. "Thieves like bus stations."

"Well, you too, then," I said, annoyed.

"Mine's steel-mesh reinforced and there's wires in the strap," she said. "National Geographic Store. Can't beat it. Here we go. Act surly; they're not gonna like me doing the talking."

"*Act* surly, she says."

Frowning and acting worried was the easiest thing she'd asked of me so far; I scanned the crowd, looking for cop hats and aviator sunglasses. A towering group of white tourists, maybe Swedish—was that the blue flag with the yellow cross on their bags?—argued with someone in an airport uniform, both in heavily accented English. I wondered if either side understood the other. A much larger group of Japanese tourists in matching t-shirts, shepherded by three guides, moved sedately towards a charter bus, shiny and green in the low, gold light. We weren't using one of those, though, Johnny had said; she wanted something less conspicuous.

I remembered, out of nowhere, the time we had been riding an Edmonton bus back to St. Albert from a book-signing and been accosted by an angry physicist, a famous one, she'd said later. "You've ruined my life!" he shrieked. "You've ruined my life! Ruined!" White hair, red bowtie, yellow teeth every which way. But he wouldn't tell her what she had done or when, and she just hung her head and apologized. She knew, though. "I was right," she whispered when he was gone. "About everything."

Johnny was yelling at the ticket agent now, her high voice carrying over the crowd; I looked over nervously, as did several other people. The ticket agent was pointing at me, beckoning me to come over. I shook my head—he probably thought I was from here, spoke his language. It was weird that I felt so out of place, surrounded by people who looked at least a little like me—some shade of brown, black hair—till I realized that it was because back home, everyone was *white* and I wasn't used to seeing so many people who weren't. You grow up with them, you assume everybody everywhere is white. Holy crap. Johnny would love it when I told her. I stood on tiptoe to see her better, about to walk over.

And in that moment I saw a face that stood out at first simply for its colour—a pale grey, bluish at the extremities—and then for what I realized, sinkingly, its familiarity: the man in the Adidas jacket. I dropped into a crouch, and duck-walked the few steps separating me from Johnny, who had stopped yelling and was instead laughing with the ticket agent, which was beyond my comprehension but also not my problem right now. She accepted a few slips of printed paper and turned when I tugged on her bag.

"That guy from the airport is here!" I whispered. "I saw him! How in the hell did he find us? I didn't see him on the plane!"

"Are you sure it's him?"

"You could believe me for once in your life. Jesus. Look, he's over there."

She glanced over, then grabbed my bag to drag me behind a concrete support pillar. I leaned my face on it and tried to watch the guy, who was scanning the crowd, a still, white point in the swirling mass of people and luggage.

"What are we gonna do?!"

"Avoid, avoid, avoid," she murmured. "Don't draw attention to ourselves."

"Did you get bus tickets?"

"Yeah, it's over there. The grey one."

"The one that's... pulling out?"

"Yup." She looked at me—for a moment the old Johnny, the one I remembered, all grin and wink—and we took off at a sprint through the crowd. I gasped at the roaring-hot air as we pounded the few steps towards the bus, which hadn't picked up much speed behind the tour bus ahead of it. Black exhaust obscured Johnny for a second, and when I could see again, she was hammering on the bus door and waving something—her ticket, I thought. The bus slowed rather than stopping, and we swung aboard, wheezing and sweating. The last thing I saw as we got moving again was the face of the man in the blue jacket—staring right at me now, the expression slack, vacant, not angry.

It was packed, the air inside a solid wall of stench, body odour, cologne, diesel, garlic, feet, even a faint smell of animal shit, like a petting zoo, although I didn't see any animals—maybe it was on someone's shoes. The bus itself was an ancient, grease-smudged Nissan that was obviously burning some of the oil it had abundantly dripped on the concrete pad at the station. Delicate towers of blue smoke rose from the holes in the floorboards.

Johnny shoved down the aisle to the back, and we sat on the floor on top of several battered suitcases, to keep our pants out of the dirt. Half the passengers turned to stare at us, nearly all the standing men. The women, sitting, seemed too preoccupied with wrangling their bags, food, kids, and each other to care—mostly kids. I thought of Mom and felt a lump rise in my throat. I had always been the one who dealt with the kids the most, but they ran to us equally when they were hurt or scared or bored, seeking the love they knew we would give them, no matter who was doing the wrangling. Christ, where were they? How could Johnny have whisked them off like that? To not know made me feel slightly unmoored, as if I might finish this trip and discover that I had no home to return to, or that I'd never had a home at all. That I was an orphan, parentless, siblingless. Sweat was trickling down my face; I wiped it on my shoulder and glanced over at Johnny.

"Hope you don't have to pee for the next six hours," she said.

"The way I'm sweating, I doubt it. Man, how did they even sell tickets for a bus this full?"

"Let's just say that not everybody here paid the same price for their ticket," she said.

We waited while I worked that one out. "Like... bribes and stuff?"

"*A* bribe. A little one."

"By your standards."

"Yeah. Not by his, I guess." She leaned her head back on a suitcase and closed her eyes. "Money, you know, it's... a lifeline up to a point, it lets you live, but after that it's a cushion. You fall, you hit the cushion, you're fine. You get right back up again. Life is softer, easier. It gives you more options than just to fall onto the floor."

"Hell yeah. What's that saying? It greases the wheels."

"Check. It won't buy us the information we need," she added, "because that's got no price but ingenuity. But it *will* help us find it."

"What if you get robbed or something?"

"What, like I've never been robbed? People try in every single country I've ever been in. Why do you think I travel with a steel mesh bag? There's always ways to access the funds."

"What a creepy, rich-person thing to say," I said. But it wasn't just access, I thought. It was that she was missing something different, something fundamental about being rich. Maybe the authority, the markers of authority: the clothes, the security, the planes and cars and jewelry. She had some of them, but still struck me as one of those bright birds that is bright to attract a mate, but she preferred to pretend she was dull because she liked the dullness better. Everyone might say 'That's because she doesn't want a mate,' even though it was more that she didn't want to be noticed at all.

But any small moving thing in the stillness would be noticed.

I leaned my head on a suitcase, shoving my hair behind my ear. "Anyway, tell me about this library we're going to."

"It's kind of an amazing story," she said. "It was started by this woman named Fatima Al-Fihri—"

"A woman? That must have been some news story around here."

"Wow, way to pigeonhole the entire population of the Middle East for all time," she said. I felt myself blush despite the heat of the bus. It actually had been a shitty thing to say; I wished I could swallow my words and just let her tell the story. Smooth move, Prasad.

She said, "Anyway, if you're about done knowing nothing about the history of human civilization, she inherited some money from her father—he was a businessman—this would have been back in about eight-fifty AD, by the way. Not eighteen-fifty, eight-fifty. It was a mosque, and then a small school, and then a university. So what we're going to is technically the university library, although it's not a university any more."

"What is it now?"

"Uh, closed. It's being restored."

"What?"

"I think the mosque is still in use. But the library, it's in rough shape—roof is crumbling, electrical system is shot, water leaks and stuff—so people aren't technically allowed in. Just the restoration staff."

"Then how are we supposed to use it?" I said. "More bribes?"

"Gather data, yada yada, improvise. We'll just have to watch out for..." She chewed on her lip, uneasy. "Fes is kind of a collection spot for magic; it rolls there like rainwater finding the low spot in the landscape. There are a couple of dozen, worldwide. Places like that attract... things like that. Human and otherwise. The minimal levels of natural magic wouldn't usually be an issue, just a curiosity. But now..."

"Now what?"

"I don't know. It's a place where magic could be used. Where if I use *my* abilities, it might be like sending up a flare. And I've been thinking about the reactor, about what Drozanoth said..."

I hated to hear its name in her mouth. The familiarity of it, the way she didn't hesitate or call it *monster* or *thing*. Her eyes were glassy in her red face, seeming much lighter than usual.

"I was running through the calculations again on the plane and it kind of struck me: where are the topographical atoms going?"

"...What?" I said, helpfully.

"They're not here. They're not in transit. They're somewhere else, but they didn't move to get there; they just flipped."

"Uh."

"Well, and my measurements were showing... it's, um, it's a little vague, but I think it might be another dimension."

"Oh," I said uncertainly. "Like from... what's that book Carla's reading in school. With the drawing. Tesseracts? Length, width, height, time, and..."

"No, not like that. But I mean, sort of exactly like that? It's not a...they're not going a *distance* away. They just flip across a plane, which is two dimensions. And then they flip back. And that's what's generating the power. I thought they were just staying in the water, but they're not. They go next door, they immediately come back."

"What's that got to do with anything?"

"I don't know. But They want it so badly. I'm missing something, I know I am. And I think They know what it is. I have to figure it out."

"Why can't you ever be normal? You don't even have normal enemies," I said.

"They say you can rate someone's quality by the quality of their enemies," she said. "Maybe that's it, though. They want quantum particles? Well, fuck 'em. That'll be us too. They'll have to use every trick up Their slee... whatevers, on us. We just have to keep moving. They might figure out where we are or what we're doing, but I'm not gonna let Them figure out both."

"Wave and particle."

"Wave and particle."

She chuckled, rested her chin on her shoulder, and closed her eyes: conversation over. As she dozed— catlike, she'd always been able to sleep anywhere, even on this noisy, fume-filled, well-over-body-temperature bus with pantslegs and skirts flapping in her face—I carefully got her notes from my bag to see if I could make heads or tails of it. It was almost impossible to read; the bus was bouncing so hard that the plastic windows were both falling open and, actually, falling out. Ochre dust stormed inside, obscuring the pages.

The destruction of Ur, four thousand years ago. I hadn't even known people had lived in cities that long. We had done mostly North American and European history in school, so I could answer bunches of questions about the Russian Revolution, but I didn't, I realized, know much about anything older than a few hundred years ago. The Sumerians wrote everything down on clay tablets, which would of course last longer than paper. It had been a long time since British archaeologists had found the key that let Johnny learn Persian, Akkadian, and Elamite. The little mounds you could find stuff in were called 'tells'—ha! Like poker. I'd have to surprise her with that one when she woke up.

And all the big men, no matter where, had made exhaustive efforts to repair, decorate, and furnish the temples of their gods, but it hadn't been enough. What the gods wanted was life force, souls, whatever was inside a person or animal that made them go. Round bowls to hold the bones and ashes as needed, to keep blood off the floor of their beautiful temples.

The old records suggested that the benevolent spirits of old, the Elder Gods, might have been able to help us fight Them—but they had tapped out many battles ago, and were all trapped, dead, or asleep. Marduk had fought Them and put Them to sleep a long time ago, but he had been put under himself, thanks to base treachery: a friend or lover turned against him. Marutukku had kept the gates shut, but he was definitively dead. Johnny had written *Apprentices?* next to this depressing fact, circled in pink gel pen.

When the Ancient Ones, enemies of the Elder Gods, first came to human civilizations, They had possessed so many people that exorcisms eventually became commonplace, till even the average marketplace soothsayer who sold onions for a living could do one. But precisely because it had become so common, no one had written down the spells.

Speaking of: more of her notes, in turquoise and green gel pen, hard to read. The Spanish Inquisition? *No.* The Salem witch trials? *Yes.* The Crusades? *Yes.* 9/11? *No? But check w/ Society.*

It had to be here... yes. More notes. Holocaust? *No.* Jonestown? *No.*

Carthage, destroyed by Them. Where in the hell was Carthage? It sounded familiar. A Carthaginian shipwreck had been found in Honduras in the 1970s, filled with gold bars and skeletons—they had gotten lost, her notes said, fleeing for West Africa, after They invaded the city.

I felt sorry for the refugees. You think you're escaping, your whole boat sinks. Awful. Jesus.

The Candlestick of the Andes in Peru pointed inland to the geoglyphs of Nazca, itself a great gate of immense power, which was why you could only see the designs from the air. A rope of astonishing, almost inhuman thickness was attached to the central fork of the Candlestick, marked as taboo by local residents, who knew better than to go near it. There was a drawing, in pink again, a series of pulleys and counterweights, maybe Johnny's idea for what the rope did. Something They would pull on, to do some dark and unknown work that even thousands of humans working together could not do.

Mu, or Lemuria, the lost continent (her note: *Island*) in the Pacific, destroyed in some cataclysm twelve thousand years ago. How had that been a civilization, I wondered? Surely we hadn't even graduated from hunter-gatherer yet? Clear signs of one of Their doomsday weapons, so complete had been the destruction. Sunk into an abyss so deep that nothing of Earth could swim to the bottom of it, and we moderns, with our remote subs and our satellite imaging and our radar, would never find anything but its traces, vanished as completely as if we only knew about the dinosaurs from footprints fossilized in mud.

The notes began to blur together, unhelped by the beginning of a panic attack. Cities ruled by 'great animals' that no one could stand to look at or touch; winged serpents; statues of weeping Gods in long, unkempt robes with bulging eyes where they didn't belong. Maps with monoliths marked with X's or checkmarks in every colour of gel pen: Scotland, Peru, Wales, France, Bolivia, India, Uganda, Australia, dozens in the Middle East, around the Mediterranean Sea. Thunderbird myths. Salt lakes. Inter-tribal, international, and perhaps even interchronological (what?) slavery enabled by Their spells. A gate in Wyoming, strange round towers, paintings of volcanoes spewing demons rather than lava. So many human sacrifices, so much blood. Kings bragging that they had met Them and lived. Festivals and ceremonies: They loved those, eating the life force of hundreds of people and animals at a time.

I put the manuscript back into her bag and covered my eyes with my hand for a second. I had thought she'd been... well, not bullshitting me about Their history, but certainly exaggerating. But it seemed that the opposite had happened, and she had been skimming over it— maybe not for my sake, maybe not even on purpose, maybe just out of distaste. There was so much out there. There was so much. Until now I hadn't truly realized how much was arrayed against us: that thousands of us had spent thousands of years throwing armies, sorcerors, intrigue, bargains, entire mountain ranges against them, and now it was down to *two people*.

The entire history of the world had been the story of Them proving that we were weak and insignificant, and that we *should* feel fear rather than hope. And whenever They saw hope in us, the only thing to do was beat it out of us, double-cross us, blow our cities to rubble and remind us that we had been conquered, till They got kicked out again.

Well, we've got something They've never had: Johnny Chambers. That means we can do this, I told myself. But it sounded fake and small even in my head.

Their own had fought Them before, and been ground into dust.

CHAPTER TWELVE

THE BUS STOPPED several times, but she'd said that Fes was the end of the line, so we simply waited while it half-emptied, refilled, swapped a few people, refilled again. It must have been a popular route. The women sitting in front of us passed around flatbread and a huge bag of dried dates, handing them directly to Johnny after staring at me for a minute, as if not wanting to feed someone so unrepentantly and ostentatiously a kidnapper of young girls.

I had lost my appetite in the heat but made myself eat a couple of dates, startled by their rich sweetness, before passing the bag on. I'd never eaten one before, and wanted to nudge Johnny and be like, "Look, I'm on my first date," but she didn't look like she was in the mood. Luckily the sun went down after the fifth stop, cooling the bus perceptibly; I was still sweating, but just my face and neck instead of every square inch of my body.

When we finally reached Fes, it was fully dark, boasting a hazy half-moon like a lemon wedge. Even so, it was crowded at the bus station, or market, or whatever—booths everywhere, all the streetlights still on, the air filled with the smell of food and warm bodies. Our fellow passengers dispersed into the arms of families who had come to pick them up, or taxis, or cars of their own, but the actual crowd itself didn't seem to thin out at all. Johnny led us away till we were in a more residential area, quiet under a single streetlight, pinky-orange like the ones back home, no different. It was still hot, but a breeze picked up that dried my soaked shirt.

"We're at Bab el-Mahrouk, *tsk*. Really shouldn't take a cab at this time of night," Johnny mumbled, studying her computer; I looked over her shoulder to see that the two black dots were much closer now, almost touching.

"How far is it to walk?"

"Just over an hour. Got that in ya?"

"Who knows." Past the streetlights, the rooftops stood out black against an intense, deep-green glow. That would be even brighter in the desert, but I had no desire to see it. "John? The northern lights... can people usually see them here?"

"Nope."

"So it's Them. Like you said before."

"A sign saying They're close. Celestial disruptions, all the rules tangled up. Solar storms and magnetosphere disturbances and comets knocked off their paths, nudged by a nongravitational force that can't be calculated or measured. Don't think about it. Come on."

I trudged after her, my back aching from being curled into a comma on the bus. Our street led into a road lined with houses and tall trees, maybe even the GMO drought-resistant ornamental ones Johnny had created a few years ago. The ever-present solar panel tiles blended into the tiles on walls and balconies; several houses had shaped theirs into pictures like the tanagrams the twins used to love: a chicken, a face, a camel, a cat. Streetlight gleamed companionably off satellite dishes strapped to stone minarets. Our sneakers were silent on the road, although we still startled a few feral cats out of garbage cans and gardens, squeezing their skinny bodies through the iron gates everyone seemed to have here. Their eyes shone from blocks away, turning into streaks as they ran. It was so quiet I could hear the patter of their feet on the asphalt.

"The—" I began, and froze. A fat, low SUV had pulled silently across the road twenty yards ahead of us, scattering the cats. I couldn't read the text on the door, white against navy paint, or see lights or a siren, but I knew cops when I saw them. My senses had gone berserk from fear and I could smell their exhaust from here, sharp and greasy over the chrysanthemum odour of Johnny's fresh sweat.

Steps sounded behind us; Johnny rose onto her tiptoes, hands spread.

"Don't run," I whispered.

"I won't."

"Don't."

"I won't, I won't."

"How did they find us?"

"Beats me."

Dark forms emerged from the alleyways, cheerful, teeth gleaming like their reflective badges in the faint light. They were shouting, not in English. I didn't need to ask Johnny what they were saying. They had guns; so much for *protective custody*.

I exhaled slowly as they approached, five cops, surely far more than was needed for two teenage runaways. Or were they arresting us for prostitution or whatever? Damn, should have worn fake wedding rings or something. Don't move, I ordered myself and Johnny, lips moving silently. Don't give them an excuse to shoot us. Don't give them an excuse to Rodney King us. Don't move.

Instead of handcuffs, they used plastic zip-ties, three around my wrists, two around John's, as she gritted her teeth against their touch. I rolled my eyes when I knew they weren't looking. It was her they had to worry about escaping, not me. The plastic was tight as all hell, my fingertips beginning to tingle before we had even been bundled into the cage of the SUV. Maybe she couldn't get out of these after all.

I shut my eyes as we pulled out. It had all been so fast. Johnny had insisted that our positions and trajectories be indecipherable even to ourselves—waves not admitting we were particles, particles denying being waves—but we'd been caught no more than fifteen minutes after getting off that bus. We tumbled around in the cage, seatbeltless, as the cops chuckled and joshed and slurped from their travel mugs, occasionally jerking a thumb back at us. The interior stank of coffee, body odour, and stale urine—about the way I expected a cop car to smell.

What now? My mind began to race, just like on the plane. Oh God, back to the station. Split up, me in a crowded cell yelling for someone who could speak English, demanding my one phone call, a cop-show fallacy that they would laugh at if anyone understood me. And who would I call anyway? Johnny somewhere else, arguing in ten languages, pulling whatever cards she could for either of us: the fame card, the kid card, the Canadian card, whatever might help. Would it be enough?

The darkness in City Hall. The faceless men, the press of our space, shoulders and hands, the sour smell of children, the smell of fear. A dark smallness, a small darkness. *No one came for us. No one protected us. We were alone in the dark, us and the dead.* I shut my eyes, waiting for it to pass.

"What are they saying?" I whispered when a sharp left threw us against each other, quickly jerking my knee back from hers.

"Blonde jokes," she said grimly. She was watching the street signs outside, though I couldn't understand how she could read them, they were going by so fast; tricky things in French and Arabic, some not even on real signs but made out of mosaic tiles, unlit and stuck to the walls. We barrelled down the empty streets, watching the occasional pedestrian leap back. Rutger's name fell into the cops' conversation once, hard in the flow of the soft language, like something silvery leaping out of a stream: *Rutger Giehl*. I looked at Johnny, but she was still staring out the smeared and barred window. I knew she'd heard it, though. That *fucker*.

The station was huge, so big I would have assumed it was a bank or office building, spotlit with amber lights and surrounded by different colours of cop cars and cops, struggling or resigned people in handcuffs or plastic ties, whole families, everyone waving their fists and pieces of paper or wads of cash, talking at the tops of their lungs. Cats perched on stone barriers, smugly grooming themselves and watching the crowd.

Our doors opened before the SUV had even stopped moving, and hard hands dragged us out, stumbling, up a flight of curved stone steps. We had to fight our way through the mob—hard elbows and chins banging into me, voices in my ears, breath of spices or mint—just to get to the glass doors of the entrance. Only the weight of my bag banging against the back of my legs told me it was still there. Where was Johnny? I twisted to look for her, earning only a harder squeeze from the cop. Something creaked warningly in my elbow.

By the time I caught my bearings again, we'd been stowed in a small, wood-smelling office with brick walls, as if it had been built onto the exterior of the building, barely bigger than the kids' bedroom back home. I panted, looking up at the flyspecked fluorescents, the ceiling fan, the stacks of paperwork and books. Johnny stumbled in a second later, pushed from behind, and the door slammed shut. In the abrupt silence, we both listened to a deadbolt turn from the far side, then fading laughter.

She had a bloody nose, though her hands were loose, two angry purple stripes on her wrists. "I leave you alone for two minutes..." I said.

"He was asking for it."

"You and your kung fu," I said. "You don't even have one single belt. Not one."

"A technicality. Just because I didn't want to do the exams. I still know all the *stuff*."

"No you *don't*."

She quartered the room, mostly looking up at the high ceiling. "Damn. That's pretty high. Well, they made the classic mistake—"

"Took their eyes off you for half a second?"

"Check." She quickly dug in her bag, flipped open her cell phone and dialed so fast her fingers were a blur. I watched hopefully as she held it to her ear, but she hissed in what sounded like real alarm. "Shit. No signal. It must be reinforced concrete behind the brick. Maybe I can improvise an antenna, put it up against the window..."

"Who were you calling?"

"Put the phone down," a strange voice said, and I jumped, falling against the wall. Johnny looked up, then slowly wiped blood from her nose with the back of her hand, letting the drop slither into one of the purple ruts.

"How very unfortunate that they have locked you in

here with us," she said. I held down a frantic sob or guffaw as she pocketed the phone and looked up at the huge man who had stepped out from behind a pile of books beside the desk.

"Yes," the officer said in a heavy accent: *Hessss*. "I heard. You were videoed, you know, at the airport. Shame on you."

"Shame on *them*."

He shook his head—a tall, muscular man bulging from the seams of his navy uniform, stained black with sweat at groin and chest, with a thick black beard and moustache.

"We received information from multiple agencies concerned for your safety. So, you are in custody until we have made contact with your guardian or your parents," the officer said. "No harm will come to you—unless you cause it," he added, tilting his chin directly at Johnny, who glared at him.

I sensed, almost felt, her resist an impulse to look at her watch. It had been about half an hour since we'd gotten off the bus. Not too long a delay yet—but we couldn't afford any more, not if the alignment was as close as she kept fretting about. We had to get out of here, and it couldn't wait until they got ahold of Rutger or her parents. They wouldn't be able to get ahold of mine, not that they knew that. I hoped that wouldn't cause even more of a delay.

The big cop glanced at me, as if reading my mind, and ran a hand caressingly along the butt of the pistol in his chest holster, one of three visible on his uniform. For all I knew he had one strapped to his shin, too, like the movies.

"The airport security, they made a mistake," he said. "Dealing with a little rabid dog. Having reviewed the footage, I will not. Please, sit. It may be some time."

He gestured at two empty wooden chairs on the far side of the desk. I immediately collapsed onto one; Johnny sat more slowly on the edge of hers.

"Can we at least get these off?" I said, waggling my arms hopefully. "I can't feel my hands."

"No."

I opened my mouth again, and stopped. The pain in my hands had gone from a numb buzz to a roar, creeping up my arms. That wasn't fair; Johnny's hands were free. Shouldn't point it out, though. A heavy silence fell, occasionally punctuated by whatever noises could penetrate the thick wooden door. At least there was that. We were in here, not out there—other cops might take our bags, grope Johnny, there would be fights, chaos, and we'd never make it home, let alone to the great gate. Jesus.

"I have to go to the bathroom," Johnny said.

"There is a bucket in the corner."

"...I changed my mind," she said.

After another few minutes, she said, "How did you find us?" I almost laughed; her pride had been hurt. As if we were international spies and not a couple of highly visible teenagers on the run.

"We are not having conversation," the cop said. "Shut up and wait."

"That zapper you're carrying? I invented those."

"Be quiet."

"We don't have time for this," she muttered.

The cop shrugged, eloquently implying with the single gesture that he too was wasting his time looking after us in this cramped office, instead of filling out forms or working on his novel or emailing his friends, but we all had jobs to do, and the best thing to do would be to not complain about it. And at least he wasn't interrogating us, or rifling through our bags, both of which I expected to happen any minute now. Think, think. How could we get out of this? Johnny had a plan. Must have. She was always the one with a plan, no exceptions.

Except for the guns. The guns made an exception. What good was it trying to break us out of here if one or both of us got shot?

And I thought again, coldly: Yes, but if *I* got killed, she would simply take my bag and go. You don't mourn the pack mule. You just keep going. The gate has to be shut. Has to.

We would not have come all this way if she didn't truly believe that the gate could be shut.

"Could we at least have some water?" she said.

The cop sighed, the ends of his moustache flapping, but maybe we looked dried-out enough to be pathetic; he opened a desk drawer, took out a bottle of water, dipped his head as he dug deeper in the drawer. Johnny tensed. I held my breath, waiting for the leap, the collision, the gunshots.

But she let him get all the way back up again before she pounced, and I stood up, yelling her name, crashing against the desk and dancing back as they struggled. It wouldn't have been a fair fight even without the size difference—the desk was in the way, they were fighting around it, sickening crunches of arms and legs against the wood. I could see that he didn't want to hurt her, which was unfortunate, since she certainly wanted to hurt *him*, and it wasn't till he finally held her down with one hand and went for a gun that I leapt.

We collided harmlessly; I felt the breath of air as he evaded my headbutt, the only move—from watching the kids—that I reliably knew in a fight, and then it was just a mad tangle, him throwing me easily to the floor, the casters of the desk chair bumping into my ribs. But Johnny got a hand in, somehow, and drove his head against the side of the desk with a horrific *crack*. He slumped next to me, and we stared at each other for a moment before his eyes slowly, dreamily closed. I tried to get to my feet and found that I couldn't.

Johnny pulled the chair away and stood panting while I got my back against the brick wall and clumsily walked myself back up. "Oh my God, oh my God," I gasped. "Holy shit. What the hell was that? What is this, a kung-fu movie? How are you still alive?"

"Don't jinx it!" she wheezed, quickly frisking herself. Bruises were already developing, and there was a small, dripping wound on her temple where a fingernail had caught her. She stooped and I strode over and hip-checked her.

"We are *not* travelling with a gun," I said. "Especially a stolen cop gun."

"But what if we need it?" She fished one out anyway, and—I assumed, having never seen it done in real life— put the safety on, then tucked it into the waistband of her khakis, where it promptly tried to pants her, exposing penguin-print panties that I looked away from in horror, too late. The fate of the world rested on someone in novelty underwear.

"I'm gonna need some eye bleach."

"For what?"

"This is going to end *so badly*," I said. "Come on, get me loose and let's bail."

She cracked the plastic ties on my wrist using a boxcutter from the desk, and then went for the door, where we both stopped. I bit down a rising scream as blood returned to my dead fingers, shaking my wrists to distract myself from the pain.

"Maybe that's not such a good idea," she murmured.

"Plan B?"

Plan B wasn't as terrifying as I had expected—I was thinking air ducts, squeezing along past whirring fans, like in *Aliens* or something. But we simply stacked boxes till we had stepped shelves high enough to reach the high, small window that led outside. We reluctantly played rock-paper-scissors to decide who would go first.

The cop was stirring and moaning by the time I managed to get the painted-shut clasp open. I could have fainted in relief. When you knock someone out for more than a couple of seconds, that's bad shit. We would go from whatever minor crime faking a passport entailed to a manslaughter charge and—whatever came with that. Helping or whatever.

"Move it!" Johnny hissed, as if reading my mind. "I don't want to hit him again."

"No, because you might *kill* him this time," I muttered. The window had one of those levers on the side that could, in theory, prop it open, but it was bent and not working. I let out a few other choice phrases as Johnny started to mount the boxes behind me, her next words drowned out by banging on the office door. I whirled just in time to see her start, lose her footing, and fall the few feet to the tiles, the gun sliding out of her waistband. It hit butt-first and went off, so loud I yelped, a puff of brick dust floating down onto my hair.

We were still staring at the hole in the wall, a foot from my face, when the cop finally either unlocked the door or busted the lock. Then he stared at it for a moment too.

"Get down, little dog; and you, too," he said sharply, a youngish guy, thin, with sharp black facial hair, as if it had been drawn on with a marker. "You are being moved to Station Zoor. For... protection."

"Please, protect me from *her*," I murmured as he approached us with another set of zip ties.

"But that's halfway across town," Johnny said, frozen in what seemed like shock as he bound her wrists again.

"Very good. Move." He glanced down at the unconscious cop, then looked up again, at me. I shrugged.

"You don't understand," Johnny said. "We can't."

"Uh huh."

Shit. I didn't know how big the city was, but her worry couldn't be good. The time to transfer us there, whatever time she needed to break us out, whatever time to get back to the library...

"Who gave the order to move us?" she said.

"Move, I said." He still hadn't pointed his own gun at us; it seemed inert, heavy, very small in his hand. I wondered what it would feel like to have it aimed our way. "No trouble, understand?"

"You're supposed to return us unharmed, though," Johnny said. "That's why they put us in here. You're not going to shoot us. There would be an international incident."

"Oh? Move." He paused, and met her gaze, then flicked it down to the big officer on the floor, getting to his hands and knees, trying to focus on our faces. "Quickly."

The new cop led us out into the hallway, as crowded as the front of the station had been, and down a set of newer concrete stairs into a car. We'd grabbed our bags, but hadn't taken the water. My mouth and throat felt so dry that I thought I might start coughing and simply choke to death on my swollen tongue. And as soon as I'd thought it, it was all I could think about. Panic placed a hand over my face and pressed down.

Through graying vision and the thick plastic grate between us and the new cop, I heard Johnny say, "Who sent you?"

"You know who."

"No, I mean who *specifically*. They hardly have

enough power to let you pull something like this, do they?"

"No, we do not; and some argued against using it at all. But the cats have been reporting unusual sightings lately," he said, quietly, in perfect English with a faint French accent, his voice much deeper than before. I bit down a gasp as I watched his face shift and blur in the rear-view mirror, as if he'd been wearing a thin mask that had suddenly floated away. "They saw you come into the station."

"Lucky," Johnny said. "Can you give us a ride to Al-Qarawiyyin?"

"Tariq has asked to speak to you."

"We can't spare the time."

"I know you cannot," the cop said. "Not if even half the rumours are true. They will raise the alarm at the station at once, and then there will be a city-wide alarm. I do not know if anything can be done about that. We cannot be everywhere at once. But I agree with their decision to bring you, and we are going all the same."

"Sightings of what?" she said thoughtfully, evidently agreeing to disagree with the last part of his statement.

"...Impossible things."

He fell silent then, and refused to answer any more of her questions. After a few blocks, we pulled over and he bought water and a bag of smoked almonds at a haroun, then ducked into the back seat and sliced through our zip-ties. Johnny opened my water and fed it to me in little sips while I tried to get circulation back into my fingers.

"What's going on?" I said as we got going again, cold water splashing down my shirt. "Don't really care who answers. Pick someone."

"You'll see," Johnny said, staring intently at the front seat. "Almond?"

CHAPTER THIRTEEN

I WAS ABOUT to doze off when the car stopped, and we stepped out into the coolness and silence of a back alley, ending in a one-storey white clay building.

"Where—" I began, and flinched as the headlights turned on; we both turned and watched the cop car reverse out. When I looked back, dazzled from the light, Johnny was already disappearing into the building's open door.

We crossed a small round courtyard, then entered a hallway, dim and heavily scented—roses, pine cleanser, herbs. There was another odour underneath it, though, as if someone had hosed the place down with air freshener to hide something. I felt my hackles go up. The walls were hung with several layers of rugs, the floor white tile. Light came from a few dim, wide lamps, barely bright enough to show the rich colours of the rugs. A small movement as we passed showed a gray tabby darting down one of the hallways. *The cats have been reporting unusual sightings...*

I shook my head, and we emerged into a low-ceilinged room ringed with wooden benches, the floor covered in more rugs, cushions, and blankets. The walls were plaster interspersed with dark wood beams. A small metal cart held a duplicate of Johnny's coffee machine from back home, blue enamel instead of red.

"Tariq," Johnny said, her voice inscrutable. I strained to hear something in it: hope, excitement, happiness, fear.

"Joanna. What a long way you have come. I almost did not believe it." A tall man emerged from another door with his hands out, so suddenly I thought for a second that one of the shadows had stepped away from the column. He was dressed in a flowing, grey-pink robe and matching headwrap that accentuated the absolute indigo darkness of his grave face, his long hands. Something swung on a chain around his neck, hidden in the folds of his robe. As he moved towards us I gagged on the smell of roses. Johnny didn't take his outstretched hands, waiting for so long it became awkward. He finally put his hands back into his robe and smiled.

"Sit, sit. Both of you. Coffee? Tea? Have you eaten?"

"We don't have time."

"Of course not. We will be brief."

I flopped onto a bench and, seeing Johnny do it first, unhooked my bag from around my body, groaning with relief. I had been wearing it so long that there was a grimy stripe across my neck from the strap, and I felt unbalanced on one side. Tariq sat across from our bench, arranging the robe over fancy sandals decorated with blue and white stones. I sniffed the air again, uneasy.

"And this would be the famous Nicholas," he said.

"Pleased to meet you," I said automatically, almost before I was aware I'd opened my mouth. We shook hands, his grip cool and strong. Famous? To who?

He laughed at Johnny's expression. It did nothing to break the tension building between them, like a wall going up brick by brick between their stares.

She said, "Thanks for sending Omar to come get us. I mean, we were almost out on our own, but thanks."

He waved a hand. "You know already what I am going to say, before I say it."

"Yes."

"Which is what?" I said, loudly, when neither of them spoke again.

Johnny didn't even look at me. "That that was as much help as this chapter is willing to offer," she said. "Not *can*, but *will*. Isn't that it? Why did you want to talk if that's the case?"

"You are a terrible scientist because you think everything is simple, Joanna," someone said; the heavily beaded curtain at the other door parted with a clatter and revealed a woman, much shorter than Tariq, beautiful, compact, maybe in her seventies, long silver hair visible through a translucent silk scarf. A white cat followed her, gaunt, with one blue and one green eye. It studied me for a minute, then jumped up onto our bench, as far away from Johnny and me as it could get.

"Helen," Johnny said. "You're a long way from home, too. When did you get here?"

"We have questions for you to answer, not the reverse," the woman said, glancing at me and dismissing me in the same glance. "And you have brought them upon yourself, starting with that ridiculous phone call." She remained in the doorway not as if she were uncomfortable or awkward, but as if she expected this conversation to be short, necessarily so, because there was so little to say. If so, I thought, she didn't know Johnny very well.

But the way they looked at each other spoke to me of a strange, deep knowing—almost the way she looked at Rutger. I wondered who this Helen was, so erect and pale in her royal-blue dress—and where she had come from. As far as us? Her voice was unaccented to my ears, which meant she was from Canada or the States. It made me homesick suddenly—longing for a place where there was more sky than building, where I could understand people, where things were mostly decades old instead of millennia, where a building made out of baked mud would disintegrate in a month, where magic didn't roll downhill.

"Things are more complicated than when I first called," Johnny said. "And you guys are complicating them even more, with all due respect."

"With all due respect," Helen repeated. Her face was

cool and hard. "*Now*, Tariq, she speaks to us with respect."

"*Of* respect, I think," Tariq said, smiling, or smirking.

"Yes, ha ha, kids these days," Johnny said, getting up and gesturing at me. "I get it. Again, thank you. Nick."

"Sit," Helen said. Johnny's legs snapped out from under her; the bench vibrated as she landed on it again. I looked at her instinctively: her face was white and startled, as if she too had not expected to obey.

"Out of nowhere you call us, demanding information from our most closely guarded archives," Helen said, finally coming into the room, standing next to Tariq's bench. Their shoulders were almost the same height. "*Need* it, she says. Telling, not asking. And she can't extend the courtesy of asking, of risking a refusal, because what? Because the world is about to end. And she knows this how? How does she know this, hmm? Upon what is this based?"

Johnny looked up at her mutely, as if waiting for it to be over. I recognized that face and wished I could surreptitiously squeeze her shoulder or touch her hand, the way I did with the kids when they got yelled at. Especially because no one ever spoke to Johnny like that. She wasn't the one who would come home with low grades or truant notices. No one, since the day she'd begun speaking, had ever accused her of being a terrible scientist.

"But you believed me," Johnny said. "Or you wouldn't have let Omar come for us."

"We believed at the time that you were credible. Then

we began to make our own inquiries," Helen said.

"So you know what's happening."

"No. Nothing is 'happening,' Joanna." Helen crossed her arms over her chest, the pale scarf spilling over them like milk. "There... is a little more raw material around than usual, but well within background levels."

"Background levels for *here*. You need to get out of the city," Johnny said urgently. "There's so much that Nick can see th... can see things."

"The uninitiated cannot recognize the products of magic," Tariq said, still smiling. "Not even ordinary trickery. Pick a card, mm?"

"Don't talk down to me," Johnny snapped. "Listen, if you would just let me *look* for the scrolls—"

"Absolutely not," Helen said.

"Why would I lie to you?"

"Lie, perhaps not," Tariq said soothingly. "Exaggerate, surely. There have been alignments before; you said as much. And I, in my lifetime, have seen three. They are asleep, Joanna. For what we understand as sleep. For what They understand."

"They're about to not be," Johnny said urgently, leaning forward on the bench. Her bag slid off and landed on the floor with a thump that sent the cat careering off into the scented darkness, slinking back slowly. "Did I not make that clear? That They're awake, that They're coming? Would we have come all this way for a—a—a *vacation*?"

"Ah, but it is lovely here," Tariq said.

Helen ignored him. "*Would* you?" she said. "Why

would They target this alignment out of all others, why even approach? What have you seen?"

Johnny hesitated, visibly. Maybe not a bad scientist, but a *terrible* poker player: I knew that already. And Tariq and Helen looked like they suspected as much. If Johnny admitted what we knew, she might also have to admit, cagily, to being the one whose invention had awakened Drozanoth from its shallow, watchful sleep. To have, even without meaning to, drummed on the membrane between our two worlds, sending the sound as far and as deep as the dropped stone in the Chamber of Mazarbul in *The Lord of the Rings*. Not a hero selflessly saving the world from a random disaster, but someone frantically trying to clean up her own mess.

Johnny swallowed, and hung her head. "We need to find and shut a great gate somewhere near here, and soon. When I called, I didn't say what I meant. What I meant was, will you help us?"

Helen fell silent, watching Johnny's face, still ignoring me. "You are too used to living a life without help," she said. "Before you reply, no, you are wrong, Joanna. Hiring people is not help. Who would help you without recompense?"

"Is that what you're asking for?" Johnny said. "Recompense? Is the world not enough for you? Is life not enough?"

"It is not a matter of *enough*," Tariq said firmly, looking up at Helen. "Every price comes with a new payment. And the price can change any time; and you, little one, have changed your prices on us too many times for us to look each other in the eye. You will never change. What we do, we have always done for other reasons."

"So you say," Johnny said. "So you always say. Listen. You dragged us here to get answers, and I don't have time to give them. Let us go, if you're not going to give us anything. Just let us go. I know you're going to call the authorities as soon as we go. Do that, if you want. I don't care."

"Ah yes, the defiance that covers fear," Helen said. "Like a snake that hisses and hisses and hisses and will never bite, because it knows it will not be able to kill."

"Good one," Johnny said. "I got called a dog earlier today." But she didn't get up. My skin was crawling, and I felt woozy from the stench below the smell of roses, so I also didn't feel like moving, but there was something different about Johnny's stillness—as if she had been pressed to the bench. Tendons stood out along her neck.

"Just to clarify," I said into the silence, flinching as Helen and Tariq turned to me. "You're from that... that group that used to... worship Them. The Ssarati. Aren't you?"

"Is that what she told you?" Helen said stiffly. "We are nothing of the sort."

"Oh, the stories I could tell you," Tariq said, smiling and tapping his feet on the floor. "A girl, a hundred years ago, from my father's tribe, no older than you, who led them into the true way of the Ssarati... lured from our people by a white *adventurer*, so-called..."

"We do not have time for those stories, Tariq," Helen said. "Thousands of years have passed under our supervision, young man. We once fought Their incursions; now, we cloud Their curiosity and hand down the old ways. We guard the gates, monitor various indicators, keep the wards and sigils fresh, discourage tourists and adventure-seekers, strengthen the spells where we can, preserve the old scrolls and tomes, copy and disseminate. We are a society of knowledge and wayfinding. We are scholars and guardians."

I had run out of nerves, and could only nod as they lost interest and turned back to Johnny. Tariq's gaze remained on me, though: amused, even delighted.

"But we did use a cloaking spell to get you out of that police station," Helen said sharply, "and *if* what you are saying is true, we will attract more attention than is our due."

"What do you want, an apology?" Johnny snapped.

"We want merely to know what you know, so that we may decide what to do next," Tariq said, soothingly.

"That's not what you want at all," Johnny said. "No matter what I say, you won't pick a side."

"Don't be ridiculous. We are on the side of the preservation of humanity, as are you. You are no... lone light in the darkness, Joanna."

"You're not on *our* side."

Tariq said, with a note of pleading, "We have asked you to join us many times, we have asked for use of your facilities and the academics who work for you; we have never asked you to use your great intelligence for us directly. Why have you always refused? Why do you even deny an association with us?"

Johnny stared mutely at them.

But I knew the answer she could not give them: that if they were allowed to close the distance between them, they would know what she really was, and how she had become so.

They would know she owed everything to something they had spent all their lives fighting.

The air seemed to darken; hidden in its nest of pillows, the white cat bared its teeth. Something screamed at the back of my neck, not merely itching but burning, the half-healed welts on my cheek where Drozanoth had touched me beginning to burn too. I got up slowly, aware that Tariq and Helen were staring at me, and slung my bag over my head. "Come on, Johnny," I said, hearing my own voice thin and brassy. "We have to go."

"Check," she whispered, but still didn't move. Tariq got up, though, and crossed the room to me, hands out.

"Nicholas, sit down, let us talk like adults," he said.

I retched from the smell as he approached, and backed away, getting between him and Johnny. "Don't," I said. "Let us go."

"No one is keeping you here," Helen said icily. "Go, then, if you believe your own tale." I looked up at her, and back down just in time to see Tariq reaching for my chest; casually, not fast.

I got a hand up and found the silver pendant half-hidden in his robe, seized it—a blinding burst of pain, as if I'd grabbed a wasp and had the sting driven into my palm—and yanked, snapping it from the thin chain and dropping it on the floor, then kicking it under the bench. Tariq's hands stopped moving; I looked into his baffled eyes, the confusion slowly turning to anger. Under the bench, something was screaming, a tiny noise, that too like a wasp.

"Your name is known to Them," he snarled, unmoving. "Yours, boy. It hangs about you like a cloud. In Their books, hidden in a dark place, in an obscene script, it is written that your time will end in sorrow. Leave her, before it is too late. Stop paying her price."

"I picked my side," I whispered, much more quietly than I intended. Some hero. "Come on, John."

I slung her bag on the same side as mine and reversed out of the room, not wanting to turn my back on them. They watched us go, till I fumbled at the door, emerged into the cool night air, shut it behind us. The last I heard was a soft voice, so quiet I didn't know whose: "*No. Let them go.*"

I didn't know which way we were supposed to go, but I needed to get Johnny away from there; she was wheezing, half-canted over, as if with cramps. I walked as fast as I dared, making sure she kept up. Wherever Omar had taken us, it was as busy as the bus station—despite it being long past midnight, there were still people up, talking, smoking, eating, haggling, turning to look at us. Two kids in a dark alleyway. Great.

But no one approached us—maybe I didn't look touristy enough, I thought hopefully. Maybe I looked like a guide, like one of the guides who had yelled and gestured at us when we'd first gotten into the city, trying to get us to come with them. And if that was the case, Johnny looked like my customer, and they wouldn't horn in on that. Thank Christ, if it was true.

When Johnny's breathing finally eased, we turned down another alleyway, into the meager yellow light from an all-night tailor, printing its list of prices in shadow on her face. It was just enough for her to look at her map and for me to check my hand. I was sure there would be a cut, or at least a burn-mark, but there was nothing. "Weird," I said.

"How did you know?" Johnny said, looking at my open palm as I held it between us.

"I have no idea. I think it was the smell coming off it."

"The smell?"

"You didn't notice? Like Theirs, under all that air freshener?"

She looked up at me, obliquely, like the cat, and then got her laptop out, balancing it on one forearm while she used the other to scroll and tap.

I said, "Do you think they'll turn us in?"

"I don't know. They don't like interacting with authorities, they like to fly under the radar. Maybe they'll get someone to do it anonymously."

"Who were they?"

"Tariq lives here—he's been head of the Fes chapter for four hundred years. I wasn't expecting Helen at all; she lives in Prague now, she was there when I spoke to her. When she came in the room, I thought... I mean, she'd come all this way because of what I told her. I got excited, thinking she'd come here to help us."

"Guess not."

"Thanks for getting us out of there," she said. She was really rattled, despite her casual tone; her hands shook on the keyboard. I tried not to let on how utterly horrified I was in turn. Whatever had happened in there, she had expected none of it, and they had expected all of it—everything she'd said, everything she did, even me being there.

"What were they doing to you? Us? Just you?"

"Immobility spell, I'd guess; meant to keep me there till they got the answers they wanted. That wouldn't have worked a week ago. Those fucking liars, they know there's magic pouring in, they're even using it. Background my ass."

"Jesus. It's like *Harry Potter* up in here."

"Nothing so organized, I'm afraid." She clicked the laptop shut. "The Ancient Ones and all Their servants have senses we don't have, their consciousness, their bodies work in different ways from ours. When they move They aren't moving like us. Parts of Them can be places, Their consciousness can be split up, some awake, some asleep, even their memory, even their desires; some of Them can control people, some of Them can't even control how solid They are, how They interact with our world, our rules, gravity, inertia, time. We can't understand Them. We never will. We *cannot*, not if everyone on Earth dedicated the rest of our lives to studying them for a million years. They can't be understood, even by each other. Only obeyed." She glanced back at the direction we'd come. "You have to wonder about people who spend all their time thinking about Them. About proximity effects."

"They said... my name was..."

"No. It might look that way because you're traveling with me. Layers overlap and blur; things become hard to distinguish. Don't worry about what he said. Anyway, we've been walking in the right direction, at least. Come on, we might be able to get a taxi here."

CHAPTER FOURTEEN

THE LIBRARY TURNED out to be embedded in the middle of a complex of buildings, through which we walked as inconspicuously as possible, dodging the crowds, until finally there was only darkness, silence, us. The mosque reared above everything, cool and symmetrical in white, slightly insubstantial in the dim light, backed by a million stars. I stopped to stare suspiciously at some large, bright ones that I didn't recall seeing a few nights ago, tinged with blue and green.

"Johnny—"

"I know. Seeing the birth and death of stars is a bad sign, since they're all millions of light-years away. The time dilation effects of transitory magical particles and the... listen, just don't look. They'll pull on you."

"Pull?"

"Don't look."

On either side of us stretched neat brick walls, pierced with round-topped doorways, all shut, many with signs on them that I couldn't read but could guess what they said: *No Trespassing.* Or, *No Admittance If Not A Student.* We'd seen a lot like that so far, Johnny walking blithely past them, hopping gates and picking locks. The mosque looked as big as the Coliseum back home—maybe bigger. How many people had I seen at the hockey games on TV?—no, it had to be bigger than that. The roof was dark green, lit up only here and there from streetlights in the darkness. The annex next to it was covered in fantastic tilework, colours muted, bordered in carved cedarwood and flanked by big black pillars. I inhaled the wood scent deeply, wondering that I could smell it at all. You probably couldn't during the day, when it was busy with tourists and students and worshipers. "That's the Medersa el-Attarine," she whispered. "Not us."

"What?"

"That's for tourists. Sorry. *This* is us."

"This is... much creepier."

The door, flanked with UNDER RESTORATION: DO NOT TRESPASS signs in a dozen languages, was big enough to walk an elephant through, but shut so tightly you couldn't fit a piece of tissue paper between the joints. Johnny ducked under the barricades and pushed anyway, then pulled, to no effect. I ran my fingers gently along the complicated carvings in the dark wood, touched here and there with gold or enamel. Everything was mirrored, balanced, mathematically precise. It looked like the doorway to a very fancy hotel, not a place where you could find books on monsters and mayhem. But how would we get in?

Johnny looked up appraisingly at the roof and said, "Oh man, they are not gonna like this."

"I haven't even heard the idea and *I* don't like it."

"You're gonna like it even less in a minute."

We circled the annex to a cluster of support buildings, low sheds and quonsets. Johnny stopped at a random— or so it seemed to me—shed and flexed her fingers for a minute. "Boost me up," she said. "If I can get up and over the roof, then I'll figure out how to let you in."

"Are you... no way. I'm almost a foot taller than you, I've got way more reach, and what if there's guards or something inside the wall? I'll go. You, stay put. I'll let *you* in."

"I'm lighter! You'll sound like a marching band crashing around up there."

"And you'll sound like one when you fall off the roof. We need you alive to save the world or whatever, we don't need *me* for anything."

She glared at me. "If you're so unqualified, why'd I let you come?"

"Dunno. Guess if we get stuck in the desert you can eat me?"

"Gross. Like that Guy Pearce movie."

"I'm way more food than Guy Pearce."

"Look, if I don't make it, *then* we can—"

"And if a frog had wings, it wouldn't bump its ass hopping."

"Shush."

I cupped my hands in front of me, let her step in, and shoved her up onto the roof of the shed, my amulet-stung palm bursting briefly with pain, gone when her weight left it. I heard her scrabbling for purchase for a second, then looked up to see her standing on the roof, arms out. "There's kind of a dip in it," she said in a loud whisper. "Ugh. Didn't figure on that. See you on the other side!"

As she got a running start for the next roof up, I felt my face stretch into an involuntary grimace of horror, like watching the boys dart into the road with their hockey sticks, not watching for cars. But she leapt and landed, dusted herself off, and looked up at the next roof, close but high. It was too dark to see what she was doing, but I heard clinks and thumps, followed by the discreet but highly identifiable sound of plaster crumbling. Then more scrabbling, her worn-down Pumas trying to get purchase on the wall. Then silence. I realized, morbidly, that I was waiting for a thump.

But she had chosen her path well, to coincide with roofs and distances that someone her height could get to—prodigy mode again, I figured, rather than any native athleticism—and in a few minutes I saw her spreadeagled on the shiny tile roof, lit up in moonlight so bright, now that my eyes had adjusted, that I could see the sweatstain on her back, black on the grey t-shirt.

She crawled carefully up the tiles, knocking a few loose that slid rattlingly down to lodge in the gutter— rather than smashing to the floor, thank God—and disappeared over the other side. No one came to investigate, unbelievably; I wondered if there were spells already on this place, spells not of immobility but hiding, veiling, something to protect the books she wanted. Or... guarding, defense. What had we walked into?

I went back to the main door, since she hadn't told me where else to go, and put my ear to the door to hear the small, measured strides approaching it. Then: "Fuck!"

"Oh my God, you can't say 'fuck' in a mosque."

"Well, it's not... *fupping* locked, but there's a... *furking* big wooden bar here across the door and I don't think I can lift it. Hang on."

"Bullshit. I've seen you lift the back end of a Ford Focus six feet in the air. You're an ant."

"*You're* an ant."

I listened to her grunt and strain for a minute, faint scraping noises coming from the far side of the ornate door. I hoped she wasn't damaging any of the carvings. Then I heard her leaving and returning moments later, followed by a louder scrape that could only have been the bar she'd described. The door swung slowly open. I walked in and tripped on a long piece of plywood, incongruously bare and raw-looking on the incredibly complex tile floor.

"How did you—"

"Physics, my good sir."

I picked it up and propped it against the wall. We walked across the moonlit floor, my eyes swimming at the patterns and colours till I realized I was actually becoming dizzy. I focused on Johnny's back instead, a solid colour, moving quickly towards another door, marked with caution tape and barricaded with more light planks. Building materials—bags of cement, stacks of tiles, cans of paint and epoxy, pallets of lumber, copper coils, solar tiles, and power tools—were locked up in a wire cage next to the door.

"It's very old," she whispered as we approached the door, and hesitated. "They've been working on the restoration for years. Apparently I actually donated some money for it, Rutger says. Through one of my academic charities, to fund doctoral students studying rare books or something. But there's..." She frowned. "This isn't right."

"Aren't we in the right place?"

"We should be, but..." She stared around us, visibly evaluating and dismissing each of the other doorways. After a minute, she snorted in frustration and ordered me to turn around, digging in my bag. With the brick of notes she had brought from home, she sat at the corner of the wire cage and began paging slowly through them with a penlight, cursing under her breath.

I walked around while she read, admiring the tile patterns, the lacy work of the doorways. Everything looked impossibly delicate, and yet that wasn't what the restoration seemed to be working on. How old were these carvings, these patterns, these arched roofs? With a little jolt I wondered whether anyone in my family had ever seen this place, generations before mine. I didn't know much about my background ("India," my uncles told me when I asked, "and then Guyana," as if I had not known that already). So little had been written down both before and after the British had brought our ancestors to South America. What if we had, some of us, one of us, walked in this place a millennium ago, spoken prayers here, read the books…

The tiles were hypnotizing in the moonlight, making me dizzy. I slowed my walk, tried to concentrate on one pattern at a time. Starbusts, whirls, stepped spirals, marching squares and triangles in perfect symmetry.

And there it was.

No. Gone.

I took a few steps, stopped again, baffled. Tired, low blood sugar, eyes unfocusing, nothing more than that. But I knew I had seen something.

Ceramic smooth under my fingers; I started a little, unaware that I had even reached out towards them. Still warm from the heat of the day, they were slick, spotless, absolutely regular… no. Not absolutely. I slowly ran my hands over the spirals of black and white and green and blue, feeling something arise from it, shutting my eyes, trying to let my fingertips read it. Straight lines, curves. Letters? Words?

"…John?"

Even after I had explained it to her, she said she couldn't feel anything in the tiles, and I had to do it again and again, and finally write down what I had felt on a scrap piece of paper. It still made no sense: six horizontal lines, one straight one piercing them like a spine, and two random rectangles that I was sure I had drawn incorrectly.

"Holy shit," she whispered, holding the drawing in one hand and absently trying to stuff the wad of notes back into my bag with the other. I took it myself and zipped the bag shut. "It's... I think it's the missing part of the floor plan. The Room of Protection for unholy documents. The whole wall's got natural wards on it. How in the hell did you find it?"

"I don't know. It kind of... you know, like those Magic Eye things?"

She stared at me appraisingly. "I can't see it."

"Yeah, Brent and Cookie can't see them either. Just me and Chris." But their names felt like poison in my mouth, and for a moment I almost felt crushed with grief—that I had left them, that they couldn't see this, that I couldn't protect them. As if everything were normal until I spoke the words. I looked away, wishing I could have had even one more moment of feeling proud about finding the secret room before it had turned to bitterness.

We followed the map through the door, down the hallway, and to a tile wall that Johnny confidently walked up to and threw her full weight against; it moved perhaps a half-inch. I gestured her aside and leaned on it till it opened its full width. She shut it behind us as we entered, waving her tiny penlight ahead of us in the perfect darkness, counting under her breath as the saucer of white light played over more bright tiles and then thresholds of perfect darkness, doorways that did not lead to where we needed. At six, she turned right and pushed open a set of wooden doors.

I knew it was the right place; a breeze blew from it

like a breath, cold and heavy with the odour of old paper and mould. It smelled like the ghost of a library. The darkness was near-absolute here, only the thinnest bars of grey light filtering through gaps in the roof onto shelf after shelf of books and scrolls. They rose in the darkness, intricate shadows, the only brightness from masking-tape labels attached to some of the scaffolding, most labelled with dates—indicating, I supposed, when they had to be moved to continue the restoration project.

"They're still working in here," I said. "They'll have guards."

"Not sure I care. They'll have lights too."

"You have a real authority problem," I whispered as we tiptoed into the darkness. "Only Child Syndrome."

"Oh come on, that's been debunked a hundred times. Where did you learn that, high school?"

"At least I *have* a high school diploma! What have you got?"

"And *you've* got a problem with authority, too."

"That's because you're a bad influence."

SHE HAD BEEN working for two hours, with a caged fluorescent worklight dragged from the hallway to her study carrel, when we started hearing the noises. I snapped out of my uncomfortable doze (*the indigo water, the dust, silvery dust on all the cities of the world, raining down, some dust, some ashes, some spores, some cells*) and looked around. Outside the blinding circle of the worklight, it was pitch black, not even moonlight visible. We had both lost whatever remnants of our night vision remained, whatever handful of rods or cones, I couldn't remember which, and couldn't get it back while we crisscrossed from floor to floor, room to room, trying to find the books Johnny wanted in the complicated shelving.

"Hit the light," I said, knowing it wouldn't help. "Someone's coming, we'll get in trouble."

"I need it," she said, pointing at her laptop and the growing pile of notes beside it. "I know when the alignment is and we are going to leave an inch of rubber on the road to make it in time. And I still don't know how to lock the gate or where it is, exactly. But the way to calculate the coordinates is here. It's got to be. I can't stop. Not right now."

I stood up and wavered for a minute. God *dammit*. Weren't you not supposed to split up in horror movies? Finally I headed back to the entrance, wriggled a two-by-four loose from the hastily-made barricade, making sure it still had a nail in it, and set off to find the source of the sound, hoping it was just a stray cat that had gotten in. I didn't want to smack it or anything, even one of the Society's nark cats, but I was so jittery that anything seemed possible.

My feet sounded very loud on the slick tile, tempting me to take my shoes off and walk in my socks. But whoever was in the library with us was at least as loud, though it sounded like they were heading away from the Room of Protection. They wouldn't know how to get in there anyway.

I stalked towards the noises, board raised over my shoulder like a baseball bat. *Never* split up in a horror movie. Something is always going to get you. Who didn't know *that?* Even the kids had already watched movies where that lesson was taught. It didn't have to be *Evil Dead* or whatever. Like, this was *Land Before Time* territory.

Worse yet, while I was bumbling around in the pitch blackness, following whatever I should have been running away from, Johnny was alone, head down, not listening for danger, surrounded by those weird books and scrolls, some of which had seemed to be faintly flickering or not really there, or had hissed at her from their chains, or were definitely moving slightly. Dammit.

Maybe it was a decoy, meant to lure me away from her, as if she were not the one compared to a dog and a snake and an ant, all things that could defend themselves. As if I had ever been able to defend either of us.

I wavered. Still. Still. She was the thing we had to protect, not me. Finally I turned away from the noises and walked swiftly back to the room—just in time to spot a shadow emerging from a corridor, heading for the secret door. Though briefly silhouetted in the moonlight, I knew who it was at once—the face was blinding in its whiteness now, as white as a mushroom, as if not even a trace of blood could be persuaded to move in the veins.

"Hey!" I yelled. "Get away from there!"

He growled, a prolonged, deep-throated noise that made the hair on my neck stand up. And then he was shambling towards me so fast I barely had time to get a hand up in front of my face, feeling his fist sink into my stomach. He hadn't hit quite low enough to wind me, but I staggered back and—well, you swung first, pal—tagged him with the two-by-four, aiming for his head, managing a glancing blow off his shoulder instead.

He screeched, an inhuman noise of insult and pain; thick, clotted drops of something spill to the floor. I must have caught him with the nail. But he was coming at me again, roaring. I backed up, swinging the board in warning. "We don't want trouble!" I shouted. "Just leave! Leave us alone!"

He grabbed my shirt, getting a handful of skin; I blinked in shock. How had he gotten inside the swing of the board without my noticing? It was like Drozanoth in Ben's room.

But it didn't matter; his hands had found my throat and we fell thrashing to the slippery floor. His fingers were icy, strong and slick, but weirdly unformed, as if the bones were embedded in wax. Cold battled the burn in my throat as everything went dark.

Fading... dying?

She's not going to come get me

She's not coming for me

Do something

But it was dark, and warm, and the pain was fading into the distance like an echo, and...

Didn't think

Got caught

Do s—

I jammed a hand under his chin and shoved, feeling something grind under my palm. His grip loosened; I rolled free, weakly grabbed the board, and clocked him in the head.

He flopped onto his back, more clotted grey stuff flowing from his mouth onto the intricate tiles. I stood panting for a second to make sure he wasn't going to get up, then ran back to find Johnny, where she was fighting in silence with someone else, a tall woman in a long red-brown robe, hair a wild, dark cloud around their heads. I stepped forward with the board, then hesitated—what if I hit Johnny with that nail? Would she catch something? Some contagion of Theirs, making humans into these grey things?

A second later the question was moot; Johnny threw the woman over a chair and kicked her so hard in the face that I heard a rattling crunch, as if she'd stepped on a cockroach. The woman tumbled to the ground and rolled, fetching up against a man I hadn't even seen, already fallen. Johnny was gasping, one hand still extended protectively towards her pile of books and papers.

"What the fuck was that?" I croaked. "Are you okay? Are you hurt?"

"I'm—they—are *you* hurt?" she said, grabbing the light and holding it over her head. "You've got marks on your neck."

"I'm okay." I giggled hysterically even before the next sentence left my mouth, feeling it as both a gag and a *gag*. "Think I just murdered a guy though, the airport guy—or I dunno, if he's not dead, he'd better be able to live with part of his head on the floor."

"Nick, don't—"

"'Mamaaaaaa,'" I sang, "'just killed a man—'"

"Nick!"

"'Put a gun against his—'"

"Stop butchering Queen and calm down for a second, all right? They weren't alive any more."

"I killed a dead guy?" That did stop me, and I stared at her, the green eyes glittering not with tears but with prodigy mode, now that I knew what I was looking for. Yes, there—the halo of golden dust, her time ticking away. It faded as I watched. No wonder they had found us. She'd been using it since we got in here. And the longer she used it, the brighter it must have been to them, like a searchlight beaming into the sky. "You said human servants."

"I didn't say alive ones."

"What are you supposed to do with a dead servant?"

"The Ancient Ones used to do it all the time," she said. "Tariq is the expert, but I gather that human thralls, they're called *y'tan rek'wh*, they're not dead, they're not alive either, they're not *lalassu*, spirits in human form. All their life force is drained out of them, fueling the magic of their master."

"An Ancient One."

"Drozanoth, more likely." She took a breath and let it out in a long fluting whistle, like a strange bird. "It'll need to start over now. It's spreading itself thin, even with these increased levels of magic. Trying to keep a lot of plates spinning, keeping its thralls going, preparing for the alignment, calling out to Them, finding us."

"Is that what the cats saw?"

"Probably. The Society uses them as spies because they can see magic and magical beings. It would probably only work in Fes."

"So. But. I mean. The upshot is, I'm not a murderer?"

"No," she said sharply. "Don't think it. Drozanoth is the murderer here, not you. Not us."

"Jesus," I said. "I just do not know how you, as a scientist, handle this shit. I just don't."

"If anything, I think it informs my science," she said. "I'm always looking for the explanation that rules Them out, since I can't deny that They exist. I want to know Their purview. Where Their limits lie."

"Because They're where science stops and magic starts," I said. "And you went ahead and became a scientist anyway."

"I had to. I had to prove that there could be *one* covenant that didn't go wrong. And I can still prove it."

The last fumes in my tank ran out and I simply sank to the chair at her study carrel, trying not to look at the bodies behind her. What about their families? How would they find out? How were we going to get rid of the bodies? What were we going to do, what incriminating evidence had we left behind? This was far worse than anything we'd done so far, no matter what she said. They would still be alive if we hadn't come.

I was shaking so hard my teeth were clattering together in a steady buzz and my stomach hurt, a long dull ache like a noise in the distance, like the buzzing, furious chant I thought I'd heard for a second just as the board connected. I hadn't even realized I had picked it up with the nail end out. I hadn't even looked. "Oh God, what are we doing here?" I whispered as she turned back to the pile of manuscripts, putting her elbow down hard on one that was trying to crawl away. "What are we doing? Wasn't there anyone else who could do this?"

She didn't answer. After a while I turned away, put my head down on my arms, and waited for her to say my name and tell me we could leave. I had to keep my eyes open, because every time I closed them I saw the thick fluid spilling from the airport man's head, covering the tiles. Hiding their beauty in his contagion.

She still didn't say anything when I began to sob, but I hadn't expected her to.

CHAPTER FIFTEEN

WE LEFT AROUND dawn—Johnny had transferred what she needed onto her computer, packed my bag with more notes and a carefully hand-copied map, and generated a new laptop map. When I had gone out into the hallway to find a bathroom—no way could I bring myself to just find a handy corner, not here in a mosque or a library—the airport man had disintegrated to a muddy black outline on the tiles, only scraps of his Adidas jacket remaining, bubbling slightly, moving as if it were filled with maggots. I had been preparing to have a conversation about body disposal, and was relieved that I wouldn't have to.

We headed through a tiny side door into a walled garden or park. I gasped the relatively damp, cool air gratefully and looked up at the palm trees swaying in the pale, pink light of dawn. A few stars glittered on the horizon, hot and blue. Everything smelled of cinnamon, flint, and leaves. I hadn't realized how stifling and musty the library had been. "Did you find what you wanted to find?"

"The alignment isn't in our solar system," she said. "It isn't even in our universe. I knew that, but I also didn't know where it was. Now I do. And we are screwed. Absolutely screwed."

"Tell me something I don't know."

"We have till about dawn on July fifth," she said. "Today's the third."

"But... did you find out how to shut the gate?"

She shook her head; the light wasn't even touching the dark circles under her eyes. I probably looked even worse. At least I didn't have her beauty to lose; start lower, not as far to fall. "But I know who's got the set of records I need. Duplicates, but they'll have to do, we don't have time to track down the originals."

"Where are they?"

"Ireland. But they've got good copies at the University of Carthage library." She snarled with frustration, and dug a foot into the thick grass. "We can't waste any more time on buses; we're chasing daylight now. We'll have to take our chances at the airport here."

"But the cops...?"

"Depends largely on Omar," she said. "If he shut up that big cop with the moustache and told the others he transferred us, it'll be a little while before they realize we're not there. It's easy enough to lose track of people in custody."

"Jesus, let's hope. What about trains?"

"No trains. You gotta zig where They think you'll zag. Plus, trains mean tracks. Too easy to find and you can't bail if you need to."

To my immense, almost tearful gratitude, we found a cafe to have breakfast in first—or whatever meal we were supposed to be eating after skipping so many. The tables were small and round and perfect as backgammon pieces, real marble or a white stone that looked a lot like it, the plastic chairs a little incongruous next to them. She ordered in French and paged through her notes while we waited, my forearms resting on the smooth edge of the cold stone.

"What did you order?"

"Dunno. I said 'the usual.' Too bad, because I really wanted real couscous here—not the box kind you get back home. But that's not really breakfast food. I just want something hot from the big pot in the back."

"How do you know there's a big pot in the back?"

"There's always a big pot in the back."

Eventually a tray of sticky-looking glasses and a tall silver teapot appeared, as well as one plate of what looked like samosas and another of flat bread with hummus, and two big bowls of bean and tomato soup sparkling with olive oil. The server poured our tea with an extravagant flourish, not spilling a single drop.

"Eat," she said. "For the next ten, fifteen minutes, all we worry about is our blood sugar. Do you have to pee?"

"I peed back at the library. Not a bunch. Think I might be super dehydrated. You too, incidentally."

"Check. I feel like a raisin."

"You look like one, too."

I chuckled, and right on cue felt my lips crack. Johnny dug in her bag and solemnly handed me a lip balm, the fancy brand her mother sold at her spas. I debated asking her if it was one of those sneaky ones that looked colourless but then turned pink, then decided I didn't care and smeared some on. She used it herself before putting it away. It was, I thought bleakly, the closest we'd ever come to a kiss.

The tea wasn't what I expected—mint, hotter than napalm and almost as thick thanks to all the sugar. I guzzled it anyway.

"I packed Tudela pills, but you should get something in your stomach first or you might get cramps," she said. "We'll be able to drink the water after that."

"Good thinking," I said, emptying another glass of the tea. Super dork. Naming her traveler's bacteria pills after some medieval nerd who traveled around and then wrote a book about it back when no one else went further than a half-day's mule ride from their house (half, she'd explained, so's you could get back before dark). I wondered who else in the world would have got that joke. Then I wondered if Helen would have gotten it, and managed to startle myself with jealousy just thinking it.

The tea was like hot mouthwash and I didn't feel like it was hydrating me at all, but the shakes stopped and I dug into the food, soup first. After I finished mine, Johnny let me scrape out her bowl too. The triangle things turned out to not be samosas but some unbelievable device with tuna and a hot, runny egg in it that exploded down my arm.

"Oops," she said, reaching for one. "Should have warned you. Briks usually have an egg in them."

"You're the worst." I licked off as much as I could, dried my arm on my t-shirt, and devoured the emptied thing, then two more before digging into the flatbread and hummus. At least I recognized that.

We each took two of the pills, washing them down with the tea. I felt like I was still sweating out half a glass for every one that I drank; my blue t-shirt was black with it, surrounded by high tide marks of salt. Classy. I doubted anyone would care, at least. This place was sweat central.

Afterwards, we found a drugstore and Johnny bought water, sunscreen, toilet paper, and packaged snacks— "So this doesn't happen again"—and loaded up my bag.

"Do you need to pick up girl stuff? You can go back in, I'll wait here," I said.

She gave me a look so long and loaded that I felt sweat start to trickle down my back again in the coolness of the alleyway. Oh God, stop talking, stop talking. I said, "I'm trying to be, you know, helpful. You don't have to PMS at me about it."

"First of all," she said, "I suggest you never again ask someone if they've got PMS, or whether it might be responsible for their behaviour, lest you get murdered to actual death. Second, not that it's any of your business, but I don't need that any more."

"A... any more?"

She rolled her eyes. "I patented an annual shot five years ago to get rid of periods."

"Why?"

"Because they're a pain in the ass, and some people don't want to bother," she said, her voice getting icier by the minute. "I could ask my marketing people for up-to-date information, but last I heard, about fifty million of them are being sold every year in North America. It was all over the news. And you had no idea, of course."

"Why *would* I have any idea?"

"Exactly," she said, darkly. "Anyway, how about you choose life by shutting up, and we figure out how to get to the airport and act inconspicuous? I'm getting a lot of flak for being a white girl, traveling with a brown boy, with no wedding ring."

"You kind of look like a boy with the scarf," I said.

"Stop trying to be helpful, Nicholas."

"Sorry. I just meant you don't have any tits, which is good."

"I could buy some when we get home."

"That's true."

She was right about the flak: I'd noticed a lot of dirty looks and whispering as we'd been moving around in public, even some yelling. I had guessed at the meaning, but she had obviously understood.

I was dark enough to fit in with most of the people we saw on the street, a mix of tans, browns, beiges, blacks. There were quite a few white people, I wanted to point out, but they were traveling mostly together—not in mixed groups. One of those subtle call-outs that other countries saw more clearly in tourists, I supposed. And of course, it did help to be a dude. Nowhere in the world you could travel that it was easier to be a girl.

At the same time, though, what the hell? Was this really the first time she'd seen shit like this? Maybe it was, now that I thought about it. It was like both our lives had been designed to be obstacle courses by people bigger and older and meaner and smarter than us, and you had to jump through so much shit to live—for me, being young, being dumb, being poor, being brown, not knowing languages, not knowing manners, not knowing *anything*; and then for Johnny, what? Basically, being a girl, being famous. Her obstacles were tiny and easy and had a net below them, so that she might bounce back up laughing, and she had money and looks and genius and a staff of people rushing around to ensure that whatever obstacles did come up, she might not even see them. It was like she'd gotten to build her own course, instead of having it handed down by family, prejudice, geography, history. Here maybe, truly, was the first place that I was better off than her, in one way. I followed her, and pushed down a small, mean wave of satisfaction.

FOR A CITY of a million people, Fes had a podunk little airport crammed with tiny planes like a parking lot, with a single, though elegant, concrete building. My stomach lurched. How were we going to go anywhere in one of these tinkertoy gliders? When she'd said 'airport'

I had pictured big planes, like the 747 we'd flown here in from home. Hundreds of people—safety in numbers, anonymity, the bland process of booking and confirming and going through security checkpoints in long lineups with everyone else, throwing away hand creams and baby bottles, no liquids allowed now at all, filing into our assigned seats, even if we had to do it all under fake names, and with cash. But these planes suggested a sort of Wild West chaos, pilots picking and choosing their own passengers, everything jumbled together.

I waited for her outside the main building with a few dozen other people in a boiling wind tunnel, where the captured breath of the planes and the roaringly hot air of the nearby farms was caught in a kind of vortex that pulled the end of my scarf straight up. The other travelers ignored me, after a token glance. A relief, to not feel watched for once.

I found myself scanning people's faces all the same, watching for anyone who stared, who was too pale, who moved like a shambling marionette in a kids' show, their strings pulled at a distance by monsters. It helped make me feel at least a tiny bit useful, while Johnny did all the work here, less like the dead weight I knew I was. Quantum, I thought. Quantum, quantum. Stay in motion.

I didn't even know what quantum *meant*.

When she came back out, she was already rolling her eyes. "You ever get the feeling that you're trapped in a *Star Wars* movie?"

"Yes," I said, with conviction.

"So it's normally about a six-and-a-half-hour flight to Carthage," she said. "This guy? Claims he can do it in five."

"Gee, that sounds both safe and pleasant," I said. "And likely. I bet his Millennium Falcon is a shitty little cargo plane that in no possible way could go faster than a 747."

"Right? Lying right to my face, after I paid him all that money, Jesus. Anyway, go use the bathroom, I put toilet paper in your bag, and then get ready to hold it for probably about—"

"Eight hours."

"Exactly." She pointed at a tiny, shit-brown painted turboprop parked on the tarmac with something blue written on its side in Arabic, and a clunkily painted logo of a shark. "That's our plane, our pilot's name is Hamid. We're leaving in fifteen minutes."

"Are we? How much did you pay him?"

"I dunno, probably more than the plane's worth, but we're *kind of* in a hurry." She pointed peremptorily at the concrete building, adding something I barely heard as I walked in—maybe 'Don't get caught.'

As I washed my hands, I wondered how much the plane was worth. Johnny was rich, of course, the kind of rich where she didn't actually *have* to patent or produce or publish things any more, the money simply multiplied like the heads of a hydra, no matter how fast she dumped her profits back into science stuff: labs, chemicals, telescopes, researchers. So this wasn't much, probably—a crumb, not a chunk, that would go unnoticed in her annual budget, something Rutger would write off as 'Misc.', like giving a couple of million dollars for grad students to study ancient documents.

But it was goddamn infuriating that she had made it legitimately and now this guy had received it via, basically, highway robbery. It wouldn't take much to see how rushed and desperate we were, or to demand more knowing that we were kids and could get in trouble for even trying, knowing that we couldn't really negotiate, not *really*. And I hated people who preyed on need like that. Hell, it'd happened to us often enough after Dad left. Little things like the phone and cable companies who wanted to charge us to cancel accounts, big things like our house getting broken into. Kicking people when they were down, that was the worst.

As I was walking back, I passed the office I'd seen Johnny go into and craned my head to look in the small, reinforced-glass window out of sheer curiosity—would it be modern, did they have computers? It was empty, covered with stacks of paper and maps of various vintages, some yellowed with age and falling apart, which I hoped Hamid wasn't using, and... a stack of money on the desk, lazily covered with a single sheet of paper, several bills poking out, US currency. That had to be part of Johnny's bribe—to the airport people, at least; Hamid's was a lost cause. Had to be, or else why would it be out there? They had just gotten it a few minutes ago. I wondered if they had even bothered to lock the door. I could get it back for her, just hand it to her nonchalantly, right a single wrong in this world.

My heart hammered as I went back in, briskly, trying to look official; no one glanced twice at me as I tried the door of the office. Locked, but loose. If I just leaned on it hard enough...

Someone grabbed my belt; I whipped around with a yelp, face flaming, and looked down into Johnny's furious glare. "Outside. Now."

CHAPTER SIXTEEN

"THE FUCK WERE you doing? Were you doing what I think you were doing? Because you better not have been!" she yelled over the sound of the wind tunnel, holding her scarf down with one hand.

"Trying to get your bribe back!"

"*Why?* That's the whole *point* of a bribe, Jesus Christ."

"Because it looked like a fuck ton of money!"

"It wasn't!"

"Not to you, maybe!"

"I can't believe that you were about to get us stopped, probably arrested, probably thrown into a goddamn Moroccan jail, which we *just* escaped from, for a lousy couple of hundred dollars! No, wait! I *can* believe it! Because you don't have any self control at all! It's like traveling with a toddler!"

"Oh, yeah? Not like you, not like Little Miss Deal With The Devil?" I shouted. "You want to talk self-control? You want to talk about controlling yourself?"

"Maybe I do! What are you saying?"

"What am I saying? This is all your fault! If you had just turned that goddamn thing's deal down, none of this would be happening! None! And you're the one who—who called Them here! Who sent up a goddamn *billboard* inviting Them in, and you already knew They were watching for *exactly* the kind of thing you were doing, you already knew that! You knew that your whole life! You practically knocked out a wall and rolled out a red carpet for Them to walk on! You don't have the self-control God gave a bag of hammers!"

"Yeah, and if I *had* turned down the deal, millions of people would be sick or dead! And now I could save even *more* lives! How about you think of them for a change, instead of yourself?"

"Millions of people are *going* to be dead, Johnny! Maybe *billions!* Because of you! Because you wanted to be a hero! Because you wanted to be famous and rich and on the cover of *Time* magazine! Who's thinking of themselves now, huh?"

"I didn't ask for *this* to happen! I wanted to help people! Don't you know what getting the world off fossil fuels could mean?"

"Oh, I guess *not*, because I'm obviously too stupid to have read up about global warming and air pollution! *You're* the only one who knows anything about that!"

"I wasn't implying that! Or that you were stupid! But

if I did I think I'd be justified, based on what you just almost did!"

"What *I* almost did? Aren't they tracking you every time *you* use your *stupid powers*, which you are obviously not doing now?"

"Are you suggesting I'm being *stupid* about this? Me? Are you sure it's me and not *you?*"

I took a deep breath and started coughing on a lungful of dust, which was lucky, because I could feel veins throbbing in the side of my neck and wondered, dimly, how close I was to simply having an aneurysm or some damn thing. And Hamid was approaching, it must have been—short, fiftyish, a bright ring around his eyes where the olive skin had been protected by his mirrored shades, potbelly straining at a black *Ziggy Stardust* t-shirt tucked into severely drop-crotch jeans.

"You coming?" he said, cheerfully. "You can keep fighting aboard, no problem."

"Come on," I muttered. I stomped ahead of her to the tiny plane and climbed inside to discover that there were no seats inside, just a jumble of boxes and bags. Everything reeked of cigarette smoke; the inner walls, painted pale grey, were turning yellow in an uneven gradient from the middle up. Johnny pushed past me and settled against a big bag of something or other—I couldn't read the writing on the sack, but it must have been comfortable. I picked a similar one and settled back. It felt like nuts, something light, round, and hard. They'd be smoked nuts by the time they were delivered, I thought. Gross.

"Ey, you kids, no touch in the back," Hamid called from the front. "That valuable stuff. Big money!"

"We won't," Johnny called back.

"Nah, I know what you are. Rich babies travel on your 'gap year,' hey? You think I don't know that word? No, I learned it from other kids. I know them all, English, French, Spain, everywhere. I fly them all. Always good times to fly on your gap year, see new places. Then go to school. Hey?"

"Yeah. Gap year."

Her voice was strangled, as if she were holding back tears. I found that I didn't care. She'd dragged me halfway across the world, taken me from the people I loved, didn't even care that I didn't have a house or a job to go back to. After all, she had always been surrounded by people who could just buy a new house if they needed one, and who had never even heard of jobs. She'd taken everything from me, and I'd taken nothing, and I had tried to make a gesture to show her that the world didn't have to be as unfair as her money let her pretend it wasn't, and she'd yelled at *me*. Asshole. Let her cry, if her feelings were so hurt.

The plane jolted forwards, then back, so sharply that we were thrown onto the diamond-plate floor, and then we were bumping, at a sedate walking pace, away from the asphalt pad and towards what I assumed was the runway. As I regained my feet I glanced out the window to see three men racing across the tarmac towards us, not in official uniforms, just shirt and ties, one of them waving a piece of paper with two dark squares on it. I felt my blood run cold for a second—were those our photos? had we been caught?—but the angle was wrong and they fell behind us as we taxied, picking up speed, and finally lurched heavily into the sky at an angle that threw me back amongst the boxes and bags.

"Ey! I said no touching!" shouted Hamid. "My *deliveries*!"

We rolled and pitched as we rose to whatever minimal altitude the little engine could manage. As the cabin filled with diesel fumes, my stomach announced that it was going to empty itself at the earliest opportunity and that I should find an available corner. I gritted my teeth and imagined being a statue, Han Solo frozen in carbonite. Don't move anything. Not a finger, not a knee, not your tongue, nothing. Maybe the message will get passed down.

Trying to reorient my eyes and brain, I stared out the small, greasy window at my shoulder, the size of a paperback book. Yellow sand, smoke-grey mountains. Maybe just hills, back home; it was hard to tell from up here. We were still so low that you could identify specific animals—camels, donkeys, a dog running ecstatically from the road towards a farmhouse and a boy's waiting arms.

We'd never had pets, growing up; in the Caribbean, Mom and Dad always said, animals were dirty and belonged outside with the rest of the dirt, and they were either food or pests. You'd never have one living inside your actual house. A few rich men had pet dogs or cats, but Dad in particular dismissed that: "They bathed them constantly, cleaned house constantly. Who's got time for that?" We begged, but nothing doing. Then after Dad left we moved again and again, and there just didn't seem to be room for one more living creature anywhere. The kids would have done a shit job looking after a pet anyway, even a guinea pig or a fish. They just lavished love on whatever animals they met or saw, and spent a lot of time with their friends' dogs.

The thing about Johnny, I thought, was that she had never been loved enough, never accepted enough love. She had bailed on her parents so young, only seen her dad a handful of times since the divorce; she treated her mother as an acquaintance, scheduling lunches with her weeks in advance; Rutger was more a robot than an employee; she had no other friends. Even Ben's adoration only went one way. Always it had just been her and me, me and her—a claustrophobic togetherness that, if she hadn't been away so much, would have driven us both insane. Or maybe it had and we hadn't noticed, so stifled under the creeping sense of wrongness that a friendship that had begun in blood and bullets should have lasted so long and been so steady and unshakeable on such a foundation. A near-death experience was no basis for a friendship.

And yet she was the only one who ever let me in, the only one who didn't leave me alone and outside of herself, the only one who didn't think it was okay to leave me outside. Because that had been my whole life: on one side of the glass, staring in. She was the only one who said, again and again, *Come be on my side of the glass. Come be with me.* No matter what I did.

We'd even sworn a blood oath once, when we were about seven. I was sure I still had the paper somewhere at home, the red-black *J* on it cracked but unfaded. I remembered how she had insisted we sterilize the knife we had used, remembered the faint *pop* as it parted the skin; I thought it would happen in silence. Did she still have the blood 'N' somewhere in that wedding-cake fortress of a house? We had been so brave, so swaggering, so young. I couldn't even use the stove or do long division, and I had cut into the palm of my hand at her suggestion.

We glanced furtively at each other at the same time, and laughed. Her nose was red, but her eyes were dry.

"Oh, you're kidding me," I said. "Were you crying?"

"No!"

"Pants on fire," I said. "Listen, I'm sorry I... did some stuff back there. You're right, I wasn't thinking. I just wanted to get your money back. Because it's really yours, not theirs."

"I guess it makes more sense if you look at it that way," she said. "I just kind of saw it as... this stupid, risky, dangerous thing that might slow us down. And I thought any new barrier, anything, when there's so much already in our way..."

"I mean, it's just the whole world."

"Yes."

"So I guess it's okay that you were mad."

"No, it's still not okay," she insisted. "I shouldn't have yelled. I'm sorry."

"Look at us, all grown up as shit, apologizing like grownups."

"As grown up as *shit*." She sighed and leaned her head back on her bag, sending up a puff of dust. "We didn't use to fight this much when we were kids."

"We're still kids. And anyway, what was there to fight about?"

"You know what I mean."

"What are we looking for in Carthage? Your duplicates or whatever," I said, settling back into the bag. The sunlight coming in the windows was hot, but the floor was freezing, and I couldn't get comfortable. My stomach still felt like a kettle at full boil.

"Oh man, *hope* is the word," she said, grabbing a new handful of papers from her bag and lurching closer to show me—more drawings of pottery shards, half-legible scribbling that changed from English at the top to sticks at the bottom. "Oops, I started writing in cuneiform. Don't pay attention to that. Translated from something else. You can't write in Their language, it... changes things."

"Oh. Yikes. Don't do that."

"No no, I'm being careful." She pointed at one of the fragments, the edges obsessively delineated. "We need to find a book that has the text that's on this tablet, first of all, and we need to find the book that tells us how to find *that* book. That gives the old name of the city the gate was in—I know it's in Iraq, what we call Iraq now, but I don't know where exactly, and we could be looking for months if we can't find that book. One of the big problems with the transliterations of the names, translations of translations, it's hard to wayfind now. The locals wiped all those places from their records and memories for self-preservation, but now it means all the names are changed. And I haven't found any navigation spells yet, let alone how to use them properly. Second, I still need to know how to shut the gate."

"Kind of important."

"Check. Now, I've found some warding spells—minor ones—that might give us a bit of protection. Mostly calling on the powers of Nariluggaldimmerankia and Asaruludu, who used to help the guardians of the gates on our side. Those spells will have to work harder as more of Their magic comes into play though. And…" She paused to catch her breath, and then blinked several times, as if dust had fallen into her eyes. "What did you say earlier?"

"Uh."

"About… about knocking out a wall. That I hadn't just called to them, but…"

"I was mad," I said. "I was yelling. I don't know. It doesn't mean anything. I don't know why I said it."

"Hm." She shook her head. "Anyway, when we land, we have to find a permanent marker, first thing."

"What?"

"Warding spells are small potatoes. What I'm looking for is the big potato, the ur-spell, the Heracleion Chant complete and in the earliest possible translation without modifications, if we can find that. But it's a powerful, powerful spell, more like a weapon, and it has to be right. Not sort–of-right, right-right. And it'll cost me."

"Cost... what?"

"I don't know. I hope just time. I'd pay in years. But it could be anything. It could be life... whatever They take that makes the difference between alive and not-alive. In that case I hope I have enough."

So, I thought, you'll have to make a sacrifice too. Mine was my family; yours could be your life. But the world needs you. It doesn't need me. You say it all the time, I've heard you say it, you said it when you cured HIV: *The world goes on without you. That is all it knows how to do.*

I said, "If there's a way to, uh, to help pay... to split it up between us... when the time comes..."

"Thank you. I mean it."

Her eyes were green in the light from the windows, as green as the forests I had seen from above, steady and unafraid. And I thought again about death, the pond, all those years ago. We had almost died. She went through with a crack and a splash, not even time for a scream; just *gone*. All unthinking I raced for the hole—a sickening lurch beneath my blades as the ice tipped me in with her *oh my god oh god I'm falling I'm falling*— then the cold hit me like a car, not temperature at first, just impact, and my numbed hands found the space-age parka, locked tight, hauled her small deadweight up into the air. With chest and pelvis I smashed through the ice to the shore, legs going like a boat prop, our faces turned to the night sky. Stars were the last thing I thought I'd see.

We had to crawl up the slope to the shed, legs already too cold to hold us up. It was minus thirty and her lips were lavender, like the frosty lipsticks the girls wore at school. When we got the electric heater started, we simply looked at each other in wonder for a long time, taking in the frozen hair, the white ears.

"No more skating," she said drily.

"*Yeah* no more skating."

Turned at forty-five degrees to each other, we stripped off our wet clothes, put our coats back on for decency's sake, already far too old to be doing that, and huddled in front of the heater, filling the shed with hot fog.

I remembered it now, still staring at her, no need to look, knowing every inch of her—the length, the weight, the width, the colour, the scent. How I had known exactly the moment that my hands would find her coat. And we had been tricked, we had guessed wrong, we made the mistake that all kids make, of thinking things could be negotiated. The ice had seemed safe—in fact, as I had crashed through it, I remembered thinking how thick it was, wondering how it could have broken under Johnny's weight. We had been wrong before, gotten in trouble before, gotten spanked or yelled at or chased before, but we had never come so close to death. At least we were together, for a mistake like that. And here we were, together again.

"I love you," I said. "I won't leave you."

"I know you won't," she said. There was a pause while I thought, wildly, Oh God, I said it, kill me, I hope she says literally anything next except that she loves me too, because when we die, when They destroy us, I will have to remember that lie as being one of the last things I heard from her lips, it's the lie I'll remember, it's the lie.

The plane bumped with turbulence; she was up in an instant, staring out the window as if she expected to see something. "Knock it off," I called. "I'm paranoid enough already."

"You never know when your life is going to turn into a *Twilight Zone* episode," she yelled back.

"What? No, don't tell me. Didn't it already?"

"We're not getting paid, if it did." She stooped, hanging onto the window's edge with her fingertips, staring for what seemed like too long. The plane kicked like we were driving fast down a gravel road, back wheels about to slide out from under us. I put a hand over my mouth.

She sat back down, gave me a sympathetic look, and said, "You've probably already figured it out, but part of my covenant with Them, what I hammered out, was that They cannot kill me. That's stealing time and that's not part of the agreement. I have to live exactly as long as I would have lived, except for what I pay to use the powers."

"Then why are they—?"

"Loopholes. They're dumb and evil and single-minded and ravenous, but They're also old, very old, and even the slowest of Them has got a kind of cunning that takes millions of years to develop. They don't sleep the way we sleep. So They find loopholes. They can't kill me— but They can slow me down. They could batter me into beef tartare and I wouldn't die. Not till I was supposed to. I'd just... linger, alive, in pain, till the right time."

"Oh, Jesus."

"I know. Disgusting. The other big loophole, of course, is that They could get someone else to do it. That's not part of the deal, technically."

"You just said you couldn't die until you were supposed to."

"I said They couldn't *kill* me. I can die, no problem."

"Holy shit." I felt cold despite the close heat of the plane, and gave in to an all-body shiver, nausea gone, replaced by a kind of frozen heaviness, an extra weight pressing me into immobility.

"What if They, what if... what if They cheated somehow? If one of Them..."

"The universe isn't set up that way."

"...Exsqueeze me?"

"The conditions of a spell... okay, let me use an example," she said, using her finger to draw in the dust of the floor—just a circle. I looked up when it seemed as if she wouldn't do anything else. "The universe exists under certain conditions, can we agree on that?"

"No. What the hell?"

"First premises, Nicky. It has to run a certain way or it won't run at all. Now, when They came to our universe, They set up a new one and destroyed the old one."

"*What?*"

"That's what any spell does," she said. "My covenant included, the little warding spells included. It's always the same, even something as small as the old songs to make milk sour or cure a flock of sick sheep, to travel long distances in a single night, to call up the wind to get you back to Valparaiso, to move a coin a couple of inches on a countertop. A blink, a change. The old world gone, the new one in place, with the spell running and all its associated conditions."

"Wow."

"So, for example, once upon a time, the universe was set up so that iron could defeat any magic. If you drove an iron knife, even a nail, into a magic circle, that would be the end of the spell—and, sometimes, the end of the person casting the spell. No one knows who created that condition, but it was unbreakable; it was simply the way the world worked, like gravity. And then a very, very powerful wizard in about 1100—some scholars think it might even have been Morgan le Fay, King Arthur's sister—*did* manage to break it. Some say she got hold of secret scrolls looted from the Holy Land during the Crusades. Anyway, the universe changed, and iron lost its power. Now you could drive a steel I-beam into a magic circle and it would crumple like tinfoil before the spell failed."

"So what we're trying to do," I said slowly, "is... create a universe... where the gates are closed and They're gone?"

"To be honest, I think that's why we got a head start," she said. "Because They didn't think we could. At least for a little while it wouldn't have occurred to Drozanoth at all."

"But the universe that's currently set up has your covenant in it," I said. "Could you change that?"

"I can't break that. Only They could. All I can do is work with the parameters of the spell *I'm* doing."

"Shit." I chewed on that for a while, rubbing my back, which had begun to ache against the sack from lack of support. "Listen, I hate to say it, but what if we... what if we can't? Or we're too late? Or the cost is too high for us to pay? I mean, I know you're thinking about all the things that could go wrong. What's our backup plan?"

"What do you think it should be?"

"Nuke 'em from orbit," I said promptly. "It's the only way to be sure."

She laughed.

"No, seriously," I said. "Is that a thing? Could we do that?"

"All joking aside, I *could* pull some strings to get a nuclear strike," she said.

"No. Fuck off," I said, forcing my jaw back up. "You can't, though."

"Yeah, I can. I'm in Bilderberg—"

"Which is what?"

"...Not important. Let's say a group of mostly very nice people who aren't necessarily *seen* running things. They asked me to join in 1994, and I've got some favours to call in, if I needed to. If."

"Jesus Christ." I pushed down an enormous wave of nausea and tried to think clearly. Thinking of her making a phone call and then that Ray Bradbury story, with the silhouettes burned on the walls. The photos from Japan in 1945. The one thing we had all agreed, worldwide, that we would never do again, no matter what. How in the *hell* did a seventeen year-old get into that position, prodigy or not? "But that would be a last-ditch effort."

"Yeah. A nuke might not even have an effect on the Ancient Ones themselves. There's a chance it could kill some of the smaller ones, what They call the Lesser Angels. But the old records, of course, can't show what a modern weapon would do to them, because they weren't invented yet."

"But we know what it does to people." I closed my eyes, picturing it: the mushroom clouds, people blurring, vanishing, like in *Terminator 2: Judgment Day*. Sarah Connor's hands vanishing from the fence. Some favour. "What else could we do?"

"How *do* you kill something magical? Something that could come from the sky, or from the ocean, or from right next to you? Something bigger than your field of vision can take in? Something that could destroy a whole city in minutes? That could drive people to riot and murder, that could control minds, get into dreams, poison the water and the air before we could instigate a plan B? I mean, assuming that a nuke can't do it, let's say."

"I don't know."

"Me neither. Nukes are the best we've got, the best the human race has. To be honest, maybe weaponizing the reactor *against* Them would have worked. But that ran the risk of it falling into Their hands. Claws. Tentacles. Whatever. And that's a risk I wouldn't take. I'd kill myself first."

"Don't say that."

"I'd kill myself first," she repeated. "Believe it."

We sat there for a few minutes, just listening to the words bounce around us. I wondered what power even saying something like that might have. Finally I said, "Hey, John?"

"Yeah?"

I pointed behind me. "Nut sack."

"*Nicholas.*"

CHAPTER SEVENTEEN

DESPITE THE JOLTING, the noise, and the stench of the smoke and fumes, I managed to sleep briefly on the elderly turboprop, waking to screaming wheels and a half-remembered vision of something dark reaching for me, something with eyes and claws. When we finally stopped, it was sudden enough that I was thrown forward almost to the cockpit, and had to crawl back to my bag. "How is it, exactly, that you didn't throw up your lungs on that plane ride?"

"I'm doped to the gills on scopolamine," she said. "Didn't you see me putting it in your bag at the drugstore?"

"Oh man, I can't even answer 'yes' to 'Did you pack this luggage yourself?'"

"Don't worry about it. I'll take the rap."

"Damn right. You could have offered me some, by the way."

"You were asleep!"

We had to get out on all fours, I was so cramped up and Johnny was so woozy from the Gravol; Hamid waited at the bottom, perkily, his post-flight cigarette already down to the filter. "What I tell you?" he said, delighted. "Fast like hell."

"Amazing," she said.

"Hold on," he added, as she began to stagger off; we both turned to look at him. Another bribe, I thought. Of course. Not worded as such.

"I know you," he said slowly, stretching out each word, staring at Johnny. "I do. Where do I know you from? You're not a student, hey? Traveling with local boy?"

"Sure I am."

She sounded innocently dismissive; I felt my skin prickle though. Had he seen something? A wanted poster (did people still do those in this day and age, with the Internet?), a news spot about missing children, a police alert in the airport?

"The singer," he said, delighted. "Her! The girl in the short skirt. What did you cut your hair for?"

"Britney?" I said, and flinched from the blast furnace of her glare. I gave him a half-hearted wave and dragged her off before she killed him.

"Uh huh," Johnny said, staggering off. I exchanged a look with Hamid, we shrugged, and I walked after her.

WE GOT A cab at the airport, Johnny switching languages easily when the cabbie struggled to understand her and tried to get better directions from me. In a combination of English and French, he vented about the sinkholes opening up all over the city, the ineffectiveness of the city government at fixing them, how one had eaten his friend's car, his livelihood, five children, how will that man live now? Perhaps if the rich tourists felt like sending some money his way, not for the friend, you understand, but for the children, until a new car could be—

I half-listened and stared wildly around myself, trying to get my bearings. At home I prided myself on having a good sense of direction and a better one of time, often able to guess only a few minutes off from true, but here I felt untethered, actually unmoored, as if something were flapping loose behind me. The buildings passing on either side of us were low and brown-grey, like something left too long in the oven till it dried out, punctuated here and there by stubby grey-green trees and the occasional vigorous-looking palm. People watered potted plants—cactuses, palms, spiky aloes—on the open rooftop courtyards, partly shaded by soft white netting. All the plants looked like tiny monsters under their white canopies. The crisscrossing transmission lines looked as perfectly organized and purposeful as a spiderweb. I wondered if I had culture shock, if it was finally kicking in.

"We can do this," Johnny said. "Stay cool."

She sounded very sure of herself. I nodded and watched the cars passing us, the hungry-looking succulent gardens, razor-sharp green leaves and grey thorns reaching for the sky, the sunlight the one thing they had a surfeit of, tall green hedges hiding main roads, a car dealership filled with new things and junky things, some bigger than Hamid's plane. Then a familiar, flapping flag: the US Embassy? Where was the Canadian one? And everywhere small mosques, clay-brick walls that I realized I was already assessing for their jumpability, climbability—could we escape, if we were trapped in one of those courtyards? Nothing is paranoia, she'd said. Nothing is, to two people trying to save the world, two people with a fear of enclosed spaces and loud noises that we couldn't get rid of. Two people whose brains had been busted when we were kids, when no part of the world could be kept out.

The university, when we reached it, stopped me in my tracks, it looked so much like a bank. And not even a real bank like back home, the low CIBCs and TD Canada Trusts I knew, but a movie bank—blindingly white, with fluted pillars and a triangular roof. Johnny laughed at my shock as we walked into the main entrance.

At the library—refreshingly normal-smelling, brightly lit, nothing weird hiding in the corners—she didn't even make it to the reference desk before people began vaulting it to get to her, talking excitedly. I looked up, seeing— not much to my surprise—a portrait of her on the wall, soft luminous oils rather than a photograph, and below that a discreet plaque with the word *ENDOWMENT*. Oops. Caught.

"Please don't tell anyone I'm here," she began, raising her voice over the din. "I'm just here to do a few minutes of research. I need access to the rare book collection, and a computer with Internet, please." The staff scattered at once, some of the younger ones shouting ahead of themselves to clear the way, running rather than walking.

"What was all that?" I said out of the corner of my mouth. "Do you think they're rushing to tell somebody first?"

"I don't think so. You can always trust librarians. They want to help, and..." She rubbed her raw, red eyes. "Memory-keepers are the pulse of humanity no matter where you go, no matter when you go. That's half the difference between us and Them. We trust our librarians."

"Uh, okay. I'll remember that. Are you okay?"

"Just my eyes. I'll be back in a minute." She vanished, reappearing—as I had predicted—with her face washed, in a clean shirt, her hair wet and slicked back.

"You know what just occurred to me?" I said. "You keep saying you like Madonna's music, but really I think what you want is to *look* like her. Like right now. The 'La Isla Bonita' video. That literally is what your hair looks like right now."

"As if!"

"Look me in the eye and tell me I'm wrong!"

"I'm not even going to dignify that with an answer," she retorted, "and furthermore, if you are trying to channel the hot guitar player from that video, you are failing *spectacularly*."

"Says you. The ladies, they love me, they all come to listen to me play the guitar."

"If I was a president, I'd be Baberaham Lincoln."

"If I was a prime minister, I'd be John Babe McDonald," I retorted in turn. "Anyway, incoming."

Books piled up, old stuff, edged in pictures or gold, smelling sweetly of leather and age. There were even a few scrolls, some treated with some kind of plastic, others still curled up, bulky and smelling faintly of something sweet and ancient. A younger man beckoned us—or just Johnny, I supposed—into a back room containing a couple of computers and some office supplies. Johnny immediately pocketed a black Sharpie, then winked at me. I gave her a crisp nod. Prepare for war, general.

After studying the scrolls for perhaps an hour, she hauled out her laptop and started drawing on the back, an astonishingly complex design that started with two circles and got more and more crowded until I found I couldn't look at it any more. When she stopped, it shone for a second, not the purple-red colour of tilted Sharpie ink, but something else, an oily white light like the surface of an opal. Or had I imagined it?

Shading my eyes with my hands, I said, "Is that it? The protection spell? I can't believe that's going to work."

"Oof. That's because you can't feel it working."

I glanced at her, alarmed; she had gone pale, her eyes half-glazed, blinking rapidly. "Holy shit," I said. "Is it...? Are you...? Is it taking your...?" I fumbled for words, and gave up. "Anything?"

"Something. Yeah. Feel tired. Like I was just running, or I had an asthma attack. But if that's what it takes to keep the spell going, that's what it takes." She sighed and rubbed a hand hard across her eyes. "Jesus."

"What's it... doing?"

"If I did it right, which it feels like I did, then fudging where we are, and hiding when I'm using prodigy-mode. It should make us harder to track. I still need to find some spells for personal warding, though."

"Can I help? With any of it?"

"Not the research," she said. "The spells, maybe; there's a way to share the load, but it was so common that all the ancients just assumed everyone knew how to do it; it would have been like writing down the rules for tag. But I don't know how yet, and not just anyone can actually access the magic."

"Okay. Stay tough, John. I'll go stand watch. Can I have some gum?"

"Here. Thanks, Nicky."

I wandered off, not attracting too many stares from the few students at the study carrels—were they still in session here?—since I was dressed virtually identically, except that they had neat, short haircuts and mine under the scarf was decidedly shaggy; I'd been procrastinating on a haircut for months. If I could keep it up I'd be well on my way to becoming the guitar guy from the video. Some looked at me inscrutably as I passed, their calm, dark eyes following me. Were they... agents? Minions? What was the word Johnny had used? Maybe not. They still looked possessed of all their life forces, their vital juices, not like the man from the airport.

I glugged from a drinking fountain in the hallway,

deliciously metallic, like the mineral water Johnny had given me a taste for back home, and cleaned up in their spotless bathroom. Everything had a curious smell to it, hot and dusty, like the dry smell of the sand at Elk Island in the summer, with an edge of toasted bread and seaweed. The smell of a new place, a city detectably at the edge of a desert as well as a sea, detectably different from the smell of Casablanca and Fes. I wondered what home would smell like when I eventually went home, my nose desensitized to familiar things. *If* I ever went home.

I did a few laps around the library, drinking every time I passed the fountain, then wandered outside, into what initially felt like the inside of an oven, full of pale brick and sidewalks, but was tolerable after a minute thanks to a constant, stiff breeze. Tiny sparrows that looked exactly like the ones at home flickered around my head. Away from the library, the university buildings were scattered amongst a veritable forest, dense trees planted everywhere except the pathways, which were lined in white concrete pots filled with succulents. I had gotten so used to the heat that it actually felt cool in the shade. There were more students here, dispersed amongst the trees or napping in the lawns. Despite the heat, the grass was green and lush. Tuition dollars, I thought without humour. You pay your bucks, you get the receipt with the word *Degree* across the top, you get the green, thick grass.

Two girls in sundresses, one red, one purple, were dancing to music coming from a small stereo in the grass, giggling and stepping adroitly over their textbooks. I stopped to watch, jealous of their education, their bare feet, the expensive sandals discarded on their bags—even the boombox, remembering my broken one back home. Students were the same everywhere: rich and bright, and not purposefully ignoring but not actually *able* to see people like me, as if they had some filter for people who were lesser than they were, that they might try to break down over the years of their schooling or they might not.

The big difference between me and Johnny, I thought as I kept walking, not wanting to be branded the campus pervert, wasn't race, wasn't money, wasn't gender, wasn't looks, wasn't intelligence. It was that she thought the world was, in general, improvable, and I didn't. We'd both extrapolated from the people we knew, from personal to global, and just veered away from each other like lines on a graph, never able to come close to touching again. I'd seen enough of people to know that they never changed. And she'd seen enough to think that they did.

But she was wrong, fundamentally wrong. I'd tried to change people, and failed. And I didn't know anyone who had succeeded, not one single person. Yet she persisted in believing that she could do it—and not one or two, here and there; everybody, everywhere, for all time. That was why the press loved her, that bullheaded optimism that would have looked like actual insanity in anyone else, but who had the patents and the labs to back it up, who had designed valves for the Canadarm as well as wheelchairs, who had drugs for Alzheimer's and multiple sclerosis and malaria and sleeping sickness and cancer, who had created both extra-caffeinated coffee beans and vitamin-enhanced rice, who had a giant thing that only transported photons and a tiny thing that only killed potato pests. No strata of society had escaped her vision. She saw a shining future, and I saw more of the same. But both of us couldn't be right.

I headed back to the shade and sat under a tree across from three young guys in button-up shirts quizzing each other with flashcards. Same everywhere you went, everywhere. The ground was cool under my jeans. Should have been like Johnny in her khakis. They showed dirt quicker, but she was a hell of a lot cooler on this trip than me. I looked up through the soft leaves—no, needles. Some deep-green tree with sweet-smelling needles. My entire body relaxed in the humid, scented air as if someone had cut the strings making it go. I leaned back on the trunk and looked up, listening to air hiss through the trees.

the sky is
he has come! he calls!
shadows with no shape
voices with no voice
every light a star, every star a god

I opened my eyes to darkness, a blood-black sky pierced with crimson stars, burning with a violence that stung the eyes. Panting, I stared around myself. Had I slept, under the fragrant tree? Had the sun gone down, or had I somehow missed the disaster that was expected to happen, had Johnny's calculations been wrong, was this the end? What had I *done?*

I tried to get to my feet and pitched forward as if I'd been thrown. My weight was wrong, or the air was wrong, or gravity was wrong. I floated as if I were in water, but there was nothing around me but warm air and silence. Dreaming. Dreaming?

The trees and lawns and students were gone. Nothing but the dark sky, the hot stars. Below me, far below, as I contorted myself to look, lay a plain of reddish sand dotted with white, so that for a second I thought it was calm water reflecting the sky, but they were stones. The stones were blue-white, tall and conical, like skyscrapers, blunt and—I somehow knew—ancient. They had been sharp once, as sharp as knives. Chiseled to a point long ago, chipped and shaped like a Neolithic spearhead. An indigo sea chewed away at the edge of the cliff, showing long, rippling strands of something in the water, like streamers of bull kelp, though mushroomily pale.

We greet you and salute you, human

I tried to turn, failed, hung panting in the thick air. Wake up! Wake up! Don't stay here! They are a contagion, creeping, They have crept into my dreams—

We wish to offer you a proposition

A covenant! Just like Johnny said! They would offer a covenant and oh God, They have crept or crawled—not walked—into here, into my head, get out, wake up, wake up, wake up, wake up

We are not now that strength which in old days
Moved earth and heaven

Wait, I know that, I know that line, get out of my head! You stole that from Johnny's favourite poem! The one she quotes at award shows!

"No," I said, half-gagging on it. "No, whatever it is. I said no before. I'm going to keep saying no. You'll... you'll have to kill me."

We will not

"You're going to have to. Do you hear me? Believe me? Or is it that you're still too weak, you can only walk in our dreams, use humans as suits; well, listen up, you're not going to get any stronger, we're going to stop you, Johnny's going to stop you—"

We want what she made

"You can't have it! We destroyed it!"

Then kill her, kill the maker, kill the child

"No!"

Stop her
Stop her
Then stop her only, forget the made thing
Only you can stop her
Only you

Something was approaching behind me; I flailed, succeeding only in turning myself half on my stomach, folded over and hanging in the sky above the stones. My skin felt the pressure as it came closer, slowly, the touch of the thick air. In a moment I smelled it—different from Drozanoth's deadly reek, this was like a stagnant swamp, bubbling and fermenting in the August sun, dead from dangerous bacteria, never to return, changing colours and killing everything in it, fish, snails, insects, everything. I held a hand over my mouth.

"Get away from me! The answer is still no!"

A green cloud enveloped me—the stench made visible, making me cough and retch, my eyes burning. How close was it? Were there tentacles reaching for me now, or limbs, or segmented legs, a carapace of some kind, were there dripping claws—?

But nothing touched me. Infinitely worse somehow.

Kill her

Kill the maker

Kill the child

It is not difficult

"No!"

In the new world we create, you could be king, ruler of many humans, powerful, wealthy, protected

Yes, we would protect you

Forever

It would be the work of

Of

Of moments

The simplest of works

"What don't you understand about 'no'? Fuck off! Leave me alone! This world doesn't belong to you, and neither do I, and neither do my dreams!"

The new world would be a beautiful dream, filled with

"You're going to destroy it! Just like you tried to destroy everything before!"

According to whom

According to the child?

Is that what she said?

Make your own choices, human, choose your own way, make your own

Yes, your own

Yes, do not listen to her, she is run by older magics than even we, the Great Old Ones, the Watchers, she has ever been their thrall

"No she isn't! She told me the truth about you!"

She has not

Told you

Everything

I opened my mouth to reply and everything went white.

CHAPTER EIGHTEEN

FOR A SECOND I thought I was paralyzed—nothing moved, nothing felt—but then I realized I could feel, and what I felt was something repeatedly tapping or poking me on the shoulder. Were my eyes working? I tried opening them, experimentally, and saw blue sky peeking through thick, green needles. All right. Woke up; calling that a win. After a moment I managed to sit up and paw at my shoulder, only then realizing that someone was squatting beside me and prodding me with a pen. We stared at each other.

"Er," he said, a zitty young guy maybe five years older than me, in a white t-shirt and khaki shorts, with a wilting moustache. "English?"

"Yes?"

"Uh. The lady inside, uh, uh—"

I nearly groaned with relief. "Johnny sent you to come find me."

"Yes! Miss Chambers. Doctor Chambers? Miss Chambers." His relief seemed as great as mine as he helped me up from the needles and we walked back to the library. My head and back hurt, and my eyes were burning; I wondered if I'd slept with them open. How long had it been? I didn't feel refreshed by the nap, and now I was embarrassed that he'd been sent to find me. Some lookout I was. Jesus. Slacker.

My face burned as I came up behind Johnny, who was staring at something I couldn't see on the computer monitor, obscured by the brown-sugar hair sticking up where she had run her hands through it. She looked a bit like Leonardo DiCaprio about to freeze to death. "We've got trouble," she announced as I came in, about to tell her about my dream.

"Wow. Didn't even turn around. Do I smell that bad?"

"Well," she said, "I'm pretty sure we both smell."

"You don't."

"Anyway. Would you, perhaps, if you're quite done, like to hear about the trouble?"

I sat as she gestured the student out of the room, then pointed at the computer, where she had a dozen Explorer windows open. "Look at this. Giant oarfish washing up. Indonesia, the Philippines, the coast of Chile. Do you know how deep those live?"

"Oh sure, I just wrote a whole book about them."

"Sinkholes in Siberia and Patagonia, and the middle of Australia. One of them, they're saying, was filled with CO_2—a herd of over five hundred cattle died instantly, and the three ranchers that were out there. And an unconfirmed one in Maine."

"All right, but—"

"Look." She started clicking feverishly through the windows, so fast that I couldn't read the headlines, just a barrage of pictures, none of which made any sense. "That was all in the last couple of days—starting within *minutes* of pouring water into the reactor. This too: a meteorite landing in the ocean near the Rock of Gibraltar. Hasn't been recovered. The resulting tidal wave swamped the tourist launch, four hundred and eighty people were washed away, drowned. Another thousand or so in hospital. A windstorm of two hundred miles an hour is revealing new Nazca lines, reported by a local pilot. Archaeologists who rushed out to see them— that was this morning—haven't been heard from. Look. Look. The Shinano river is turning red. No bacteria, no dyes, no industrial effluents that they can think of, they keep sampling it and they can't find anything. Bright red. Look, it's almost orange. It happened in the space of an hour. They're having seismic events there. In fact, seismic activity is increasing all over the world."

"Johnny—"

"They're rising," she said, turning back to me, her pale face glistening with sweat. "This could all be random, right? But all at once? How random is that? And this is just stuff that's being reported, no one knows *what* they're reporting or what's *not* being reported, they can't see the pattern—this giant eye found on the beach in California, this rain of metal spheres onto Madagascar, this boiling lake in Namibia, villages spontaneously going dark in—"

"All right, all right, all right," I said, holding my hands out, stopping myself a second before I covered the screen. "Okay."

"Thousands of people have already died," she said. "Nicky, the gates are all thinning. The alignment means that a dozen old spells slot into place, not just one or two. The Ancient Ones, They're shifting, moving, crying out, like human dominion over the Earth is just a bad dream They're having and it's about to end. Magic is *pouring* through, not seeping. Magic and danger and evil and filth. People are getting contaminated already, other things, canaries in the coal mine, chemical indicators, that fucking *oarfish*. All my theories were way off-base. I can't... there shouldn't be... we have to go. Now." She began to cram her notes into her bag, hands shaking. "There's only one place left that might help guide us to the great gate. It's just damn lucky he lives in Carthage now. I left a message—"

"He? He who?"

"Friend of a friend of a friend," she said. "Used to work for the Department of Antiquities in Baghdad. His name is Akhmetov—"

"Not from around here, I guess. Is he one of those secret society people? Does he know about your covenant?" I said, and felt a slow flood of vertigo rise from my ankles up. I was glad I was sitting down, and watched as my hand white-knuckled the table, holding me upright. The word. A cov... an agree... someone had... someone in a dream... I fell asleep outside and... "Johnny, I..."

"What?"

"Nothing. Sorry. You were saying?"

"I wasn't saying anything," she said. "Are you all right? You look sweaty. Are you going to throw up?"

"No, I..." I looked down into her impatient, terrified face. Something felt different. Subtle, as if I had done no more than walk through a mist of something that had evaporated at once, only the memory of it on my skin. I felt... important. Seen. Something had spoken to me directly, not through her, something had tasked me with... with something. Something essential that only I could do. Something about saving the world. Better than her. For once, better and cleaner and easier than anything she had suggested. And I couldn't quite remember what.

"Anyway, he's got a private library that you kind of have to see to believe," she said. "And if it's got the last book we're looking for, then we're in luck."

"We've been lucky so far," I said. "Librarians want to help, like you said."

"Well. He's not a... librarian, really. He's just a bibliophile."

"What's the difference?"

"You'll see."

"And if he doesn't have it?"

"Time to make some more phonecalls," she said, standing, swaying, and grabbing at the back of the chair. It promptly tipped, and I grabbed it before both she and it toppled to the floor. The spell was clearly taking it out of her—but after a moment she looked steadier, and her cheeks went from white to pink again. "I've already talked to people who have confirmed that there are warships gathering in the Gulf: American, Russian, and French. Tensions are running high. No one seems to know who gave orders for those ships to be there—"

"*What?*"

"—but no one's moving, either." She slung her bag over her shoulder and patted her pockets for the Sharpie. "I tried to buy some time before they begin hostilities. Begged, really. Till the afternoon of the fifth, I said. But things move so fast when they start going wrong."

I watched the back of her neck as we walked, where the skin was tanning darkly instead of burning for now, fuzzed with fine golden haze that disappeared up into her hair and down into her t-shirt, wanting badly to touch it, comfort her, but also wondering how delicate it was, the spine, the spinal cord below it, how it might crunch and pop in my hands. How if I took her around that slender throat quickly enough I could crush her windpipe, make the sides stick together. She'd suffocate at my feet without landing a single blow.

"You coming?" she said, and I realized with a start that I had fallen far behind; she looked up at me from a dozen steps down, small, expectant. So much smaller than me. That sixty or seventy or eighty pounds that she didn't have, that inertia that she didn't have. My hands began to shake. If I pushed her here, and she rolled another... eight steps, to the concrete below...

"Yeah. Sorry. Thinking about stuff."

"Drink some water," she said. "You still look sketchy."

"Yeah."

SHE CLAIMED IT was walkable, but I was slow, disoriented, helplessly bumping into things as if I wasn't sure where my feet or hands were. We passed the glossy buildings and factories, the rich houses, the poor houses, a lot of suburban-looking houses, too many trees, the businesses and shacks and markets till everything was whirling in my head in a blast of heat and spices and neon signs and bright fabrics that seemed to be everywhere, and finally Johnny paused and said, "We're almost there. Let's stop for a minute."

"But it's getting late... won't he be...?"

"Yeah, but you're going to die and I'm starving."

"I'm not going to die."

"You look like you might," she said. "No offense."

"*I'm offended.*"

The place she took us looked like someone's house, complete with a couple of old ladies staring at us and kids playing with plastic toys in front. "Are you sure we can eat here?"

"Says 'café.' Trust me."

We sat at one of the low tables and Johnny called out to the man behind the counter, a riot of blue, white, and green tile, glossy and clean despite the dust everywhere else. The old women and the kids mysteriously vanished when I looked again, a robot figure that looked half-familiar—one of the shows the kids watched?—spinning in the grass. I realized, by degrees, that I was shaking. My nails chittered on the worn wood of the tabletop. Something wrong, something very wrong. The memory of how I'd felt when I'd woken up, when I'd gone into the library, had faded, and everything else had changed too. I grabbed for the memory and felt it slip through my fingers. Only that it was both good and wrong. That I was useful not to Johnny but to everything, to history, to the future.

After we ate—fish and chickpeas with lemons piled on couscous, more egg pastries, and another huge pot of aggressively minty tea—we walked in silence through thinning crowds as dusk approached. Suddenly Johnny stopped and beckoned with a finger at her lips; we crept sidewise to one ancient-looking clay brick house and peered through the front window at their bigscreen TV. I stared at it in something approaching horror but also embarrassment, a sense of immediate vulnerability, as if the TV had reached through the glass and with a single gesture shucked off all my clothes.

The photographs of our faces—Johnny's a professional headshot, mine my school ID—looked pale and shiny, like they were physical copies and had been re-photographed with a flash. They were followed by thirty seconds of black-and-white footage—oh shit, the airport. Johnny attacking, me puking. Through the rising lump in my throat I still had to hold down laughter, and clamped my hand over my mouth. After they showed a map of Morocco with a couple of arrows on it, Rutger came on, his face stuttering in the flashes from a dozen cameras, composed and handsome, each flick of light illuminating a patch of grey in his hair that I had never seen before. Then Johnny's mother, then her father, in separate cities, begging for us to be returned. I hadn't seen them for so long that it took me a moment to remember their faces. I glared at the screen till Johnny tugged at my sleeve.

We tiptoed on, now looking at everyone around us as if they might tackle us, turn us in. No one gave us a second look. There were fences everywhere here, some brightly painted in blues and turquoises and pinks, and lots of murals, some I assumed by children, shakily signed near the ground. Far in the distance, above the tops of flowering cacti in people's rooftop gardens, I could just make out the silhouettes of mountains.

"Oh my God," I said.

"Did you see the reward?" Johnny said, faintly stunned. "A *hundred thousand dollars* just for *information*. That could be millions of dollars by the end."

"For you, maybe. I'm worth about the same as a box of Cinnamon Toast Crunch."

"It said for both of us." She paused, and frowned. "I wonder where Rutger is taking the money from."

"You're paying for your own reward?"

"Oh, sure."

"People run away every day," I said. "They're only putting this up on international TV because you're rich and famous and loved, and you know it. And I'm... whatever. Collateral damage. Did it say anything else?"

"Just that all relevant authorities are actively engaged

in the search, and that given the state of your house and the disappearance of your family, foul play is suspected," she said. "At least we're not in Morocco any more, but I mean..."

"We're bounty now! There'll be bounty hunters! Like Boba Fett!"

"The police will definitely get it if they can. That's a lot of money back home, but it's a *hell* of a lot of money over here. The cops would never let Boba Fett even try to claim the reward. We'll have to watch our asses. Keep an eye out for cameras."

"Shit," I said. "People find missing kids all the time."

"Well, and a lot of kids stay missing, too."

"Because they got *murdered* or whatever. Christ. If we—"

"Anyway, we're not kids. We're adults."

"*You're* still a kid. And I've only been, technically, an adult for three fucking months! Rutger fucking sold us out," I said. "We didn't say it before. But it was him."

"Not necessarily."

"Yes necessarily," I said, stopping to face her, too close, watching as she backed up. "He was the only one who knew you weren't just going on a business trip. And he's the only one who *would* report it to the police. And that's why we got caught at the goddamn airport, and again in Fes."

"Oh, so it couldn't have been buddy in the blue jacket?"

"He couldn't even *talk!* He was *dead!*" I spluttered.

"If it *was* Rutger, he was just doing what he thought was right. We didn't say that before, either."

"Who cares? He promised. We all promised. You *made* him promise. And he said yes. And now we're worth *money*. He broke his promise. Not breaking your promise is the whole *point* of making one!"

"What do you want me to do about it?" she snapped, her eyes bright with tears. "It's done!"

"I want you to say you were wrong for once! That you trusted the wrong person!"

"We both did!"

"*I* never trusted him!"

"It's done! All right? Will you just shut up, because it's done!"

"How about you don't tell me to shut up again, and we could maybe have a civilized conversation about this?"

"How about *you* try to understand something about him?" she shouted. "Like, I'm sorry that you never liked him, that you never trusted him, but you don't know *anything about him*. Do you even know what it meant for him to—to leave his family, and come work for a *six-year-old*? Not just personally, but I mean how that looked to his parents, how that looked to the other students, his professors. Everything! And for him to come with me after succeeding year after year, acing all his entrance exams, getting into the university, getting his PhD, and then being *homeless*, do you know what that *means*? They ask him about it in interviews and he always just says, 'I could no longer live at their house, I could no longer,' and his face, Nick, his face is like..."

"What do *you* know about *any* of that? And who *cares*

what they do back *home?* You can't take your country with you when you go!"

"I suppose you'd know a lot about that! You were born in *Canada!*"

"And what does that have to do with him *selling us?* Please explain, because clearly you got saddled with the dumb guy again! Like always! Why don't you just get rid of me and do this on your own? Why did you let me come with you? Why did you even *ask* me to come?"

"Why do *you* think?"

Someone from another house shouted something even I could understand, demanding that we either take it inside or shut up, and the *bang* of their shutters was like a pair of scissors cutting off the fight. I stared at her for a second, chest heaving just as hers was. I knew it. I knew I was a liability rather than an asset. She hadn't brought me along because she thought I could help. Not even to keep me 'safe.' She just wanted me to do what I was told, like always.

"All right," I said after a second. "Let's go."

"Fine."

I had to trot to keep up with her, our shoes still silent on the cobbled street, surrounded by low graceful one- and two–storey houses with geraniums spilling out of their windows behind brightly-coloured curtains. Dozens of dark doors nestled under curved and carved arches, some hosting small kids that waved at us as we passed, unafraid. The air smelled of frying food and the leaves of the low, grey-green trees lining the street. It was so peaceful, and I was so *mad.*

Goddamn little know-it-all, thinking she's better than me. Any of these alleys, I thought, kept thinking, couldn't stop thinking. Any of them, I could drag her down them, I could... something about... red sand, blue stones... white-blue stones, as if their raw surfaces had been chipped away by something as big as a battleship... this would be a good alley, no windows. This would be a good one, there's a dumpster there. This...

"Are you even going to *try* to keep up?"

As before, I looked up and saw her almost at the far end of the street. I thought: If I had a gun, I could shoot her from here and hit her.

And then I began to shake, realizing what had happened, the depth of the contagion. How the tendrils of it, finer than hair, had infiltrated the tiny, stifling space that we now inhabited together, how I had been not corrupted or turned but *polluted*, dusted with their filth in the space of a dream, not realizing that it was spores instead of dirt. Not realizing that waking up couldn't brush it off, that it had sunk into me somehow. How much stronger would these urges get? They were at the 'thoughts' stage, they were pictures in the head, not even as real as a puppet show. But what came next? A shove, a slap? Would it just... accelerate, then, like a dropped stone reaching terminal velocity?

I had always thought my only good quality was loyalty, that I was the attentive dog to her don't-touch-me cat, that the best thing about me, maybe the only reason we were friends, was that I was the one who was steadfast and true, true to her, and she was true only to the world. I paused and listened to my breath snort frantically in and out, like a bull. Like the red bull in *The Last Unicorn*, the embodiment of evil, which had scared the kids to tears for weeks when we rented it. Johnny wrapped in a blanket on the couch between Carla and the twins, equally horrified. Darkness, the flickering screen, the red monster. Me. I.

"Nick?"

"I'm coming." It was an effort to get my legs moving again, but I forced them up the street towards her, in the thickening dusk. "Sorry."

"Stomach again, mm?"

"Uh, yeah."

"I should have gotten some antacids at that drugstore. Remind me tomorrow when the stores open."

That was her version of contrition. I knew that. I followed her unspeaking, hating myself, not fearing myself. Yet.

Around the corner, a sudden blare of noise made me jump, as if we'd walked into a marching band, only muffled by the thick brick walls till now. I clamped my hands over my ears instinctively, taking them off to yell, "What the hell's that?"

We turned the corner into the wall of sound, and I saw I wasn't too far off—a dozen men were blowing trumpets in the crowd, and other instruments I didn't recognize, made of animal horn or wood, at least three people holding boomboxes in the air, like in that movie, some random people were carrying hand-held drums, and everybody was singing. Only about half the crowd was singing the same song, but Johnny, at my side, back to the wall, yelled, "I think it's a wedding! They're singing a pretty rude song!"

"You think everything's a pretty rude song!"

"Well I'm a delicate goddamn flower!"

I backed myself to the wall too, laughing as a wave of people surged past us, hundreds of laughing mouths and clapping hands, giving us only a cursory glance in the darkness. Across the street I saw flashes as tourists got their cameras out, the white light bouncing off glasses and jewelry, polished brass, the metal edges of the drums, buttons on hats. Flower petals rained onto my face, making me shut my eyes for a second against the soft assault. It was like being caught in a parade, arms brushing past me, feet stepping briefly on my own, smells of steaming food and armpits and the musky cologne of old men. Faces blinked in the streetlight, visible for a second and then gone.

"What are they singing about that's so rude, anyway?" I shouted, and glanced down to see that Johnny was gone.

My head jerked up automatically, a flinch of shock and guilt, as if I'd lost one of the kids in the mall. *My responsibility! I'm the grownup here! I failed!*

Wait. Stay put. Like I told the kids, not that they ever remembered. If we get split up in public, stay right where you are. I'll move, not you. Two moving things will never find each other. One still thing and one moving thing might.

I hoped that she too would stop moving, just let the

sea of people wash past her and leave us together in an empty street. But they just kept coming. I could see over most people, impeded somewhat by a few tall formal hats, and scanned the crowd for something small, blonde, swept away from me as if in a riptide. My heart was beating so fast that when I opened my mouth, a purring noise came out. Shit. Shit. Jesus.

She'd lost her shield—the so-called 'guide' I represented, that kept others from harassing her—but so had I, the person who knew where we were going and spoke the languages I didn't speak. I felt as if I'd stepped out of a suit of armour I hadn't even known I was wearing. Everyone seemed to be staring at me, even people who weren't even looking at me, glued to the wall in the darkness, just a pair of staring eyes and an open mouth in the noise.

Finally the mob passed—the bride and groom last, obviously exhausted and lagging behind, dressed in sweat-soaked finery and trailed by a half-dozen professional photographers. When the clicking and flashing and singing and honking was gone, I scanned the empty street. She was gone.

A prodigy, right? A genius. Someone who knew damn well that she should stay put even if she got caught up in the crowd. Someone who would wriggle or fight free, and come back to the last place she'd seen me. So if not...

Had someone *taken* her? Or something?

There were no rules against that, were there? Were there? Not for Them. Not even with the warding spell she carried on the back of the laptop, not the... the warding spell that was no longer protecting *me*.

"Shit, shit," I whispered. I dug in my bag for the cell phone I had put in the front pocket—nothing. I frantically rummaged through the bag's interior, fingers running across paper, sodden clothes, a smooth surface—the phone? no, a water bottle—pens, cardboard, receipts, garbage, a package of cookies. Lost. Or taken. More likely taken. I wanted to dump the bag out and search properly, but knew already that the phone wasn't there. I hadn't even gotten to use it.

The silence was stunning after the wedding parade. Normal sounds slowly returned: the chatter of the remaining tourists, the hushed hum of traffic in other streets. The brick of the wall behind me was cool under my palms. True night, heat escaping the day-baked clay and cobblestones. A sharp movement across the street was myself, reflected in a mirrored diadem decorating a doorway. And for the first time in my life I was alone in a strange country, functionally voiceless and voicelessly functionless, and lost.

Stay, I told myself. She'll come back for you.

Minutes passed, my breath and heart eventually slowing. This solved the problem, though, didn't it? Of wanting to kill her and not wanting to kill her. Of wanting to so much as touch her, which would have gotten me ineptly but immediately beaten up. Of saving the world. Of being part of this, drafted like an unwilling soldier, fighting an enemy I didn't know in a war so big I couldn't even see the edges of it; nothing but machine-gun fodder. I wondered why I hadn't thought of it sooner.

I gasped at the humid air and began to walk, taking turns at random. I kept looking down at either side of me, glancing back into my blind spot. It was as if I'd lost a limb. But—maybe a rotten limb, I thought. Something amputated for my safety. An operation I'd looked at with terror beforehand, relief after, knowing that I didn't have to worry about it any more. I'd compensate with the others, I knew I could. She wasn't the only tough one here.

The renewed noise echoing up the street alerted me to having caught up to the wedding party. I trailed it discreetly—where were they going? Would someone there know enough English to be able to get me to, say, the Canadian embassy?

They were heading to what looked like an event hall, a lot like the ones you'd see back home on the south side of the city—low, frosted white with stucco, pierced with dozens of round arches, surrounded by dark greenery and drooping rosebushes. Someone grabbed me around the shoulders, singing loudly, a blast of bad breath into my face and a blur of golden skin and black moustache; someone grabbed me from the other side at the same time. I yelled random noises, blending into the din, automatically putting my arm around the first man, my fist grasping for puchase on his robe, rough with silver embroidery. Here for the first time I heard women's voices rising over the crowd, high and joyful. How would I find so much as a single person to talk to in this crowd?

Inside, I tore free and beelined for a table covered with coffee urns and glasses of juice. I chugged a glass of what tasted like apple or pear juice, refilled it with black coffee from the urn, and leaned against the exterior wall while everyone went past. My eyes still crisscrossed the room, searching for a blue t-shirt, blonde hair. Wait. Had she still been wearing her scarf? Dammit. Knock it off, I told myself. I'm *free*.

Coffee sprayed across the white wall as a cold arm wrapped across my throat, and for a second I froze, unable to breathe, choking on my mouthful of coffee, someone being a little too friendly, or maybe drunk. But the grip tightened and I felt myself being dragged backwards, shoes skittering on the ornamental gravel. Panic overtook me like a wave, suffocating, *I'm drowning I'm drowning I can't breathe*, pain across the bruises still on my throat from the fight in Al-Qarawiyyin, *I've never been in a real fight*. Instinct threw the remainder of the hot coffee into the face behind me, the glass following it, connecting with a crunch, shards of glass sticking to my palm. A bubbling scream tore my ears apart.

For a split second I realized I was waiting for rescue—someone heard the noise, someone would come see what was happening—but the grip slackened slightly and I shot my hands up into the half-inch of space, breaking the arm free and running helter-skelter into the darkness without even looking to see who or what it had been. A single glance behind me as I ran showed me precisely what I had feared, lent wings to my battered runners: the white, damp, pearlescent face of one of the thralls.

It was like a bad dream. Like the kids waking, crying out, *a monster was chasing me, I couldn't see it but I knew it was there*. My chest was already burning from thirst and exhaustion as I ran, dodging corners, hearing the slap of its feet. It wasn't fast, but I wasn't as fast as I normally was either, and it was gaining on me despite my feeble zigzagging. Turn? Fight? No. I'd lose that, too.

A crowded area, that's what I needed. Back to the wedding? But I didn't know where I was now, and the streetlights showed people in ones and twos, who utterly ignored me as I ran. I cried out for help as I went past, but was ignored. The cobblestones became dark ahead of me, outlined in green moss, as if paint had spilled there, slick under my shoes. Another white face shambled out of an alleyway nearly in front of me, ten or twelve feet ahead—lumpy and fungoid, black mouth thickly drooling. I sucked air and pivoted the other way, realizing that they were trying to flank me, surround me. Battle tactics. *Find your fort, General*. Shit, shit, no, I wished Johnny was here, running by my side, fighting with me, shit.

Somehow, I had been herded into a space where no one walked, no cars parked. I stopped out of sheer shock and stared around in the darkness, eyes refusing to adjust. Shadows approached, unhurried, shuffling. Like zombies in the movies. I spread my legs, raised my fists, pretended I was in not a zombie movie but some old kung-fu film showing at three in the morning, something where they made the sound effects by wrapping celery in a towel and pounding it with the microphone. I could taste blood and bile and juice in the back of my throat. Last stand?

"Nick!"

A girl's voice, in the darkness ahead of me. Not Johnny's. For a second I was so confused I stalled out, like hitting the brake and the gas at the same time, and then the courtyard lit up with green light.

I blinked away afterimages, then gagged on the greasy smoke that had begun to fill the small space, backing out the way I'd run in, then bumping hard into someone. I screamed, my fist shooting out automatically, connecting with thin air.

"Wow, holy shit," Johnny said.

I spun. "Holy *you're* a shit," I gasped. "Where the fuck were you? What happened? What's happening *now?*"

"You screaming like a little girl," she said matter-of-factly. "Come on."

"'Like a little girl,' she says. Like I'm the one who cries every time I hear a Simple Minds song."

"Not *every* time."

It was as if an invisible hand had taken my leash again; I followed her dumbly back into the street, into the orange and pink streetlights, aware I was on the verge of tears. I'd never been so glad to see her—or possibly *anyone*—in my life.

"I thought you got kidnapped," I said. "I thought one of Them got you."

"You thought right," she said. "It was camouflaged in the wedding parade. One second I was standing there, the next I was fighting it off."

"Son of a *bitch*," I said.

She rubbed her arms, where black bruises were already developing like a Polaroid. "Anyway, I got loose and ran, but a couple of *y'tans* came after me, and then someone cast a fire spell from behind me, and here we are."

"Here we are? Someone? What?"

"All of us," she said, and pointed as, from the courtyard, dusting her hands, walked another girl about Johnny's and my age, pretty, coppery-brown and dark-haired, in a loose pink and green dress topped with a white scarf. "And you are?"

"A helpful local?" the girl said hopefully.

"Nice try," Johnny said. "You're from the Society. Why were you following us?"

"Why do you think I was following you? A 'thank you' would have been nice too, you know."

"Thanks. Come on, Nick."

"Wait a minute," I said, as Johnny turned away. "How did you find us?"

She shrugged, a little cagy. "There's always information. But I mean, the two of you... it was like following a trail of explosions or something.

Johnny turned, interested again, and returned. "Who are you?"

They glared at each other. She wrung her scarf in her hands; her nails were painted a frosty pink, some of the polish scorched off at the tips. After a moment, clearly making a concession that she expected us to notice, she said, "My father said—"

"Who's your father? Do I know him from a hole in the ground?"

"Louis D'Souza."

Johnny groaned. "That explains everything. Yeah. Okay, Sofia. That is you, isn't it?"

"Yes."

"What does he want from us?"

"Johnny!" I said, startled. "She just *helped* us. She saved our lives. That doesn't mean—"

"He just wants to know what you know," Sofia said. "The Society has a stake in this."

"The Society gave up its stake," Johnny said.

"No, it did not. I just helped you. Like he says. We bought a stake with it."

"That's not how this works. You can't expect to be paid for helping. You don't *buy* a stake in someone else's business."

"Why not? Everyone who helps you is paid."

"Not me," I said. They both ignored me.

Johnny crossed her arms over her chest, beginning to turn away again. "Ask Helen. Ask Tariq. They'll tell you everything."

"We did ask them. Why do you think I'm here? We need more information."

"Yeah? Trying to buy a way out of the end of the world? We don't need any more help. You'll only get in the way." Johnny turned her back on the girl, and glared at me. "Where's your phone?"

"I lost it."

She gave me a look—not anger, just disappointment, like the old cliché, knowing that she'd warned me about pickpockets, and probably also knowing that I'd put the phone in the front of my bag, where the bulge would show. "All right, let's go. That was as scary as shit, and I don't want to get separated again. Especially if I can't get ahold of you."

"Seconded, *Mom*," I said, pleased by her eye-roll. "I mean, check."

"Check."

"Check."

"Check."

But Sofia followed us as we headed back down the street, more paranoid now, even my sweat smelling different, acrid with fear.

"Magic is coming in," she said, walking a few steps behind, her voice pitched low. She had a slight accent, perhaps French. I wondered if she was local. "Please, listen. Listen for a second? There are monsters in the city. I've seen them. People say they are in the ruins, smelling with their heads down, like dogs. I wouldn't even have been able to cast that spell if so much magic weren't coming in."

"Don't doubt it," Johnny said, not even slowing down.

"Something is coming. What is it? My father said—"

"Cosmic alignment. Morning of July fifth. Hope that helps."

"Let us help," the girl said, trotting to keep up in her heeled sandals. "Father said—"

"A lot of things, probably," Johnny cut her off, glancing up at a street sign. "Helen talked to him, eh? And he talked to you. 'Oh, if they need help, do what you can.' And by a huge coincidence, we were tracked by the *y'tan*, we needed help."

"Oh, shit," I said, more loudly than I had meant.

Sofia glared at me, then caught up to Johnny, panting. "Listen, the Fes chapter—all right, Father said there have been questions about them for a long time now, about their loyalty, because of what the city was built upon. But we're not like that here."

"Cool. Especially that Louis didn't want to tell me about these, uh, questions."

"Joanna, they were rumours, no one knew for sure, and there would have been... splits in the group, people wouldn't have liked it."

"No shit, Sherlock." Johnny finally stopped, out of breath, and turned to the girl. It struck me as deeply weird that they were probably the same age, maybe to within just a few months of each other, and yet Johnny seemed like an adult and Sofia a child. Maybe that said more about me, about the company I kept. "Go home. Don't get in our way. This warding spell isn't enough to protect all three of us—especially now that you've been casting shit."

"You called us for help!" Sofia protested, voice breaking.

"Yeah, and then I changed my mind," Johnny snapped. "Like I told them in Fes."

"Johnny, wait a minute," I said. "You did say we needed the help. You said we needed as many people as we could get, and that no one would help. Well, now she's saying that they will. And it's kinda ungrateful to—"

"Yeah, thanks but no thanks," she said. "That kind of help we can do without. Come on."

You don't get a vote, is what she was really saying, and I slunk after her as she briskly kept going, Sofia falling behind us in the dark, just the shine of her earrings and sandals fading into the blackness, and then she was gone.

"What will happen now?" I whispered.

"Did we just make an enemy, you mean? I don't know. But we don't have time to play nice."

"Afterwards, though."

"I'll fix it if it needs fixing. With any luck I'll never speak to them again." She hesitated, and glanced up at me. I stopped too, in the shade of a drooping tree, like looking out of the mouth of a cave, while she dug in her bag for water.

After a minute, I said, "Remember when we first met?"

"Of course."

"They separated us from the adults. And the adults let it happen because they thought it would be better, that we'd get hurt. Remember that. Remember that they couldn't do anything, that they did what they were told, that no one tried to be a hero. Not even for us. Their children. Their most precious things. No one even *tried*. Because that's not what they do. They just wanted to negotiate, beg, try to 'appeal' to the humanity of the people who had locked us in that closet. And that's the way it always goes. It's up to us to do something else. I understand what you're doing now. And what you're saying by doing it."

She looked at me appraisingly, and smiled. "Attaboy."

CHAPTER NINETEEN

WE STOPPED AT a big, nondescript house, white brick and red tile just like its neighbours, with its own rooftop garden—swaying green leaves, black against the indigo sky, with stars visible through the drifting fronds. Calling to me, the stars. A dog whistle, nothing Johnny could hear. I gritted my teeth against the noise. She warned me they would pull. It seemed stronger now, impossibly so: like a string attached to my head, dragging me up, cutting in.

Contamination, I thought again. She carried with her the pure heat that would burn the infection from the world. I carried something else. I was sure of it. The stars said: *You are the infection now*. Whatever that meant. I wondered that she could not see or sense it. But where had I gotten that idea?

The air smelled of roses and the old, sweet scent of

books. There was no sign saying *Library*; in fact, there were no signs at all, just a locked metal gate leading to a courtyard in front of the house. The house was dark except for small lamps on either side of the big, arched door, gleaming off bronze studs set in wood that looked older than the house itself.

"We're too late," I said, grasping the gate and jiggling it in case the catch released. "He's closed."

"He knows what's at stake," Johnny said grimly.

"Yeah, must be why he locked the door and turned off all the lights."

She got out her cell phone and pressed what seemed like two dozen numbers on the little orange-lit pad. "Ha, wow, look at that. Forty-five missed calls. None from Mom."

"Yikes. Anything from... from my mom?"

"Rutger would never let them. I'm sorry, I know it's scary, but... hello? Igor? It's John... at your front door. Yes, Tunisia. Yes, on the street. You can go right back to bed after. I need to... Yes. It's what we talked about. No, I know it's crazy that I'm here, with my body, at your house. I know."

A light went on in an upstairs room. Further down the street, silent, I saw a flash of blue and red—cop lights. No way a cop would let a bounty hunter get that money, I thought. She'd said so. The Society, maybe. Without speaking, we moved slowly into the shadows beneath the big tree by the gate. That, too, quite a coincidence. The society people again, Sofia the Suspiciously Good Samaritan? Secret detective work? Or was it just that millions of perfectly random people had seen us on CNN today?

Finally a dark shadow padded through the courtyard—a stocky man barely taller than Johnny, in a loose white robe and slippers, holding a lantern with violet glass in the panes. As he got closer I saw designs etched into the glass and wondered if it meant something or if it was just decorative; everything seemed like a system of signs now. He was mostly bald, dark hair cut short where it remained, scalp visible through it.

"Stand back," he said, and I followed Johnny as she backed into the street. We turned just in time to see a blue-white flare, like the light of an arc welder, fade from the gate's heavy lock. "Quick, quick. Who's this?"

"He knows," she said, as if that were an answer. As we passed under the gate I felt a bone-deep tingle, as if I'd been briefly electrocuted; the air shimmered in front of me. Johnny's hair rose for a second, then settled back down. She said, "Protection?"

"No. Who is so strong? Not me. A glamour only, to hide the call of the books. I put it on days ago, when you first called. Shouldn't have worked, should have needed too much power. Hmmph." He unlocked the front door with an ordinary key, but tapped the brass studs quickly in a pattern almost too fast to see before he opened it. Inside, it smelled like fresh, unfired clay, books, and incense. Broken-up sticks of the stuff lay unburnt in flat bronze dishes hanging on chains from the ceiling. Bad place for open flames. The walls were bare, white clay, undecorated with the tiles I had seen everywhere else.

He looked at me. "You. She didn't answer the question."

"Nick Prasad." I looked down into his face, creased and squashed with sleep, his eyes blue but surrounded by pink, bleary.

"Where you from? Here? Assyrian, Akkadian? Not a Hittite."

"Um," I said. "We're from Guyana. I was born in Canada."

"Guyana? You don't look African."

"Guy-ana," I said. "Not Ghana."

"Then you don't look South American." He turned to Johnny, face pleading. "Look at this thing you drag with you, full of lies."

"Guyana is crammed with Indians that the British brought over to work on the sugarcane plantations," I said, annoyed. "Read a book sometime."

"Uh-huh," he said. "Speaking of which, *don't* touch the books. And as for you"—he held the lantern closer to her, so that the lavender light joined their faces, matching expressions of anger and impatience—"you say you'll make this right."

"I said I'd try."

"On the phone. You said. You knew how to do it."

"I said I knew how to find *out* how," she said. "You're splitting hairs. Are you going to let me down there or not?"

He chuckled, a thick, angry noise. "Some choice. Some choice you give me."

The plain white hallway led to another big, studded

door, this one locked top to bottom—seven locks, all different and some as big as a Frisbee—and barred with a wrist-thick iron rod. He continued, not looking at either of us as he fumbled in his robe for a keychain: "I watch the news too, I see what they say. I get emails from all over. I got yours, for example."

"Well, there," Johnny said. "Why lie? Why come all this way to lie?"

"Who knows? I thought: Famous scientist wants to dabble in the occult. Stupid, awful kids nowadays. It wasn't you that convinced me, you know. You, the prodigy. It was seeing all these things. It was seeing everything... thinning out, getting soft, *thin*. You know the locals finally finished pulling out all the logs in Estaqueria, the circle there? They burn them for charcoal. Tsk. Spell's broken for good."

"Forever? Was it weakened after they changed it from a sigil to a circle?"

"Think so, yes. It was good protection. Gone at last. When we needed all we could get."

"Suspicious timing."

"Those weirdo people, what do you call them. The Committee?"

"The Ssarati Society."

"Aren't they supposed to be preserving those things? Their local chapter. Buenos Aires or such. What were they doing, huh? They knew it was getting weak."

"I don't know."

"What you doing here, anyway? They send you to fix this?"

"No one sent us." She opened her mouth to say something else, then shut it again. Smart, I thought. Maybe no one else has figured out why she's involved, but she'd only need to say one wrong thing.

He fell silent, working at the locks. Some of them unlocked with a puff of smoke, or a burst of light, or a hum that set our teeth on edge, or a faint, faraway shriek. Finally, he tried to lift the iron bar without putting the lantern down; I let him struggle for a minute before helping get it off and slot it into the holder next to the door. The door swung open, emitting a surprisingly cold draft, reeking of mould and books.

"I'm going back to bed," he said. "Be gone by dawn."

"We'll be gone long before then," Johnny said. "We have to get to Iraq before the alignment."

"*Iraq!* Good luck with that. Don't you know it's a tinderbox over there? Saddam, you know? You don't know about that? You don't read?"

"Can't be helped."

We crept down the stairs, clay wall to one side, empty air on the other. The lightswitch at the bottom lit a roomful of books with a handful of low-wattage bulbs encased in heavy-duty glass, giving everything a wavery, underwater glow. Akhmetov shut the door behind us— slammed it, actually, with a reverberating thud that I felt in my back teeth.

"What an asshole," I ventured as we looked up at the towering piles. A path about two feet wide threaded through the books, most of which were unshelved and stacked with the spine in, presenting us with walls of yellowing paper. Sprung traps with desiccated mice in them littered the floor, so that we had to nudge them aside as we walked.

"He's worried," she said. "If he's watching the local news like he said, then he knows how much the reward is, and he knows he can't turn us in, and he's sick about it. He's missing out on more money than he'll make in twenty years; but what if we're right? We have to trust his uncertainty."

"Do you?"

"No."

"He sort of... gives the impression that he trusts yours."

"He should. Mine's *researched* uncertainty." She skirted a stack of wobbling books smaller than the palm of my hand, and glanced back at me with her sharp-edged smile. "You're an asshole when you're worried, too."

"Yeah, and you just become nicer and sweeter and more accommodating of all these assholes we're meeting," I said. "When you start sounding like Shari Lewis, I'm gonna find a bed to hide under." I ducked under a low arch and followed her into another room of books, this one lit with just a single bulb. "But Saddam, he... they... nothing's going to happen to us, right?"

"Couldn't say."

"I read that the UN said they were going to go look for weapons of mass destruction there," I said.

"They're not going to find them," Johnny said. "Or, at least not the worst ones Iraq has. Because that's what *we're* looking for. Big Man syndrome again.

Conventional weapons aren't what the world needs to worry about anyway. I don't care what he's got, frankly."

"Yeah, pretty sure the Ancient Ones aren't on the UN list." We stopped, and I stared around at the endless maze of books. "Jesus, how are you going to find what you need? We'll be here for *days*."

"We don't have days."

"Once again, the question is not answered by you, a genius. Thank God you're not out to take over the world."

"Pinky and the Brain, we're Pinky and the Brain," she sang absently. She found a pair of wooden desks and chairs, one with a desk lamp with an old-style green glass shade. Switched on, it contributed little to the watery dimness. "We only need to find one book," she said, "and I'm going to need your help. It's the one that contains the key to finding the other things we need."

I tried not to puff up at her asking me for help. God, get a grip. Show some pride. "Which book?"

"It's in Latin, it was written by a Carthaginian monk in about 1357. You'd translate the title as *Celestial Observations*."

"That doesn't sound like—"

"I know. But he was offered a covenant."

"Like you." I ignored the fresh drumbeat of words in my head at the mention of it, as if it had been a lightswitch that someone was fiddling with, a dog drooling for a treat. Something there. If only she could see it. If only I could see it. I held down my worry and tried to listen.

"Yes. And he did the equivalent of wishing for more wishes: He bargained for the ability to do what Drozanoth does. And They allowed it."

"Why? That seems like a stupid move. Like a... a country with nukes giving one to a country without any. You could cause a war, disaster. Kill millions of people."

"Of course. But you can't tell people what to want. You can tell them it's stupid and horrible and destructive and self-serving, but you can't tell them not to want it."

"I would."

"I know, but you can't expect them to stop wanting it just because you did." She sighed. "They love to make covenants and then wait to see them go sour, knowing that human nature guarantees it. Like mine. They like to see what evil comes of trying to do good. It's the way They play, amuse Themselves, over the millennia."

"Did it? Did he fuck himself up?"

"Sure did. Died young. He wasn't dealing with Drozanoth back then anyway, but Nyarlathotep— someone with whom you do *not* want to fuck, and humans rarely do, fortunately."

"Why?"

"He's bad shit. He's still asleep after his last banishing, thank God, but he's really nasty stuff—he likes appearing in human form, which is a problem on its own, of course, but he also likes to have human servants, companions, apprentices, cults. For all intents and purposes he's the Lucifer of their pantheon. Drozanoth idolizes him, rather than its own master Azag-Thoth, who's technically more powerful. Nasty politicking there, if the old stories are true."

"Is there anyone more powerful than Nyar... ghh?"

"Just Azag-Thoth. And one more, with no name, the most powerful of all, there's hardly anything written about that one. The oldest, most powerful of all, old, old, old. It's just a thing with a yellow, silk mask over its face that doesn't touch its features, because not even They can look at it. Don't let's talk about it."

"Let's not. Tell me about the monk who wrote this book we're looking for."

"He asked, he received. He saw so many things, some of which he didn't even understand. At the end of his life he frantically wrote everything down, encrypted it, and sneaked it into the appendices of a completely unrelated book. There's only one copy. And it's here somewhere."

"What does it look like?"

"No one knows. I only know about it because it was written about in other books. The way books always call out to each other, even if the book doesn't exist yet, or any more."

"Well, that can't be true," I said, irritated. "One person knows—Akhmetov, because he got the book and put it down here."

"He probably doesn't know he has it. In times of normality, the book can't be known as what it is. But if you find it when the barriers are too thin, when there's enough magic in the world, it'll fight you—and it'll call for help. It'll call to Them. That thins the walls between our worlds even more, as more of them wake up in response to the call and press against them. If you find it, yell for me. Don't touch it. Actually, don't touch any of them. Like the old man said."

"If *you* find it, will you be able to touch it?"

"Should do. There's enough for me to get a spell of subduing on it. I just need to get it back here into the light."

She took out her Sharpie and drew two complicated magic circles on the backs of her hands, slightly different, unmatched. I felt woozy looking at the designs, which shifted as I watched them, like gears. A solid circle in the centre of each winked suddenly at me, and I flinched.

"Protection against whatever might come when I touch the book the first time," she said. "More warding. Different kind. Don't look."

"Can I have one?" I said, pointing.

"I can't power it for both of us, sorry," she said. "It'll be okay, Nicky. Just call for me and I'll come."

I hadn't really wanted one of the ugly, alien things, and barely knew why I had asked. Helpless to contradict anything she'd said, I moved off into the stacks.

Dust motes swirled in a golden darkness; I smelled mould and felt a bolt of terror. Leaving home had heightened my senses for... not danger, precisely, but reminders of my eventual fate. Not the vague one that awaits all of us in some way, but the specific one that awaited us right now. I knew the likely day of our deaths, the time, even who would be responsible. Only the manner was unknown, and I didn't want to think about it.

After the heat of the day, the cold, silent breeze should have been refreshing, but it wasn't. If it had been just cold and still, that would have been one thing—we were underground, after all—but it felt like water continuously trickling on my face. I began to shiver as I moved carefully around the teetering stacks, eyes beginning to tear up from the dust.

Everything in me wanted to start turning them around so I could read the titles on the spines, but both Johnny and Akhmetov had said not to touch the books. I was less inclined to believe the grouchy Akhmetov, who would have said it just to be a pain in the ass, but if Johnny said not to touch them, I'd be damned if I would. It was slow going though, especially as the paths narrowed deeper into the stacks, so that I had to suck in my gut and contort my shoulders not to touch the crumbling paper.

"We'll *know*," I muttered. The increasingly slender main path branched off into dozens of even smaller ones, some delineating stacks just a couple of books wide, others big enough that the path slipped out of sight. It occurred to me that this place was like Johnny's house—carved out underground and far bigger than the house on top, like an iceberg.

I shivered and walked, walked and shivered. If I could just touch the books, I could see if they were in Latin at least. Maybe similar languages would be grouped together. Arabic with Arabic, Latin with Latin. Whatever pointy stick language Johnny had been learning in the other libraries before we left. Akkadian? Sumerian?

What had she called it—coneform? Comic-book stuff, time of legends, Conan the Barbarian, King of Cimmeria. A time of beasts and monsters and wizards and magic, but also the time, it seemed, that people learned the words to speak of Them, write of Them. Maybe the time humanity had invented writing specifically to banish Them and record what They'd done.

I thought: If the plan works, no one will ever know. They'll just know that Joanna Chambers, child prodigy and scientific entrepreneur, had run off with a boy for a week, or been kidnapped by a boy for a week, and beat up some people in an airport, and then meekly came home. My name won't even be remembered. We'll never be in the history books for this. *If* it works. If the plan works. It will be our secret, another one to keep. Like the bullet that still invisibly joined us. Like falling through the ice. Like the wasps, at the Creek, and looking at each other through the clear water. Like the kite I'd broken at her house, a gift from the Emperor of Japan that I never should have touched.

Like thirteen years of friendship with the glass wall of her secret between us, like the barrier separating animals and humans at the zoo.

And yet here we were, nine thousand kilometers from home, together. A girl and her dog.

I took random turns, left here, right there, waiting for a book to... what, jump out at me? Be so amazingly gorgeous I couldn't miss it? Speak to me? Light up? The mouldy smell was intensifying too. I pre-emptively told my stomach not to be a dick, held my hand cautiously over my nose, and kept going. With everything looking the same, it was hard to tell whether I'd been through a particular path before. If I could just... turn some books, make kind of a code, like a half-turn so it stuck out an inch would mean I'd passed it and a full-turn, like two inches, would mean I'd passed it and come back around as well...

It was deathly silent, nothing but my shuffling footsteps. I couldn't even hear Johnny, who had gone in the opposite direction. Worse, the deeper I went, the darker it got. I wished I had asked for a flashlight or one of those glass lanterns. But realistically you'd never want to take a flame into a place like this, even enclosed. You'd burn to death in moments, long before you ever found the way out. I ignored the fear creeping up my throat and forced myself to keep walking. The light of the single bulb was long gone and everything was lit by its reflected radiance, so that I moved through pools of completely black shadow interspersed with the various greys and browns of exposed paper.

I hoped Johnny would find the book first, but I also— slightly less—hoped that I would. Be first, for once in my goddamn life. The stench was a solid wall now, and my hand did nothing; I pulled the hem of my shirt up to make a half-mask. Gawd! It was like something had died in here. Bigger than a mouse.

I stopped the moment I thought that, heart pounding. It *did* smell as if something had died. Died, and was rotting slowly in the cold. Not a mouse. Not a dozen mice. Nothing so small.

The ground was changing under my battered runners, going from the hard, smooth clay of the walls upstairs to something more raw, crumbly and uneven—gravel and stones, then sand. I stopped and stared at it. Definitely sand. Fine, black sand. They hadn't said I couldn't touch that, so I did, scooping up a handful and letting it run through my fingers. It was even, dry, and so cold that my hand went numb.

I teetered on the edge of the gravel, wondering if I should turn back. There were a dozen or more of the tiny book paths that I hadn't followed, in other directions, some heading back towards the light. The book could be there. Or maybe Johnny had already found it and had dragged it back to the desk, silencing its screams for help with the black-marker gears on her hands until she could subdue and open it, not wanting to waste our precious time looking for me. Maybe she was just waiting for me to come back.

No. Come on. Fucking coward. At least go look.

I headed into the darkness. All around me I could still feel the barely-visible pressure of the books, like a crowd of people that had shuffled just close enough that I could sense their presence but not feel their breath. The sand hissed softly under my shoes.

I ran out of light so gradually that at first I didn't realize what had happened, only that the looming mass of the books was gone because I could no longer see them. Just the barest grey light still somehow reached me, bounced off the edges of a billion pages. I turned, and stopped dead.

Because the rest of the library was gone. There was nothing but sand dunes, lit faintly by the impossible light of a few dull stars.

I STOOD THERE with my mouth hanging open for what felt like far too long. The smell of mould was powerful here, fresher, harsher, mixed with a dozen other unfamiliar stenches. Nothing I could identify. The closest I'd come had been a dead deer in the woods by the Creek. Decaying flesh was not something a city boy would have much experience with; the occasional chicken breast gone green and blue in the fridge, that's all.

I took a few tentative steps back the way I'd come, my footprints clearly marked, but when they ran out into clean sand, I felt panic rise over my head and threaten to pull me under. The books were gone. Everything was gone. In the silence, my gasping breath whistled through my nose. Too fast. Might faint. Okay. Calm down.

"Johnny?" I called. "John!"

Nothing. The dark stars ate my voice.

I called for several minutes, not even hearing echoes off the dunes. How was this possible? I had to still be in the library, there must just be some... some *spell* that made me think... that I wasn't, that I was outside in a desert, on a night with no moon (but there had been a moon last night) and only the faintest of stars (when they had shone so brightly that I saw constellations I should never have seen).

The sand began to hiss, then boom and roar, as if something heavy were driving over it. I stood poised on my tiptoes as my eyes began to adjust to the starlight. A whirlpool formed in the sand, grew, hungrily ate its own crumbling edges. Sinkhole!

I turned to run, slid backwards. Yelling, pumping my arms and kicking my knees almost up to my chin, I scrambled up the shifting slope and got back onto firmer ground, then watched in terror as the sand drained away my remaining footprints. There was something in its centre, something dark yet emitting its own dark light, like ultraviolet, something that my eyes couldn't perceive but something else could, my skin or my inner ear or my pineal gland, something that made me turn away uneasily.

Finally I studied the thing through slitted fingers, feeling again that sense of disorientation or illness, like looking into a malfunctioning strobe light, barely lessened by the narrowness of field. And there it was. Had to be. The book.

It was the size of an ordinary paperback, emitting that pulsing throb of ugly light, its cover illegible but marked, clearly, with *something*. Swirls and circles, probably meant to be models of stars or planets moving, with a darker purpose that anyone casually looking at it wouldn't know. But I recognized magic circles now.

It took several more long peeks to realize, with a little involuntary yelp, that it wasn't sitting in the sand on its own. I wasn't alone here in the desert. And I had spent so long feeling unwatched that it seemed to come as an extra shock to see someone there watching me just as I was watching hi... it. No gender seemed right.

It was curled in the sand, its limbs not human, more like paddles, webbed and cracked where the starlight touched them. Its face was a smooth slate of black stone, like an obsidian arrowhead. That was the only smooth surface—its hunched back was irregularly lumpy, as if it had both wings and legs under there, or—I shuddered—a whole other monster. Like Master Blaster in *Mad Max*, but dead and rotting, maybe forever.

It spoke to my entire body, every cell, every muscle, in a way I couldn't even articulate properly as fear, more like a reflex—like shading your eyes against the sun. My entire body wanted to turn and run so badly that my thighs trembled with the effort of staying still. But we needed that book. We couldn't do anything else without it. If I couldn't get it, I may as well give up and allow the end of the world to happen.

I edged towards the pit, kicking at the sand to make a ramp. The light burned and throbbed as if it were physically trying to push me away. But I didn't dare close my eyes as I walk-slid down the slope, shoes filling with the black sand, in case I overshot and collided with the dead thing holding it. Between the smell and the light I found myself retching emptily again and again. Everything about the thing and the book seemed to want me gone. But knowing that was half its power. I wondered what would happen to someone if they simply wandered in here and didn't know what the book was, not that Akhmetov would ever let that happen.

It was flatter at the bottom of the pit, where the thing holding the book sat and rotted half-buried in the dry sand. I held my breath, reached for it—then paused. She'd said not to touch it. They'd both said not to touch it. But what choice did I have, if she couldn't find me here?

I unwound the scarf from my head and wrapped my hands in it, making a sling, and reached out again.

"Who are you?" whispered the dead thing.

CHAPTER TWENTY

I SCREAMED AND leapt backwards, my head crashing onto the sand. Above me, the stars in the flat, charcoal-gray sky grew marginally darker. I scrambled up, groping for the dropped scarf and clutching it to me for what scanty comfort and protection it could give, like holding up a blanket against a nuclear bomb.

"I'm..." I hesitated. Tricksy things, she'd said, the Ancient Ones. They'd studied humans for a long time and knew that words were our biggest weakness. "Who are *you?*"

"My name, once, was Namru," it said. The voice wasn't like Drozanoth's—this was dry, without weight, the sound you'd imagine from the mouth of a mummy rather than a swamp monster. No muscles to push air out of the chest. Or like an insect. Something making noise by rubbing something together, not with the wet red springiness of vocal chords.

"Why are you here?" I said, not sure why I was asking.

The blank, mouthless face tilted down protectively at the book. "I was... something else... in another time."

"What were you?"

"A guardian. Protector. I think." The voice clicked and grated randomly, then resumed. "They... tricked me. Trapped me here. I once was the God of Knowledge, many prayed to me, their voices... I heard many prayers. Scribes and priests and beermakers and engineers and sailors. They prayed to me for numbers, letters, seals. They prayed to know. But now, nothing... no one. I am here, dying. Forever. Alone. At Their behest."

I stared at it. There was no good reply, least of all sympathy. I knew what had happened. A covenant had gone wrong, a loophole had been found. Namru, who once had been a smaller spirit like the one Johnny had called on for her warding spells, had been betrayed and imprisoned here. I wondered when it had last seen a human being, heard a voice like the prayers it had once received. Poor thing.

"I'm here for the book."

A long silence. The smooth face turned to me. Every moment that passed, I seemed to see the countdown on Johnny's computer. The clock in the corner like any other clock, but heading towards death and disaster.

"What will you give me for it?" Namru said, pulling it closer.

"The... the owner of the library said we could take it."

"He is not its owner. I am."

"I don't have anything I can give you for it."

I waited for Namru to counter, to tell me what it wanted so that I could hedge and negotiate and maybe talk my way out of it, but it simply said, "Then you cannot have it."

We both stalled out. My neck was hurting from turning my head away from the poisonous light. I glanced back to make sure it was still there. When it wasn't speaking, it was utterly silent. More silent than death, with its chemical gurgling and maggot chomping and gases bubbling. More silent than the desert. No real desert was so still. Johnny and I had watched documentaries about it. Thousands of things live in deserts. Quietly but not silently.

"I don't want to take away the only thing you've got," I said.

"You speak truth. You have a good heart."

"But... but I will if I have to. We need it. Terrible things are about to happen."

"Do not. It will break your heart. Trade me. Trade."

"Time," I said. "I... I could..."

It was impossible to gauge the thing's reaction. But time was the only currency Johnny said she'd ever heard of them asking. And time was all I had to give. I could not offer my life.

"I need not time here," the thing said, and this time the stone of its face moved slowly, as if something squirmed beneath it. I quickly looked away again, kneading the scarf in my hands. "There is no time there. But there are... other things..."

Something was approaching in the distance, hesitantly,

slipping on the sand. In the starlight it was impossible to see what it was until he had come within the radius of the book's unnatural illumination. We stared hungrily at each other. I felt my vision narrow to a pinprick.

The thing chuckled. Actually laughed, as if it were human. "This knowledge is not yours to have," it hissed. "And the world not yours to save. But you could have *this*."

"This," I croaked. "What... what are you... what is this offer? How...?"

"That you stay," it said, finally extending its front limbs with the book on them. It was absurdly small. If I'd had my jacket with me, it would have fit in the pocket. Tears blurred my vision. What if I was wrong? What if Johnny was wrong—wrong about everything? She had admitted as such earlier. That she was wrong about something. About...

But no. The way the world had become, I felt more certain about some things. It must have been like this in the old days, I thought suddenly. When magic poured through for us and our enemies to use alike. When the end was near. When everyone knew the end was near. When they could feel it in their marrow, smell it in the air. When deals could be made and broken. "If I stay, you're saying... *he* can go."

"Go?"

"Back to the world. In my place."

"Better." It made a complicated gesture with something that wasn't an arm, and a door opened, a rip, ragged at the edges as if the dark desert was a torn piece of cloth. I shut my eyes against the sudden brightness, but not before I saw what lay on the other side: blue sky, green grass, the pale trunks and golden coin-like leaves of aspen in the fall. A breeze cut through the creature's stench with the sweet smell of leaf litter and clean air. "This one. Do you see it? I still have power left... to do this thing."

"Nice try," I said through a throat suddenly so dry with want that I almost fell to my knees at the bottom of the pit. I clutched the scarf. "Back to a world you'll destroy."

"A different world. One where the walls have not been breached between us by something that should never have been made. One where it was never made. Never even conceived."

"They say..." I swallowed, my throat clicking again. Desert dry. Not like the other world, with its damp leaves, its blue sky. "They say the universe is a certain shape because it was made to be so. It is a shape because it is made to do a certain thing. Like a tool."

"Yes. This is not that universe. This was shaped a different way." It held the book up higher, flaring the many-coloured light across my clenched face. "Only agree to take this from me, and agree to stay. Be custodian of the knowledge in my place. Guard it from thieves and villains. Forever."

"And where will you go?"

"To be again with my kind. Just as he will be."

I looked at the other Nick, silhouetted uncertainly at the hole in the world. Sunlight spilled across the sand at our feet, showing how matte and absolutely black it was, without a single sparkle of quartz or mica. The shadows of leaves moved easily on the dark dunes, dappled and brisk.

Why was it always me who was tempted, who was offered these things? Why me, who constantly had to pretend to be Jesus on the mount, resisting the Devil, and not her, goddammit? Fucking *why*?

Because she had already been tempted with all they had, I thought. And she'd said yes. They had no more to give her.

But to tempt me, there was still so much. So much. This Nick, and the kids, and Mom, and their quiet life.

The other Nick, in the other universe, looked good. Healthy, scared but calm, clean-shaven, cowlick tamed, the disproportionate features—wide mouth, big nose, huge eyes, no different. The same face I'd seen in mirrors and windows and puddles all my life, not one molecule different. I wanted to talk to him—didn't even know what to address him as. Nick? Me, I? He looked into the rip, the whispering aspens, then back at me. I couldn't read his face. But there was no love there. I didn't blame him. Are you real? I wanted to ask. Are you real enough for me to swap? Is it enough?

In my head I heard Johnny's voice, clear and far away: *Do you trust me?*

No, I thought. But. We were running out of time. I had already paid him more time than the book was worth.

No you didn't. He said you had a good heart. Now you will not pay his price.

No. I will not.

And I darted forward, slapped the book out of Namru's grip, and wrapped it in my scarf. Both custodian and book screamed so piercingly that it seemed impossible to bear, and I screamed too as my ears buzzed in agony. Something crashed into me—the other Nick?—but when I opened my eyes I realized it was cold clay, the floor of the library, and I had fallen heavily to the ground, wrapped around the scarf and the howling book, unmuffled by my weight on top of it.

I scrambled to my feet, took two steps, and saw Johnny sprinting around a corner, knocking books aside in her haste. Black tentacles swirled at the edges of my vision.

I thrust the bundle at her, not wanting to touch it an instant longer. The fall had cut the inside of my cheek on my teeth, and my heart was beating so hard I thought I would faint. I swallowed blood and braced myself on a pile of books, uncaring whether I touched them now. Don't faint, don't faint, don't faint, I told myself. My shoes were heavy with gathered sand.

Her mouth was moving but I could barely hear her over the screams of the book. As she unwrapped it and pressed her illustrated hands to the front and back covers, holding it awkwardly like that, the sound droned away to a buzz, mixed with the ringing in my ears.

"What the fuck, Nick! I told you to fucking call me when you found it! Jesus Christ! Are you taking this fucking seriously? *Are* you? After everything we've seen?"

I looked back to where I had crossed into the desert,

seeing nothing but the clay paths bordered by the labyrinth of books. Then I rolled blood in my mouth and spat crimson into the corner. Onto the floor, not near the books, in case they ate it. The blob gleamed for a second, then sank into the clay and dried to a flat, dull stain. I hoped it would be there forever. I didn't know what I had given up, or what I had gained, or what had happened to the other Nick, if he was real.

The blue sky, the gold of the aspen. The round leaves like coins in the sun.

"I called for you," I said, unsurprised that my voice rasped in my dry throat. "You didn't come."

"Bull-fucking-shit. Bullshit. I would have heard you even in the other corner of the room."

"Not from where I was." I toed off one shoe and tipped it over with my foot, not daring to lean down. We both watched the black sand pool on the floor. After a moment, when it seemed clear that she had nothing to say, I put it back on. I'd empty them out properly later, when we weren't about to have an army of Ancient Ones called down upon us.

She stared up at me in the dim light, her mouth half-open. "Where... did you...?"

"I don't know. I don't know where I was. But come on. Like you said, too late to do anything about it now. Whatever it called, it called. Whatever's coming's coming."

There was nothing else to say; the damage had been done. I followed her slowly back to the two desks and slumped into the free chair, watching her through heavy eyes until sleep pulled me down, swallowing my own blood like a baby nuzzling a bottle to drift off. At the last moment I thought: Breached the walls. *Breached*. It said... she had...

> *we are*
> *the heart that beats*
> *still*
> *in the corpses of dead worlds*
> *and it is your heartbeat*
> *we desire to eat now*

CHAPTER TWENTY-ONE

I AWOKE TO thumping, and a thin fall of dust on my face, like fingertips. My eyelids felt as if they had tried to stick together the moment they closed. Next to me, Johnny was writing fast in one of her notepads with one hand, typing with the other. Her face was as hard as a skull, white and harsh in the light from the lamp, carrying around it a halo of gold. So much magic in the world. Like dust. Had it been a dream? One of those scary, real dreams she said they could give you?

Another thump put paid to that. No, I was awake.

I got up, heart hammering. "What's that?"

"They're trying to get in," she said.

"*What?* They're trying to—but there are spells here, to protect the books, you said, Akhmetov said—"

"Yep." She hadn't looked up; I wondered what minuscule portion of her conscious mind was having a conversation with me, and what percent was still frenziedly working on the code, the key, or the map that she had hoped to find in here. The stack of books next to her had grown while I slept, and she had built a jointed cylinder out of cardboard and paper, covered in dense writing in blue ballpoint. For decryption?

The next thump was louder, and this time a dinner-plate sized chunk of the clay ceiling joined the falling dust, landing with a sound like bells on the books next to me. I yelped involuntarily. "Jesus! Come on, we gotta go."

"Can't. Need to finish this."

I hesitated, physically twisted between chair and doorway, unable to leave her. She was right, I was right. For a moment I heard only my wavering breath, and then the room shook again and more chunks of the ceiling leapt free. This was worse than the library in Fes, far worse.

I covered my head with my arms as fist-sized pieces of clay hit them, coating us both with fine white powder. Johnny paused only to tilt the notebook, clearing the page, then began to write again. I half-expected to see the pen nib smoking. Full prodigy mode. Time off the end.

Time. That was all I could buy her. They were coming in over us, so if she wasn't there, they'd have to find her again. I panicked for a second—why on earth was I, the sidekick, the non-genius, having to come up with a plan? I was terrible at thinking on my feet—and said, "Okay, you're not going to be *able* to work in a minute. Can you touch those books?"

"Yep."

"All right, grab 'em, come on."

She didn't move.

I grabbed the notebook away from her, leaving her with the pen, and then seized the laptop when she didn't move; finally she looked up, dazed, her face red and hectic under the white clay like a china doll. "The light—"

"Fuck the light! Come on!"

Finally she took the cardboard cylinder, the top three books from the pile, and the still faintly yelling one I'd taken from the monster in the black desert, and followed me at a twitchy sprint through the stacks, retreating into the darkness. The thumping and crashing receded behind us—supplemented now, terrifyingly, by an occasional gurgling scream. The hair on the back of my neck was standing up. It was like being in the zoo and having the tiger stop and make eye contact with you: a much older part of you than your conscious mind is responding to being prey. How long had They been teaching us how to fear?

"I can't work here, I can't see, and I need to break the code, I need—"

I shut my eyes, opened them to a darkness not too different from the inside of my eyelids. Just... yes, the computer in my hands, smash her skull in, keep pounding till it was done, till the deed was done. Circuitry embedded in the greatest brain the human race had ever seen. The brain got by illicit means, by dealing with monsters, pulling them as close to us as if we were waltzing at a party. The brain of...

She was still talking. I snapped back to myself, gasping, looking down at her in the last of the light. Books toppled gently around us, making me dance back to avoid them.

"The spells," I said. "You saw hundreds of them today. And I know you didn't try to memorize the ones you didn't need, but I know you did anyway, because that's how your memory works. Can any of them get us out of here?"

She stared at me, the whites of her eyes wild. "Yes, but they would take us to—"

"Don't care. Does it have light? Can you work? Can you get us back?"

"Yes, maybe, if there's enough magic—"

"Do it. You just need to squeeze what you need out of those books and then you can bring us back. It's either that or try to fight in here, and you know we can't win that."

"It's dangerous!"

"And this isn't? Do you know what's coming through the ceiling onto us?"

"No—"

"Me neither. You need the time. Quick!"

She grabbed the Sharpie, juggling the books awkwardly to her chest, and started drawing on the floor. The initial circles showed up on the clay as strong black marks, but they grew progressively fainter as the clay sucked out the ink. My stomach somersaulted. She was working feverishly, her arm a blur. It glowed faintly blue when she was done, but the last marks couldn't be seen at all.

I hoped she had dug them into the clay or something. I didn't want to know what an incomplete spell would do.

Behind us, in the darkness, something growled.

"Get in!" she cried, and I stepped onto the circle, colliding with her just as a claw swiped at my back, missed.

And we were surrounded in a wash of light that was not light.

WE LANDED HARD; I tucked and rolled instinctively, protecting the notepad and computer, feeling something slash at my jeans. When I finally stopped and creakily rose, ankles aching, Johnny was a dozen yards away, curled over the books she'd grabbed. I hoped she'd taken the right ones.

My jeans had been cut by a glossy, slaty looking black surface, ridged with sharp edges. Cooled lava, maybe? I'd seen something like it in a textbook. And there was light, cold and pale as a winter day, from a greenish-grey, tornado sky. There was no sun. The back of my neck burned and prickled.

"John," I said as she got up and limped towards me, "where are we?"

"You know where we are," she said quietly, sitting down on the cool stone and spreading out the cylinder and books, the screaming one last. I resisted an urge to kick it.

I handed her the notebook and computer, and looked around—nothing but stone and silence as far as I could see in any direction. But the sunless sky worried me, the shapes of the clouds roiling like a thick liquid, occasional hints of... something sharp, something curved, something straight, something dark. It was better to not look right at it. I felt completely exposed, standing out there under that sky. Sweat broke out under my shirt.

"We're where They sleep."

"One of the places. Yes."

"Did you pick this on purpose?"

"No." She wasn't paying attention to me any more, so I let her work and started walking. My heart was still pounding from the escape, unburned adrenaline eating away at me like acid. I wanted to run for miles, jump, scream. Instead I just sped up, occasionally looking back to make sure I still had Johnny in my sights. The sand spilling from my shoes made faint scratching sounds on the stone. My God, she'd taken us into the belly of the beast. Escaped the monster in the lake only to run right into the Balrog. I laughed into my cupped hand, still scented with death and book dust. Good one. Should go back and tell her that one.

I turned again: still there, a small lump in the distance, kneeling over her books. Knowledge is our only power, she'd said. The *only* thing we had. A tiny fragment, chipped off the tremendous knowledge They'd accumulated in Their millions of years of existence.

And in all those millions of years, had They been evolving too, like us? Had They been getting worse? Surely not entirely. Not all of Them. Nothing could evolve all in the same direction like that. Some of Them must have been getting... better, kinder, must have split off from the angry, vengeful ones the way we'd split off from chimps. Maybe some of the Lesser Angels were secretly on our side, and presumably those were waking up too. Maybe when They all came through the gate, I could ally myself with those ones, the good ones, the ones that Johnny kept denying existed. How could the entire population of any one race, albeit a race of monsters, be exactly the same? Logically, it wasn't possible.

They'd make me something important, raise me up. Let me live. And not just live. Live in glory, like a king.

All I had to do was fulfill my half of the deal. I had said no again and again and again, but now, I could do one thing to show them that I had really meant yes...

I glanced back one more time, my huffing breath the only sound in the sterile landscape. No weapons here. Could I smash her head on the stone? Strangle her? They would be able to bring me back, and then I could find Rutger, force him to give up Mom and the kids... protect them while everything happened, and then we'd be all right afterwards, They would make sure we were, in a new world, with no bullshit jobs, no worries about school, no cable bills, no...

A great wave of calm flowed over me, like warm water, a bath for my brain. Five minutes. That's all it would take. Just surprise her, and five minutes later, everything would be all right. For once in my life, I would have done the right thing. For everyone.

I walked back slowly, feeling the ripples of that beautiful calm flow around me, washing away my pain and silencing the rabble of voices inside. It was so strong I almost thought my hair was blowing back. The crunching of my shoes made her look up; I wrestled a smile onto my face and waited for her to smile back.

"Whoa," she said. "Are you okay?"

"Are you almost done?"

"Yeah, we should be able to go back in..." Her eyes crisscrossed my face, anxiety written in her gaze as clear as the Sharpie on her hands as her voice trailed off. I took one more step, watching the clouds of gold swirl and evaporate around her head, much clearer now than before, in Their place, engulfed in an atmosphere laden with Their magic, and found that I couldn't move. With a great effort I managed one more step, then stopped, heart pounding from the force needed to move my legs.

It took me a second to realize what had happened: the warding spells. They had warded me off. *Me.*

Behind me, I sensed the eyes turning, lids and membranes opening, focusing on us, our little drama, the two warm, live bodies on the bare stone, seeing us as They saw us: the bright dots, so close together. Awake? Asleep? Still dreaming? Did They dream They saw us, or did They know?

Out of nowhere, I remembered something I hadn't thought about for years, as if it had been projected onto my mind: her grandmother's funeral. Thirteen years old. How we had faced each other afterwards, and love had blown through me like all four winds, and I knew it for what it was, for all that we stood there now, turned away from each other like bullfighters, poised for horns and spears.

Outside. Always outside, except for her. Never belonging, except that I belonged with her. Belonged to her.

The sky roiled behind me; I didn't need to turn to see it. Definitely awake. A low, rumbling roar began, like the prelude to the kind of thunder that would knock out the power and slap shingles from the roof. We stared at each other as I knelt next to her, no longer pushed away.

And I knew she knew what I was thinking, exactly what I was thinking, and how the hold had been broken, and why she had lied to me when I had asked for warding spells of my own. She knew.

"One day, we'll have that conversation," she said, as if I'd spoken. "But right now, They're realizing we're here and we should probably bail."

I opened my mouth. The discussion *did* need to happen now, goddammit, and I was sick of her pushing me around, more sick than I'd ever been, but at the same time I felt somewhat infected by her pragmatism. I had robbed someone for taking my time earlier; I could not waste it now. "Jesus, yes. Don't know if we're going back to anything better, but—"

She looked over my shoulder and her eyes widened. "Don't turn around," she said, so of course I did, and saw the sky splitting, something mistily emerging from it, long and thin and dark, flapping like a tapeworm, flying towards us. Dozens of eyes opened, popping audibly even over the noise of the thunder, a buzzing roar like a billion voices saying something different all at once.

"Johnny!"

"Handled," she said, and instead of reaching for the marker like I thought she would, she snapped a hand up and sketched something quickly in the air, then said something guttural, deep in her chest. Everything folded inside-out, so suddenly that my own scream seemed to hang in the air far behind us.

WE DESCENDED INTO chaos, books tumbling everywhere, and the rapidly closing orifice that we'd tumbled through was disgorging—that was the only word for it—vomiting things, fast-moving shadowy things like the black ghosts of wolves, running towards us without faces but with fangs and tattered skin revealing glistening sacs bulging with cloudy fluid.

"Stairs!" I yelled.

The ceiling crumbled as I turned, fridge-sized chunks of clay and wood crashing into dust on the floor, mostly missing me. One of the black monsters lunged out of the corner of my eye. I spun and managed a clumsy kick that knocked it back, but it recovered and bit down on my ankle with a crunch. Johnny ran back at me screaming and tore the thing off, spilling glittering fangs onto the floor. My jeans had taken the brunt of the bite, but it hurt like crazy as I ran after her. I wondered if it had broken skin, injected some nightmarish venom into my bloodstream.

She pattered up the stairs ahead of me, then said "Duck!" and I saw her hands begin to move. I dropped flat and covered my head. Even with my eyes shut I saw the blast of purple light, searing my retinas for just a blink, about as long as the screaming lasted. When I got up again Johnny was sagging against the door, exhausted and bloodless, her fingertips either steaming or smoking. I stared for a second, then pushed at the door, still half-blinded by the falling clay. It opened an inch, then stopped. I looked up, shading my eyes, and saw the bar down on the far side. The things behind us were still coming, crawling clumsily up the stairs; not enough had been blasted by the light.

"The locks are still open but the door's barred! Can you get it open?"

"Maybe," she said faintly. "Hold my bag."

"Can I help?"

"Behind you!"

Something yanked at my leg again—not the wolf things, but something else, a whirling mass of tentacles and claws of a dark, burnt red, with a single huge baleful green eye in the centre. I lost my grip on the stairs and went bumping down towards the opening mouth, no teeth but a ring of grinding plates making a sandpaper noise as they circled each other. As I slid, I kicked out, sending chunks of clay and stray books into the mouth, choking it. It reared back in surprise and a solid kick sent it flying onto two of the wolf things, scraps of their dark skin simply tearing loose and spattering the walls.

Something swooped towards Johnny, a hovering

creature that seemed to be mostly teeth, like a flying shark, and I hurled 'pieces of debris at it till it came for me instead, the end of its beak stabbing me in the collarbone as I dodged. I grabbed its head, smashed it as hard as I could on the edge of the stairs, and kicked it down onto the others, who immediately turned on it.

Panting, I scrambled back up to Johnny, who had somehow succeeded in melting rather than burning a hole in the door on our side, through which the bar was just visible around the smoldering, liquidized wood. The other monsters had already finished their fallen victims, and were coming back for us. I kicked futilely at them, and covered my eyes as Johnny let loose another blast of flame, but worryingly weaker now, smaller, less virulently bright.

Looking at the burn marks on her arm, I saw the problem. Her reach wasn't long enough: she could grab the bar through the hole but couldn't push it up, lacking both the leverage and the strength.

I balanced on the top step, just a few inches wider than the others, and reached through the still-hot wood, banging my hand at once on the bar; she'd guessed pretty close to where it was. I pressed my entire body to the door to get the heavy bar up, straining to pass the pivot point where it wouldn't simply fall back, listening for the *clunk*.

The door flew open, letting in a welcome breath of clean air that blasted my hair back. I grabbed Johnny's shirt and hauled her after me, jerked back in a moment and losing my grip as something behind her seized her leg. She shrieked and fought at it, nothing coming from her hands now. I seized the bar and brought it down on the thing's head, sending it shrieking backwards for just long enough to shut the door. I threw the bar down, and we raced through the darkened house.

She paused at the last moment, near the gate. "The books! I could—"

"We are *not* going back for any books, you fucking dipshit!"

"Let's just get out of here," she gasped, wheezing from the dusty air. "Wait. What's..."

Akhmetov was curled up in a corner by the cement wall, far from the house, shivering and clutching his purple lantern. Inside, the noises had ceased, replaced by a faint, high chant that sounded painfully familiar, though I wasn't sure from what.

The look on his face. The monsters hadn't dropped that iron bar; they'd come in from somewhere else. Perhaps only haste or a last glimmering of conscience had stopped him from resetting the locks. I wondered what They had offered him to do that, and to take off the protective glamour, to let Them in. His uncertainty, Johnny had said. Trust that. And we hadn't; and we were right not to.

It didn't matter. I glared at him as I towed Johnny away, a limp bundle barely able to walk, and kept walking till we found a public park, collapsing onto a concrete bench under a dozen tall, dark trees. The air was cold and clean, the cinnamon-sand smell muted by leaves. Far below us, the dark streets were outlined in pink and orange, gleaming here and there off solar panels, some larger buildings—castles?—lit up more extravagantly still, with coloured spotlights.

I was shaking and had barely caught my breath; she looked as if she were barely breathing. Her bag was twice the size of mine; she must have stuffed the books into it. Well, a small compensation for what had happened; Akhmetov deserved to get robbed.

"Peter was betrayed three times," she said, and laughed wheezily, a chiming noise like the asthma attacks she used to have as a kid. "At least we're only up to two."

Three if you count me, I almost said, then shook my head. "Your chest doesn't sound good."

"Boys. Always obsessed with chests."

"Did you bring an inhaler with you?"

"I haven't needed one for almost five years," she muttered, pushing herself upright on the bench. "Thought it was gone. I just need a couple minutes."

I took her bag strap off my shoulder and passed it over my head, so it was across my body, like my own. Could at least let her not carry a literal weight. My chest screamed as I settled the strap across my collarbone.

I gingerly lifted my jeans leg to see where the thing had bitten me—three dark, clearly teeth-shaped marks, bruised and rippled, and—yep—blood, soaking into my sock. It seemed to have stopped, though. Something shone in the wet denim; I leaned down and picked a broken tooth out of it, faintly shocked, staring at it in the moonlight—the first real evidence of Them that I could touch. It was translucent, with blue-black veins running through it. I rubbed it in my fingers, feeling the fine serrations along the edge. Like the tooth of a T-rex. A steakknife built to cut meat away from bone. The universe is a certain shape because it must be to do its job.

"Can I have that?" Johnny said. I handed it to her and she examined it the same way I had. Her hands were bone-white, trembling, and she almost dropped the tooth a few times. "Look, a real *allu* tooth. Servants of the God of Prey. Amazing. I've never had anything of Theirs to analyze before."

I looked over at her. That would be her god, wouldn't it? If she wasn't an atheist? And the only real relationship in her life, ours, was that of the predator and the prey, wasn't it? The most intimate of relationships, closer than twins. The one that had life on the line. When we talked, when we ate, when we danced, it was teeth versus hooves, claws versus horns, parrying and thrusting, giving ground then taking it back. Kids watching nature documentaries think the contest can only end one way, but it's not true. Prey fights back. Has been given the tools to fight, even if it is eventually killed. She would know that, being a predator herself. Even her vulnerability was not really vulnerability, not what you would see from other humans, but the curiosity and innocence of a dangerous wild animal that has wandered into a camp of hikers or farmers, all sides unarmed, seeking simply to see what they are and how they might react to a monster in their midst.

A made thing. Like any made thing.

"Give me that. It's not good to touch it." I didn't know if that was true, but I didn't like the way she stared at it. I took the tooth back and put it in a tiny pocket inside my bag, and we listened as, down the street, Akhmetov's house collapsed, sending a cloud of white dust into the sky. I wondered if anything had been killed, or if it was crawling out now, sniffing for us. I found that I was too tired to care.

"I found the gate," she said after a minute. "It's buried at Nineveh, under the old city."

"Wow, you could have made a bigger deal about it. Where's that?"

"Northern Iraq, not too far from the sea." She reached for her bag, then dropped her hands back to the bench. "They destroyed the city, and of course the great library of King Ashurbanipal, but one of the sorceresses that worked for the king was able to drive Them away before They destroyed the entire valley. The spell she used was hidden in a secret chamber below the king's tomb, but as far as I can tell, it hasn't been found. We'll need that. It'll be close to the gate."

"As far as you can tell?"

"Nineveh is an archaeological site now," she said. "Local academics have been working on it for years, bit by bit, depending on funding and permission. But I don't think they've found that chamber—there's no mention of the spell tablet in any of the literature dating back to the earliest days of the dig, and it's not in their current catalogue."

"Or it doesn't exist."

"Or somebody took it that wasn't part of the dig," she went on. "The chances we take."

"Well, isn't that what we're doing? Grave-robbers. Cursed. Like the—what do you call it. King Tut. We learned about that in school."

"We're not robbing the grave. We just need to read something written inside it."

"How's that different? We're breaking in."

"It's a library," she growled. "We're using it."

"All right, all right." I paused. "Come to think of it, you stole from Akhmetov's library too."

"He deserved it."

"And that's it," I said, trying to fight down the hope that insisted on rising in my chest, like the small, guttering flame of a lighter. "That's all we need?"

She sighed. "There was more I had hoped to find. How to make the spell permanent, how to power the spell—the sorceress used twelve apprentices, apparently—"

"Ew. Apprentices are people too."

"— but you don't need to if you can find an amplifier device. But we don't have time for that. We need to get out to Nineveh and find the tablet and not get killed or caught."

"Right. By cops, by the airport staff, who probably have our faces plastered all over the place now," I said, counting on my fingers, "by Boba Fett, or by Drozanoth, its buddies, Their dogs, or any of the other Them."

"Correct."

"Whoooo." I rubbed my face, feeling clay land on my jeans. For a moment I wondered if I would, physically, be able to get up off the bench. The silence around us pressed in, close, cold, lit by so many stars I wondered if I'd ever seen them properly before. Not back home, definitely, The new ones, malevolent and oddly-coloured, blazed like eyes through the leaves. What would Dad's old astronomy group make of that?

Johnny's small voice rose beside me, steady and brave, tinny, as if it were coming from a radio far away. "I know you're tired. I know you're hungry. I know you're burnt and bleeding and a little bit busted up. I know we're headed into dark, small spaces, and I know those scare you, and I know we should have been diagnosed—formally—with PTSD years ago, when we should have been helped. But no one did. No one did. The people that should have been protecting us and making sure we were okay just didn't. We can't count on anyone else to do it either. Just ourselves."

"I know that."

"I know you're sick of being away from home and stuck with me. Me too. Me too. Me too, *all* of it. But whatever is in you that can fight needs to stand up and fight. We're the only ones who can."

"I will," I said, and forced myself to my feet. "I can." I held out a hand to help her up; she looked at it for a second, white in the moonlight, and then stood by herself, shakily, straight as an arrow.

"One more day," she said.

CHAPTER TWENTY-TWO

WE AWOKE TO screaming and for what seemed like minutes I had no idea where I was or what time it was or what was happening, and when I remembered that we were on a plane I still had no idea. Johnny scrambled out of her seatbelt despite the plane's jolting, and grasped the cargo webbing to climb to a window, immediately jerking back and falling flat onto the floor.

The screaming was coming from up front, but in the darkness I couldn't see who it was. I reluctantly unclicked my seatbelt and went to look.

After the last few days, what I saw barely surprised me. I had felt real anticipation, getting onto this plane— it wasn't a commercial liner, but it was comparatively big and sturdy, the neatly boxed cargo was fastened to the floor with webbing as well as bungee ties, and the pilot—old, lean, unflappable—struck me as eminently more trustworthy than Hamid, which already seemed like a thousand years ago. We even had a few people riding with us this time, a middle-aged married couple that seemed to be local as well as a young tourist from New Zealand, here on her gap year.

They were all screaming now at, I assumed, the glowing, dangling white shapes pacing the plane on either side, eyeless and essentially shapeless, like snot. Something rocketed out of one and smacked wetly against the plane. I stepped back as the window began to bubble and spit.

"Oh, I've seen this," Johnny said, faintly. "Xenomorphs."

"Gross. Get away from there."

Up front, the girl was yelling "Monsters! Monsters!" and I could hear the pilot reply at the top of his lungs. The plane rolled slightly to either side, but the flying shapes simply sped up, getting ahead of us, perhaps a dozen of them. I didn't need to understand French to know what he'd said: the cargo plane wasn't a fighter jet and there was no way he could simply outmaneuver these things. The noise of the engine suddenly got much louder and I felt us start to descend.

"Is that going to get through the window?" I said, unnecessarily, as Johnny was already dismantling one of the boxes to get a flat piece of cardboard. I helped her rip off the final seam as she rushed back to the window and slapped it against the still-intact plexiglass.

"Don't know, but our nice oxygenated air could all spill out if it does and if we're too high, then—oh, there it goes. Yup."

The hole must not have been very big, though; the cardboard bowed noticeably, sucked to the hole, but held. We stared at it for a second, hands out as if willing it not to move. The plane was still descending—not, I thought, crashing, just getting lower and lower, the cardboard bowing less noticeably, beginning to slide. Something loud crashed against the opposite side and a window went dark. Below us I saw the beginnings of a city—roads, streetlights, even a few cars still moving around, a dark shining line that could have been a river.

"Are we going to, like, *do* something about this?"

"Don't think I can," she said. "We'll see how much danger we're—"

There was a wrenching yowl from the back end of the plane, a noise that sounded so uncannily like a human being that we both leapt back from the stacked boxes, but it was metal ripping. The jellyfish-fungus things were stronger than they looked. The tail of the plane disappeared and spiralled out into the darkness, its signal light flickering just once, like a head still blinking as it fell off the guillotine.

Now air did begin to roar out, fast, the metallic edge of the pressurized climate replaced with Their smell of death and decay. I covered my ears, not sure what else to do. It seemed clear that we were going to crash— just as I had predicted, not even knowing what other flights we might take before we were done. The noises blended into a white noise of crying, praying, cursing— the pilot—and the roar of the air and some of the less-tightly-staked-down cargo pouring from the rent at the back of the plane.

"We're almost there," Johnny said, dreamily, hanging onto the back of the seat where an exposed metal bar made a good handgrip. "If we can land—"

"We're going to *crash*-land," I said. "We should get back in our seats."

"No, I don't think we are," she said.

"Is that the prodigy talking, or the optimist?" I said, sliding into the back of the seat and grabbing another metal bar that creaked alarmingly under my grip. The plane was now shuddering so hard I could barely see, except for the glowing, greenish tentacles trying to find their way over the tops of the boxes. I grabbed the handle of Johnny's cargo pants to pull her into the aisle, away from the grasping, prehensile things.

"Neither. I can see the runway. Hang on."

"You can crash into a runway!"

I turned back as the plane bumped and landed, throwing me into the air and snapping me back down to the floor, and immediately slewing sideways as if we'd hit a patch of grease—maybe we'd dragged one of the flying monsters under the wheels? The praying couple were thrown forwards in their seatbelts, and the tourist was hurled into the cockpit, her scream cut short. The wheels howled on the runway as we spun, spilling boxes from the back where the acid must have eaten at the webbing, wings screeching and sparking as they hit the asphalt on both sides.

We slid to a sideways stop on the runway. My stomach

bucked but kept its load of bile and water—it had been a long time since I'd had anything but gum. More pressing at the moment, I'd hit my head on the metal bar and my leg had started to throb; I hadn't said anything about it. I kept thinking: blood, venom. Should have gone to a hospital. But told them what? Bitten by a dog? Stung by a scorpion? The wound looked like neither.

"Ready?"

"Ready for what?" I said, automatically slinging my bag across my body.

She pointed at the runway, ten feet below the torn steel.

"No," I said, "we'll break our ankles."

"Grab the webbing, it'll slow you down," she said.

"So we can't use the door?" I said, glancing up to where the pilot was vomiting into the empty co-pilot seat and the three other passengers were clutching each other and sobbing.

"Nope," she said, pointing again. I squinted and saw the police cars approaching the front of the plane, flanked by three airport security vehicles, clearly marked. "We got rumbled."

"Christ, update your slang. What year is it again?"

"Come on!"

She was right; we'd have a short head start if we bailed out the back, where they couldn't see. The drop was sickening, and even with the webbing I landed with a revolting crunch, tearing open more skin on my palms on the tarmac and feeling pain shoot up both shins.

Johnny landed more lightly and took off at a dead run.

It wasn't quite dawn—the stars still shone balefully in a dark green sky—and I wondered how visible we were, me in my jeans and blue shirt, her in her khaki and gray. Our bags thudded against my back as I followed her, hoping she knew where she was going.

She did not, judging from the language. "Shit! There's no gate in this fence."

"Well how's a gate gonna help?" I panted. "They lock those at airports."

"Hey, there's no razor wire over here. Come on."

"What?!"

She went over the chickenwire fence first, and as I tossed the bags over I glanced back at the wrecked plane, now brightly lit with a couple of light stands, more being rolled over by the airport staff. The open back end was surrounded by milling people, many in uniform. We had indeed taken one of the things down; something thrashed furiously under the wheels, shooting blobs of liquid that sparkled in the halogens, occasionally lashing out a tentacle that shrieked as it scraped against the asphalt or the hood of a car.

Now they would know. Everyone would know. Whoever had doubted would no longer have any doubt, not with those things on every news channel in the world. Final days, I thought. Like seeing that darkness come over the hill.

As I started the climb up the fence, the squares bowing under fingers and toes, the shouting redoubled—and everything suddenly turned white. My eyes adjusted after a second to see Johnny frozen in the spotlight, my shadow printed across her like paint. "Quick!" she yelled.

I scrambled, now hearing footsteps behind us—or maybe my senses were so sharpened by panic that they sounded closer. Anyway, no time to look back. The links were too small to fit my shoes in, and my arms trembled under the effort as I clawed up the fence on sheer adrenaline, blinking frantically in the blinding light. My jeans snagged at the top, refusing to rip as I thrashed and pulled, unable to get a leg over. The voices became words as I struggled: "Stop! Halt!"

"Nick!"

"I'm *stuck!*" I couldn't look now even if I wanted to, I was so twisted, the wire stabbing the one knee I'd swung over the top. Finally I wrenched free and toppled from the fence. I glanced back to see the officers, silhouetted in the spotlight, hesitate, clearly torn between chasing us and returning to the monster under the plane. I made their choice easier, racing after Johnny in the darkness, wiping my bloodied hands on my bag; everything hurt so constantly now that I had barely noticed catching them on the ends of the chickenwire.

"How in the hell are people going to explain *that* thing?"

"Depends on if we fail or not," she gasped. "Remember—history—written—survivors."

Back around the front of the airport, neat and quiet in the early-morning chill, its blue neon sign winking unsteadily, we pounded to the cab stand and hijacked a cab right in front of a pair of British tourists, who were too stunned or polite to yell at us as we slammed the door.

We were, she said, headed into the city of Erbil, which was a translation—or did she say transliteration?—of 'Four Gods,' which gave me the creeps.

"Which gods? Good ones? Or the other kind?"

"Best not to know."

Many of the buildings looked unbelievably old, too old to still be standing as proudly as they did, towers and arches, domes and walls all the same soft, tan brick, noticeably incongruous with the modern asphalt roads and concrete barriers we passed on the way. We had made cityscapes like this in art class, all rulers and compasses, here a dome, there an arch, nothing flat and boring.

The cabbie dropped us off in the downtown, still quiet at this hour, people walking around sleepily—either getting ready for work or just getting off a night shift. I breathed in deeply: car exhaust, dust, spices, a strange smell of lanolin or perhaps just sheep, fresh paint, a whiff of detergent from a laundromat's exhaust vent. The sun was coming up as we walked towards some huge round fort, surrounded with stalls and vehicles, studded with domes and tall minarets as sharp as knives. A riot of colour, the even, crisp bricks, the high wall.

"This is the Citadel," Johnny said. "There's a market here, we'll be able to get some supplies before we head out to Nineveh."

"Which we are going to do how?"

"You're not gonna like it."

We bought new shirts to replace our ripped and bloodied ones, taking turns changing in the seller's tent, emerging into a sunlight that made Johnny visibly uneasy. "We're burning daylight," she said.

"Please stop saying that."

"Tomorrow," she said. "I'll stop saying it tomorrow."

I happily rubbed the logo on my new Transformers t-shirt as we walked deeper into the marketplace, which was starting to fill up. She seemed to have some internal list that the stallkeepers were happy to help her complete: bottled water, a bag of salt, a package of markers, a flashlight and a handful of lighters, two shovels wrapped in canvas and string so they formed an unwieldy bundle rather than two razor-edged weapons as we walked through the thickening crowd. The streets were made of uneven, square-edged little cobblestones, not rounded like other places we'd been. I wondered how old they were, how often they had to be re-laid. If it all came from the same ancient quarry.

There were more stalls than there appeared from outside, with herbs and dried flowers and spices and random leaves, deep-fried street food spitting hot oil, signs and pots and plaques with sayings on them in a dozen languages, huge tapestries and tiny ones the size of a mousepad, some showing disquietingly familiar tentacled things that, upon closer inspection, turned out to just be scenes of mixed seafood. White piles of what looked like porcelain were nougat, studded with nuts. Pigeons ran nimbly underfoot, iridescent, unafraid, driving away the sparrows.

We stopped underneath a pointed brick archway that ran the entire way around the place and ate pieces of baklava and then bean soup so thick it was more like a dip, pooled with oil and dotted with garlic slices, scooping it out with our fingers and a piece of bread. My hands were filthy despite borrowing Johnny's hand sanitizer whenever I remembered. Guess I hadn't remembered enough. Oh well—at home, Mom would say that was what our immune systems were for. Like that time Chris came in bragging that he'd eaten a spider.

But thinking of Mom and the kids made something curl up inside me in pain, like a nerve poked with a needle while trying to find a vein. I looked around for distraction, eventually settling on the stall next to ours. It was staffed by an old lady dressed in black, squatting on the ground in front of dozens of incense cones and sticks, bottles of dark oil, balls of scented wax, and a handful of clear bags of what resembled candy, like the honey candy you could still get at the museum. "What's that?"

"Mm? Oh, in the bags? That's frankincense, she's a perfumer. Want to smell it?"

"You mean, like... what... they brought for Jesus? The Three Wise Men? Gold, frankincense, and... uh..."

"Myrrh." Johnny knelt on the dusty rug in front of the old woman, who grimaced at us as Johnny picked up a bag of the frankincense and handed over a small American bill. I wondered how it was that no one seemed to mind American money over here. Weren't there economic sanctions against Iraq right now? Well, not Iraq really, just Saddam. Or the Taliban or whatever.

We kept walking as I opened the zippy bag seal and breathed deep—an amazing, sweet, musky smell, like cut wood but also like pine needles, or like the air of an evergreen forest, the clear lacquer on the pews of the church at home. "Oh, man! Thanks. What do they do with it?"

"You can burn it just as incense, if you like. Or you can use it to disguise smells—the smell of a cremation, for instance. They also sometimes breathe in the smoke because it's good for the lungs."

"Is it?"

"No; all smoke is bad for pulmonary tissue. Polycyclic aromatic hydrocarbons and fine particulate matter. Oh, or you can chew it—you've got a good-quality selection there, lots of clear and light-coloured pieces. It's just tree sap, after all. *Boswellia sacra*. You can burn the wood too, it smells nice."

"Is it?" I felt obscurely disappointed. "I thought people like, uh... I don't know. *Made* it, somehow. And it was valuable because it was so hard to make. Like, this amazing, rare, secret substance that practically nobody knew how to make. So that's why it was one of the things the Three Wise Men brought."

"Where did you get that idea?"

"I honestly don't know. Twelve years of Catholic school and everything gets kinda muddled."

"Oh, Nicky." She smiled up at me, tiredly. "God's not gonna get us out of this one."

"I thought you didn't believe in God."

"I don't believe in that one," she said. "I believe in the other ones."

I smiled back and thought again of her grandma's funeral. That was the frankincense doing that—the smell of the wood just like the smell of the clear crystals.

Afterwards, when everyone had headed to the church basement for cold lunch, we stayed behind in a back pew. She kept turning over the program, the thick paper muttering against her gloves. Lots of people had worn gloves to the ceremony, and in my teenagery way I had assumed this was a mark of money, just the way rich people mourned. Johnny's were black lace, a pattern of swirling paisley leaves, closed at the wrists with three crystal buttons.

Leaning back in the pew, I looked up at the roof of the church and the stained glass, the stations of the cross. I hadn't spent much time in churches, but it had mostly been in this one—a small but tall Catholic church, built in the twenties, solid, high ceiling. The pews had a sweet, cookie-like smell, and were lacquered so thickly that where it had chipped, you could count how many coats they had put on.

I took the program from Johnny's trembling grip and accordioned it out between our laps.

Joanna Marya Ziegler, 1921—1998. One older photo, one newer, one showing her as new, one as old. I liked the older one, a pretty wartime blonde with an amazing resemblance to her daughter, less to her granddaughter. Bold, movie-star looks—sharp brows, plump lips over a fur-collared coat. The newer photo showed her at some kind of family party, a skinny old lady smiling benevolently at a kitchen table. She had ignored Johnny the few times I'd been in the same room as them—not hateful, it seemed, but disdainful. I was used to it from the rest of her family, so the grandma didn't seem unusual to me. I assumed that was why Johnny hadn't seemed too upset. I didn't know much about grief back then. Or women.

"Did they name you after her, or was that like a huge coincidence?" I said.

"They named me after her. I used to wish they had given me her middle name instead. I thought Marya was so pretty."

"Meredith isn't so bad. What's that, the other grandma?"

"Great-aunt. Dad's mom's sister." She let go of her end of the program and I folded it back up. "We're not so good on original names in my family. We're better at recycling."

"Very environmental of you. Who started calling you Johnny, then?"

"Oh, that was my dad. Ages ago. You know that group, the Waterboys?"

"Nope."

"They had a song before I was born. 'A Girl Called Johnny.' You know, it was about Patti Smith and it was supposed to be kinda sad—but my dad liked it. And later he told me a Joanna is a big lizard, like they have in Australia, not a little girl."

"Oh, yeah. Like in that movie. Joanna the goanna."

"Yeah. She—Grandma, I mean—she *hated* it when people called me that. I mean it wasn't just that it had been this big deal when they gave me her name, but that my nickname was a boy's name, she just hated that. Very big on traditional gender roles and performance. And she hated... she just hated things about me. Not disliked. Hated."

"It doesn't mean anything. It doesn't mean we thought of you as a boy. It's just a song. Sheesh."

"I know. It's without meaning and weight. It's just who I am, that's all. Not her. Never her. Just me. Always."

She took another breath, as if to continue, and burst into tears. I popped her purse open and got out a pack of kleenex. One quick glimpse of the rest of the contents—a few pens, a handful of coins, a notepad that had flopped open to reveal a page of equations with the question *BUT NOT MUONS??* written at the bottom, a tube of her sticky pink lipgloss, her massive keyring clipped to a sparkly killer whale keychain. She hadn't rigged the house electronically back then and there were dozens of keys to get at all the different levels and labs. I used to joke that I hoped we got mugged when we went into the city, so she could smack the muggers with her purse. Knock them through the nearest building, I said.

I went downstairs first and filled a plate for myself, then her, and was able to hand it to her just as she came in through the door. She gave me her smallest, bravest smile—tired, just like today in the marketplace.

Afterwards, we had walked behind the church to

listen to the bells. It was so cold that the sky was clear and blue, but it was still snowing—tentative flakes that crystallized right out of the air, the last little bit of moisture unable to stay up. Johnny shivered in her thick black peacoat, like a drawing of a kid out of an old storybook. You expected her to pull a wand from her pocket and sail off with the pirates or fairies or wizards.

"At least there's no wind," she said, half her face buried in her scarf. "Don't walk home in this. Let Rutger give you a ride."

"It's not that far."

"You'll freeze! I don't want to go to another funeral so soon after this one!"

"Who said you were invited?"

She giggled, caught off-guard, and when she looked up at me I saw her eyes were dry and cloudless again. Glassy-green, drained of colour and personality by the snow.

I did a quarter-turn away from her, and she from me, and we stared intently at each other's shoulders, knowing that there had been a lot of hugging at the funeral, but that we hadn't hugged today, or ever, and would it be weird, or did one of us need the comfort?

"Joanna! Come say goodbye to Aunt Rose!" someone yelled behind us. I waved at Johnny, stuffed my mittened hands back into my coat pocket, and started for home at a fast trot, not quite a run. Pointedly, I didn't turn and look back.

Love. That's when I knew it was love. Then, and every day after, and here, now, so far from home, about to head to our deaths. And she didn't love me back. And the only people who did love me were who knew where. Now, I had to carry all that with me, and she had to carry nothing.

"Nicky?" she said, stopping to wait for me.

"I'm coming."

"THIS ONE," JOHNNY said. "I saw the owner leave."

"We can't. Can't."

"This, you're going to protest? After everything?"

"There's got to be another way!"

"Shush. Look casual. If I can do it fast enough, no one will even look. Just walk. Keep your head up."

I preceded her to the glossy black Range Rover, looming over us as we approached. Keep your head up, she'd said; only my eyes were racing back and forth behind my new sunglasses. I blocked her from view as she jammed something into the passenger side door with a crunch so loud I was sure everyone would stare at us.

But I continued standing there, chin up, leaning on the door to show ownership, proprietorship, *something*, focusing through the shrill whine in my head that assured me we were about to be arrested, that literal strangers were about to run over and ask what we were doing, with our bundle of supplies and spots of olive oil on our new shirts, one girl who looked twelve years old and like a white tourist, and one boy who maybe was from around here but then could not be reasonably associated with a twelve year-old white tourist except as a miscreant, stay calm, stay calm...

"There. I'll pop the back; load up while I get the engine started."

"Since when do you know how to hotwire ca—"

"Same place I learned the handcuff stuff. Move."

The hatch cracked a half-inch; I opened it, not rushing, affecting boredom in fact, sighing like a longsuffering guide, and loaded everything in. As I slammed the door shut—yes, surely everyone would look now, I would hear shouting, sirens—and got into the other side from Johnny, the engine was already running.

I felt safer behind the tinted glass, but the fact remained that we were about to steal—or had already, in fact, stolen—a car. I looked down, expecting to see stripped wires dangling near my knees, but everything looked more or less intact; although she had jammed a strange arrangement of nail files and bobby pins into the keyhole, from the pink Hello Kitty grooming kit I'd wondered about her buying earlier.

"You don't have to hotwire most cars," she explained. "It's enough to get the tumblers to turn in the keyhole. Come on, let's go. Not fast, don't jerk when we start—"

"Hurr hurr hurr."

"Focus!"

I adjusted the mirror and pulled out as smoothly as I could, following the cars that were leaving ahead of us. The huge SUV was quite something after so many years driving my tiny Geo Storm, though they maneuvered about the same. Like steering a cow.

"Where are we going?"

"Let's get out of here first, and then I should be able to navigate you."

We emerged into full-on rush hour, and my breath stopped in my throat. There was nowhere to go if we got caught, nowhere to turn and escape. We inched along in the procession, waiting as people crossed the road ahead of us, leisurely, chatting to each other, smoking, waving their arms, talking on their cell phones, one old guy in a black robe and the most fabulously ornamented camel I'd ever seen, silver coins dangling over red velvet and dozens of stitched scenes on its blanket. The camel stopped in the dead centre of the road and looked around.

"Stay calm," Johnny said. "I can hear your stomach from here. Stay cool. No one will hit us."

"You sound like my old driving teacher."

"Johnny?"

"Yes?"

"You are getting a *huge* zit next to your ear."

"Oh, eat my entire ass with Grey Poupon. You don't think I know it's there? It feels like a redhot grape. When we get out of here, we're both going for facials."

"But—"

"Both of us. Drive."

CHAPTER TWENTY-THREE

BUT I DIDN'T calm down till we had left the city behind—with only one incident of prolonged honking, not at us but in our immediate vicinity, something taxi-related, which had shredded my nerves—and were out into the desert. Johnny had said it was virtually a straight shot on one road, and she'd tell me where to turn; I watched the road steadily, grateful that they drove on the right here, ignoring the huge oval of sweat on my back that had formed even though we had the air conditioning on, running intermittently to save gas. There was very little traffic on the roads to or from Nineveh; I wondered if that was usual. Why weren't people fleeing the incoming disaster? If the gate was buried under the city, didn't they know what was about to happen?

Johnny carefully drew a magic circle on the glove

compartment door, the marker-tip squeaking on the leather.

"Oh my God," I said. "Vandal. We'll never be able to give this back now."

"Nonsense. We'll give it right back as soon as we don't need it any more, *and* he'll be safe from eldritch monsters."

"Those writers... Lovecraft and Lord Dunsany and them, the ones that were in your notes... how did they come to know the Ancient Bastards? They wrote stories about them, for Chrissake. They got paid money. And everyone said, 'Oh, they're making it up.' Did they make covenants?"

"No. They were society members, that's all. You can learn a lot from those guys. I mean, the head of the Rio chapter is over a thousand years old."

"How come they don't get caught?"

"They're good at flying under the radar. And it's hard to get a straight story out of them, as you've noticed. Good thing too, because a few of them got institutionalized for talking about it."

"They're gonna institutionalize *us* when we get back."

"Well, *you* should've been locked up long ago."

"But they knew," I said. "They really knew."

"Yeah. Luckily they had the good sense to make up languages for their stories. Can you imagine having that many copies of real spells spread around the world in pulp magazines?"

"They knew better than that."

"Yeah." She shook her head. "What's bothering me

now, though, is that said Ancient Bastards have no reason, none, to not know where we're going. If They aren't tracking us directly, They could easily track the magic we've left behind us. Are we headed into an ambush?"

"Yes. I've seen a lot of kung-fu movies."

"'It's a trap!'" she said in her best Admiral Ackbar voice, brushing her fingers across the magic circle, glowing blue in the centre. "What I'm creating is enough to blur where we are exactly, I think. The spell itself says something like 'The enemy will not know on which side of the river you lie, but it will know from which river your army drinks.' So we're visible, but not that visible. Just our final destination. They'll know that. They can't not. You wouldn't have to be Sherlock Holmes."

I risked a glance over at her, the determined profile, small jaw jutting like a bulldog. But her eyes were jittery and bright with fear, darting around the empty landscape around us, all wheat and sand and small concrete barriers, not a living thing for miles.

"They like deserts and oceans in particular," she said, "and mountains. They like to see what's coming up on Them. Even though They're the apex predator wherever They are."

"Hey," I said, "you're not... steaming. Pollinating. Whatever. In genius mode. So this is the real you?"

"I'm always the real me."

"No, I mean, the you that's you when you're not... using Their magic."

"That's still me." Her voice had gone up an octave,

tense with pain. I opened my mouth again and stopped. After a few kilometers she said, "Nicky, remember me like this. As who you've always known me, not who I am when I'm Theirs. Whoever that is. Whoever you think that is."

I started to agree and choked on something thick in my throat, then nodded. We would not remember each other. We would die at the same moment; or if not, if one of us survived, it would be her. Not me. She would let me die if it looked like it might interfere in her plan.

Heart pounding, I drove on, into the desert, towards our deaths.

STEPPING OUT OF the air conditioning was like walking into a lamp post, just the shock of a heat so intense I wondered if I'd ever been this hot in my entire life. It seemed an entire order of magnitude hotter than anything we'd encountered yet. On the far side of the Rover, I heard Johnny simply collapse into the sand. I walked around the hood, feeling the soles of my runners heat up, and squatted next to her, pushing up my shades.

"Oh my God," she said, muffled, head in her arms. "We're not going to make it. We're not going to make it in time."

"Says fucking who?"

She got up, kneeling in the scanty shade of the Rover's side, her face already red. "We can't excavate in this. We shouldn't be doing *any* physical activity in this! We didn't bring enough water. We'll…"

"Johnny," I said as gently as I could. "Hey. Come on. Listen."

"Mm?"

"Somewhere in my house," I said, "there's a videotape of you dancing to 'Get Ready For This.' Okay? And if you don't move your ass, I'll find a way to release it on the Internet."

"You wouldn't dare. You wouldn't *dare*."

"Pelvic thrusts and everything," I said. "In my parents' basement."

"Shut up."

"In a *New Kids on the Block* sweatshirt. I'll do it. You know I will."

"Shut up."

"Come on. Up we get."

Sniffling with laughter, she got up and untied her scarf from around her waist, putting it around her head again. We cracked open the Rover's hatch, releasing a final sad blast of cool air, and I hauled out the supplies while she organized her notes.

"Here. The dig hasn't reached the mound, I think, where the king was buried. They're still quite a ways away. We'll need to go into the ruins and come in from beneath."

"Grave robbers. Cursed."

"I know."

I couldn't make head or tails of the hand-drawn map, which she had annotated in so many places that the drawing under it could barely be seen, but I figured I was just there for moral support and brute force anyway. "Sounds good."

I looked around at the ruins while she frosted herself with sunscreen. We were at the outskirts—presumably to avoid disturbing or getting 'rumbled' by the dig staff, even though I hadn't seen any vehicles—and so it was hard to see just how big it was. It was surrounded by a chainlink fence we hadn't had to even stop to open; it had been left wide open, the gate half-buried in sand. The old city, she'd called it. One of the oldest in the world. Where They had sensed our gathering numbers, and swooped in to investigate, all those years ago.

There were tall, square structures with delicately stacked bricks on top, a soft pinkish brown, pierced with arched windows and gates; dozens of walls were decorated with brick and carvings, and the stick writing as well as Arabic. The ground was pocked with dozens of holes—many neat-edged, square, with ladders leading into them and grids marked with string or tape, but many fresher-looking, messy, with damp dirt piled at their edges. Those made me uneasy. It looked as if something had dug up from below—something with enough violence to rip out the turf instead of making a burrow, like a rabbit would have done. How thin were the doorways here, near the main gate?

The low walls near us were covered in carven writing—spells or instructions, I wondered? Classifieds, *Ahmed was here*? They looked much older than the rest of the buildings, which had been worn by the gentlest breezes, the least lading of sand, over thousands of years, to nubs that stuck just a few feet out from the dirt. The higher walls seemed weirdly... layered, as if they were stone covered by something else. I pointed it out to Johnny, who shrugged. "They used to put cement on top of stone so they could write and paint more easily on it," she said. "Especially the steles—those tall things. They were like bulletin boards, they'd have important public information on them."

"Hey, look," I said, standing on a statue base with two broken-off feet on it. "Holy shit! It's just like the poem."

"'Ozymandias'?"

"Yeah, Ozzy Osbourne. 'I met a traveller from an antique land, who said...'"

"'Two vast and trunkless legs of stone stand in the desert,'" she finished.

"Nice. Does this say whose feet these were?"

"Nope, sorry."

"Too bad," I said, and meant it. I had liked the poem when we did it in English class a few years ago, and the discussion afterwards where we had argued whether Ozymandias was a bad guy or not. A tyrant? Or a good man with an ego? Our teacher had eventually argued that it didn't matter, since all that was left of him was the name and the smashed statue, but it had mattered to me.

Loaded with our bags and the shovels, one each, we walked up the slope. There was a constant low noise, like a generator running slightly out of sync, that made my jaws ache and my eyes water; I looked around, but couldn't see anything. "What's that noise?"

"It's not from here."

"Well no, there's no one else here."

"I mean this dimension. You're hearing something that can only be heard near the end," she said quietly, looking down at her map. "This way. Watch for foggaras, aqueducts—there's one, there's another one. They're pretty sturdy and they run in straight lines; if we have to run, they'll give better footing than the sand."

I looked at the biggest excavation, gridded perfectly with wood. "What's down there?"

"Regular city stuff. That's not what we're looking for." But she hesitated as she turned away, and turned back. I followed, worried by her worry. There was a brand-new notice tacked up, written on a piece of printer paper in several languages, the green marker so scribbled that even I could tell how rushed the writer had been. "Hm."

"What's that say?"

"It's from three days ago. Telling students and staff that the dig is closed indefinitely, due to safety issues. Wildlife attacks, it says."

"Wildlife?" I looked around at the still, silent site. Even the scanty grass was barely moving. "What lives out here? Anything big?"

"Shouldn't think so," she said. "Don't think ecosystem dynamics could support anything big enough to be really dangerous, and the area's got a constant human presence. I don't know, at least we've got some privacy and we're not gonna get arrested for interfering with the dig. But keep your eyes open."

"Yeah, as if that wildlife is really 'wildlife.'"

"As *if*."

Following her map, we found a maze-like complex of low enclosures, none higher than my waist. She kept stopping to copy things off the walls, grousing under her breath at how worn-down and illegible they were, except for some of the carvings—lions, warriors, flying arrows, monsters.

"What the hell is this?"

"A minion," she said, pointing. "There, it says... *O Lesser Angels—fly the wide world—and bring me back a new heart—unstained by the blood of yesterday.* Sort of. 'Angels' isn't quite the word, but you see here, where the wings are over the face? That made it into the Bible. An angel, well, you don't know what an angel looks like. Maybe it looks like one of these. In it goes."

"Jesus."

The wind pushed sand into and out of openings, pushed the grass against stone and cement, tilted the steles so that everywhere we went I heard not just our footsteps but eternal scritchings and sighings and gasps. My nerves felt stretched hair-thin.

And it wasn't just that: there was the heat, which continued to feel like some huge animal stalking us. The wind brought no relief, drying the sweat that formed in my hairline and on my neck in seconds, but drying it like a hairdryer, well over body temperature. We drank our water as sparingly as we could, every mouthful tasting as exaggeratedly sweet as Gatorade, but my throat felt full of mucus, my tongue swelling. How soon could you die of dehydration here? Or would we go from heatstroke first?

Scritch, scritch, scratch, behind us. I spun, shovel up; still nothing. The wind plastered itself to me like a plate of red-hot iron molded to the shape of my body. We stopped to rest in a patch of shade, a few degrees cooler. Johnny's chest was squeaking like a bad fan belt.

"I outgrew it," she finally said, answering, I figured, the look on my face. "I did. I swear. Years and years ago. I didn't think I needed an inhaler."

"Take it easy, take it slow," I said. "I don't need to tell you this. Stop and rest."

"I can't. We don't have time. I'm going in circles trying to find clues as to where the king's burial chamber is, and how to get in, and they all refer to each other on purpose, like a riddle..."

"Drink some water."

"And half the words are missing, either buried or just worn away, and what if what I need is just under the sand? Do we dig? What if something collapses on us? What if I write down something wrong? What if—"

"Johnny! Drink your water. I brought the salt, have some salt."

Instead of putting it in her water bottle, she poured some out into her dirty palm and darted her tongue into the little pile, like a snake testing the air.

"Weirdo," I said. "Everything you do is weird. But everything feels kind of..."

"I feel it too. The salt might help."

"I thought you got it for like, dehydration or whatever."

"That too." The bags under her eyes had gone from simply dark to actually black, like she'd been struck hard on the bridge of the nose and blackened both eyes. What were the spells taking out of her?

"*What if* a lot of things," I said. "Just keep doing what you're doing. We'll get everything we need in time."

"Yeah." Her head was bobbing with exhaustion, not really nodding, the scarf slipping over her ears. "Yeah. We will. Yeah. Gotta."

"Fix your scarf and let's go."

We copied from broken tablets and scribbled brick, ran black crayons over papers to take rubbings from the walls. They didn't, to me, look as if they could be assembled to a coherent whole, but Johnny assured me that wasn't what they were for. "They do form a picture," she said. "Taken together, not separately. They did that on purpose—the sorceress and her assistants."

"What was her name?"

"Nuphel-Don, I think would be the closest rendition. But she also went by Ben'nest Soth Nothnal, a transliteration of the Old Language, and also Brac-gha Nothnal. Those weren't different titles and they didn't refer to different people, as far as I can tell; she just kept using different names. I wish I knew why."

"Would it help us?"

"Don't think so. Knowledge for knowledge's sake. Anyway, she loved the king—no, not like that—and didn't want anyone to find his tomb. But she acknowledges—here, at the bottom of this stele—that one day there might be need, and so she has given us, the future, the tools to do it. I trust her."

"Why?"

"Because she fought Them too." She sighed, weighing a palm-sized piece of red clay in her hand, the writing still sharp and crisp, something we'd had to tug free from beneath a round stone written, she'd said, with terrifying warnings. "This says the entrance to the tomb's labyrinth is underneath the statue of Nanna, but it's locked for eternity. Another one—that one there, with the blue paint—says the statue was destroyed in the realm of Alalngar. So that doesn't help us, unless we can find the old base—they often built a new statue on the same base as the old one, because this area is so poor in good stone. And that tablet says the statue of Nanna was located next to the shrine of En-Lil, so maybe it would be easier to find the shrine, which wasn't destroyed."

"Were those shrines and statues to the... to Them?"

"Some of them. Some of them are Elder Gods. Similar to but different from Them. Mostly dead now."

"Are those Their real names?"

"No. I promise." She ran her forearm over her face, scattering sweat-salt like snowflakes, and trudged off towards a low, broken white brick wall. "Somewhere here. Let's just dig till we hit something."

"My least favourite sentence today."

But it took only an hour of careful digging, interspersed with excursions into the volcanic heat-sink of the dig site to steal timber to shore up our excavation, to find the shrine and then the door into the labyrinth. It was narrow, arched as all the doors were here, so that I wondered whether I might go back home and find rectangular doors strange. It was also heavily carved with writing on every available surface, so that the stone looked textured instead of written. Johnny stood panting as she scanned the door top to bottom, writing on her notebook without looking; I glanced down at it, but she wasn't writing in English.

The broken bricks at the top and bottom of the door looked so much like jagged teeth that once I saw it I couldn't stop seeing it, and I hesitated before following Johnny across the threshold. There was a faint suggestion of faces as we walked into the darkness, the daylight following us in for inches at most.

The floor was covered in sand, not very surprisingly, since it had been incidentally buried in sand rather than deliberately buried in dirt. Turned on, Johnny's flashlight produced a white light that washed out all the writing on the walls, gleamed off the clean pale sand. I played it up and down, keeping it off her face, feeling my heart speed up.

There was writing everywhere, even the ceiling, except on the statues lining the walls, bearded men wearing elaborate headpieces, something severely wrong with their lower bodies. The earth above it seemed to press down on us; I swung the flashlight up and saw a dozen places, dark places, where the light never seemed to touch. I kept my arm still, training the beam on the darkness. Not a hole. Not a crack. Not a shadow. Just a place where the light couldn't go.

Johnny caught my gaze and looked up. There was a long silence in which I thought I might just go screaming back out into the sunlight, but it was too late. The darkness shifted slightly as we walked, keeping pace with us. I took a deep breath. The darkness, the bullets coming through. All those years we had run and run and run and now we were somewhere we could not run from danger. Just like before. Helpless in the dark. A dark that shifted, following us.

"Ignore it," Johnny whispered.

"What is it?"

"Don't look at it." Her voice was trembling; I felt the presence of the darkness as a physical thing following us, about to clamp around the back of my neck. Whether a thing of Nuphel-Don or Them, I didn't know. I only knew, somehow, absolutely, that it was meant to push people out of the labyrinth, to give them the fear that emptied bowels and stopped hearts, and it would only get worse as we got deeper. Just like Akhmetov's library.

"Do we have a map of this place?" I asked, keeping my voice down.

"No. It's a labyrinth. And I do not like those statues at *all*."

"You sure? I dunno, we could steal a couple, stick them in the Rover, put them on your lawn at home—"

"Scare the neighbours, yep, I'm down for that."

"What does this writing say, all this writing? Why did they write on the ceiling and everything? They had a lot to say."

"It's a story," she said softly. "About how King Suen-Ngir accepted the worship of these new gods; how a pilgrim came from the west and told them of it, gave them tapestries and statuettes. Then how the gods gave the king power and wealth in return for a few people a year, how the demands got more and more, and then the shrines were destroyed by the prince when he came to the throne. Finally, the gods destroyed the city, and Nuphel-Don and her apprentices flung them into a place of imprisonment and slammed the gate shut."

"If the Gods destroyed the city, who wrote...? Oh."

"Yeah. I'm sure there won't be anything left of them by now," she said, not entirely reassuringly. I thought of the brave Nuphel-Don, devoted apprentices at her side, in the elaborate draped clothing I'd seen in the frescoes outside, feverishly inscribing, lit by candles or torches, as the air ran out and the remnants of the city trembled outside, guardians forever of the king's tomb, and forgotten or even cursed by everyone except Johnny, who had dug up her story.

After what seemed like forever in the long entrance hallway—and hang on, how big *was* this place, anyway? The site itself wasn't that big—it finally branched, a Y-shape rather than a T, curving rather than straight. Both branches held a blackness so solid it was like asphalt rather than air, and something deep inside me, seeing the light of the entrance recede, whimpered—a dark room, the sound of bullets resounding, echoing, a darkness punctuated only by lighters, matches, strange men.

It was so quiet I could hear Johnny's watch ticking. Once we turned the corner, even the grey light from the entrance would be gone. We would just have our flashlight.

Johnny turned left, and I followed without protest. One way was as good as another down here. The air, amazingly cool after the furnace outside, smelled of dust or sand and nothing else. Johnny and I had been so thoroughly sandblasted that even our sweat smelled of the desert. If They tracked by smell I didn't even think They'd be able to find us.

A slithering bump behind us; I whipped around with the flashlight, seeing nothing.

"Nicky." Her voice steady again, though very high. "I need the light."

"Sorry."

I kept it on the walls and floor as we walked, taking turns at what seemed like random, often backtracking, our footprints already smudged by other tracks. From the corner of my eye I saw dark shapes moving and thought: Just do what she said. Ignore them. Do what she said. She's got you this far. Plus maybe you can smack it with the shovel. Whatever it is.

I was very aware that we had no way out down here, that it would be the work of a moment if one of Them wanted to block the doorway. That we'd never leave.

Clicking, behind us, distinct now. I turned again, unable to help myself, shining the light quickly around, up, down—still nothing. But the air in the clay-lined tunnel felt different, had mass, weight, had pressure, the way you know someone's home when you open the door whether you can see them or not.

"John. There's something in here with us..."

"I know. Keep walking. Don't run." She sped up,

though, so I had to lengthen my strides to keep up. "Not all of Their servants could be seen. That's mentioned in some of the stories out of China and Egypt and the Aztecs. Atlantis, too. Numerous accounts later saying that what destroyed many homes and temples couldn't be seen."

"I hope it's not one of those things. I hope it's Boba Fett."

"Me too."

"I mean, not to say that getting caught by Boba Fett would suck more than getting caught by... whatever that is."

"Yeah. And I wouldn't have to pay out the reward money either."

"That's true."

A left, a right, a left. Back again, the invisible presence receding, as if mocking us. A left, a left, a right. A room with a shining black table in the centre of an old, wavy-edged brown stain, tapestries in the background still bright and clean, gold threads winking like neon signs in the single pass of the flashlight. A room with stone chairs, carved with sea creatures, sharks and octopi, lobsters, things I didn't know. A room with battle scenes on the wall, incised hard into clay, not carved into stone—horses, chariots, arrows, spears, an enemy obscured by the shadows as we rushed past it.

Something glittering in another room, barely glimpsed before we turned—vases, masks, horns, cups, all made of gold, clean and smooth and menacing, decorated with bright blue and green stones. The sand on the floor ran out and we were walking on bricks, the flashlight glittering off something in them, maybe flecks of mica, like Johnny's granite countertops back home. Whatever was behind us, the legion behind us, grew; I felt the air grow crowded with their presence, refused to turn around and look. We doubled back, crisscrossed, circled.

"Are we lost?" I whispered at last. The air felt heavy, charged. Even if I had not known something was coming, the signs were becoming physical, impossible to ignore.

"Yep. And we can't waste any more time on this. We're going to have to ask for help," Johnny whispered.

"Won't that attract... attention?"

"I know, but there's nothing else I can do. Help me get the sand off part of the floor."

I held the light in one hand and helped her sweep with my foot, then her scarf, till we had a clean spot on the floor. Dark stains were still visible in the cracks between the flagstones. What had happened here? "Who are we... asking?"

"Marutukku," she said. "He helped keep the gates shut. Nuphel-Don may even have called to him for help directly."

"Is that what *we're* doing?"

"No, I can't summon him the way she would have been able to. And it would draw too much attention to where we are in the maze. I just need wayfinding help. We can't do this alone." She was drawing on the floor with a marker, bracing herself over it with one hand as if she might keel over. Her cardboard cylinder came out too; she rotated it, muttered, wrote. Brown dust fell onto the circle. How many spells was she running right now? I opened my mouth and shut it again. The sacrifice. *Everything will be taken from you.* They'd said so.

"Okay, here goes," she said, and leaned close to the stone, whispering into the centre of the circle.

Nothing happened; the space between my shoulderblades prickled as the things behind us watched the spell fail. "Oh shit," I said.

"No," she said, almost a sob, catching in her throat. She leaned forwards, pressing the palm of her hand to the design. "Marutukku..." She gasped, pulled her hand back just a fraction, and then pressed it to the stone again, hard. As she whispered again, a plea in his language, I assumed, the circle on the floor glowed. Something hummed above us, smug, discordant.

"Come on, Johnny," I said. "We're on our own."

"Wait..."

Finally she simply collapsed onto her side, the marker circle fading as if we'd poured rubbing alcohol on it. I stared at the empty space on the floor, then down at her hand, which was turning blue on the palm, a powdery sky blue as if she'd run out of air. Then lines began to coalesce on it, dark, sweeping in from wrist and fingers, into a new magic circle very different from the one on the back of her hand. The centre was a painful, bruised purple.

After several agonizing seconds, she got up, cradling her hand to her chest, steadying herself on the wall with her other hand. "Come on," she said hoarsely.

"What just happened?"

"We'll have guidance for a little while," she said, stumbling along the hallway again, away from the noises behind us. "So we're going to have to hurry."

"How long?"

"As long as I can keep it up."

CHAPTER TWENTY-FOUR

"There." Her voice was barely audible. The wall we'd finally reached curved inwards like an eggshell, carved with something so complicated that my eyes couldn't even follow the story. Bearded men with long curly hair, and more curls in the air, like smoke, or fog, or mustard gas, and everywhere people running, speaking, each carved figure in the clay matched with its little block of writing the size of my hand.

"Nuphel-Don said it would be locked," Johnny said.

"This is it? For sure?"

Her small, dusty hands moved gently over the surface of the clay, tracing a particular inscription. She must have known it would be there, so tangled it was with all the other writing. I felt the old awe, the old envy, return. You are too young to know so much; you have always been too young; and yet here we are. The wise child, the holder of knowledge.

"She and her assistants left help. In case anyone made it this far—and, you know, knew what they were doing."

"Do we?"

"I hope so. But you have to make sure, right? That only people who are... qualified. Can get in. And see it. Not just anyone."

Her voice was muffled; I looked away from the carvings to see that she had slumped forward into the recess, forehead-first, breath ragged and slow. My relief turned into alarm. "Johnny? Are you all right?"

"Just tired," she slurred, trying to push herself away from the wall; I hooked a finger into a beltloop and pulled, freeing her face. "Have to find the locks. Have to get the locks open. They would have made them hard to lock. Hard to open, too."

I trained the flashlight on the wall, seeing how pale her face was, how it too glittered like the floor, how she seemed actually translucent now—seeing veins in places I hadn't seen them before, standing out sharply on the backs of her hands and on her silky temples, lavender and green.

A dark place, a long time ago, the smell of blood. I clenched my back teeth and tried to keep the flashlight steady. We were almost done. Home stretch. Just... get the spell, get back out, wait for the gate to begin to show itself, shut it. Lock it.

The sense of company in the hallway faded abruptly, as if blown away by a sharp wind; I turned my head, seeing nothing in the dark, but in the silence, far away, there was the distinct sound of screaming, as high as a whistle. Sweat broke out on my forehead. Where had they gone? What was the screaming about?

Something screeched so loudly that I dropped the flashlight, scrambled to pick it up while Johnny muttered against the wall. The walls or floor shook from invisible impacts hard enough to make us sway in place, followed by a string of words in the Old Tongue, far away but easily recognizable, freezing my blood in my veins. "The shit was that? They found us?"

"Sounds like it."

I spun sideways and got my back to the tunnel wall, one hand on the flashlight, one hand on the cool ceramic, feeling the sharp edges of the writing under my fingertips. The entire place was shaking now, irregularly, as if someone were pounding on it with their fist. But the Sumerians had built the place strongly, and nothing came down on us. Clicks and clunks sounded behind me as Johnny worked on the locks, cursing quietly, either unbothered or not actually aware of the continuing commotion. Golden flecks swirled around her head in the half-dusk of the flashlight's reflection. The carvings on the friezes seemed to crawl, their edges crackling with blue light, like static electricity on a dry day.

"One more," she said. "Gonna need some blood though."

"You might be able to get a whole bunch of mine in a minute," I said, watching as greenish, sickly light began to fill the blind corner, shadows overlapping, bumbling, as if it were unused to enclosed spaces, or limbs, legs, gravity.

"Well, if you've got any to spare sooner than that…"

I peeled a hand away from the wall, picked quickly at a scrape on my arm—a bright flare of pain in the just-knitted flesh—and held it out, still trying to keep my back protected. She gingerly dipped her index finger, then touched it to a part of the door that, I saw with shock, was actually moving—slowly, but detectably, turning, like an embedded gear.

The blood stuck for a second, then dribbled down, and there was a heavy thump as something moved deep inside it. Pink light shone out, brighter than the flashlight, illuminating the hallway behind us at last. It was filled with horrors, more legs and eyes than anything should have had, antennae, tentacles, other things that weren't either, but mostly teeth—lots of teeth. I swallowed a reflexive scream, and spun back to Johnny.

The door wasn't opening, but the turning stone had sped up. It wasn't going to be fast enough. I stooped and picked up the shovel just as the first thing leapt, connecting not with the end but with the wooden haft, slapping it against the wall. It lay stunned for a moment, and something else jumped, shooting out a long, ropy tentacle to grab the shovel.

"Ha! Saw that coming, motherfucker," I shouted, dropping the flashlight to get both hands on the shovel, connecting with the glistening limb, the metal slicing almost through it, clinking musically against whatever it had that passed for bones.

"Holy shit," I said dazedly, adrenaline making everything buzzy and distant. "They're like, fuckin, uh, Jell-O. Johnny, look, they're like Jell-O."

"Nick! Get in here!"

"Can't. Too many of these, uh, jelly mofos." Something was reaching for her ankle where she knelt in front of the half-open door, which I wouldn't have fit through anyway, not yet. I brought the shovel down, cutting through the limb and sending up sparks where I hit the floor. They all screamed in unison, almost making me drop the shovel. A white light wavered into my face and away—Johnny picking up the flashlight. I felt her, or something, pull at my t-shirt.

Something dark dropped in front of my face, a glimpse of red eyes, and there was a tearing pain in my shoulder. I heard its teeth rip into fabric and then flesh, not the pain at first of being bitten but of burning, searing, so that I groaned rather than screaming, and instinctively bodychecked it into the wall, hearing it squeal and pop, thin fluid running onto my shirt, into the bite wound, down my arm.

"Nicky!"

Her voice rose over the screaming. A perfect descant. Her mom's church choir, when we were kids, the rows of grumbling kids in white skirts and black pants, everyone in white and black, a black bow at their throat, clipped on, not tied, so they wouldn't have their air restricted, and John with the descants in the back row, you only needed three of them to be heard over the—

"Nick, goddammit! Please!"

I turned, barely able to hear over the roar in my shoulder, hit something at shin-height, and fell through a membrane of pink light, into the clean embrace of sand.

MY EARS WERE ringing. I slowly returned from half a blackout, the ringing receding, to see Johnny framed in rosy light, sobbing and dabbing at my arm with a shirt—one of hers, from her open bag on the floor. The flashlight lay next to it, lens cracked but still shining.

I fumbled for the shirt, trying to get her to stop. "...Ow..."

"Shush!"

"What are you crying for?" I said cautiously, pulling the t-shirt out of her hand and pressing it hard to the bite. I was sitting on spotless white sand, not like the sand outside. Like playground sand, the kind you could buy bags of in Home Depot. "Should I be crying too? Are we in the right place?"

"Yes..."

"The tomb? The king's tomb?" I squinted, seeing dozens of tall, stone boxes, glittering in the flashlight's circle. The statues encircling them were smooth black stone, ornamented with gold, their heads disappearing into a dome so high I couldn't see the top of it. Beyond the light, the door closing back into stone, the frustrated growling and screaming so high it stung the ears. Then the stone closed completely and we were left in blessed silence. I wondered if she was crying simply out of relief. I knew how she felt.

"Hey," I said. "John?"

"What?" she said, face still in her hands.

"If the world makes it, where do you want to go?" I said. "To visit, I mean. Not for work."

A long pause, emphasized rather than broken by her muffled sobs. "...Petra," she said. "I always wanted to go there. Touch the pink stones. And the Giant's Causeway."

"Where's that?"

"Ireland. It's these tall basalt columns all together, like—"

"Why do both of your places have to do with rocks?"

"Well where would *you* go then?" she said, drying her face on her t-shirt, leaving translucent smears of blood and tears and snot.

"New Zealand," I said. "I want to meet a hobbit. Antarctica, so I can meet penguins, which are the hobbits of the bird world. And the Exclusion Zone."

"Me too. Like it's gonna be worse than here."

"Yeah, at least you can wear badges that say when you've got too much radiation," I said. "You should've invented a badge that showed when we were getting exposed to too much magic."

"I will if we get back."

"*When*," I said. "Come on. Up."

She walked off slowly, bag bumping at her side, flashlight held high. After a minute I got up and followed her, not wanting to be so close to the door. Who knew if those fuckers could open it again somehow? We were stuck in this dome, like a spider under a cup, skittering around, waiting to see daylight again. I swallowed hard. Best not to think about it.

There was no mistaking the king's tomb—it towered above the others, wild with shards of gems and gilt, and the baked glass stuff that Johnny had told me was called faience, as colourful as a painting. We approached it reverently, churchlike, shining the light low rather than high. Ancient plants crumbled as they felt our breath, dried rather than rotten. The reddish dust of petals, the golden dust of pollen. Someone had laid flowers on the king's tomb.

There. I had been expecting it for so long that when we finally found the first skeleton, I exhaled sharply in relief. The bones had crumbled so dramatically that it was more of an outline, though some of the bigger bones remained—pelvis, skull, part of a femur. Teeth scattered like pearls. All were surrounded in a soft, bluish-pink glow, showing the remnants of a dark blue gown, jewelry—earrings, necklace, bracelets—shining in the dimness. Even a few scraps of dark hair remained on the sand. It was sitting up, leaning against the tomb. They hadn't been lovers, Johnny had said; but she'd stayed, she'd put the flowers there. More than one kind of love. Remember that. Loyal to the end. Past the end. "Thank you," I whispered as we went past. Had I imagined the light flickering, just for a moment?

Johnny got her notebook out and scribbled briefly on it as we walked around the tomb, then stopped at one of the flat faces, which had a small door on it, maybe six inches high. "Here goes nothing," she said, and leaned close to whisper something at it—the Old Tongue, I knew at once. I backed away as she finished.

A minute went past, then two. Just as she began to say, "Maybe I wrote down the—" the door opened. We stared at it. I had been expecting lights, fireworks even. But she reached inside and came out with a small clay ball, maybe the size of her hand, the seal on it so distinct I half-expected the clay to be damp. "Is that it?" I whispered. "That was disappointing."

"This is how they used to seal important documents," she said. "The clay ball proved that no one had tampered with it."

I held my breath as she tapped it against the side of the tomb, breaking the clay like an egg and extracting a tablet with the same seal on it—an animal, horned and winged. There was just one line of writing on it.

"It's the Word of Power," she said softly. "All we need now is the *hua-shinoth*."

"Whatever that is. You could just be making shit up at this point and I'd never know. Is that here? How do we get out of here?"

She glanced at the shut door. "Not through there," she said. "It's locked from this side, too."

"So we're hooped."

"...Let's just walk around and see how hooped we are."

Finally, I found a tiny staircase and called Johnny over, pointing up at the dome, the darkness uninterrupted by so much as a speck of light. "They wouldn't have built a staircase if it didn't go out."

"Are you *out of your mind?*"

"A little bit. But we can always climb back down, right?"

I let her go first, then crept up myself, able to hear faintly again the pounding outside the burial chamber. We had gotten our break, our little vacation from danger, and now we were headed back out. Story of my life.

I gritted my teeth and followed her up the narrow staircase, maybe just a foot across, leading impossibly, terrifyingly to the top of the dome, into the darkness. The faces of the statues loomed over us, then drew level, staring with eyes made of a stone so blue they seemed like summer sky, then fell below us. My stomach was spinning even though I couldn't see how far down it was. Johnny held the flashlight between shoulder and ear, needing both hands and both feet to climb.

"Well, they did put a door up here," Johnny called down; I had fallen several steps behind, my shoulder screaming with pain, hands sweating and slipping, the shovels scraping against my back where I had tied them to the bags.

"Great," I panted. "Probably under a ton of dirt."

"Probably."

"And outside of which, the entire Polyphonic Spree of the Them could be waiting, because we've been down in this thing for hours and have no idea what's up there any more."

"Could be."

"Fantastic. Can't wait. Do you want a shovel?"

"No, I'm going to see if there's a lock. Can you hold the flashlight on it while I look?"

She crawled down a couple of steps to hand it to me, but somebody fumbled it, and it plummeted to the ground hundreds of feet below, not breaking. The light shone on the king's tomb, small and clear, sending crescent flares of gold onto the colourful stone.

I looked over the edge, carefully, and sighed. "I'll go get it. I dropped it."

"I did. And anyway, forget it."

"Forget it? It's pitch black up here!"

I heard the rustle of her clothing, and then a click and a moment of bright light. I realized she'd gotten her cell phone open and was holding it in her teeth to look at the door. "Mmph. 'Ep. Ooh, another ten 'issed calls. And a lock."

I watched the tiny, bluish light waver as she put the cell phone back into her pocket. "Cover your eyes," she said, "and get low."

With my head buried in my arms, I barely heard the lock opening and the noises above us—hissing, chittering, clicking. But there was nothing we could do about it; I followed her into a brick-lined conduit that led up to a trapdoor, which we both had to pry at with the shovels to get open. I heard it flop onto the sand and weeds outside, and then Johnny:

"Shit."

"Considering that your ass is directly in my face, yes. What are we dealing with up there?"

"Uh... can you pass me a shovel?" she said, beginning

to climb again; I could see her hand in the bright sunlight, and handed one up. I had to push everything else up through the square opening to get out myself, or I would have gotten tangled, and emerged into light so bright I couldn't see at all for a minute, just—through slitted lids—a kind of blur hitting something with the shovel, something I couldn't see.

I scrambled up out of the tomb, letting the trapdoor shut again, and stumbled to help her, still half-blind. More of the *allu*, the skinless dog-things, more like jackals in the daylight, long-snouted, eyeless, crusted with sand. She whirled and connected, sending one howling, actually airborne. The ground was crawling—rats, scorpions, spiders, snakes, tangled together, many attacking each other. I stood back to back with her, careful not to let our backs touch, lest I get hit with a shovel too. The smaller vermin was too terrified of the lunging, snapping predators to be much harm; I stamped and kicked, clearing a circle.

It was good to have a weapon, get some reach. They screamed and snarled, trying to get inside my swing, but I'd seen that before and was watching for it now. One managed to latch onto the wooden handle, but I got a foot up and kicked it in the chest, dislodging it enough that I could back up and get a clean hit. At least with these you didn't feel bad about hitting them, hearing them shriek in pain; at least you didn't feel like you were hitting a human. Johnny blasted a few of them with green fire, sending them scurrying.

When it all seemed to be over, we stood catching our

breaths in the low sunlight, reaching at once for our bags and the precious water bottles still left. The corpses of the skinless things had already begun to bubble and melt into the sand, sending runnels of black liquid down the slope. The surviving creatures, wounded and maimed, were slowly retreating for the most part, teeth bared in their skull faces. I looked away.

The sky was filling with tall, liquid-looking, greenish-grey towers, too regular to be clouds.

"Please tell me that's totally normal," I said, gesturing with my bottle.

"Wish I could."

"Hey, we're the opposite of grave robbers now," I said. "We left something *in* there. We're grave *gifters*."

"At least I have an excuse for all the missed calls now."

"So, what are we looking for now?" I said, looking around at the quiet site; ten yards away, a jawless, bleeding *allu* sulked under a bush. I shook the shovel at it.

"We have almost everything we need," she said. "Just the very last part of the spell to go, and I know that's not here in the compound. The *hua-shinoth* is basically an amplifier—something that would let us shut the Great Gate. You wouldn't need it for anything else, not even the big one in Nazca."

"I thought you said Nazca was... was a magic circle, not a gate."

"It's both. Most things are more than one thing.

Anyway, without an amplifier, we don't have the reach. It's an artifact that contains the concentrated remnants of Their magic, Their darkness, and it'll act as a megaphone. No, don't give me that look, I know what a red herring is. This isn't one. You always use what They are to destroy Them. Evil to destroy evil."

"I thought good was supposed to destroy evil."

"Not when there's more evil in the world," she said. "Not when it's got all the power. In a way, we humans are lucky; we happen to live in a universe where there are specific things we can use—circles, colours, words of power, places, idols, life forces—that could help create the universe we want. One where the doors and gates are securely locked. Or have enough bars to keep Them from getting in even when They have the key."

"And we can do that."

"Us? I don't know," she said. "I hope so."

"Oh, Jesus."

"We've drawn a lot of attention to ourselves trying to find everything; things are probably converging here, knowing that. And They'll know just as well as we do that I can't cast the spell without help. I mean, the principle is sound. It would be better if I could sacrifice a bull or something, get all the life force out of something at once, but..."

"We could have bought that fancy camel back in town."

"That was the *fanciest* camel."

She dusted off her hands and looked around, chewing on her sunburned lower lip; as I watched, a droplet of blood emerged and slid down her chin, glinting transparently in the low light like a ruby. I realized with a start just how long the shadows were. How had so much of the day slipped away? We had only a few hours left.

"It's not here," she said, "but it's close."

I followed her out of the perimeter of the ruins and stood carefully on the wooden catwalk, listening to faint, high sounds in the ruins—bats, maybe? Getting ready for a night of bugs? *Close* meant nothing. It meant the desert, the scrubby grass and gravel around where the dig had collected a bit of dew or rainwater, and then nothing but sand, sculpted into low dunes that I knew would be exhausting to walk on.

And I was so tired. Not as tired as Johnny, probably, who had been clambering up and down the ladders and ramps all day with legs much shorter than mine, and with fewer reserves of body fat. But we were running out of time. I thought again about the timer she'd put on her computer, discreetly set at the corner of the screen, counting down. Like something dark and poisonous in there. A scorpion, under the tough waxed canvas.

A tiny bat, barely mouse-sized, swooped past my head; I caught a glimpse of one shiny eye, bright as a droplet of water, before it vanished into the open desert. Johnny balanced on the catwalk next to me, which creaked slightly under our combined weight.

"Do you know where to look?"

"I set up the spell to help find it, but it's only good to within... a slightly weird measurement. Works out to about ten meters and then we'll have to dig for it."

"What's the measurement?"

"Uh, the actual monster who cast the spell came up with it, so it's his wingspan. Tip to tip. Part of what I had to look up to do kind of a conversion. All the sources said different things. So I don't even know if it'll be that accurate."

I shook my head. "Monsters and their egos."

She laughed. "Worse than scientists, even."

"Worse than geniuses."

"Let's try here," Johnny said. She set her hand-drawn map down carefully in the sand, weighting it down with a brick, and we started to dig. The sand was so soft and dry at first that it was more a case of pushing it aside, under her direction, into a big wide pit, eight or ten feet across. Then we hit a harder layer and fell silent, joshing done, waiting for a telltale *clunk* or chime as we hit something that even she had admitted she was barely sure existed. She called a halt after an hour, at four feet down, and I had to pull her out of the hole with her shovel handle.

"Okay, next one we dig a ramp, because we are obviously the hottest but not so smart," I said. "Where do we... Johnny?"

She was crying again, quietly, her back to me. In the absolute silence of the desert, her squeaky sobs were barely distinguishable from the faraway cries of the bats. I hesitated. I'd never seen her cry as much as I had this week, and my God, I was so tired of waiting it out, of waiting for both of us to pull our shit together. By *far* we were too young for this. By *far* we had not seen enough of the world we needed to save. Our bones and teeth and brains weren't even done growing yet, how could we bear this weight? This pain and fear? How could we form a structure that could bear it together? No one built great houses or churches or ships out of saplings. They waited till the trees were old and strong. What kind of fucking world was this?

My own eyes filled with tears as I came up behind her, some kind of sympathetic magic. I wondered what I could say that would move her. Or me. Or just keep us going a bit longer. "John," I said. "We can do this. But I can't do this alone. Tell me where to dig next."

"...Little bit east. This way."

"I know which way east is, thank you." I clicked my shovel handle against hers, like patting her back. "Hey. Come on. Don't waste water crying. Dig."

"X marks the spot," she said through her tears, walking about twenty yards away and plunking her shovel into the sand. "Let's try here. We're not far, I swear."

After a while my shovel clinked against something again; I stooped and gently pried out a ceramic mask. I laughed when it came to light, unable to help myself.

"What is it?"

"Just a mask," I said, putting it back in the hole.

"Pretty."

"I honest to God thought when I turned it over, it was going to be you," I said. "I don't know why. Maybe because that's what would happen in a movie."

"I don't think there's any Sumerian in my family, Nicky."

"What does this thing, this talisman, look like, anyway?"

"It's a magic circle, a solid one. It won't be clay or glass or cement or stone. It won't be anything you know. It'll look weird. Very weird. I don't know how big it is, though. And, I guess, one more thing: this close to the alignment, it might be glowing. Or it might not. Just keep an eye out."

"Ark of the Covenant," I said firmly. "I'll know it when I see it." I paused for effect before I began to dig again. "Is it going to melt my face?"

"It might melt your sperm."

"Son of a..."

The sun was actually down now, and I could feel the air cooling by the minute. But it had been so hot earlier in the day that I doubted it would get cold enough to make us uncomfortable. I kept digging while Johnny dragged brush from the shrubs and fallen trees near our pit, and lit it up with one of the lighters in her bag. It was good to have the light, and it burned without smoke, a pure, clear blaze. When she wasn't looking, I fumbled the bag of frankincense out of my pocket and threw a few of the honey-coloured crystals onto the blaze, waiting for the smoke to blow to her.

"Ha," she said a few minutes later, turning around; her face was wan but pleased in the golden glow of the fire. "Good one."

"Mm. I guess it's an okay gift for the son of God," I said. "I mean I guess it's better than, like... a sheep or something. Or a goat. Or a fancy hat."

"I guess. You'd get him some shit from San Francisco, wouldn't you?"

"Novelty t-shirt," I said. "Obscene magic 8-ball."

"Shot glass set."

The ground trembled minutely, transmitted up the haft of the shovel into my hands. I paused uncertainly. "Johnny? Did you feel that?"

She looked up instead of down. "Oh, shit."

CHAPTER TWENTY-FIVE

AT FIRST I thought it wasn't alone, had several more things like itself concealed in the huge raggedy cloak, had brought an army, but then I realized that it had just grown to fifty times its size. What had looked like an overcoat at the Creek was now clearly wings, spanning half the horizon, obscuring the first stars. I froze, as if we were in *Jurassic Park* and staying still would help.

Between the wings was a tangled mass of gleaming tubes and tentacles. The pale face was not a skull but shards of bone arranged around flaming eye pits—black flame, the light all wrong. I looked down, trying not to meet its gaze.

"*You dare*," Drozanoth cried, hanging there, billowing. "This, you dare. To interfere with Our realm, you and your dog."

"It is not yet yours," Johnny said, her voice very small

after Drozanoth's. I saw the circles on her hands light up as it drifted closer, and saw her visibly sag. The spells, drawing out more power. Jesus. The fire flickered as if it too had suffered a loss.

"You cannot stop Us. No one can," Drozanoth said. "We will take back what is Ours, and you animals will once again find your proper place."

"This world isn't yours," Johnny said. "It's never been yours. Find some other world."

"'*Find some other world.*' But you invited Us to *this* one, child. You and your... toy."

She was kneeling in the sand now, face a mask of shock and fear; my stomach twisted. What did that mean? The reactor, yes, but...

A screech of laughter. "Do you not know? Can you not guess? With the gift We gave you, which you have been so assiduous not to waste?"

She stared up at it, a small patch of light in its darkness, the robe flapping mere feet from her face.

"I... my calculations..."

"Were correct, of course. Little monster, is *that* what you feared? That you were merely *wrong?* Is that all you fear in this life? They were correct. But you did not go far enough."

Something else in her face now. Something that sent ice through my veins. I knew that look. "Johnny," I whispered. "Don't listen to it. Let's go. Run. Back to the..."

"Finish," it whispered, its voice thick, gloating. "Finish it now. You stopped at—what? Where it fit your human ego? Where you thought you could save the world, where you thought *They will call me now a god.* Now go on. Let them run. We do not; Our minds do not work that way. We know it in the other way of knowing. But you, you will not believe me. Finish it in your head."

It chuckled, rising to a howl as Johnny stared at it, through it, the golden glow rising above her head and quickly ripped away in the strengthening wind, as hot as the breath of a bonfire.

"You see?" Drozanoth hissed. "You do, I see it, I even smell it from you."

"Johnny!" I grabbed her t-shirt and pulled, but she seemed fixed to the ground, not even noticing me as the seam along her shoulder ripped, exposing skin, blood, the ancient scar.

"You opened not one door or a hundred or a thousand but a number you cannot even *conceive.* And you opened them into one of the few places—and there are so few now! —where the chanting that lulls my masters to sleep can be heard with human ears."

The noise, I thought. Oh God. We heard it. We both heard it. You lie, I wanted to shout, you lie...

"Yes," Johnny said dreamily, still staring blankly up at it, her face suffused with internal light. She looked like she had the night she'd discovered the reactor. When I had seen her in her silver dress. "Yes. Microportals. Of course. Opened briefly and randomly by the flipping of the electrons. I thought it was into one dimension, the closest. But it wasn't. It was all, all of them. And it let everything through. The reactor wasn't a call but a—"

"—an invitation. Not a—"

"—gate, but a road."

"Not a road. You know that, my child."

"A ship to fly," she said softly. "Between places you often travelled, and had become overgrown. Wings, and—"

"—the power to soar between the places. Carry us, O—"

"Lesser Angels. Carry us. Carry us down the meeting ways."

I looked between them with revulsion, listening to them finish each other's sentences as if they were singing a canon. Old friends. I let go of Johnny's t-shirt and wiped my hand on my jeans, only half-aware I was doing it.

"You didn't save the world," it finally said, trailing closer; I backed away instinctively lest the dripping liquid touch my skin. "My unwilling apprentice, you carved it and served it to Us on a plate. What will they say when they know? And after you have spent so long keeping your secrets. What will become of you? Ripped to pieces by a baying mob? Well, you need not worry about that, little godlet. No one will ever know. You will not leave this place. Nothing of you that can be torn apart will leave this place. And We will take you for Our own, and you will re-make your toy, and We will use it to go between the darkness and the light as We wish. Forever. Effortless as the flight of a star through the void."

"No," she said, and shook her head sharply, the

scarf sliding free and landing next to her. Freed, her hair crackled at the tips with black and violet light. "It doesn't matter how it happened. It won't matter. You'll be gone. We are sending you away."

The sand below us trembled again, more definitively this time. I fell to my knees, got up. The sharp bone face swivelled to me, casting inexplicable shadows on the sand, flickering at the edges, all wrong. I resisted a powerful urge to jump into the hole I'd just dug. It doesn't matter how it happened, she had said. Of course it did. She said it only because it was her fault. Hers. Her doing.

"This world is as much Ours as *he* is *yours*," it said, drifting even closer, till I could hear the wind through the shredded edges of its wings. I continued to stare at the sand. Stay calm. What did it mean? Stay calm. It knows it's almost defeated, it'll say anything, try anything. Slippery, slimy, the better to fit through loopholes.

"Did you not know that, human?" it went on, the gloating unmistakeable now despite the scratchiness of the voice, the lack of humanity. I turned my head away.

It said, "I thought not. Witless creature, pathetic lapdog. What drives a man to become? Tell me, you who think you are a man, not an animal. Is it guilt? Greed? Lust? Is it different from her? Yes, I think it is."

The sand was trembling now, rocks dancing half an inch above the surface. I unlocked my knees and straightened my back, trying to ride the waves, my bad ankle shrieking in pain, about to give. I ignored it. Not going to kneel in front of you again, asshole. What in the hell was it implying? Had it come here simply to harangue us about its impending failure?

"Don't," Johnny said, sharply. Of course. Figured it out before me. Prodigy. But what?

"Don't? You little lover of truth, so you say, how long have We watched you? And you have never told him. Let this then be the last thing he hears before We rise. If he is the one you wish at your side when it ends. If he is the one you wish to witness. Is he?"

Close now, so close the desert couldn't cover its smell, so close I could see the things that made up its wings, not skin at all but thousands of blind, black, leathery creatures clinging to one another. I gagged, recovered, finally found words. "Whatever it is, I don't care. I don't want to hear it."

"No," it said, "you do not. Had you wondered why you were not killed at once? Why We allow you to live? Why you see Our truths in your dreams?"

"B—because..."

"Nick, don't listen to it," Johnny shouted, her voice thick with tears. "It's lying. You know They lie."

"I did not lie about your device. Did I?" Drozanoth flapped a wing negligently, sending a wave of sand and stones towards her, crashing against the invisible barrier of her warding spells. Enough got through that she went down, coughing and spitting, nearly into the half-extinguished fire. I turned towards her as if on a string, then stopped. Drozanoth was chuckling.

"You were *part of her covenant*," it cried; the ground cracked as if in response.

"Wha..."

"O witless one, perfectly matched! She feared, when we first came to her, that she would spend all her life alone," it said, laughter now coming from its wings, its chest, the creatures that comprised it all delighted, laughing together. "Thought that Our gift might leave her bereft of love, her great works unadmired. And so she asked for a present. We believe, in fact," it chortled, bringing its face within feet of mine, "that she wanted a sister. What she got was you."

"How?" I said, aware of how faint it sounded. All the blood in my body seemed to drain into my gut, all the blood in brain, heart, hands. Everything trembled around me, dark around the edges. My body was lead, sinking into the sand. The buzzing voice seemed to come from inside my head, it was so close.

"We... made arrangements. Planted seeds. Covenanted with others. Arranged a performance. And after you were struck by the human weapon that had struck her, she summoned us and said. Him. He will never leave me. Put him under my protection. You cannot kill him just as You cannot kill me.

"And We *always... keep... our word.*"

Memory exploded back, driving me almost into the hole; I felt my head slide over the edge of it, hair hanging. Darkness, the smells of blood and piss and cigarette smoke, the dim light of the windows, rough voices. The agony in my shoulder, screaming till I lost my voice, the explosions that had taken off the walls and doors. Two survivors. *Two survivors.* Bullets striking the small, bloodless corpses. The lie that only ugly things are evil, that only beautiful things are good. The lie, the lifelong lie.

"No," I said, struggling up, balancing again on the seismic sand.

"Yes. Ask her if it's true. We are not the ones who lie. *She* lies."

My head turned of its own accord to look at Johnny, getting to her feet, scarf gone, her hair sweat-soaked and dark. "Nick," she said. "I can explain, it's not the way—"

"Twenty-seven children died that day," I said, the words dragging up like vomit. "Were killed because of you."

"I..."

"You could have stopped Them," I said. "Before it happened. Isn't that true? You could have stopped Them. Told Them to do something else. Some other day."

She fell silent, and in that silence I thought: Dog. I was always meant to be her dog. I never had a choice but to love her, I never had a chance. We never had any other friends. Look at the others who tried to get close to her, and I never saw the pattern, only she would have: suicide, accident, relocation, incarceration. Look at the people who tried to get close to *me* and couldn't. She took up all that space. The dog that gets kicked and kicked and kicked and still comes back for another kick. She took me away from my family, because that's what you do with your pets. You take them with you and you erase their kin. Their own kind.

"You were a made thing," Drozanoth hissed softly, just louder than the wind now. I stared up at stars, at the corner of its wing. "No better than a dog. Little better than a *lalassu*, which at least is shaped like a man. Had you never wondered why she could not love you?"

"No," I said. "I didn't."

"Because she made it so. There," it said, "die with that. Or leave. Whichever you choose. For now you know, and you have the choice. Do you not?"

Its flapping wings had laid clear a perfect path to the Range Rover, blowing the sand away, subsoil gleaming in the starlight. I glanced back at Johnny, pink-faced and shaking. "Yes," I said. "I do."

"Nick, wait," she said, stumbling over the dunes towards me, ducking under Drozanoth's wing as if she had not seen it. "Wait, listen to me. It's manipulating you, it *wants* you to do that, since when would you do anything *that* thing wants? This is the world we're talking about, how can you—"

"It's always been the world," I said. My blood was heavy in my veins, weighing me down. "It's always been the world, not me. How could you have stayed my friend for so many years, knowing that? Knowing what you did? And knowing that I couldn't leave?"

"I... listen, it's not as simple as that, it's not as black and white as that. You know there's so little that's black and white." She was hurrying over her words now, the green eyes wide and terrified, not remorseful at all. That cinched it. But I thought I would let her finish.

"What I've done for the world," she said, "you, you're

part of that. *You've* made me what I am, not Them.
Showed me what humanity is and could be. Made them
worth saving—all the people I never would have worked
for if not for you. I know it... it sounds as if... it sounds
bad, the way everything began... I thought I would miss
out on the chance to save the world. I changed the lives
of so many people—extended my share of lives, by
millions or billions of years. When it would have been
so easy to become a force for evil instead of a force for
good. So it's not so bad, is it? You're... the centre of that,
the *heart* of what I've done..."

"You had no excuse," I said. "None. None, to make
me your slave."

"That's not what you are!"

"Sure," I said. "Don't you remember what my family
came from? That we *were* slaves, born of slaves,
shipped over from another country filled with slaves?
The British gussied it up, changed the name, made us
'colonials,' part of their empire. Said we were part of a
great undertaking: that we would change the world. Just
like you. But there was no way home. Not then. I have
one now, though. And that's where I'm going."

"Nick, you can't!"

"I can't? I *can't?*" I said, watching as she stumbled to
her knees. Her eyes were dry. I found myself unsurprised.

"Don't you know what it's like?" she cried. "Having
the whole world tell you the same thing, tell you that
you can do *anything?*"

"Do you know what it's like having the whole world
tell you that you can do *nothing?*" I said. "All right.

So that's why this fucker went after Ben instead of me. When I was standing right there. That's why my family almost died. Why my *family almost died*. I thought: Oh, yeah, They're leveraging the leverage, trying to make me more compliant. I didn't know They couldn't kill me. All right."

"I *need*—"

"Because this is your fault, you can't even tell me that you're better than Them, different from Them," I said. "The world can end. So long as you're in it when it does. Or save it if you want. But you'll have to save it without me. This isn't love. This is Stockholm syndrome. I was so wrong. Neither of us knew what it was. Now I'll never know."

"Nick—"

I turned again, heart hammering, summoning every last ounce of breath in my body. "*Don't talk to me!* Don't you say another *word* to me, you son of a bitch! You bastard son of a bitch, you murdering motherfucker! I *hate* you! I wish everyone knew the truth, so they could hate you as much as I do! Now fucking *die alone* because it's what you deserve!"

They both turned to watch me go. Neither followed.

CHAPTER TWENTY-SIX

THE ROVER WAS as hot as an oven; I aired it out before I started it, then turned up the air conditioning to MAX. Half a tank would easily get me back to Erbil, to the airport, to civilization again, even with the AC that high. It was just an hour away. An hour to things that were two and five and ten years old, instead of six and seven thousand. To where I could die with humans around me—people, instead of the apprentice of monsters and its own little monster apprentice. I was shaking uncontrollably, as much as I tried to clamp down on it, trying to control the big vehicle on the empty road. The lane markings wavered in my headlights, then went steady.

I only had to pull over once to throw up, and then it was a straight shot back; the city lights were warm and welcoming. In the centre of the city, several mosques and part of the Citadel had been lit up in blue and pink and green; maybe an art installation, or maybe just something they did because it looked nice. It looked like the northern lights.

I had never felt so free as I turned into a parking lot to get my bearings. We had left this way; which way had the cab taken from the airport? I closed my eyes, retracing it. Didn't need her for everything, leading me around the goddamn Middle East by the nose like a donkey, carrying her shit, silently following her, no reason to be here except that I could drive and lift more than her. Pack mule, human luggage, an ancient image in a racist encyclopedia of a brown boy in a sugarcane field, hefting a sack on his shoulders. Let the prodigy go her way, and I would go mine. Unprodigious. Human. All human. Forever, however long 'forever' was. Maybe just a few hours.

What would my life have looked like if it had truly belonged to me? I could have had friends, even girlfriends... I could have made my own decisions, gone my own way. I could have heard voices outside the soundproofed echo chamber that was her and me: a single other voice would have been enough. No chance now. The years she had taken from me—I would never get those back. Who could I have been if I hadn't simply been a mute, shapeless stone to sharpen the blade of her mind against, wearing away under the harder material of her genius? What could the world have been? I would never know, no one would ever know.

Dad had hated her, quietly, and me through her. Never

hid it. Because 'gifted' was what he wanted *us* to be, and we turned out so ordinary. Screaming at us for anything less than 90 on a test, when our white friends would have pizza parties for marks like that. He thought we were going to be special, exceptional: doctors, lawyers, scientists. And then we were washed out in the glare of his son's best friend, the prodigy, the false god. I wished he was here so I could have told him she had been truly false, a liar, a made thing. So that he could have hated us less. Hated himself less for failing us. It hadn't been him who had failed.

And she didn't need me now anyway. Had there not, in fact, been a moment when I had the power of life and death over her, there in the ice? Or more than one? I should never have let her live, I should have... I should have killed her, then myself, to cancel out the guilt of whatever role I had in creating the monster, in giving her permission to be what she was.

The city was effortlessly normal around me, not sharing in my disaster; people still walking around, smoking, eating food out of twists of newspaper, hawking things from the marketplace—shoes, electronics, fruit, nuts—under the orange sodium streetlights. No one even looked my way, parked in the empty lot in a stolen car.

If I could get to the airport, I thought, I could find someone who spoke English, get in touch with the Canadian Embassy in Iraq, get home somehow. Ask them to call in some nukes. Ask them to move the warships. Well, they would hang up on me, but maybe I could trade on that little motherfucker's name one last time. Taste the bitterness of it in my mouth, the taste of betrayal and poison. What had they taught us Socrates drank in the end?

"Shit, yeah," I murmured. A relief to have an actual plan, with steps in it that I could work towards. One, two, three, four. Even if they took me into custody to claim the reward, I'd still be on my way home. They wouldn't mistreat me. And I wasn't the one who had beat up those airport security agents back there, so even if they wanted to charge me with something, I could say that it had all been her. And it wouldn't be a lie.

I slumped in the warm seat, feeling unburned adrenaline rush through my body till I was shaking again. Shake away, be my guest, I thought. Not doing anyone any harm here in the shadows. Let it all out, body. It's okay. The truth set you free, and yes, it is gorgeous, it is the first time in your life that you can say it. But when the shaking was over, pain overtook me again, the t-shirt ripping loose from the bite-marks on my shoulder, fresh blood oozing. Yeah. Better go to the airport, find help. Antibiotics. Yes. Good.

The Range Rover's owner had left, as I had suspected, some emergency or toll or snack money in his glove compartment. I sneered at the magic circle on it as I slammed the door and walked into the thicket of market stalls, ignoring the stares, my scowl apparently just enough to forestall any questions.

Three of the colourful bills and a lot of pointing got me a tall bamfoam cup of coffee, a paper bag of flatbread, and a tub of hummus, which I took back to the Rover to eat. I felt safer with the doors shut, invisible behind the tinted glass. Like a dog in its crate, I thought; and I felt hate boil up from my stomach, almost sending the coffee back up. I took another sip, defiantly. Shut up! I'm allowed to hate whoever I want to hate. Literally anyone.

On the drive to the airport, after buying a blurry, inkjet-printed map off one of the street vendors, the sky was visibly changing—not black with stars as it had been before, but boiling, charcoal clouds that could have been mistaken for rainclouds if they were not moving so fast, lit from beneath in greens and blues, sickly, weak lights, blotting out the stars. Everything racing towards the alignment, everything that had not already come through the microportals of the reactor.

I felt oddly calm and light about it, almost buoyant: evil begets evil, and now evil was being called to account for it, being taken to task, as it should be. As was right. Why should she, who was responsible for all this, beg off or outsource the responsibility for fixing it? Polluter pays. Just like she always said.

The tiny planes parked at the airport trembled as if they were about to take off, their wings rocking in unseen currents, slightly too heavy to be sucked upwards. The bigger ones weren't moving. That was good. I wondered if I would be able to fly home from here, or if I would need to go to a bigger airport, if they would take me to somewhere more central. I was nauseated and shivery with pain, though I could feel the food settling my stomach. If only they didn't put so much olive oil on everything; they were used to it, but for me it was just a delicious mouthful of grease that gave me heartburn. But the coffee, the strongest stuff I'd ever tasted, had helped a lot. My shoulder and ankle thudded in time with my heart as I drove, my torn palms so swollen they looked like gloves.

I pulled into long-term parking and shut the Rover off, the engine winding down, ticking sharply in the cool, dry air. The low concrete building ahead of me was a bastion of friendly, twinkling lights. At this hour there were few fliers, virtually no one to witness me turning myself in, begging for help, far from home. Maybe I could even toss a call in to Rutger somehow, demand to speak to my family. I could be with them soon, comforting them at the end of the world. Mom's soft arms around my shoulders, the feel of the kids' hair under my fingers.

Far away, a noise began: the long, low call of a horn or some brass instrument, resonant, grating, a warning. I waited for it to die down, entranced. People left the airport and examined the wooden poles outside, each crowned with a bouquet of megaphones—even putting their hands to the wood—to see if it was air-raid sirens. It would have been so easy to just tell them what it was, and wait to be disbelieved. "That's what it sounds like on the far side of the gate," I'd say. "Don't you know that?" Knowledge long her only power, now mine too. To have something that no one else had.

Enough. I got out, dragging my bag, coins jingling in my pockets, change from the hummus stall. Whoops. Get flagged going through the metal detector for that. Even in this place full of young brown men, what they feared at the airport would be a young brown man. We were what the whole world feared now—for a few minutes more. Soon enough they would fear other things.

I turned my pocket inside out, finding the coins and something soft—the ziplock bag full of frankincense. I opened it without even thinking and dug my nose into the warmed contents. Sap, she'd said, the sweet smell of the deep desert and the blood of wood, a perfume I'd never known. Would never have known, if not for her. The most precious gift anyone could think of to give to the baby they thought was their prophet, their saviour, their messiah, the one that the star shone upon, telling them where He was. As precious as gold. Given to me with barely a thought, for a couple of American dollars, simply because I was curious about it.

(That time we'd gone to see *La Dolce Vita* at the Metro. Her uncharacteristic silence afterwards when I had asked if she'd liked it. "Yeah, I guess." And weeks later, she'd asked me what I'd gotten from it.

"I don't know," I said. "Mainly that nobody is really meant for each other. And that love isn't enough."

"Enough for what?"

"Anything, I think. What about you?"

And she'd said, "I cried. When I got home, I mean. I was trying not to in the car. Because what I got from it was that if you ever choose, you get trapped in a cage, so it's better to go on forever never choosing."

"You can't go through life like that," I said.

"I know. Not choosing traps you too. But the cage is bigger.")

And now, holding the frankincense, all I could think of was the cage she'd locked herself in by her choice, the famous prodigy, how They hadn't waited till she was an adult and could make real choices, how They came to her as a child too young for preschool, how she'd made the choice based on such simple math: Her or the world. The world or her. The biggest cage in the world, but still a cage. Not the sweet life. Just a life.

I'd chosen too, of course; chosen to leave. But how much of that choice had been mine and how much had been Theirs? How much had been love, how much the death of love? How much had They counted on me leaving when I knew her secret? Counting on Their gifts to go wrong, waiting for the inevitable. Laughing to Themselves. Hoping for that pain. Their trump card, saved for the final hand. Rules for her. Rules for me, too.

She had changed the whole world. Everyone in the world had been touched somehow. Everything in the oceans, everything in the skies, everything under our skins. And she had *chosen* the world. Did I dare make the same choice? As a salute to hers, as an acknowledgement only, not as an honour. Not to say that it was her I might choose, here at the end of all things. But to say that it was the world.

I said *I love you, I won't leave you*. And then I left. But you *should* leave your enemies, goddammit; you should leave the people you hate, the ones who have wronged you, ruined you, stolen from you. You not only should but *must*, or else what kind of life can you live?

And yet.

I hated more than one being here. Many more. More hate, maybe. Hard to say at this point but... yes. I did hate Them more. Maybe I could make a difference. Maybe I couldn't.

But I wasn't sure I wanted to die not knowing.

I mean, I was going to die anyway, right.

It wasn't forgiveness. It wasn't love. It wasn't even hope. It was the great uncertainty. The only thing I felt certain of was that she was still fighting. Alone.

I rolled a piece of the frankincense in my fingers for a minute, scenting my hand with it, waiting for it to soften, but it didn't.

Then I got back into the Range Rover.

THE DRIVE BACK out to the Nineveh ruins went straight through a violent sandstorm; my headlights—expensive, powerful—penetrated a foot or two into the swirling sand and stopped, as if I were traveling with a couple of lighters attached to the grill. I slowed to twenty klicks and white-knuckled the steering wheel, glancing over again and again at the circle Johnny had drawn on the glove compartment. It was glowing blue-white in thin, piercing lines, as if it had been incised with a scalpel. Occasionally the car was buffeted by something that felt far bigger than sand—something I would have assumed was a tarp or a plastic bag until one of them briefly stuck, in the swirling vortex, and stared at me for a second before disappearing again.

It was okay. *Would* be okay. Just gotta... get there in one piece, not a bunch of pieces. One piece. Fine dust filtered in through the vents even though I didn't have the air on; I eventually shut them, watching it continue to drift in and fall, softly, like baby powder, onto the upholstery.

The city looked abandoned—no lights, no cars. Maybe the sandstorm had simply knocked the power out. Occam's Razor, Johnny would have said. I crept through the dark streets in low gear, the sand lessened here, blocked by the dark, silent buildings, towards the archaeological site.

The Rover's powerful four-wheel drive gave out on the ramp leading into the dig, now buried in fresh sand. I reluctantly shut off the headlights—the only light for miles except for the stars and the undersides of the ugly clouds—and got out into the dark and grit, shuffling my feet. Where the hell was that huge open excavation, with its grid of planks over the top? If I fell into that, it would be all over.

The wind screamed over the sound of chanting from the other side, the Ancient Ones awakening, pushing on the door, waiting for its new thinness to bend under Their weight. No real weight but the weight of Their malevolence and magic, the weight of Their will, pushing. Everyone in the world must be able to feel it now, that terror, as if hearing something outside scratching at a door they didn't even know existed.

My foot caught on something thick and I pitched forwards, muffling a scream; reaching down cautiously, I felt something leathery, rough, my fingers unable to make sense of it. Like a dead bat but inches thick. And then they hit something wet, cold even in the warmth of the night, and as I drew back, my shoes finding the extent and folds of the thing, I realized that it was one of Drozanoth's wings, torn completely off. Next to it lay Johnny's music player, the wood cracked and the interior filled with sand and molten globs of something. "That's my girl," I muttered reluctantly. What had it cost her? Best not to know.

I shuffled faster towards the top of the king's mound where I could at least get a better view, hoping my eyes would adjust to the thin, greenish light. My skin stung from the sand, the grains redolent with Their stench now, or the smell of Drozanoth's amputated wing.

All my night vision vanished in a crack of lightning that came from both up and down, meeting for a fraction of a second in mid-air. I squeezed my eyes shut too late and had to study the scene in its afterimage, burned into my retinas: a wall, a cloud, a hole, a girl.

Johnny had somehow climbed to the top of the tallest structure, the arched brick gateway we'd seen on our way in. Straight ahead, if I could keep my bearings in the sand. There was more light now, heavy and venomous to the eyes, like staring into a UV bulb—like the lightning, it seemed to be both seeping up from the sand and down from the clouds. As headachey as it was, it did make it easier to see, but it also meant that the alignment was close—that I had perhaps even missed it, and Johnny was up there because she couldn't get back down. Shit.

I screamed her name and waved, but she didn't respond, unsurprisingly; I couldn't even hear myself over the noise. The chanting was building into a roar now, the sound of a packed stadium, rushing in synchronous waves, as if millions of voices were crying out the same thing, pausing at the same moment. A choir, unholy, unblessed, singing songs of praise for evil gods.

I stumbled over the sand till my feet hit something hard—an aqueduct, thank Christ—and sped up along the solid length till I reached the base of the arched building. Think. Look. Someone five feet tall with asthma and several recent injuries climbed this in the pitch black, dragging a laptop computer and a ton of clay tablets in a bag behind her. Where did she get up? Where did she start?

I jogged around the building in three frustrating loops. Where? Where did she get a hold? Jesus, hold it together, hold it together. Nothing. Time was wasting away. Jesus. Move! I threw myself at the wall, skinned fingertips unable to hang onto the jointless brick and stones, nails shredding. The pain woke me up, and I stopped, hands to my face, protecting my eyes. My heart pounded as the air around me thinned, breath replaced with sand.

Wait. There. Two boards torn from the excavation and propped against the side of the building, making a steep ramp just high enough to reach a ledge, from which you could climb on the protruding broken bricks till you got to the top, if you were very lucky, or very light, or both.

Being neither, I kept spilling off both the boards and the ledge, each time landing on my back not as hard as I thought I should—something had gone wrong with gravity, tangibly, as if the ground were pushing up on everything that was on it. My fifth try took, though by then my fingers were cramping and my legs trembling from the effort, and I finally made it to the roof, nearly toppling at the last minute as I swung myself over the edge, coughing.

Johnny's face was inscrutable as she turned, no expression at all. I wondered if I looked the same way. Whose betrayal was worse, I couldn't say. And what help I could be now that I was here, I didn't know. Maybe I was worse than useless, to have come back. A distraction. Too bad.

I crossed the roof to stand next to her, my feet sliding on the sand as if someone were pushing me backwards. Her nose had been bloodied again, I saw, not quite dried, crystalline with adhered sand. It was quieter up here, only the howl of the sand rather than the constant hiss, though the chanting was louder. I waited for her to thank me for coming back, even though I knew she wouldn't. At least, I thought, an acknowledgement that she hadn't expected it.

"What did you do to Drozanoth?" I said after a long time, when I couldn't stand to stare up at the curdled sky any longer, bereft of stars. The clouds were so wrong, moving in ways clouds shouldn't ever move.

"Only what was deserved."

"Good." I paused, and added, "Fucker."

"I couldn't find the *hua-sinoth* in time," she said. "I knew I would have to stop looking and prepare to just... do the spell without it."

I stared at her, suddenly dizzy, and put a hand to the rough brick roof to steady myself. My stomach was flying up like the rocks below us. "But you said... it wouldn't work, it wouldn't be powerful enough."

"I know. But I have no other choice."

"No, can I help? Is there anything I can do?"

"I don't know. I'm sorry. I thought there would be help from Nuphel-Don or her apprentices, but there wasn't. I don't know how to open that valve. I can't even see it. I'm sorry."

I swallowed. We would be beaten because we deserved to be beaten. Called Them to us. Handed Them the power to get in. Didn't find help in time. And the world would never know. "Shit, son."

She smiled at last. "Well, at least we'll die doing what we loved."

"Standing on a roof in a sandstorm?"

"Swearing."

"Oh. Yes. That." I looked down at her computer, protected from the sand inside a slipshod hut built of clay shards and tablets, its screen dimmed. Reference material for the spells to shut and lock the gate. Except could we shut it now, without an amplifier? Or would it fizzle out, like those fireworks that pop into the air and fall back to earth, charred instead of alight, while its fellows illuminate the entire sky?

"Got any last words?" she said after a minute.

"Nothing I'd want printed on my tombstone."

"Me neither."

We stared upwards, helpless, frozen, as the sky ripped open—tendrils of blackness parting like torn flesh, not light and air at all anymore, a membrane, shredding, and through it crowding nightmares. I cried out and shut my eyes, turning away, but it was too late, I had seen the legion of teeth and tentacles, eyes and brains, like nothing we had seen yet, nothing the Earth should ever have had to see.

The noise of Their side rose to a scream; I slapped my hands over my ears and sank down behind the wall, dimly seeing Johnny still standing, her hands up. The building we were standing on began to rock and sway with real violence, sending her down on her knees beside me, whimpering in pain from the broken brick. I looked over the edge to see a huge crater forming in the ruins below us, tentacles as thick as schoolbuses reaching up from there too, as if about to grasp the ones curling down sinuously from the sky, a deadly handshake of congratulations at overtaking the world.

Johnny was wrong; she did have last words, and they were about to be in the Old Tongue. She shouted into the wind, hands still up, palms out; a long crack of red lightning hit and enveloped her. For an agonizing moment she hung suspended in midair, and then the lightning blasted outwards into the sky with a noise like tearing metal.

The tentacles responded with a shriek and withdrew into the darkness; a moment of blazing hope, seeing two stars—ordinary, white, twinkling stars—in an ordinary black sky. Johnny collapsed next to me, her breath leaving her in a long, forced wheeze, as if she'd been punched.

I glanced down at her for just a second—because the building was rocking now, shifting sharply; her laptop slid to the lower edge, cracked against the brick, and flipped over, disappearing into the maw of darkness below.

Then the chanting faded and resumed even louder, pounding against my head. I screamed, barely aware of the noise coming out of my mouth. She wasn't moving.

"Johnny! Get up! They're coming back! It didn't work!"

She muzzily rose, blood spilling from her nose and ears, and slid as the roof tilted even further, fetching up next to me with a boneless *thud*.

"Do it again!" I screamed.

"Can't," she said; I had to read her lips for that one. "Nothing left."

"Not nothing," I said, using her t-shirt to haul her to her feet. "Not nothing. You still have me. You always have me."

She turned to me slowly, tentacles reaching not everywhere now but coming for *us*, a few tiny orange flowers bursting far away—someone must have gotten organized with a tank or an RPG or a fighter jet or something, to no effect, the scaly bubbles of skin weren't even singed—and I heard a voice as clearly in my head as if we were alone in a silent room.

Whatever is in you that can fight
Whatever remains
Let it step forth and fight
Let it step forth from the darkness into the light

Take it, I answered, and snapped my arm out; Johnny's hand locked onto my forearm and everything inside me lurched towards her, as if blood, soul, weight, mass, thought, were all on separate planes, dragged by different forces, blue light churning from her clamped fingers and up into her arm. Her mouth moved— nothing audible above the undiminished roar. Saying the spell? How would we know if—

I howled as it turned me inside out, heart, guts, everything, eyes pressing in then out, something fleeing me in gouts, a ribbon spiraling out for miles and miles, into the darkness, red and pure, bonding with the spell and whatever remained inside of her, detonating in the centre of the abomination in the sky. Blue light surrounded her, and her hand on my arm blurred, becoming translucent as her mouth continued to move.

A bright bolt of agony in my leg; I forced my head back down, realized that the ledge was crumbling, shards of ancient brick both dropping and soaring, swirling around us in a razor-edged hurricane of edges and sand, tentacles and eyes. One upward-flying chunk of brick missed me by an inch; another clipped Johnny square on the chin, staggering her. The blue light wavered. My stomach heaved as we dropped a foot, then two, and then a shocking lightness—freedom— only pain and sound and air and bricks.

I felt my heart flutter and pause. Dying.

Well. We always knew we were going to. Only the time unknown, and the time was now, and she was falling, mouth still moving.

No. Cannot be. Falling. *Finish! Finish the spell! Finish!*

I grabbed Johnny and wrapped myself around her, fingertips touching a scar I knew, a round scar, a moon, full not crescent, images flashing behind my shut eyes, the kids' faces in winter sunlight, Mom laughing as we chased her with the hose, Carla's braids, Johnny's small, knowing face under the pyramid as we looked at the century plant, the faces of others, only others, all the light outside of me where it belonged, all the love, my emptied heart gulping to a stop.

With my last breath I whispered her name, unheard beneath her loud, pure voice still crying out the spell, cut short by the stunning impact, an explosion of pain, light, and sound.

CHAPTER TWENTY-SEVEN

Silence.
  Darkness.

CHAPTER TWENTY-EIGHT

LIGHT. THE PALEST and purest of golds trembling, flecked with black, long, curved spikes coming for my eyes. Dull, unceasing thumping, like the march of an army. The light wavered, rolled out, vanished, rolled back in.

I slowly came back to myself—not just senses but words, memory, coming back bit by bit, creeping back to me—and realized that everything hurt. Maybe that meant I wasn't dead?

"Blink, blink," someone was saying, far away.

I blinked obediently and something warm moved across my eyes and face, making me sputter. I forced myself to sit up. Johnny knelt at my side with a water bottle; I realized she had been washing sand out of my eyes. Everything looked gold and pink.

"Can you hear?" she said.

"What?"

She handed me the bottle and I drank deeply, the plastic-tasting liquid as hot as tea. How long had we been knocked out, in the silence and the dark? The sun had come up, night was over. I looked around; the ruins were gone, or at best more ruined; we lay in the bottom of a vast crater of sand and gravel and broken clay bricks and scraps of toppled steles, surmounted by a circle of perfect, beautiful blue sky.

I stared at it. The thumping was my heart, irregular but strong. I listened to it while I stared, marveling at the cleanness and evenness of the blue, unmarred by even a single cloud or bird, let alone the things we had seen.

God! Those things. I wondered if I would see them every time I closed my eyes for the rest of my life.

"We won," I said, trying to make it not sound like a question.

"For a given value of winning," she said. "The gate was open a long time. Too long."

"I don't care. I'm calling it a win because we shut the fucking thing," I said.

"Well, then it's a win," she said. "You're bleeding."

"So are you." The cut on her chin had bled in a wide delta, soaking into her t-shirt, and she was covered in fresh scrapes. A blotch on her dusty hair resolved into a bloody handprint—mine, too big to be hers. Tear tracks had sliced through the pale dust on her face and washed away the crust of the nosebleed. I imagined I looked worse, having fallen who-knew-how-far onto a pile of ancient bricks. Had I broken bones, protecting her from that fall? Concussion? Shattered spine? TV had led me to think that I wouldn't know till I tried to move.

I looked up, where the circle of sky had finally been crossed by a handful of sharp little planes, silver and black and green. "Are we about to be bombed?"

"Hope not."

I stood, ignoring her protests, then swayed and went down again, trying to catch myself on a pile of sand instead of bricks. I landed on my ass with a puff and missed her next several sentences through ears ringing with pain, gritting my teeth.

"Anyway, you did it," I said when I could talk again.

"*We* did. I asked for everything at the end. Everything inside of you. And you gave it. And when we fell..."

She started to sob, one hand over her face, the other waving at me. Inanely, I handed her the water bottle. She dropped it and lurched forward. My arms came up reflexively, catching her tense body as she collapsed onto me. My God, she was so fragile, she was so light; as small as she looked, I had no idea she weighed so little, as if the desert had dried her out like a leaf.

Her hands formed fists in my t-shirt, as if she were literally fighting tears. Against my chest, her heart was going so fast I thought it might burst out of her. How soft her hair was. The fur of some predator. Like petting a cat, aware that it's a carnivore, that its ancestors leapt and slashed, that it only seemed tame. I thought, clearly: You did this to me. And you have been doing this to me all my life. You expect a dog to love you back. All the different definitions of love and I never realized that you engineered mine.

But I couldn't push her away.

After sobbing for what seemed like forever, she simply went limp; I sat there with her silky head tucked under my chin, rocking slightly, smelling blood and sand and the faintest edges of ozone, as if she were carrying a thunderstorm within her, and a whiff of frankincense as it warmed against my hip.

There were awful conversations ahead, I thought. About how to get out of here without dying—how would we find the Rover? how would we find our way back?—and then assuming we could leave, we still had to get home, release my family from witness protection, fix things with the reward and the missing persons report, fix things with the airport security guards, fix things with Rutger, fix my house. Grown-up things: credit ratings, jobs, reputations.

But for now, there was silence, the slight coolness at the bottom of the blast crater, the warm bricks. And there was knowledge. I knew that she too had never trusted, that she too feared that if she dared love anything, it would be taken from her. I knew her great fear was not so different from mine: that we were always too late, too slow, too cautious, that our hearts did not even belong to us. At last we were neither particle nor wave moving in an unknown trajectory. We had come to rest.

I felt her hands move tentatively up my arms and onto my shoulders, as if there were still a chance I might push her away. She reached up and cupped the back of my neck.

"Wait a minute," I said, but it was spoken into her open mouth, sending a shock all the way down to my toes—no one had told me a girl's mouth was so soft and warm, no one had told me you could kiss someone and taste their blood, no one told me the edges of her predator's teeth were like a razor. I told myself: *Remember this. It won't happen again.* Her hand in my hair, her heart wild and loud, the satiny skin under my nose, the softness and sharpness of it.

This couldn't be love. Anyone else would kiss you with such yearning tenderness as proof of love, but not her. Always she had only loved the lie and, loving it, loved only herself.

We finally peeled apart, gasping, and she wriggled free from my hands and stood up. "Think you can walk?"

"If I can't, can you carry me?"

"We could have a conversation about dragging."

She didn't look like she could drag a helium balloon, but I gamely got up again and teetered for an uncomfortably long time. The first few steps shot iron bolts of pain up both legs, but nothing gave way.

The crater's edge was more sand than brick, and more glassy, burnt stuff than either; Johnny scrambled up first and waited while I dragged myself up the few pieces that looked as if they could hold my weight, slicing through my shirt and leaving thin obsidian grooves in my stomach, like claw marks.

The air was an oven again, but had lost that heavy, leaden feeling that had both flattened us to our knees and lifted the ancient bricks, and it had lost that awful, damp stench from the place where They slept. At the top, my legs gave out and I ate sand.

It took an eternity to force consciousness into my deadened limbs, feeling heat and blood draining onto the ground below me. Johnny grabbed my wrists as I struggled up, my head gonging in a whirling circus of darkness, and by bracing her feet and leaning back like the prop on a tug-of-war team she somehow got me vertical. I rewarded this feat by collapsing directly on top of her; she grunted with the effort, but stayed upright, and slung my arm around her, shoving her shoulder into my armpit to take my weight. I felt bad for weighing as much as I did.

"Is your touch phobia over now, or what?"

"It wasn't a *phobia*."

"We've *had* this conversation."

"Walk," she said. "It's not far."

Lying: it was miles and miles, a sea voyage, crossing the entire desert, the thousands of miles of it. My vision narrowed to a pinprick. I watched her feet and mine, in our similar blue runners, and tried to sync my steps to hers. It helped to have something to focus on. Focus on something, anything, doesn't matter what. Just has to be something different from what you're doing. Step. Step. Step. The sweet smell of her hair. How was she holding me up? Step. Step. My body roared and grated as I walked, the pain mounting with every step, slowing me as we trudged towards the barely-visible top of the buried Range Rover.

I stopped and lifted my head, scenting the air like a

deer. We really had won. It smelled just like air. Just ordinary air.

"I know," Johnny said, turning her face up to the sky. "I know, I know."

EPILOGUE

"Doorbell!"

"It's too early!"

"*Nicky! I can't find my wand! Did one of the boys take it?*"

"Ew, boys!"

"I can't find my shoes!"

"*Doorbell!*"

"*We know!*"

I pretended to jam two fun-sized Tootsie Rolls into my ears as I waded through the chest-deep sea of kids, some of whom I didn't even know—Carla had invited a ton of her friends over so they could coordinate who was going as which princess, except I couldn't figure out who on earth was supposed to be a princess with a wand, was there a *Harry Potter* princess?—and clung to the doorknob like a drowning man.

It *was* too early; most trick-or-treaters would have waited till it got dark, a couple hours from now. Maybe some parents with a baby or toddler, too young to go out alone.

I wiggled the chain off, ignoring the hands pawing at my back, and said, "Trick or... oh."

"Treat!" Johnny said, and plunged into the crowd, balancing a box teeteringly filled with bags of chips and full-sized chocolate bars and Skittles and Jolly Ranchers and Bonkers and all the weird candies I'd ever imagined in the desert, where I only wanted food from home and thought I'd scream if I had to eat one more date. For a moment I was too stunned to speak. We hadn't seen each other in months. But the kids were pushing past me, yelling for her.

Johnny said, authoritatively, "Pregaming, you guys, that's where it's at."

"Auntie Johnny!" screamed Chris, and ran for a hug before I could stop him; she dropped the box and threw her arms around him, which was Brent's cue to sidle up and snuggle for a minute.

I glanced back at Carla, smiling uncertainly in her pale-blue dress and tiara. I wondered if Carla would ever forgive her. I knew without asking—because I hadn't asked—that *I* had not been forgiven.

Yes, they had returned without incident, the house had been renovated without comment, Mamoru invisibly intercepted and paid all our bills now. But no one talked about the new arrangement of reparations, and no one talked about when it would end, or what we had exchanged for this new ease, this peace that was so gorgeous and abundant and felt so rich and effortless, the sour cloud of anxiety gone from, I thought, everyone, because our bank accounts were full now.

But other accounts had been emptied. Nothing you could check. Nothing you could prove. Except here, maybe, seeing Carla's cool smile and Johnny's supplicating eyes. There would be no hug between these two. The boys had thought their time away (in what turned out to be Sweden, of all places) had been a glorious holiday to get away from house monsters, somewhat in the way that you would stay at a nice hotel if your house was being sprayed for bedbugs. They had spent the few days excitedly eating berries and marveling at the unsetting boreal sun; but Mom and Carla had been so terrified that even now, the fear and shock could be seen on their faces in unguarded moments.

"*Oh Henry Bars!*" someone squealed, and Johnny ducked out the door before the riot started. I squeezed past them and followed her outside, ending up on the front sidewalk under the big poplar tree. She glanced at the scratches on the bark, the exposed wood yellow now, like a cut apple, still sharply visible.

"Happy Halloween," I said. "Who are you supposed to be?"

"I'm Frodo, from—"

"*The Lord of the Never Getting Laid?*"

"Har har. Who are *you* supposed to be?"

"I'm handing out candy! I don't need to be in costume."

"You do so!"

"Fine, Frodork, I'm dressed as a semi-pro candy-hander-outer." I flicked the ring hanging from the chain at her neck, both of which turned out to be plastic. "Man, this isn't gonna last long in a volcano."

"Good." We both paused appraisingly at the sounds of shrieking and thumping in the house, but before I could bring up that hyperactivity study from way back that she'd told me was a fraud, she said, as casually as possible, staring at the grass, "Just so you know, I came by to—"

"Get the kids hepped up on sugar? Thanks a ton."

"—say goodbye."

"Oh, yeah? Where you off to now, Carmen Sandiego? Lecture tour? Lab visits?"

"No."

My dinner—mostly chocolate—crept slowly up from my stomach and lodged smouldering under my breastbone like a coal. Yes, the barometer, the burglar alarm, never wrong. I had to swallow several times before I could speak again.

Johnny let the silence stretch out, knowing what I knew. Knowing *exactly* what it meant. Had the wind grown colder? Was that the whisper of a language no one knew, hissing through the brown leaves in the gutters?

I had never found out what she had done to Drozanoth, nor how, nor what it had cost. Only that the universe would not have let her pay for it with anything but time. In my absence, I still wondered what horror I had missed. And in turn, she had never found out that at those last moments, I had heard another voice speaking the words she had once said, in my head; that I still woke up dreaming of them, full of terror that my courage might fail. I did not want to tell her that I had heard it. If she hadn't said it, then who?

Rutger had parked way down the block, the silver Lexus already becoming soft-edged and ghostly in the coming darkness, smudged by the drifting smoke of leaf fires; he was leaning against the door, curled up on himself in misery. So she had told him, too. And perhaps told him goodbye.

"I recalibrated the reactor," she said quietly. "It only accesses a 'pocket' dimension now: more or less next door in the topographical material. And I've tested it extensively. It's ready to move to the next phase."

"Does it... still make the noise?"

"No. Not any more. All the same..." She sighed, and closed a hand around the plastic ring hanging around her neck. "No one else can get it to work. There was a test last month where I—"

"I know. I saw it on the news." She'd been asked to prove that her reactor wasn't a fraud, like the cold fusion excitement years ago, and had agreed to build one completely from scratch in a random laboratory in New York, filmed the entire time and using only the materials provided by the lab. It had worked, but no one could explain why. And if she had told them it was because she alone stood at the interface between the science and magic that let the reactor work...

"So I'm a fraud," she said. "Or a wizard or something."

Godlet, I thought. That's what it called you. Don't think I'll forget. Don't think I'll forget what you did. You wanted to be a god and that's how they got you. And now I see you haven't stopped. Won't stop.

"But this is more important than what people think I am," she added, looking up at me from under the brown curls of the wig. Her face was fearful, eager. For what, I wondered. My approval? I couldn't give her that. I used to think I was incomplete without her, and now I understand that that was her design all along. I looked at her differently now. I had to. I felt more complete now, even as I tried to rebuild my relationship with my family; she seemed not quite herself too, more ruthless rather than less, more arrogant rather than less. Even if this was a function of her running out of time, I wasn't sure I could forgive her for it. Any of it. "It's more important than ever that we try to focus on the future now. I mean, since the Dimensional Anomaly," she said quietly, using the term that everyone used now, since it seemed that the entire Northern hemisphere had seen the things reaching down from the sky. "We're free. Safe. We just have to work together to turn the tide against everything we've done."

I nodded. I hoped she meant 'we' in the global sense. That she knew that I was done with her, with all this. I was satisfied with a life without her, for the first time I could remember. Covenant or no. I would never be dragged into her manipulation again. Even that kiss, I thought. We'd argued about it quietly and coolly, both holding back tears. I didn't mean it like that, she'd said.

You put your tongue in my mouth, I argued; it has to mean that. It *didn't*, she said. I was just... overwhelmed for a second.

We both looked back at the house at the same moment, golden light visible through the repaired front window, black silhouettes of princesses and ninja turtles behind it, a waving wand. As if staged: light in the darkness. Hope, in the fading day.

Maybe she'd finally realized what she'd taken from us.

But I doubted it.

"Good luck," I said.

She looked up at me, green eyes faded with fatigue and fear, but still the eyes I knew—beautiful, hopeful, watchful. That gaze would never change no matter what we looked at. No monster could take it away, no danger dull it. The ring on her chest was caught for a moment in a stray beam of light, and glowed as if it were on fire. "I'd better go. Say goodbye to everyone for me."

"I will."

Someone was calling me from the house; down the street, clear against the setting sun, I saw groups of kids already walking between other houses. I stuffed my cold hands in my pockets and took a deep breath of the cool, smoky air. Where would she go? When might she smell it again? Had she dressed as Frodo on purpose, hoping that I would be her Sam?

How hard would it be to stop her now, as she walked back towards the car, just put a hand on that small, cloaked shoulder, and say, "Stop, I'll take you back." How hard would it be to say, "I still love you, I forgive

Beneath the Rising

you." Even though neither of those things were true.

But I let her walk, and went back inside, and watched from the window as she got in, not looking back, and the car pulled away. Someone sidled up to me, rested their head on my arm; I embraced whoever it was absently, then looked down to see Carla, her face covered in glitter.

"We're ready," she said. "How do I look?"

"Princessy. Very princessy. The most princessy of all. I have literally no idea who you're supposed to be."

"What did Au... Johnny want?"

"She just wanted to drop off the candy. That's all."

And to say goodbye, I almost said. Goodbye to me, to you, to Chris and Brent, to Mom. To say goodbye to us as a part of her life, and to the idea even of saying goodbye. To say without words that this might be the last time I saw her.

"Is everything going to go back to normal now?"

I looked at the phone, my arm still around Carla's shoulders.

"Of course it is."

Back to normal. Johnny continuing to soar into history like a rocket, the brightest star, till she could be assured that her name and her legacy would never be forgotten; and no one knowing how, the deal struck and never renounced, the evil that fueled her rise. And she would never be free from it. Only I was free. From her, and from her evil. Forever.

ABOUT THE AUTHOR

Premee Mohamed is a scientist and writer based out of Alberta, Canada. She has degrees in molecular genetics and environmental science, but hopes that readers of her fiction will not hold that against her. Her short speculative fiction has been published in a variety of venues, which can be found on her website.

www.premeemohamed.com
@premeesaurus

FIND US ONLINE!

www.rebellionpublishing.com

/rebellionpub   /rebellionpublishing   /rebellionpub

SIGN UP TO OUR NEWSLETTER!

rebellionpublishing.com/sign-up

YOUR REVIEWS MATTER!

Enjoy this book? Got something to say?

Leave a review on Amazon, GoodReads or with your
favourite bookseller and let the world know!